CITY OF LOST KINGS

KRISTEN R. MOORE

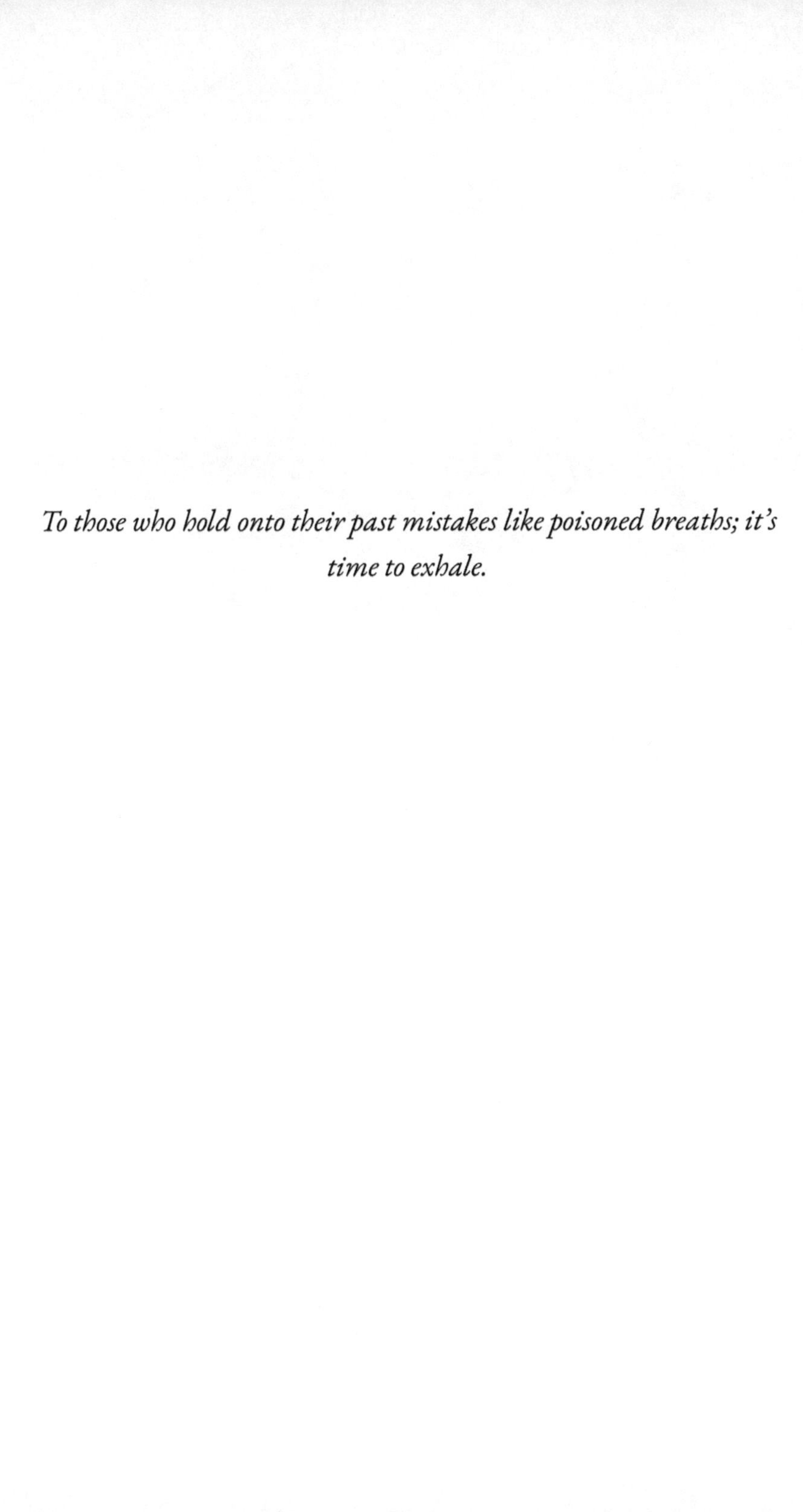

To those who hold onto their past mistakes like poisoned breaths; it's time to exhale.

THE ISLES
UNKNOWN TERRAIN
WHISPERING MOUNTAINS
NOVARIA
THE OUTPOST
PISCIS SPRING
N
VARGAH

PROLOGUE

The king always knew his slow descent into madness would one day consume him.

Destroy him.

He just did not know it would be so soon.

"You're going to be late."

The voices nipped at the king's ears as he made his way down the corridor.

"The mad king is always, always running late."

"Enough," Desmond whispered aloud, swatting at the air as if the voices had manifested like flies buzzing around his head. He burst through the throne room doors, *late*, just as the voices predicted and his heart skipped a beat.

For there, upon the dais, stood a group of councilmen and the most beautiful woman he'd ever seen.

"Finally," a councilman grumbled.

"Forgive me, I lost track of time." Desmond walked up a few steps to meet them.

"All is well." King Godrick of Novaria stepped forth. "King Desmond Orathka, I present to you, my eldest daughter, Kamari Zeliath. Princess of Novaria. May your marriage bring peace to our kingdoms at long last."

Desmond hardly heard a word the king said, too distracted by the buzzing in his ear and the erratic beating in his chest. "A pleasure." Desmond extended his hand, his heart leaping to his throat when Kamari's skin met his.

"Your Majesty." She curtsied and Desmond fought the urge to yank her to her feet, to remind her that she will be queen, and will bow to no one, including him.

In the weeks that followed, their days were filled with premarital traditions. Teas, dances, games. Normally, Desmond would be put off by the idea of being around so many people for so long, but he quickly found how bold Kamari made him.

He was enamored by her. Struck not only by her beauty but by her curiosity. Her genuine kindness. He couldn't get enough of her. He studied her like one of the maps in his library. The tiny freckle she had near her lip. The dark spirals of hair that sat cropped above her shoulders. Her eyes, the color of scorched earth, called his attention at a glance. The way she tilted her head back when she laughed and *stars*, her laugh. It was the only sound that drove the voices to silence.

So he made it his priority to make her laugh every day.

He drew her pictures. Wrote her letters and slipped them under her plate at dinner. He plaited her hair, and they swapped stories of their homes. Their childhoods and families and the duties they were born into.

Desmond couldn't recall exactly when they fell in love, only that over the year that followed, they did. Despite their marriage being forced upon them, despite the stain of war their fathers had brought to their kingdoms, it was all forgotten when her hand was in his.

"You are nothing like I expected." Kamari drew a line across his bottom lip with her thumb.

"No?" Desmond's stomach sank. Could she see him for who he really was?

Mad.

Decaying.

Slowly losing control.

"And how am I like?" he dared to ask as Kamari studied him under the soft light of their bedroom.

Desmond worried, under such scrutiny, if she would be able to see the secrets that lined his eyes or the darkness that was inked into his heart. He hadn't told her of the voices. He wasn't sure he ever would. He couldn't imagine the way she'd look at him if she knew. It would be quite torturous, he decided, if she looked at him any other way than she was looking at him now. Eyes heavy, lips parted, a smile creeping over them.

"You're kind." She inched closer until the tips of their noses brushed. "Romantic." She kissed him long and slow on the mouth. "And you make me happy." She drew back enough to look him in the eyes. "And how lucky are we to be happy, Desmond?"

Happy.

Happy was such a foreign word to Desmond, he hardly understood the concept. He spent so much of his life just trying to survive.

Survive his father.

Survive the war.

Survive the voices in his head.

Survive the pressure of being crowned a king when he was better fit for the shadows.

Kamari's lips brushed his again and, as heat spread across his skin, he decided that despite the hardships of his life, of living with a mind that didn't feel like his own, her lips on his must be happiness.

Yes, he thought. *I'm happy.*

He clung to the thought like it was something tangible.

Kamari is the light that will keep me from drifting. My moon that will keep me grounded.

And for a long time, it worked. Her laugh and her voice were so intoxicating, he hardly heard the voices at all. They were a distant memory. A nightmare he was finally free from. They fell into a routine, she at his side, making decisions together for a better Vargah. A better Novaria.

For a year they stayed this way. Growing deeper and deeper in love, until he could no longer keep the voices out.

Desmond sat at his desk shaking off another bout of fatigue.

"You cannot stay, Desmond."

He shooed the voices away, but they pressed on.

"Leave now."

"You will be better off."

"Come with us."

"I don't answer to ghosts!" He threw his pen atop his desk and stood. "I don't answer to voices in my head. I will not answer to *you.*" He glared into his empty study, but he felt their presence in the chill of his skin and the sweat on his brow. In the spiraling, sinking feeling of dread in his stomach.

Silence stretched from corner to corner, the darkness a rising storm in the small room. Pressure rose in Desmond's chest, pressing and pressing until he couldn't breathe.

"You know very well, Desmond Orathka, we are not *in your head."*

Desmond picked up his pen and sat. Scribbling any and every detail he could into the final pages of his journal. Desperate to put onto paper what he dared not say aloud. He wrote feverishly, his words bleeding together on the parchment. For years, he journaled every moment of his life because he knew, deep down, his life would not be long.

Sweat dripped from his brow. His fingers shook and ached. The darkness grew behind him and within him, gripping his chest like a vice.

Time, time, time.

He was running out of time.

But still he wrote. He wrote despite their warnings not to, he had to put it onto paper. He needed her to know. A sharp pain erupted behind his eyes. He cried out, pressing his hands over his ears.

"LEAVE ME ALONE—"

"Desmond?"

The swell of darkness retreated to the corner, shrank down until it was nothing, and Kamari was there in her silk nightgown, like a beam of moonlight, brushing his tangled hair from his face. "Desmond, are you alright?" Worry etched its way between her brows and Desmond had a thought to kiss it away.

"I'm sorry, my love." He cleared his throat and took her hands in his own. "Just getting some thoughts out." He smiled and hoped she wouldn't see the fear behind it.

"You know you could tell me, right?" Kamari wrapped her arms around his shoulders and kissed his cheek. "If something is bothering you." She brushed his hair from his face and cupped his cheeks in her hands. "If something is hurting you, I need you to tell me Desmond."

The voices were there, humming in his ears like vile insects.

"Do not tell her."

"I'm just tired, my love."

Kamari's brows pinched and he knew that she didn't believe him, but then her face softened and she kissed the tip of his nose. "Then come to bed."

When she turned to go, he couldn't help himself. He grabbed her wrist and brought her into his lap. "I love you, Kamari Orathka." His fingers tangled in her mess of curls as he kissed her. *Keep kissing me,* he thought. *Kiss me until our lips are bruised and our lungs are burning. Kiss me until we are nothing but bone and dust. If you keep kissing me, I won't lose you.*

Instead, she pulled away and because he had no power when it came to his wife, he let her go.

"And I love you, Desmond Orathka." Breathing heavily, she stood. "Five minutes," she said. "Don't keep me waiting." Her grin shone through the darkness and Desmond memorized the shape of her lips and sway of her hips before he went back to his journal.

"You know what you need to do, Desmond."

The voices were gentle now. A soft caress against his neck.

"You have always known what you needed to do. It's the only way to keep her safe."

"Safe from *what*?" He barely recognized his own voice. Weak and full of defeat.

The voices slithered up his spine, tucking themselves tightly in his ear.

"Keep her safe from the truth."

Desmond glanced down at his journal, to the nonsensical notes and drawings. *Mad*, the people called him and perhaps they were right. The truth was there, right in front of him.

He buried his face in his palms and choked on a sob. His mind had not been his own for some time now, but tonight was different. There was a sense of finality in the dark of his study that made his chest tighten and his heart race. Like if he closed his eyes, even for a moment, he'd be lost for good.

Desmond sucked in a sharp breath and shoved the journal deep in his desk, in a secret compartment he hoped no one would find. For years he had written every detail of his life, and now, what he wrote tonight, he wanted to bury it like a shameful secret. He stared at his hands, ink staining his fingers. They trembled as he wiped them against his pants.

"I can't leave her."

"Come Desmond."

"Will she be okay?" *Please let her be okay.*

"That is up to you," the voices purred.

"Come," they said again.

And this time, he obeyed.

ONE

AESIRA

Killing monsters was easier than making small talk. Which was what Aesira focused on, slicing her blade straight through the scorpion, as a new recruit babbled nonsense in her ear.

"Impressive," the recruit said.

"What?" Aesira wiped her blade clean before placing it back in the leather sheath on her hip.

"I said that was impressive. I can't wait to get my first kill."

"Report to Lieutenant Nev," Aesira said, tossing the wretched parasite over the wall. "See what she needs done this morning."

The recruit's face fell slightly but Aesira didn't have time for it. She waved her off and thankfully the recruit turned and left without another word.

She took a deep inhale of the early morning air. The sun was barely rising, a small fragment looming over the endless sand. She reached into her pocket, palming the orders she received this morning.

A new station.

A new city.

It wasn't anything out of the ordinary for the Order to keep her busy. They kept her moving. Never giving her, or any of the knights, a chance for a life to take root. That's how they kept them under control, the girls with too much fire in their hearts and venom on their tongues.

The sun stretched across the sky, tinting it orange. She filled her lungs again. This was the only time of day she could stand the Vargah heat before it became something sinister, sweltering. Truth be told, there weren't many things she cared for in Vargah, but the sunrise being closer to the west always had more of a payoff than she'd seen in Novaria. Deep pinks and light purples, the sky a seemingly endless painting sprawled across the open desert. Vargah also meant being close to Kamari and while she'd be pleased to leave the unrelenting heat, leaving her sister left a sour taste in her mouth.

She took in the last moments of silence before another sharp tailed bloodsucker crawled over the wall and ruined the sunrise for her.

"Commander, a word?"

She slammed her blade through the scorpion before turning to her knight, Rahashi. "What is it?"

"The Queen is asking for you," Rahashi said.

"Did she say what she needed?"

Rahashi shook her head, her dark skin at such a contrast to her tightly braided white hair. "She only said it was urgent." They walked in sync along the wall, passing a few other knights who were dealing with more of the large scorpions that had made their way up, including the new recruit who was struggling to unsheathe her blade.

"Was I that hopeless?" Rahashi pointed to the woman, fresh faced and untested, finally releasing her blade in time to slam it through the scorpion.

"You all were," Aesira said with a smile. "Don't worry, I was too. Keep an eye on her but first find Nev, let her know where I'll be."

"You got it, Commander." Aesira left Rahashi and the other knights to finish their work and made her descent down the narrow, stone stairway that was carved into the wall.

Her heavy boots were unnaturally loud against the hard marble floor of the Citadel, but she didn't have to wander far before she found Kamari pacing the foyer. "Have you been waiting long?" Aesira frowned but she stood straight, her arms positioned behind her back just as any soldier would. "What's that?" She nodded to a scroll clutched in her sister's palm.

"Treason is what it is." Kamari shoved the scroll into Aesira's chest then resumed chewing the tip of her nail between her teeth.

Aesira unrolled the scroll, fighting a grimace as she read the headline in bold script.

KING DESMOND; DESERTER OR DEAD?' It seems as though our beloved king has gone mad after all!

"This is just gossip, Kamari." Aesira passed the scroll back to her, repositioning her arms behind her back. "If you feed into it, it'll only get worse. It's better to ignore it."

"You want me to ignore that people think Desmond deserted them?" Kamari clutched onto the scroll, biting the tip of her nail as she paced. "Or worse, ignore that they think he's gone mad or *dead?*" The word bounced off the walls like a sadistic laugh.

Dead.

Dead.

Dead.

When King Desmond went missing a week ago, Aesira had never seen her sister so distraught. Kamari was always the picture of poise and grace, but she would allow her mask to slip when it was just the two of them alone. When they could be sisters, instead of queen and commander.

"Has he gone mad, Kam?" Aesira's voice lowered, she didn't trust all the hidden corners of the Citadel. Kamari's eyes narrowed and Aesira knew she'd asked the wrong thing. She didn't really want to ask about the king's mind, but the soldier in her wouldn't let her dismiss the question. It wasn't news that Desmond was of a different sort. Seen talking to himself, whispering in corners, face buried behind a notebook.

"Of course he hasn't," Kamari snapped. "He's perfectly fine. He just..." She cleared her throat and Aesira followed her down the hall. "It's my first meeting with the council since Desmond's disappearance and I feel like a noose has been wrapped around my neck." Kamari's fingers, visibly shaken, drifted to her throat. "I need you to find who wrote that morning scroll and bring them to me. I can't have a city full of panic on top of everything else."

"Kam." Aesira sighed deeply, which made Kamari frown. "So what do you want me to do? Find whoever wrote this and rough them up a little? Scare them? It won't change the fact that it's already written and now that it's out there, it's inevitable that more will follow."

They came to a stop in front of a set of large bronze doors that spanned from floor to ceiling, ornate with carved moons and stars to honor their goddess, Celestria.

Kamari turned to her. "I know it doesn't seem important to find who wrote this, but to *me* it is." She looked away and Aesira knew why, she was hiding tears. Holding herself together because it wasn't accepted, in her position, to be anything other than composed.

"To speak of the king in such a manner is not only treasonous but rumors in this city spread as quickly as dry-lung. It's already difficult ruling a foreign kingdom without him, I don't need a sudden surge of panic to make things worse. The peace between Vargah and Novaria hangs by a thread as it is." Kamari faced the door again, taking a deep breath. "I can't mess this up."

"You won't, Kam." Voices rose from the other side of the door. Kamari smoothed her skirts again, set her shoulders back, chin up. Aesira could see the pain in her sister's expression and immediately her thoughts turned to erasing it.

She could fix this.

Help ease her worry in any way. Because that's what she was for. The second daughter, the spare.

"I was supposed to mend our kingdoms, Aesira, and now–"

The doors swung open and a maid popped out. "Oh, Your Majesty." She dropped to a clumsy curtsey before pulling the doors wider, allowing Aesira and Kamari space to pass through. Kamari entered first, holding her skirts above the marble floor, a passive expression swept across her face.

Aesira entered next, keeping a few paces behind, eyes strategically scanning the room before eventually landing back on Kamari.

The old men and women that made up Vargah's council bickered amongst themselves, only pausing to rise and offer a quick bow before resuming.

The meeting room was lined with tall rectangular windows that let in diluted sunlight from the swirling sand outside. A long golden table stretched through the center of the room with enough chairs for each of the council members. Aesira's gaze drifted to the empty chair on Kamari's right.

Desmond's chair.

"We appreciate your haste, Your Majesty," one of the councilmen said, his graying beard and sparse hair proving he was the oldest member. Aesira couldn't remember any of their names. Or maybe it was that she never bothered to learn them since she knew she would be leaving soon.

"And what is so urgent, Councilman Sante?" Kamari declined a cup of tea from the maid, and clasped her hands together on the tabletop.

From where she stood behind Kamari, Aesira had a clear view of the room and the exits. She silently cataloged each corner, every place to hide, the different ways one could get in and out. After her sweep of the room her gaze landed back on her sister.

"If it's about the reservoirs," Kamari continued, "I've been assured they'll last through Naming Day. If the water is running low, begin rations early from Piscis Spring. Cut back on *astra* wherever we can, we don't need to cool areas that aren't absolutely necessary."

Aesira hid her wince at the mention of Naming Day, a ritual to the Goddess Celestria. One sacrifice, once a year, to prove their loyalty and the goddess would bless Vargah with enough *astra* to keep the city powered and cool and with enough water to last an entire sun cycle. With the treaty, Vargah would now be responsible for providing rations of *astra* to Novaria in exchange for extra rations of water from Piscis Spring.

The northernmost kingdom didn't need the *astra* to keep cool, their climate was much more temperate than Vargah and they used the water from the spring to power their city, but Aesira knew better than to assume her father's intentions behind this treaty were merely for peace. There was always a hidden layer with Godrick Zeliath, she just hadn't figured out what yet.

The council members looked at each other as if daring one another to speak first.

Kamari cleared her throat. "I would hope you didn't call me here just to waste my time?"

Aesira couldn't help the small smile that crept across her lips. She considered her sister a merciful queen, just as Desmond was a merciful king, but she was also a Zeliath. Ruthless when necessary and in a room full of predators, Kamari knew best when to raise her hackles.

"King Desmond has not been found," Sante said. "He has not written. No word has been sent of his appearances at the Outpost or beyond."

"You're telling me what I already know, Councilman. Please get to your point."

The doors to the throne room swung open, loudly enough that Aesira drew her sword, eyes like daggers pointed in the intruder's direction. "Forgive my tardiness." Desmond's cousin, Raffe, stalked into the room. His hair was slicked back and shiny as oil, his boots polished and teeth gleaming white. With a few bold steps, he joined them at the table, making himself comfortable in the only empty chair.

Desmond's chair.

Fuck.

She glanced at Kamari but there was no tell in her body language, no way to know if she was okay.

Of course she's okay, Aesira thought. *She knows how to lie just as well as you.*

"I believe what your councilman is trying to say is that without my cousin here, your marriage contract is null."

"I beg your pardon?" Kamari's voice held calm.

Aesira stepped forward but with a quick wave of Kamari's hand, she stepped back, falling in place behind her. She bit down on her tongue, a tiny spark of pain lighting up in her mouth, a punishment for her small misstep.

Raffe shot Aesira a grin, like he could read her mistake, before pulling out a scroll from his breast pocket.

"To cease the war between Novaria and Vargah over the rights to Piscis Spring, Novarian ruler, King Godrick the third presents his first born daughter, Kamari Zeliath under the condition she be wed and rule alongside Vargahian heir, King Desmond Orathka," Raffe read aloud.

"As you know," Raffe continued, "Piscis Spring is the only known natural water source that flows directly between Vargah and Novaria–"

"I do not require a history lesson." Kamari shook her head. "It isn't news to me that the unity of our kingdoms has brought you access to Piscis Spring. What I'm trying to understand is how you think my husband being missing means my marriage is under threat?"

Aesira craned her neck to get a closer look at the scroll but Raffe snatched it back, holding it close to his chest shooting her another grin.

Bastard.

"Ah, you have, Your Majesty," he said. "But with my cousin's disappearance, it seems a rather large part of the contract has been voided."

Kamari glanced briefly over her shoulder and in that fraction of a moment, Aesira saw what her sister wasn't saying aloud.

Kamari knew what Raffe found on that parchment. She knew and there was nothing she, or Aesira, could do about it.

Aesira's heart was a hammer in her chest, slamming over and over again, threatening to shatter.

How could I help her?

What could I do?

"In the unfortunate circumstance King Desmond should fall ill or perish, a new ruler of Vargahian descent shall take his place, ensuring the treaty remains with an even rulership. Half Novarian." Raffe's dark eyes flicked to Kamari. "Half Vargahian."

Aesira's stomach plummeted.

Damn him.

And damn Kamari for not telling me of this portion of the treaty.

She glanced around the table, at each of the councilmen. Some hung their heads, others whispered to each other. They all knew this was coming.

They all knew, and said nothing to defend their queen.

Maybe they didn't care that Desmond was missing. Maybe they only cared about their treaty. About their share of spring water and sanctioned power.

"You have a decision to make, Your Majesty," Raffe said. "Abdicate your position on the throne and forfeit the treaty. Bring war back to Vargah and Novaria. Death to the people of our two kingdoms. Destroy the peace your late husband worked so hard to gain. Or marry me, in my cousin's place."

Fear splintered like ice through Aesira's veins. The jagged shards of her shattered heart ripping and tearing in her chest. It took every bit of her training not to lunge forward and strike her blade clean through Raffe.

Her fingers ached to reach for her sister, bundle her up in her arms and take her away.

Anywhere but here.

"It's only been a week," Kamari said, her voice calm. She was like a diamond, able to withstand endless pressure. Unfortunately where Kamari was a diamond, Aesira was like a boiling kettle with the lid clasped tight, waiting to explode. "You would give up on your king so soon?"

A councilwoman at the end of the table cleared her throat, her golden hair swept back and tiny spectacles making her long, slender nose more pronounced.

"You have been here a year, Your Majesty, most of us have lived in Vargah our entire lives. We have faced many hardships with our wall being closest to the west. We have endured sand storms, monsters, and yet, the people have persevered. They have fought for a very long time to keep this kingdom safe. To keep Celestria happy. The treaty between Novaria and Vargah is new. Fragile. But it has offered them something they've never had before." The councilwoman smiled softly. "Hope. They will not receive the news well of the throne being left unattended."

"It's not unattended." Kamari stood and Aesira took a step closer, her hand drifting to her hip where her sword sat, ready. "Vargah may be missing its king but I am still its queen."

Raffe's laugh slid through the room, crawling under Aesira's armor, that boiling in her blood rising to meet the surface of her cheeks. "Never in history has our country been run without a king. Even when King Ommet died, Desmond's mother wed the following month until he was of age to be crowned. She knew her role and played it well until her end, it's time you learned yours."

Kamari sank back into her chair but Aesira didn't fall back. She kept her place, a step closer to Kamari, closer to Raffe.

They were all cowards in Aesira's eyes, hiding behind a technicality written on parchment. She shuffled another half step forward, the grinding of her armor bringing attention to her.

Good.

She wanted the council to see her. To remember that she and the rest of her knights were here. That *Novaria* was here, ready to defend themselves should the need arise.

Raffe stole a glass of water, tiny droplets sticking to the thick hairs of his moustache. "We will arrange the wedding in a month."

"No," Kamari said. She looked back to the council, some of which had the decency to meet her gaze, others kept their focus on

Aesira, worried brows bunched together. "Desmond has only been gone a week," Kamari said. "We aren't even sure if he left willingly. What if someone—"

"You can spin it any way you'd like, Your Majesty," Raffe said, "but we all know the king's mind has been deteriorating for some time. He isn't coming back and even if by some miracle he did, he wouldn't be the man you knew. My cousin was sick, and he always has been."

Tightness spread through Aesira's chest, a deep ache that pulsed in time with her heart. She could hear the words still echoing in the corridor, pounding in her ears like a pendulum.

Dead.

Dead.

Dead.

If Desmond was dead, Kamari would never recover. The treaty would abolish and war would rise.

"I don't accept that," Kamari said. "Give Desmond time to come home. Three months for us to try and search for him. Three months before we write him off completely."

Aesira ran her tongue behind her teeth, calculating.

Three months would get them past the storm season. It would give them a chance to collect a team, recruit knights from the Order to broaden the search. Three months would be enough.

It had to be.

"We can afford one month for Desmond to show," the councilwoman said. "Naming Day looms and the people will become restless. Thirsty. Celestria, while generous, has provided less and less water each year to account for our growing city. If there is word that the treaty has been broken, that water from Piscis Spring is not guaranteed, we will have another kind of war at our doorstep."

The woman leaned forward, bracing her elbows on the table, narrow eyes darting between Kamari and Aesira. "By the next Naming Day, you'll have a choice to make just as Lord Raffe has said." Her eyes met Kamari's. "One month for King Desmond to show and then, Your Majesty, the fate of our kingdom will lie in your decision."

TWO

AESIRA

Ancient spires and decorated arched windows stood tall against the morning sun as Aesira and Kamari wound through the city center. As much as Aesira resented being stationed in Vargah, where the heat was worse than the monsters over the wall, she couldn't deny the beauty of the city.

Mosaic tiles created patterns against the otherwise monotonous brown of the buildings. The looming sandstorm in the distance casted a glow over the city making everything look like it had been dipped in red dye.

Or blood.

Morbid, her mother would call her, for thinking such a thing. She couldn't help it. She was raised in blood. From the moment she stepped foot into the Order, her life revolved around it.

She was taught precisely how to spill it, how to protect it, to keep her knights and the kingdoms safe.

So when the dust cloud hovered above the city, staining it crimson, how could she not think of blood.

"Where are we going?" she asked, tightening her palm around the pommel of her sword. "And why do you have so many books with you?"

"They're not books," Kamari said, "they're journals. Just follow me and stop asking me questions. Isn't that your job, to follow me?"

"As in Desmond's journals?" Aesira had only seen them a handful of times and honestly thought very little of them. They were nothing but nonsense and drawings of moths and monsters, scribbled words that held no meaning.

Kamari waved her free hand at a few children playing games in the dusty streets. Aesira was normally able to read Kamari with ease, even when she had her queen's face on, but after the meeting with the council, she couldn't tell if her sister was angry or determined.

Both, she supposed.

"Of course they're Desmond's journals," Kamari said. "Why are you asking me so many questions?"

"My job is to keep Vargah safe, you know," Aesira said, catching up to walk in sync with Kamari. "That includes *you*. Asking questions is how I do my job."

Especially you, she wanted to say. She and her knights typically manned the wall farther north toward Novaria, but with the peace treaty, Vargah now became part of the Order's jurisdiction. They reaped the benefits of not only Piscis Spring, but the band of knights trained to slay any beasts that approached.

"I need to speak to someone, and I assumed since you're so nosy, you would want to come."

"I'm not nosy," Aesira mumbled from her side. "I just told you questions are my job."

"I thought violence was your job."

Aesira glanced at her sister, the purple dress she wore a reflection of the city colors. Of her new home. New life. "That too." Her armor was tight as they wove down a narrow alley, bypassing the busiest part of the market. "Now that we're alone, are we going to talk about what happened back there?"

Kamari bristled, her face pinching. "The moment I realized Desmond was missing, I knew it wouldn't be long before the council jumped down my throat." She shifted the journals in her arms but shook her head when Aesira reached to grab them from her. "It's like they were waiting for me to fail."

Kamari and Aesira emerged from the other side of the alley, weaving through the streets of the city, passing various food and merchant carts. Vibrant scarves and tapestries were hung by strings, shielding the vendors from the unforgiving heat. "It isn't your fault Desmond is gone," Aesira said. "You didn't fail."

Kamari shook her head and Aesira didn't press it. They were both Zeliath's. Daughters of their father. Failure of any kind was never tolerated, and the weight of perfection had been pinned to their shoulders from birth. "Did you find Nev? Is she—?

"She's looking into it," Aesira said. "She'll find whoever wrote the parchment." Though, Aesira couldn't see how it would help. News and rumors in the city burned through like a raging fire. As if the people of Vargah had nothing better to do during the hottest months other than cause a frenzy.

The heat of the desert scorched the tips of Aesira's ears, her bronze chest plate adding an extra layer to her already heavy armor. "You could have sent Hanna, you know."

"No. As much as I appreciate her, there's no one else I trust to do this." Kam's short curls bobbed as she waved to a set of workers repairing an area of the wall. "I needed to speak to him myself."

"Him? Who is *him*?" They rounded a final corner through a tight alleyway before ending at the Boneyard District.

Monstrous ships hovered above the sweltering sands. Their sails were tied down, a large "V" etched into the wood siding. The ships were Vargah's most powerful defense during the war. Fueled by *astra*, it was a luxury Novaria could never compete with though it didn't stop them from trying.

Aesira's brows rose before they quickly furrowed. Of all the places, of all the people.

"You're blushing," Kamari said with a side glance.

"I'm not. It's just the damn heat." Aesira brushed a few rogue curls from her face, willing her heart to slow down, her skin to cool. "Why are we *here*?"

Kamari ignored her question and strode forward, toward the large ships that wavered above the sand. "I've never seen you so flustered."

"I'm not flustered," Aesira bit out so quickly the words jumbled together. She wasn't flustered, except she absolutely was. Kamari laughed and if they'd been somewhere private Aesira would have kicked her. "I'm wondering why my sister, the queen of Vargah, has decided she must meet with a *smuggler*—"

"Ex," a familiar, deep voice said, raising the hairs on her arms and neck. The smuggler stepped out from behind an old tarp that was hung like a curtain, his dark blue eyes blazing in the morning sun. "Though, you already know that don't you, Commander?" He took a slow sip from his mug, eyeing the two of them over the edge.

Distorted light cut across his sharp face, catching on the jagged scar that ran from his eyebrow to his jaw. He wore a tattered white shirt and typical mechanic pants, lined in grease and dust. A pencil was stuck behind his ear and a pair of wire-rimmed spectacles sat on top of his dark, auburn hair.

"Apologies for my sister, Mr..."

"Stone Odega," he said, dropping in a bow.

Odega.

Aesira cooled her features, smoothing the deep line between her brows. Odega was the name given to all criminals in Vargah, making it easy for them to be identified and if there was anything Stone wore well, it was the name *Odega.*

"Right." Kamari took a step forward and Aesira dutifully followed, her hand tightening around the pommel of her blade. "Mr. Odega–"

"Just Stone, if you don't mind." His eyes darted again to Aesira. She focused instead on Kamari. That's why she was here.

For Kamari.

"Sorry, of course. Stone," Kamari corrected. "I was wondering if we may have a word with you?"

Aesira glanced around the Boneyard where several people had gathered. She didn't often visit this part of Vargah and she knew

Kamari didn't either. With the wandering eyes of the workers, they were beginning to make a scene.

"Maybe somewhere private?" Aesira suggested, returning her eyes to Stone whose own stare was burning into her. She bit her tongue, wincing when she hit the sore spot from earlier.

He drew back the tarp from which he came. "This way."

Sunlight beamed through the holes in the tarp as they each took a seat around a makeshift table. A few overhead lights were on, their brightness dim from the small amount of *astra* that was supplied to this part of the city.

"A drink?" Stone asked, his fingers tapping the edge of his mug.

"No, thank you," Kamari said, taking a seat.

Aesira positioned herself behind Kamari, eyes searching the room.

There wasn't much to see. A few weathered couches, upholstery worn down on the arms and back. A table with far too many chairs around it to be comfortable. Piles and piles of abandoned ship parts, buckets filled to the brim with what appeared to be gears, bolts, and tools.

"So," Stone said, "to what do I owe the pleasure of the queen's visit and the highly esteemed Commander Zeliath?" His smile pulled his scar taut, but otherwise brightened his face.

His arrogant face, she reminded herself.

Aesira glanced away, looking toward the tarp, watching for any rogue ears that might be listening.

"I have a proposition for you," Kamari said, setting the journals on the table. "As you know, my husband has gone missing."

Stone took the pencil from behind his ear, fidgeting with it between his fingers. "There's not a soul in Vargah that doesn't know the king's disappeared."

Kamari drew in a long breath. "I'm looking for someone that has the ability to navigate a ship through the stormy season."

Aesira's breath hitched, her shoulders growing stiff. Her sister didn't tell her why she was coming here and now she understood. If Aesira had known this was her plan–

"According to city records," Kamari said, "you have flown more trade runs in your time on parole than anyone else in the Boneyard District."

Aesira scoffed. "He also has more citations than anyone else." Kamari shot her a glare. "Apologies, Your Majesty." Aesira clenched her jaw, forcing her mouth to stay shut. They weren't just Kamari and Aesira here, they were Commander and Queen and Kamari outranked her every time.

Stone glanced between them before popping the pencil he'd been tapping back behind his ear. "That's because no one else in the Boneyard District is trusted to fly a ship," he said. "The only reason I was granted access was because I offered something in return. Nothing's ever given freely, especially to an Odega."

"And what was it you offered?" Kamari asked, folding her hands across her lap.

Stone sighed and rubbed a hand across the back of his neck. "A new engine model. One that can fly twice as long and run on half the amount of *astra*. A miracle the armada ever made it through the desert at all before with that primitive design. When I was released from prison, the Boneyard District was my station while on parole. Didn't take long to realize it was a fucking mess." His eyes blew wide. "Sorry."

"Don't be," Kamari said. "Please, continue."

"Anyway, the district was still running with decades old equipment. An absolute abhorrent and unnecessary use of *astra*." He leaned forward, bracing his elbows on the table. "In fact, it was King Desmond that offered me the promotion. He was generous enough to take a meeting with me and my supervisor at the time. Heard my pitch about the new model. The next day, Chap was gone and I was in charge of the lot." He leaned back in his chair, crossing his arms across his chest.

"Awfully impressive for someone your age," Kamari said.

Stone shrugged. "That's not the point," he said. "Your royal fliers have been trained on how to operate and maintain the new engines, you don't need me to fly for them anymore."

Instinctively Aesira looked around the dim room, confirming no one else was joining them. This was the kind of conversation to be had behind closed, secure doors, not behind a ratted old tarp.

"Along with an experienced flier," Kamari said, "I'm also looking for discretion." Stone's brows shot up. "As far as the council and anyone in Vargah knows, this will be a routine drop off to the Outpost. Nothing more."

Aesira's hand was beginning to ache, clenching her sword so tightly, her jaw and teeth bound together. Kamari was always the reasonable one. The one who guided Aesira and Eldrin, their younger brother, when they were lost; which for them was often. This plan, leaving during a storm season, made no sense. It was dangerous. Reckless.

"Except if it were routine," Stone said, "it wouldn't be for another few months after the sandstorms have died down." A smile tugged at his lips and his eyes drifted past Kamari, landing on Aesira. She shifted, looking away but she could still feel him staring and despite how hard she tried, her cheeks began to heat. "It still doesn't answer my question, Your Majesty. Why would you need me to fly a ship during storm season?"

THREE

KAMARI

"**I** have weighed the options," Kamari said, which was of course, a lie. There were no options to weigh. Finding Desmond was the *only* option and this was the *only* way. The thought of sending a crew farther than the perimeter had been marinating since the first day of Desmond's disappearance. Now, with the council on her back and the threat of marrying Raffe hanging over her head, she couldn't imagine any *other* option. Storm season or not, she couldn't just sit and hope Desmond would show up on his own. She had to find him.

"Our city needs its king. If you are up for the task, your crew will sail west, past the Outpost."

"Past the perimeters?" Stone's brows tugged together. Kamari nodded. There was a long beat of silence as the weight of her suggestion settled around the table. She didn't need to look to know Aesira was frowning, disapproving of her idea. It wasn't long ago Aesira would have suggested something similar but the Order had changed her and even though she shouldn't, sometimes Kamari missed the wildness of her younger sister.

"What makes you so sure he headed west?" Stone's eyes bounced between Kamari and Aesira, a hard look on his face that was impossible to read.

Kamari filled her lungs, held the breath until it burned, then released it with a silent prayer to the stars. "I brought you these." Kamari placed the stack of leather-bound journals on the table, her fingers trailing over the raised lettering that sprawled across the spines. "They're my husband's most recent journals I found in his study." She peeled one open, revealing several folded maps. "All of these maps are of the west, though they're vague as you can imagine." Her fingers traced over Desmond's soft writing in the margins. "He's written notes all throughout. If he left, this is where he was headed."

Stone grabbed the journal on top, a deep cognac color that was wearing on the corners and thumbed through it. "He kept many journals," Kamari said, filling the silence. "Always taking notes, sketching, babbling to himself." She smiled, but the last memory of him shouting at himself turned her stomach sour. "I can't be sure it's where he went–"

"Shh," Stone said, his brows furrowed.

"Excuse me?" Aesira said before Kam got the chance. His eyes snapped to Aesira's first, then to hers.

"I'm sorry, Your Majesty." He cleared his throat and set the open journal down between them. "It's just there's something interesting here." He pulled the glasses from the top of his head and slid them on, burying his face closer to the journal. Hope surged through Kamari's chest. "This, here." Stone tapped on the open page, his forefinger landing on a single word circled over and over again.

"Ravki?"

"Yes." Stone dropped his voice to a whisper which sent Kamari on edge. "This word." He pointed again to the word, rather than saying. "Have you seen it before?"

Kamari studied the word and it took her a moment before her memory came rushing back. "Yes!" she shouted and then silently cursed herself for the outburst. "Sorry. Here." She rifled through the maps until she came to the one that she was looking for. "It's interesting, I've studied these maps the last several days and none of them match any in the Vargah libraries. At least any that I could find." She slid the parchment to Stone. On the tea-stained map sat the word, worn down and barely visible; *Ravki*. And next to it, Desmond's notes.

"Through the ruins," Aesira said, reading over her shoulder. "What does that mean? I've never heard of that place."

Neither had Kamari, which is why she thought the map a farce. Sometimes, in the height of war, cartographers from the opposing kingdom would draft illegitimate maps to confuse enemy troops, purposely planting them in their camps. She figured this was nothing more than that but the way Stone tensed when she'd said the word aloud told her there was much more to this map than she first assumed.

"Listen to me," Stone said, the roughness of his voice sending the hairs on Kamari's arms straight up. "I need you to go back to your husband's study." He ripped a blank page from one of the journals and Kamari flinched. "Anything you find with these words on them, bring them to me." He pulled the pencil from behind his ear and began writing so quickly Kamari gave up trying to read from across the table. "Here." He folded the paper in half twice before handing it to her. He pushed his glasses back on the top of his head and downed the last of his drink. "I would advise you to show no one. Tell no one."

"You're speaking as if the words written in that journal are dangerous." Aesira stepped closer, craning her neck to get a look at the journal.

Stone glanced at her. "This"— he tapped the word–*Ravki*–in the journal again—"I believe, is the first clue to finding your husband. And that"— he pointed to the folded paper in Kamari's palm—"may be the whole damn puzzle." He took a ragged breath, like the last few minutes he'd forgotten to breathe at all.

"You think my husband went in search of this Ravki place?" Kamari's eyes wandered over the dull map again but they stuck on the handwritten note where Desmond had drawn circles over and over, the pencil marks so deep there was a tiny tear in the paper. "Why?"

Stone stiffened before running a hand down his face. "Ravki is a place of stories, not fact, but every myth surrounding it is the same." He looked up from the papers. "Magic and beasts that live in harmony."

Kamari scoffed, holding a hand to her chest like she'd been hit there and in a way it felt like it. "There is no magic other than that given to us by Celestria." Her body went rigid, her spine straightening. "There is no magic other than *astra*." It was blasphemous to believe in magic outside of what the goddess provided, and the thought of Desmond going after such myths... She clutched her hands together under the table.

"Like I said, it's built on old traveler myths. There's no proof Ravki even exists but to some, the promise of reward is worth more than the risk of getting there. If that is what your husband went looking for, I'm afraid to say it was a fool's errand." Stone stacked the journals into a neat pile and slid them toward her. "The faster we leave, the better chance we have at finding him before it's too late."

Lead settled in Kamari's stomach. A million questions buzzed in her mind but before she could ask them, Stone stood. "If you find anything with the words I've written, please bring them to me before our departure."

"So, you'll go? You'll do this?" Kamari knew how desperate she sounded, hated the fact that the look on Stone's face told her he knew as well. But this was her only chance at finding Desmond before her time was up and she'd be forced to make an impossible decision.

"There's no guarantee we'll make it past the Outpost during the storms. And even if we do, there's a chance that his Majesty didn't."

The implication polluted the air around them.

There's a chance he's already dead.

"I understand the risk of travel during the storm season which is why I'll pay you triple what a flight fee typically runs, not to mention the crown will owe you a favor." Nervous, excited energy buzzed through Kamari as she spoke, her knee bobbing under the table. "And as for Desmond—just find him, in any state, and bring him home. Do we have a deal?"

"Kamari," Aesira warned.

"I'll need funds to cover the cost to prep a ship." Stone crossed his arms again. "We'll want to take our best girl and she took a large hit during the last sandstorm."

"Fine," Kamari said, her heart thundered in her chest.

Hope, hope, hope, it seemed to say with every beat.

"And time," Stone continued, "the repairs are extensive."

"How long?"

"A few days." He shrugged. "Maybe a week."

"A few days," Kamari said firmly. She didn't want to waste a moment longer than she needed to. "Expect the money for your ship to be deposited tonight." She extended her hand and waited.

"One last thing," Stone said, leaving her hand hanging between them. "I'll take a crew of my choosing. Some of my best are currently residing under the city, but I won't fly that far without them."

The prisons.

If the people of Vargah didn't see her as an enemy before, surely releasing several prisoners without reason would do the trick.

"How many?"

"Three," Stone said. "I need them for the job. And after it's complete, they're pardoned. Free from any remainder of their sentencing. Free to leave Vargah if they wish."

Kamari sighed. She should have anticipated some sort of bargaining. "I will need to check their records for any violent crimes."

"They were smugglers," Stone said. "Born on the wrong side of the wall. Just doing what they needed to do in order to survive. Like me."

The wrong side of the wall.

The Outpost.

While the small colony was far enough from Vargah and Novaria to stand on its own, it technically resided in Vargahian territory and reluctantly the kingdom had supplied just enough rations and *astra* to keep the Outpost afloat, and not a pinch more.

The very least she could do was pardon a few criminals who likely had no other choice in careers. Then, when Desmond was back, she'd bring up supplying the Outpost with more humane rations. Now that Novaria and Vargah had joined forces, there should be more than enough.

"Okay." Kamari ignored her sister's glare like the plague itself. "Deal."

Stone's hand met hers, a smile lighting up his otherwise cold face. "Deal. Pleasure doing business, Majesty." He leaned around Kamari, his smile spreading. "Commander." Stone winked and Kamari bit the inside of her cheek to keep from smiling. "It was good to see you again."

Four

Aesira

"What the hell was that?" Aesira had kept quiet the entire walk back to the Citadel, not trusting for a second any loose lips that might be listening. But now that they were in Kamari's room and it was only the two of them, no roles to be played, she let her fury flow through her voice. "You've just made a deal–"

"I did what I had to do." Kamari placed the stack of journals on the desk in her room.

A wave of dizziness swept through Aesira. There were so many things she wanted to say.

How could you make a deal with an Odega?

How could you not tell me your plan?

Only when she glanced at Kam and saw the way she worried her bottom lip through her teeth, did her edges soften. She couldn't imagine the stress Kamari was feeling, with Desmond gone and the treaty threatened. Aesira was here to protect the wall, but more than anything, she wanted to protect her sister. Even when she made choices that Aesira couldn't fathom. "Are you sure you can trust him?"

"No," Kam said, "but I'm desperate enough to." Kamari pushed the curtains back, and from where Aesira stood, she could see the dust from the earlier sandstorm had settled. The red of the city now muted to a murky brown.

Aesira shifted, the bronze of her chest plate glinting in the midday sun. "I'll head to the Phoenix tonight, doesn't take much to get the people of this city talking. Someone other than Stone must have heard of Ravki."

"Thank you," Kam said. "I know the plan is outrageous but if we can find Desmond, if we can get him home maybe this can all be a bad dream."

"We? What do you mean, *we*?"

Kam sat at Desmond's desk, stacking the remaining books and journals into a neat pile. "I think you know what I mean."

Since when did Kamari become the reckless one? Since when did their roles reverse? Aesira's heart raced, a busy beating thing pressing against her ribs. "Are you out of your mind? You're going with them?"

Her sister ignored her, stacking and restacking the journals on top of the desk as if organizing them would help bring clarity to the situation.

"There's a reason no one travels past the Outpost, Kam. Sand-storms. Dust clouds large enough to take down a ship. Not to mention the accounts of many deadly beasts." Kamari flinched and Aesira knew she'd said the wrong thing again.

If Desmond truly left for the west, those were all things he would have had to endure.

Alone.

Aesira softened her voice, letting out a long breath. "Maybe if we can wait, gather a proper search team–"

"There is no more time!" Kamari spun around, a desperation lining her eyes Aesira had never seen before. The ripped shards of her heart sunk low in her stomach. "You were in that room, Aesira. You know what the council plans to do. Do you expect me to remarry so soon? Or abandon the treaty?"

"Of course not," Aesira said, tapping her boot in a rhythmic pattern. "Okay." She nodded one too many times before squaring her shoulders. It was unfathomable to even consider letting her sister join a crew of Odega's over the wall during the storm season. "I agree we need to find Desmond, but you can't leave Vargah with an empty throne. They are a den of vipers and the moment they see an opportunity to strike, they won't hesitate."

Kamari sighed, pinching the bridge of her nose between two fingers. "You're right. I just..." She threw her hands up. "I have to know where he is, Aesira."

"So, I'll go instead."

"Absolutely not. It's too dangerous."

Aesira smirked, hand resting on her sword. "And yet you would go?" Kamari opened her mouth, a snarky reply surely at the ready but Aesira didn't let her get a word in. "Let me go. That way I can keep an eye on the smuggler. Make sure he's doing what he's agreed to do. I'm sure I can be of some assistance."

"*Ex*-smuggler," Kam corrected with a hint of arrogance. "He hasn't smuggled in years. He's *reformed*, remember?"

Aesira grunted.

"And what will the Order say if they hear you've left your station?"

Aesira shrugged but she was sure Kamari saw the quick panic that laced behind her eyes at the mention of leaving her station. The Order was as rigid as the council in their rules. The knights in the Order did not make their own decisions. They were soldiers, footmen, defenders of the kingdom–*kingdoms*.

A plan stitched together in Aesira's mind and a small part of her past self unfurled inside her. The unruly part the Order had stamped down, but not killed. "The Order doesn't need to know," she said, the defiance in her statement sending a thrill down her spine. "Nev will stay behind and look after things, she'll cover me if she needs to," she said. "She and Rahashi will take care of you and Vargah."

"I'm not completely useless, you know."

"I know that," Aesira said. "But it's their job to protect you, so just let them."

"Thank you."

"What are sisters for if not risking their lives for each other?" She winked, then nodded toward Kamari's hand where the parchment from Stone was tucked into her palm. "Now, let me see the paper." Aesira attempted to snatch the parchment from her sister's hands, but Kamari was too quick, tucking it into her dress safely behind her bodice.

"Quiet," she said. "You saw how Stone acted. As if whatever he wrote on this could lead to trouble."

"He *is* the trouble."

"Again," Kamari said, "so flustered. Are you going to tell me what happened between you two?"

"Nothing happened," Aesira grumbled, flames tipping her ears and cheeks.

"Oh." Kam pinched her cheek. "Don't sound so disappointed."

Aesira shrugged away. "You'll have to show me eventually if I'm going with them so it may as well be now." Aesira was masterful at changing the subject, especially if the subject was her.

"Fine." Kamari carefully unfolded the paper and held it between them.

Of the first three words, Aesira only recognized one from earlier.

Ravki.

The next two were just as perplexing.

Whispering Mountains.

Lunaris.

But when her eyes landed on the last word, her lungs froze.

Dragon.

"This is *blasphemy*," Aesira whispered through gritted teeth. "If Stone thinks Desmond has gone looking for"—she pointed to the last word—"Desmond would be considered a *criminal* and if you think the scroll you saw this morning was treasonous, this would be worse by ten. A hundred, even."

Aesira ran a hand down her face and shook her head. "He would be viewed as a betrayer of Celestria, Kam. If he believes dragons to exist, he would defy the very religion his throne is built upon." Aesira was talking too fast, her face burning red. She paced the room, the click of her boots and grinding of her armor filling the space. "Dragons," she whispered, "are unspoken for a reason. They directly challenge Celestria."

"I know," Kamari said.

"Of all the beasts in the west…" She shook her head again. "Desmond wouldn't be welcomed back and if he managed to he would be—"

"I know." Kamari folded the paper again, placing it back in her dress pocket.

"If we acknowledge this, we may be tried as well." Aesira bit her bottom lip. If Desmond truly believed dragons to be real, his mind was far worse than Kamari let on.

"I won't make you go," Kamari said. "I won't risk your life for the sake of another's. I know you don't trust Stone, but he's my only chance."

"No," Aesira cut her off. "I'm going. I made you a promise and I plan to keep it, I just want you to realize the risks. Belief in"—she mouthed the word *dragons*—"is not just a crime in Vargah, but Novaria too."

"I know," Kamari said again. But did she know? Did she see how severe the consequences of betraying Celestria would be? The goddess blessed their kingdoms. Provided what they needed to sustain life in the barren desert. She was fickle, however. Nothing would compete with her power and anything remotely close would be abolished. Cursed. No gods or deities. No beasts with wings.

Celestria was All and they would worship as such to gain her privileges. Like the *astra* that kept Vargah running and in turn, Novaria and smaller dwellings like the Outpost. She blessed them with water that staved their thirst and kept them alive.

"They're bringers of despair," Aesira said. "I don't know why he'd wish to find such things."

Kamari glanced out the window, her eyes distant and shoulders slumped. "It seems despair has found us either way."

Five

Aesira

The Phoenix was raucous as usual as Aesira and two of her knights squeezed through the crowded tavern to find a spot at the bar.

"Any luck with the headliner?" Aesira snatched a pint from behind the counter and slid it to Nev, her second in command. Finally, the three of them had a night off, the first in weeks, and the promise of indulging in a foamy point had driven her through the last of her rounds at the wall.

Nev took a sip of the foamy ale, licking it clean from her lips. "Some young shit trying to make a name for himself. I shut him up," she said. "I'd tell her Majesty not to worry."

Aesira snorted and took a sip of the sour ale. "If only you knew my sister."

Nora waved down the barkeep and ordered another round before she'd even taken a sip of her first drink. Aesira and Nev shot her a look and she smiled, crinkling her freckled nose. "What?" She shrugged. "If I'm being assigned to a perilous quest across the least charted land in the country, why shouldn't I enjoy my last night off? It's not like the Order will know."

Nev tossed a broken piece of cracker at her twin before returning to her drink. Between the two, Aesira had chosen to take Nora with her, leaving Nev here to look after Kamari. She didn't trust Lord Raffe for a second and if she couldn't keep an eye on him herself, Nev was her next best option.

"And if the General finds out you two have left your station?" Nev asked, pulling her red hair back into a tight bun.

Aesira hid her flinch at the mention of the General, the Order's highest ranking officer. Her direct superior. The small wounds that lined her neck and arms ached, the memories of what she'd endured at the hand of the woman who was meant to be her savior rising to the surface. "She won't find out, we'll be back before our official orders are up."

"When do we leave?" Nora asked.

Aesira took a sip of her drink, steadying her nerves and numbing the phantom pains in her arms and neck. "Just as soon as that smuggler fixes the ship."

"Stone," a voice came from behind them. Aesira let out a long sigh before Stone leaned between her and Nora, sliding a few coins on the bar top. "My name is Stone, we've gone over this, Commander." A small smile tugged at his lips. "I'm wounded you don't remember." He turned his focus to Nora. "Forgive me for the reach, I just need to pay my tab."

"How civil of you," Aesira mused. "Wouldn't peg you as the kind of man to make sure his dues are paid."

"Oh?" Stone crossed his arms across his broad chest. "And what kind of man do you peg me for?"

Nora coughed into her drink, concealing a laugh. Aesira stood, abandoning her half-drunk ale on the bar. "You think you're clever," she said, "but clever men don't get caught. And if my math is right–" She held up one, two, three fingers and smiled. "You were caught three times smuggling durgi from the Outpost to both Novaria and Vargah."

Stone's smile widened, his hands raising in defeat. "That's fair," he said. "I did get caught." He stepped closer, invading her space. Grease and oil still stained his shirt. He pushed his glasses up and Aesira's eyes snagged on a pointed star inked to the side of his neck. "I also got out," he said. "I'm a free man now, Commander. As much as I'm sure that disappoints you."

Aesira stepped back, creating space between them. "You would do well to remember your place, Stone *Odega*." She spat the name like it was a curse, and to those who bore it maybe it was. A constant reminder of their past mistakes, branded into them for everyone to see.

Stone reached around her and grabbed her drink from the bar, sipping it slowly.

"That's mine."

"And where is my place, Commander? Beneath you?" Stone cocked his head to the side. The sour smell of ale drifted from his lips, and she had to wonder how many drinks he'd had tonight. The first night they met, he'd been quiet. Timid. But now he looked at her with the confidence of someone in power. Maybe it was the deal with Kamari that fueled his swagger. Maybe it was the drink he was steadily polishing off.

He swallowed back the rest of her drink and set the empty glass on the bar. "Trust me, I couldn't forget being beneath you if I tried." He leaned in and Aesira tilted back, though with the bar behind her, there wasn't anywhere to go. His lips brushed against her ear. "Admittedly, I haven't tried very hard. In fact, I'm picturing myself beneath you right—"

Aesira's short blade was off her hip and under Stone's chin before he could say another word. She pushed it into his soft flesh, not hard enough to mark him, but enough to silence him. "Finish that sentence, I dare you."

"Stone." A man wrapped his arm around Stone's shoulder, pulling him back, away from Aesira. "I think you've had enough." His dark, angular eye swept over Aesira, then to Nev and Nora, his other eye covered with a dark patch. Aesira dropped her blade. "Pardon my unintelligent friend, here. He's had a few too many."

"Queen's money burning a hole in your pocket, Odega?" Nora giggled, sipping her drink.

The man holding Stone turned his attention to Nora, his dark eye lazily taking her in from top to bottom. "And who pays you, sweetheart?" A flush of pink swept over Nora's freckled cheeks. "Exactly. Queen's money or not, it all spends the same."

Aesira tucked her blade away. "At least our money has been earned," she mumbled. Stone opened his mouth, but the man stepped in front of him. His dark hair was swept back, gathered at the nape of his neck, his frame much larger than Stone's.

"I'm Patch." He extended his hand; did he expect her to take it? Shake hands with an Odega?

"Aesira," she said, ignoring his hand completely.

"Another ex-smuggler?" Nora sipped her drink, watching the man over the rim of her glass.

"What gave it away?" Patch asked through a smile. "We should go, boss." He patted Stone on the back, gave Nora a quick wink, then wove through the crowd.

Stone leaned in towards Aesira again, "I'll see you at the docks," he said, before he left to join Patch at the back of the tavern where two others were waiting.

All of the criminals Kamari had released.

Aesira sunk back into her stool and ordered another ale.

"Well they seem fun," Nev said through a smile.

"He's a nuisance."

"I don't know," Nora said, "he's pretty cute. Don't you think he's cute, Nev? Not as cute as Patch, but cute."

Nev stifled a laugh behind her drink and Aesira thought twice about leaving them both at the bar.

"Not my type," Nev said.

"Right," Nora said through a laugh. "We know your type." She nodded to the end of the bar where a group of women huddled together, laughing and chatting. "At least be courteous and buy them a drink if you're going to stare."

"Fuck off," Nev said before downing her drink.

Aesira listened to the twins bicker back and forth, but her mind was elsewhere. The memory of her and Stone's bodies entwined together in the bathroom burned her cheeks. It was embarrassing. A regret she wished she could forget.

"He's clearly taken," Aesira said to no one in particular, brows pinching as she watched Stone from across the tavern. He leaned into one of the women at the table. Her face was slim and angular, short honey hair cropped blunt at her jaw. She was whispering something now, making Stone smile, but what did it matter? Stone Odega was the last thing she needed to be thinking about. In just a few days, they'd leave Vargah and embark on a mission she wasn't sure she believed in.

No, she was positive it would fail.

She'd never tell Kamari that. She couldn't stand seeing her sister hurt. Aesira had always done her best to avoid being the root of her sister's pain. She was determined to give this mission everything she had. She'd take all the years she spent under the Order's boot, all the training and diligence, and put it to good use.

She sipped from her fresh ale and couldn't help as her gaze drifted to the back of the tavern again.

Stone and the woman sat next to each other and across from them, another woman with deep brown skin and the man who introduced himself as Patch.

The ale was bitter, not as sweet as the last one like she preferred, but she sipped it and returned her focus to Nora and Nev.

Nothing would stand in her way of helping her sister, not even a table full of Odegas.

"Are you sure you're ready to go?" Kamari paced Aesira's small room. She was biting her nails again, a habit their mother hated when they were children.

"I'm sure." Aesira slipped her armor on, tightening the buckles. "Are *you* sure you can handle things here while I'm gone?" Kam stopped her pacing and her nostrils flared.

Shit.

Aesira was good at that. Saying the wrong thing at the wrong time. In fact, sometimes she wondered if it was all she was good at. But the heaviness of the sword at her side reminded her that she possessed more skills than being a shitty sister.

"I told you I'm not completely useless," Kam snapped. "Plus, I have Hanna. Nev and Rahashi. I'll be fine."

Aesira crossed the room and placed her hands on her sister's shoulders. "Am I not allowed to worry?"

Kam sighed and her face softened. "I'm worried too. About you. About Desmond. About this damn list and the people of my city."

My city.

Aesira didn't miss the way Kamari claimed Vargah as her own and for whatever reason it stung like a wasp, sharp and quick. She knew her sister was the Queen of Vargah. Knew she had been arranged to marry Desmond. Knew their lives no longer coincided after she took the throne but if the last few months being stationed here had given her anything, it was hope. Hope that she and her sister could still pretend they were young and careless and *free.*

"We'll find him, Kamari," Aesira said. Kam nodded, the furrow of her brows back in place. "I have to go. I'll try and send a hawk when we get to the Outpost. I've heard they still navigate through the winds." Her sister's eyes snapped to hers and her mouth dropped open. Like she had something right on the tip of her tongue but couldn't bring herself to say it. "What? What did I say now?"

Kam shook her head. "Nothing," she reassured. "But yes, hawks can navigate through the winds." Shit. Another wrong thing to say. Hawks could fly through the storms, and Desmond hadn't sent one. The door flew open and Nev popped her head in.

"I've been sent word, the ship is ready to fly." Nev stood, arms positioned behind her uniformed back.

"Thank you." Kamari pulled Aesira close and hugged her so hard she thought the metal of her chestplate might break a rib. "Take this," Kamari said as she pulled away. She handed Aesira a small blade, insignificant enough to fit in the palm of her hand.

"What is this?"

"Desmond gave it to me," she said. "It's supposed to be lucky or something." She shrugged, closing her fingers around Aesira's. "Just take it. Be safe. Be smart."

Aesira palmed the blade and shoved it into her pocket. She couldn't imagine a use for such a small weapon but if it made Kamari feel some sort of ease, she'd do it. "See you in a few weeks."

Kam looped her pinkie with hers. "Promise."

"Promise."

The Boneyard District was in absolute mayhem. Turns out, Kamari's plan for discretion hadn't been a successful one. Children and adults lined the district. Others stood toward the back, arms crossed and faces somber. It was those people, the ones with blatant doubt plastered on their faces, Aesira related to.

This won't end well, she thought. Between the piss-poor crew Stone had put together and the uncertainty of what lay beyond the Outpost, finding Desmond was sounding more and more like a nightmare.

"Nora," Aesira said, "get to the ship and see where we can post up." Nora nodded but before she left she turned to Nev. Their matched freckled faces and bright red hair mulled together as they hugged tightly.

"Don't do anything stupid." Nev pulled back. They may be twins but there was no confusing the two, not with Nev's permanent scowl and Nora's smile she gave too freely.

"Me?" Nora bat her long lashes. "I would never."

"I don't know where she gets that wild streak," Nev said.

Aesira huffed a laugh. "I don't know how it survived the Order." She turned to Nev, ignoring the rising sounds of the crowd. "You need to watch Kamari and keep tabs on Lord Raffe. Make sure–"

"I've got this, Commander." Nev squeezed her shoulder, her grip firm and reassuring. "Safe flight." Then she disappeared into the crowd and Aesira had nothing else to do but board the ship.

"Commander, you made it. I was starting to worry." Stone wiped his oil-stained hands on a rag before throwing it over his shoulder. "I take it your evening went on just fine after I left you at the Phoenix?"

She gritted her teeth, leaning into the weight of her sword for comfort. "Let's save the pleasantries," she said. "We both know you'd rather me not be here so spare me the false politeness."

He chuckled, a low and gravelly sound, before waving her forward. "Come on," he said.

Aesira stepped forward, moving around Stone blocking the walkway. "My sister may have faith in you, but–"

"I'm offended, Commander," he said. "I thought I'd earned your respect." A few Boneyard workers shuffled past, carrying crates and heavy ropes.

"If you try anything," Aesira said, "I won't hesitate to enforce the power I've been given." She glanced down at the sword at her hip and the restraints on the opposite side.

"Fair enough." Stone shrugged. "But I'll remind you, that while the idea of being tied up by you is tempting, I'm afraid I'll need both of my hands to do my job well. Now, make yourself useful and grab that crate." He nodded to a stack nearby.

"I don't take orders from Odegas."

Stone smiled, crossing his arms across his chest. "We'll see about that."

Heat bloomed over Aesira's neck and cheeks and despite how hard she tried, the memories of the first night she met Stone at The Phoenix came rushing back. Hands and skin. Tongues and teeth.

"Listen," Stone said, his tone softening. Maybe he was also remembering that night, which only made Aesira's fevered skin scorch hotter. "You're a commander and I respect that. But we don't know what lies beyond the Outpost. All I know is we'll see things." He stepped closer. "Hear things." Another step until it was just the width of the crate between them. "Feel things we can't explain." He'd dropped his voice and in a place that was so loud, she found it confusing that all she could hear was him. "The things that dwell in the desert only have one goal and that is to kill you or drive you mad enough to do it yourself. So, unless you have a death wish, I'd suggest taking some of your sister's faith and instilling it in me and my crew. I'm not after anything other than what I was promised."

"What kind of things?" She'd grown up in Novaria, a comfortable, albeit small, kingdom in the east. Aside from her training with the knights and her travels to Vargah, she hadn't seen much else of the world.

"Things not even your nightmares could imagine."

She picked up a lone crate and followed behind him. Aesira wasn't afraid of Stone's promise of deadly and terrifying things. He had no idea the types of nightmares she had or even worse, the things she'd witnessed when she was awake. But she was curious and she made her sister a promise. Find Desmond. Bring him home. So with every instinct not to trust Stone gnawing at her, she stamped them down. "Fine," she said. "We both agree to find the king and nothing more."

"Nothing more." He smiled again before turning and heading straight into the belly of the ship.

SIX

STONE

It wasn't necessarily the Commander's presence on the ship that bothered Stone, but more so what she stood for. A reminder of who he'd made a deal with.

The royal crown of Vargah.

News would spread to the Outpost that he was a sellout. Working for the very people they'd resented their entire lives. Royals. Living in excess, bathing in *astra* and water like it was luxury. As if people didn't die for the goddess they worshiped. Weren't slaughtered on stage while a crowd cheered.

Stone picked up the last of the rations and made his way below deck, setting the crate on a counter to sort through later. Aesira had gotten distracted by her knight, Stone hadn't caught her name, and he was grateful for a few minutes alone without her breathing down his neck.

"Stoney."

So much for a moment alone.

He fucking hated that nickname, but considering Birdie was the only one who used it, he let it slide. She set down a matching crate on the counter and crossed her arms.

"Provisions?" He nodded at her crate. Her dark eyes narrowed as she swept a lock of silky blonde hair away from her hollowed cheeks.

"Yes," she said. "The queen was generous." She plucked an overripe plum from the crate and juggled it between her hands. "She'll be disappointed to find out this all goes to waste considering the likelihood we live long enough to eat it."

Stone leaned against the wooden counter. He knew out of the crew, Birdie would be the most difficult to convince of his plan. But that's why he loved her. She was sharp, lethal, and the only one who called him on his shit.

"I told you last night, the amount she offered to pay us will change everything, Bird," he said. She tossed the fruit again, but he snatched it from the air before she could catch it and took a bite. "Look how much it's already changed, you're out aren't you?"

A smirk tilted up her thin lips. "You should have consulted us *first*," she said. "We always have a choice, remember?" He froze mid-bite, the soft flesh of the fruit sweet on his tongue. He hadn't expected her to use his own words against him. He chewed slowly, buying himself time.

Of course they always had a choice. He made sure of it, especially after their days of smuggling came to an abrupt halt. Growing up without a say in how they chose to live their lives, who they worked for. That was the one thing he swore to do differently when they got out of the Outpost. Out from under Vic's pressing thumb.

"Cut him some slack."

Salvation had a name and it was Bee Odega. Bee shot Stone a wink before she wrapped her arms around Birdie, tugging her close.

"Bee," he said her name like it was a refuge and in some ways it was. Her smile grew, dimpling her umber cheeks. "Your hair," Stone said. "I like it shorter."

"You can compliment the guards for their craftsmanship." Bee ran a steady hand over her head, the dark hair shorn close to her scalp. "They shaved it nearly clean." Bee turned to Birdie and kissed her, quick and expected like they'd done a hundred times before, but this time with a small pause when Birdie pulled away. A hesitation that made Stone question whether he should let them have some privacy, considering they've been apart for several months.

"Now, you two were discussing the..." Bee glanced up the stairwell, where heavy footsteps and bustling people still carried about. "The agreement?" she whispered. Birdie's face had softened as it always did when Bee was around, but as soon as the words were suspended between them, her eyes shot daggers in Stone's direction.

"Yes," Birdie said, "the agreement he conveniently didn't have time to tell us about last night."

Oh he had the time, but he figured the element of surprise was the only way to get them on board with two royal knights joining their crew. "Had too much to drink," he said, "it slipped my mind."

Birdie punched his shoulder. "Bullshit."

"Well if it isn't my favorite criminals? Who's the most hungover?" The deep rumbling of Patch's voice nearly shook the crates on the counter. "Stone?" He slapped Stone's back, a broad smile stretched over his lips. "You look like shit," he said. "I think you win."

"Fuck off." Stone slapped his hand away but a smile bloomed across his mouth.

He'd been out for six months, which only meant that the rest of them had spent that much longer in prison and that fact ate at him everyday. Maybe his plan was shit, maybe it wouldn't work with the knights here, but he got them out and for now he could at least be thankful they were all together again.

"Rule number one," Birdie bellowed from her small frame, hands on her hips.

"Here we go." Stone buried his face in a cupboard, pretending to sort through their provisions.

"Any decision that impacts the cadre must be voted on and passed unanimously," she said. Stone could admit he'd fucked that one up, but seeing them all together, on a ship no less, solidified his decision to break the rule. The queen's offer was too good to pass up and despite Birdie's frustration, he knew she'd see his reasoning sooner or later.

"Birdie–"

"The second," she said, ignoring Bee, "no matter what, we always have each other's backs. We don't leave anyone behind."

"Aye," said Patch, nudging Stone's shoulder. The second rule, Birdie failed to understand, was one of the most important reasons he insisted to the queen he needed them. If one of them was in trouble, someone would come. No questions asked. That's why he demanded their release. They were in trouble, and he came to them.

"The third and most relevant rule," Birdie said, closing in on him. Stone's grip froze around a pack of dried meat. "No outsiders."

He turned to face Birdie. His best friend. A dedicated pain in his ass. "I didn't have a choice in them coming, Bird."

She crossed her arms, tilting her head to meet Stone's gaze. "I'd bet you didn't protest it."

"Against the queen?" Bee slid her hand into Birdie's. "Come on, Birdie, what would you have done?"

Patch adjusted the eyepatch, his good eye bright and shining. His dark hair had grown longer, he wore it tied back, low at his neck, showing his matching star tattoo along with several others he'd acquired during his smuggling years. "Tell us more about the mission, boss."

Stone hated when he called him that, but he understood it. In the Outpost, Stone led the three of them as runners. They worked together, lived together, they trusted Stone then and for some reason they still trusted him now.

"Not much more to tell." Stone shrugged. "We find the king, bring him home, and you assholes are pardoned." He turned to Birdie and gave his brightest smile. "You're welcome."

"Everything is so easy for the notorious Stone Odega." Birdie shook her head. "We have a lot of terrain to cross. Plus, do you really think showing your face in the Outpost is going to be smooth as silk?"

"Sometimes the risk is worth the reward, Bird," Stone said. "That's the case now. Plus, like you said, I'm notorious for a reason." He picked up a crate from the floor and shoved it into her hands. "I'll get us through."

Everything he told the queen and her sister was true. He had flown the most miles of any current living pilot in Vargah. He had heard of Ravki and dragons. He had seen the words Lunaris and Whispering Mountains more than once in various books he stashed in the Outpost and most of all, he knew if there was anyone that would be able to hunt down a missing king and the remains of an ancient, mythical city, it was him and his crew. They'd survived hell and back being runners for Vic, they could survive a few monsters and a knight or two.

Whether he intended to actually *find* the king was a different matter entirely. One he wasn't sure he cared to do. Change in leadership always came with promise and visions of a better future. Desmond was no different. Even though it was bred deep into Stone's bones to distrust Vargah, distrust Novaria, he couldn't deny the fact that King Desmond *had* helped him. Had seen something in him and allowed him a chance at a new life.

"I'm all for the adventure," Bee said. "Beats rotting in prison."

Patch huffed a laugh, but Birdie kept her gaze locked on Stone. She was daring him to say everything he hadn't yet. That there was a real chance King Desmond wasn't alive. That there was an even better chance *they* wouldn't survive past the Outpost.

Stone went back to emptying the crate. Fruit, dried meats, nuts. He focused on categorizing the provisions. Putting his hands to work was the best way to get his brain to shut up.

Except even with the supplies in front of him, he couldn't stop the racing thoughts circling in his mind.

With the queen's promise to pay half upfront, and the ship filled with *astra*, his old ways of running through the desert came rearing up like a bolt of dry lightning. He could abandon the mission altogether and sail away from Vargah with his cadre in tow and never look back. They were already free from the prison, who cared about a pardon if they were a continent away? With the vast amount of *astra* the queen had provided, they could make it all the way to the Isles without looking back.

It could be a way for them to start fresh. Start over. Just like they'd always dreamt. But every time he thought of fleeing, of leaving the Commander and her knight in the Outpost and heading for freedom, his mind snagged on one detail.

Ravki.

Stone was a smart man, he could admit that. And the reality was that Ravki likely didn't exist. The myths surrounding the city were as ancient as Celestria herself. The stories had morphed over time. More dramatized one year to the next. And so, with his logical brain, Stone knew the likelihood that Ravki existed was slim to none. But there was always a chance–

"The man on the dock said it's time." Aesira descended the stairs, the metallic clink of her armor foreign and distracting in the otherwise quiet of the barracks. Her gaze swept over them, her mismatched eyes calculating. Cold. They landed first on Stone, then Bee and Birdie still wrapped up in each other's arms, then on Patch whose one eye grew wide then narrowed drastically.

Okay, Stone could admit to himself that he should have run the plan by the group first. They were, after all, risking their lives to seek a king they didn't consider their own. And to make matters worse, there she was. Aesira Zeliath. Commander to the Order. Upholder of the law. Daughter of the Novaria King and Queen and now sister to the Vargahian Queen. While she wasn't necessarily responsible for any of their personal arrests, what she stood for was blatant.

Order.

Conformity.

All the things they were against.

And even with all of that going against her, Stone couldn't help but track her movements as she set a final crate down on the counter. Her eyes traced the room, dark hair bound in a braid down her back, several tight curls framing her face. His fingers twitched at his sides. The same fingers that had been tangled in her hair a month ago. Then, without his permission, his eyes drifted to her lips. *Shit*. He should not have looked at her lips because then all he could think about was everywhere they'd been. How they'd tasted–

"Am I interrupting something?" There was accusation in Aesira's tone but Stone didn't blame her. He'd only ever been known to be suspicious and skeptical and in a strange way he found it comforting that she was uncertain of them.

"Not at all," he said, putting the last of the supplies away, ridding himself of any and all thoughts of Aesira Zeliath. "We've got about two hours of daylight left." He pulled his compass from his pocket and tossed it to Birdie. She caught it effortlessly and gave him a semblance of a smile. He knew letting her navigate would win him some points. He shot her a wink. "Let's get in the air."

Flying Aquila never ceased to amaze Stone. No matter how many times he'd done it, the weightless feeling of being lifted off the ground was a high he could never replace. The *astra* that was used to power the ships was often stored away during the stormy season, especially this close to Naming Day when the wells were already running low, but the queen had sent more than enough reserves to get them through to the Outpost and back. The ship roared to life, rocking gently side to side as they gained altitude.

Stone gripped the ship's wheel, the hard grain of wood pressing against his calloused skin. The people below cheered as their silhouettes became nothing but dots in the sandy landscape. He steered the ship left, as Birdie dropped down the first sail.

"Everyone in position," Stone yelled over the rising wind. "Once we cross the wall, the winds will be relentless." A loose rope whipped through the main deck. "Secure every last piece of cargo! I want nothing left to chance." The cadre got to work, Patch barking orders so Stone could focus on flying.

"Should we be worried about that?" Aesira asked from his side. He took a step backward and traced where her finger pointed ahead of them, to a massive sandstorm brewing in the distance. The monstrous clouds billowed in various shades of red and black, the winds pushing and pulling the sand in all directions. The swells rose high above the city, massive enough to engulf the ship entirely.

"No way to fly around it," Stone said. "We'll fly through."

"Through?" There was fear lined in her voice now, he could tell by the way it hitched right at the end, like she was trying her best to remain poised instead of panicked. "Maybe it's best to wait it out." Another gust shot sand up and over the sides of the ship. Stone pulled his goggles on before securing a linen cloth over his nose and mouth.

"Wait for what?" he asked, his voice muffled through the fabric. "Nightfall?" He shook his head before tightening the cloth around his mouth. "I've done this before, you just have to trust me." Their eyes met for a moment, then a gust brought buckets worth of sand over the hull. "You need to put on your goggles." Stone pulled Aesira closer, her eyes still focused on the sandstorm. "Here." He slid the brown leather goggles from where they hung on her neck and secured them around her eyes. Her mouth popped open but before he let her have a chance to speak, he tied a matching linen cloth over her nose and mouth. "For safety." Her eyes narrowed as she pulled away but when she tightened the fabric further, he took it as a thank you.

"Hold steady, everyone!" Stone shouted, his fingers gripping the wheel, steering them right for the eye of the storm.

Seven

Aesira

Sand filtered through the bands of Aesira's goggles. It tangled in her hair and under her fingernails. It crept into her armor and coated her boots. Rubbed between her fingers so badly it hurt. But as she dusted herself off, she couldn't help but marvel at the fact that she was alive. That Stone had pulled off traveling through a sandstorm. If he didn't annoy her so much, she may have even congratulated him.

"There you are," Nora said. She pulled her goggles off and tossed them aside. "There's a small cabin for us downstairs." Nora sat next to her and stretched her legs out. "It's not much. A bunk and some linens. Should get the job done."

Aesira ran her fingers through her hair, working out the tangles the sand and wind had caused. Granules rubbed against her gums, burying themselves between her teeth. She slid off a boot, emptying the sand that filled it, onto the deck. She slid off her other boot and at Nora's silence, glanced at her. Her eyes were trained on the horizon. "What is it?" She followed Nora's gaze and her breath hitched.

Aesira had been so focused on the damn sand she hadn't realized just how far they'd made it from Vargah. An orange glowing silhouette of the city stood out against the inky vastness of the desert. The massive spires of the Citadel seemed so small from where she sat on the bow of the ship and while the beauty of the city at night was something to marvel at, a knot formed in her stomach. Kamari would be alone to fend off the council and Lord Raffe.

"She'll be alright," Nora said, reading her thoughts.

She and her sister were different in so many ways, but the similarities they shared, that *all* Zeliath children shared, was their ability to bend, not break. Their father would allow nothing less than perfection and so Kamari would stay strong in her determination to find Desmond, it was everyone else in Vargah Aesira worried about.

"She's got Nev," Nora said. "That alone should give you some comfort."

Aesira smiled, the muscles in her shoulders relaxing. "Thank Celestria for that," she said. "Still, the sooner we find Desmond, the better."

Nora sighed and reclined back, leaning her weight on her palms. "So you really think the king went looking for this Ravki place?"

Aesira's eyes met hers. "Our queen seems to think so."

"And what do you think?"

Aesira focused again on Vargah in the distance, seeming tiny and insignificant beneath where they sailed, the curved lines of the city blurring together. "I think my sister is trying her best to make sense of Desmond's disappearance. I think she's clinging to the last bit of hope she has."

"Hope," Nora repeated. Not a question. Just a quiet statement. Maybe disbelief. Nora and Nev were raised outside of Novaria, in a small outpost in the northern desert. Their parents didn't have much, so when they became of age, both girls were sent to train with the Order. A place for unruly girls to become someone else's problem.

Being in the same squadron, they'd grown close and stayed that way. Everything about the Order was brutal. The training. The constant barrage from their leaders. The impossible lessons of restraint. Control. Obedience. And even though the memories were not pleasant, Aesira was grateful it brought Nev and Nora to her.

She went back to untangling her hair, the sand woven tightly between her curls. "If Desmond didn't leave to find Ravki. If he just..." She dropped her curls down and sighed. "If he just *left* Kamari and Vargah, that would feel so much worse. So, I think Kamari has convinced herself he's left to do something important." Aesira hadn't given Nora and Nev the full story of what Stone found in the journals. The mention of dragons. As far as they knew, Desmond left in search of Ravki for a reason entirely unknown. Not in pursuit of the beasts that would sever his ties with Celestria and the *astra* and water the goddess provided.

Nora nodded, running a hand across the back of her neck. Her vibrant red hair was twisted into a braid but Aesira could see where the tiny granules of sand stuck between the plaits. "We should get some sleep," she said. She stood and pulled Aesira to her feet. "Can't imagine any good will come from being above deck at night."

Sweat beaded on Aesira's brow as she tossed and turned in the small bed below deck. *"Aesira."* A voice dripped in her ears, hollow and hissing all the same. *"Zeliath."*

She sat straight up, knocking her face directly into a low-hanging beam. "Fuck," she muttered, rubbing her palm against her forehead. She glanced under her bunk, where Nora was still fast asleep. Sliding out of bed, the wooden planks were cold beneath her feet, each of them creaking as she took a step toward the door.

"Aesira." The voice encircled her like smoke, billowing into her ears, her mouth. *"Come, Aesira."*

"Stone?" She placed her palm flat against the door and waited for the voice. "I'm coming out." Her sword was propped up against the wall, she unsheathed it, then opened the door.

Darkness occupied every surface of the ship. She felt her way along the wall, creeping down the long corridor, past several other doors where she could hear snoring coming from the other side.

"This way, Aesira."

She gripped her sword in one hand, climbing the wood ladder that led to the upper deck. Hot and sticky, a breeze coated her skin, pulling loose a few curls from her bun. She adjusted her grip on the pommel and paused. One foot on the deck, the other on the last rung of the ladder. Nothing but silence and stars stretched for miles overhead. Closing her eyes, she took a deep breath. "Focus," she whispered.

The scorching wind brushed her again, bringing forth more beads of sweat on her brow and upper lip. The ladder creaked. Her heart pounded. But still, the voice didn't speak.

She opened her eyes, one at a time. Sucking in a sharp breath, she reared back but was pinned between the door jam and the creature that was now inches from her face. Hollowed cheekbones, stringy black hair, and tarnished remnants of clothing matted to a half-skeletal frame.

"*Aesira.*" Its voice wrapped around her like a noose, tightening and tightening until she couldn't breathe. Couldn't speak. "*Commander. Sister. Princess.*" It raised a knobby hand, half flesh, half bone, and stroked a line down her cheek. Aesira tried to raise her sword. Tried to remember her decades of training but she was stuck. Frozen. At the mercy of this being. This wraith.

"*Come with me.*" Despite her subconscious screaming at her to run, she obeyed, taking the final step off the ladder. Her sword fell to the deck with a sharp clatter. Her hands were too light, too empty, without it. She tried to force her head to turn toward her discarded weapon but the wraith took her hand, its bones digging into her soft flesh and all thoughts of her weapon vanished.

The wraith took a step toward the bow.

Aesira followed.

Another step.

Aesira followed.

"Close," whispered that same voice, though it was softer now. Intoxicating. Aesira could feel the muscles in her normally tense shoulders relax. Could feel a weightlessness in her chest she had never experienced before. Peace settled over her like a warm blanket, wrapping around her anxieties and duties, putting them to bed for the first time in her life.

"You'll be able to rest here, Commander. Wouldn't you like to rest?"

Yes, she wanted to say. She would like that very much because despite how much she loved her job, she also resented it. How it stripped her of everything she was. How it expected her to be everything she wasn't.

"They don't appreciate what you do," the voice whispered against the shell of her ear, as if reading her thoughts. *"No one appreciates how much you've sacrificed."* Her breath hitched, it was something she'd thought many times but never dared say out loud. A grim, oily truth that on her darkest days spun her out of control.

Only when the drinks came easily and she lay alone or beside a companion, quiet and hardly satisfied, did she let poisonous thoughts overtake her mind. Only then, at her very worst, would she let herself *hate* and be resentful. She let herself be angry for how much of herself she erased for the Order.

How many times they beat her down or made her quiet. Submissive. She resented how hard she worked to be someone she didn't care to be. How many years of her life she would never get back and for a future she'd never have, all because her parents thought her to be a burden.

Unladylike.

A thorn in their sides.

A blemish on their otherwise perfect image.

In those dark moments her resentment towards her father fueled her rage.

How quickly he dismissed her. How easy it was to send her away. *"You'll be someone else's problem,"* he'd told her. And that someone was the Order. The General. The ruthless woman who trained the knights that kept the country safe. The Order stripped away everything a person was and molded them into something usable.

A weapon.

"Almost there, pet," the voice cooed against her ear. *"Then you'll see what it means to be truly appreciated."*

Her knees bumped into something hard and with all of her effort, muscles straining for control, she looked down. The wraith had led her right to the edge of the ship. Stars filled her vision, her senses coming back to her but a wash of serenity calmed her frantically beating heart and all she could focus on again was listening to the voice.

"Step up." The wraith tugged her hand and the foreign sharp feeling of bone in her palm stirred something in her.

Wake up, Aesira! She had defeated monsters before. Had slain unimaginable creatures, stopping them before they got too close to the walls of both Novaria and Vargah.

This was different, even in her semi-conscious state, she knew this was nothing like any of the creatures she'd fought before. She had lost control of her body and some sick part of her was glad.

"You'll be someone else's problem."

Her foot hit the railing. Then, her other foot.

Wake up!

"Let go, Aesira. We'll catch you." The voice that brought her so much comfort, so much ease, quickly shifted. And now it rattled her down to her bones. It hissed and clawed at her mind. It pulled at her hair and tugged at her skin.

"No." She clung to the nearest rigging, fingers wrapped tight around the cable. Another push to her back forced her forward so she was barely balancing on the edge of the ship, forced to look down. A tear slipped down her cheek as the voices, many now, cried out around her again and again. Yelling out all her most shameful thoughts. All of her darkest truths and secrets.

"The girl with evil in her eyes."

"Who only sees after herself."

"You let him die, Aesira."

A scream burned in her throat, stamped out by fear. She hadn't let him die. She didn't–

"No," she said, but the wraith that guided her slammed its bony hand against her mouth. Dark, bottomless eyes bore into her, making her squirm beneath its touch, deep lines etched across her skin from its jagged nails.

"Let. Go."

She fought against control of her own body. Her limbs shook, her brow slick with sweat, but no matter how hard she tried, the wraith was stronger.

Her fingers slipped free from the cable, her legs weak, she couldn't stop what was coming. Couldn't fight against her foot dangling over the edge, miles above the ground. Soulless eyes and pale faces of hundreds of others watched her. Waited. Their desperation was thick in the air but it was their *appreciation* for her that caressed her skin. They wanted her. She would be helping them. They needed her to fall.

To let go.

"Save us like you couldn't save him." The wraith moved its hand away, coaxing her forward again.

"I–" Her mouth snapped shut when a strong hand landed on her shoulder and flung her backwards onto the deck. The back of her head met the ground with a loud crack. "Shit," she cursed, gripping her head. She tried to sit up, but her vision crossed, a deep ache pulsing behind her eyes.

Steel tore through bone and endless screams rang out around her. A burst of light and then an all-consuming darkness.

And somewhere among the chaos was that voice, farther away now.

"We know what you did, Aesira. We know what you are. No better than the monsters you slay."

When silence fell over the deck, she opened her eyes again, trying to catch her breath, her vision sharpening like the pain in her head. The first thing she saw was the cable she'd clung to with everything she had. The second thing she saw was him.

Stone Odega

His hair was disheveled, his chest and feet bare, as if he'd run there from sleep. Black liquid dripped from his skin, smattered across his face, collecting in the deep rivers of the scars that lined his shoulders and chest.

"Are you alright?" He extended his hand to help her up.

She swayed on her feet when she stood, a sharpness blooming behind her eyes. "I think so." A flush of embarrassment washed over her. She hadn't even been here a full day and she was already in need of saving.

Some warrior, she thought.

"What were those things?" She pulled her hand from Stone's, not realizing she was still holding it. "They knew my name. They knew–" She bit her tongue. Did he hear what they said about her? The secrets they spilled?

"Crawlers." Stone passed by her without a second glance to pick up a towel from a crate. He wiped the black from his face, then his hands and chest. "Was a matter of time before they showed up. Curious little creatures."

"What do they want?" The ache in her skull blurred her vision and she didn't remember wobbling but she must have because when her vision refocused, Stone was there, holding her up. His scarred hands were rough against her bare arms.

"We need to get you back to bed." It wasn't a question, but an order, and if there was one thing true about Aesira, it was that she knew when to follow an order. "They dwell in the deep desert," Stone said as they walked to her room. "They feed–" He glanced her way so quickly she thought she'd imagined it.

"What do they feed on?"

He cleared his throat and she looked away from his well defined frame where lines and lines of scars marred his skin. "They are in constant search of a soul to claim, to split amongst their hive." Her mind raced to the row of black eyes and jagged teeth waiting for her on the desert floor. "They feed off fear," he said. "Or at least that's what I've been told."

It was shameful to admit she was afraid. Her whole life, her whole career, was based on the virtue of bravery. And yet one night crossing the desert had left her cowering on the floor.

"The first time I saw one," Stone continued, as they crept their way down the dark corridor to her room, "Patch barely saved me in time. The crawler told me things I'd never admitted to anyone. They told me how to make my pain go away." He whispered the last part, maybe hoping she didn't hear him.

"And what did you hear tonight?" She wondered if he could hear the real question she was asking.

What did you hear about *me*?

There was a long stretch of silence before they got to her door. Stone opened it and then stepped aside. "I didn't hear a thing." He crossed his arms over his chest. "It wasn't after me. At least not this time." He pushed the door open further. "Get some sleep, Commander. Frightful as crawlers are, they're just the beginning."

EIGHT

AESIRA

Warm, orange light filtered through the small porthole window, dragging Aesira from her restless sleep. She leaned over the edge to find the bottom bunk empty. Nora must have gotten a head start on the day.

Slumping back on her pillow she rubbed the sleep from her eyes and gasped when she looked out the window. The red sand that she'd become accustomed to in Vargah had become a sea of shining black granules. Pink clouds dotted the horizon, giving a false sense of serenity.

After the crawlers last night, she couldn't look at the desert the same way again.

"I told you to fuck off!" a voice shouted from above deck. Aesira jumped off the bed, pulling on black armored pants, a short sleeve tunic with a built-in breastplate, and her boots.

"Go back to where you came from!" the same voice bellowed down the empty hallway as she poked her head out of the door. It was a feminine voice, but not Nora's, so it had to be one of the two women part of Stone's group.

An arid breeze scalded her cheeks as she climbed the same ladder as last night. Like the wind, images resurfaced in her mind, frenzied and blurry.

The ladder.

The wraith.

The loss of control over her body.

Stone.

"You! I need your help."

"As good a greeting as any, I suppose," Aesira said, following the woman. Her short, sleek hair bounced lightly as she stomped across the deck. Her angular, onyx eyes gave Aesira a quick glance over her shoulder before she turned away again. "Okay, well I'm—"

"I know who you are," the woman said. "Here, take this." She tossed Aesira a heavy rope before moving to the edge of the ship. "Get ready."

"Get ready for what?" Did the woman expect her to man the ship? While she'd flown many times over the last year between Vargah and Novaria, she'd never worked on a ship before. "Maybe I can get Stone?"

"He's busy." The woman picked up another large rope and tossed it Aesira's way, filling both her arms. "If you're going to be hitching a ride aboard the Aquila, you're going to be pulling your weight. Now get ready to toss those down."

"Down?"

"Fucksake," the woman mumbled. Aesira couldn't keep track of her. She moved like a tiny bird zipping about the deck. In one place for no longer than a second before moving onto the next. "When I tell you to toss those lines, you toss them as hard and far as you can. Understand, Commander?"

The annoyance in her voice made Aesira's cheeks heat. She was the head of her own squadron. Had moved up the ranks quickly and gone head to head with monsters–and won. Yet, this tiny woman had reduced her down to a novice. "Commander?" the woman demanded.

"Understood," Aesira said through gritted teeth. The ship swayed slightly, creaking and groaning as it sailed around a cluster of pink clouds. But other than the noises of the ship and orders from the woman, everything else was eerily quiet. "Where is Stone? The rest of the crew?"

The woman finished tying off one of the lines. She glanced at Aesira, putting her hands on her hips. "They're busy, like I said."

"And my knight?"

"She's busy too." The woman was fiddling with something mechanical, not bothering to glance her way.

"Then who were you talking to earlier?" The woman stiffened. "I heard you shouting, so if it wasn't to one of the crew, who?"

Her eyes narrowed but something scraped against the side of the ship, drawing her attention. "Toss the lines," she said. "Now!"

Aesira took two steps toward the bow, the heavy ropes bundled in her arms. Dry, scorching wind seared against her lips, but when her eyes tipped down toward the dark sand, she froze.

"Commander. We waited for you. We'll always wait for you."

The crawlers from last night.

Fear lodged in her throat, her grip loosening on the lines.

"Drop the lines, Commander!"

"Come."

"Let us heal you."

"Let us take your pain away."

Something about the last words shook Aesira from her stupor.

"They told me they'd make my pain go away."

The same thing Stone had told her last night.

"Commander! Drop the fucking lines!" The severity in the woman's voice was enough to wake her up. She shook her head once and tossed the heavy lines over the sides of the ship with all of her might.

It wasn't until her arms were empty that she realized what she just did.

"Wait!" Aesira spun, finding the woman next to her, as if she'd flown across deck, peering over the starboard bow. "Haven't we just given them a way to get up here?" Panic leeched the color from Aesira's cheeks, her stomach dropping.

"Patience," the woman said. Aesira glanced down at the crawlers and just as she suspected, they began to climb. Their skeletal bodies moved with unnatural speed and even more unnatural angles. Bending and twisting, oily strands of hair swaying in the breeze, bones cracking, teeth chattering.

"Shit," Aesira murmured. She gripped the pommel of her sword, letting the bite of cold metal be her anchor. The crawlers screamed. Over and over again they screamed. They screamed her name. Her secrets. Her fears.

She drew in sharper breaths, and as the first wraith's hand reached for her, a burst of heat and light dropped her to her knees.

Flames engulfed the crawler. Its shrieks grew higher and more piercing but through the horrific sound, a laugh rose in its place. Aesira swayed on her knees, her hands pressed tightly over her ears and when the noises began to dwindle, she pulled her sword and stood.

The woman stood tall, boot propped on the railing, a machine Aesira had never seen before aimed over the bow, flames shooting out, torching everything below.

A lone crawler had escaped the woman's wrath, its empty eyes narrowed on Aesira. The crawler launched, but Aesira was quicker, slicing her blade clean through its middle. Inky ichor spilled on the deck. The crawler howled, something low and deep until Aesira used her blade to finish it off.

"Nice work," the woman said. Together they pulled the dead crawler from the deck and pushed it over board. Heat singed the hair on Aesira's arms as she peeked over the bow, down to the scrambling wraiths below. The smell of burnt hair and rotted remains drifted through the black smoke. Aesira wiped her blade on her pants and turned to the woman at her side.

A satisfied smirk was slashed across her thin mouth, a quiet chuckle escaping her. The same laugh, she realized, she'd heard among the carnage. She pushed her goggles atop her head and lowered her weapon, her gaze drifting past Aesira. "Convenient of you to join us just as all the hard work is done." Aesira turned in time to see Stone taking a few strides toward them.

"Smells terrible," Stone said, peering over the edge of the ship. "All of them?"

"All of them," the woman said, raising her chin.

"Well done, as usual." The compliment sounded strained, as if it pained Stone to admit it. "That's new." He pointed to the flame tipped weapon the woman still held tightly in her grasp. Aesira had never seen anything like it. The mechanics of it. The flames. She was trained using traditional weapons; blades, arrows, her hands, and poison when necessary. She admired the weapon as the woman slung it over her shoulder.

A weapon like that could change everything in the face of war, Aesira thought. The ease with which it annihilated an entire hive of crawlers. It was too dangerous.

"Had a lot of time to think in Vargah." The woman pulled the weapon off her shoulder and cradled it in her arms, admiring it like one would admire a newborn baby. "Didn't take much to make with all those supplies so graciously given by the queen."

Stone glanced at Aesira, maybe waiting for a comment about the underground prisons, or her role in placing so many people there. Or maybe he didn't think she should know of the weapons being made with Vargah's money, but he turned his focus back to the woman. "Tidy up," he said. "Meet me when you're done."

Alone again, the woman led Aesira to an area where they kept cleaning supplies; mops and buckets stacked on top of each other. "Thanks for the help," the woman said. "I'm Birdie, by the way."

The hours melted into one another with various tasks Birdie assigned to Aesira. Never mind she was the least experienced flyer on the ship. Never mind that she was the queen's sister and royalty herself. In the few minutes she managed to sneak away, she found Nora who'd be assigned below deck, prepping meals and organizing their rations.

Aesira wouldn't have been bothered by the work in any other circumstance. She liked keeping her hands occupied. Appreciated the sweat that built on her brow and the dull ache of her muscles as she dragged herself to her room later that night.

She wouldn't have been bothered if not for seeing the work for what it really was. A way to keep her and Nora busy. Keep them distracted from whatever Stone and the rest of his crew were doing beneath the ship.

"You didn't see them all day?" Aesira asked as she and Nora slid into their bunks.

"Once," Nora said through a yawn. "When they came to get their meals but they were quiet so I didn't bother making conversation." Nora poked her head out of the bottom bunk. "Stone asked about you, though, wondered why you weren't eating with us." Her grin spread the freckles across her cheeks.

"And did you tell him it's because I find him repulsive?"

Nora laughed and rolled back into her bed. "Of course not, Commander. You know I'm a terrible liar."

The small window in their cabin let in the last of the day's golden light. A few moments later, Nora's soft snores drifted up from her bottom bunk, and despite the sleep clawing at her eyelids, Aesira couldn't settle.

Tonight, however, it wasn't the wraiths or nightmares that occupied her mind and made her restless. It was the nagging feeling that this crew–Stone–couldn't be trusted.

She'd seen him only once throughout the entire day, after Birdie set flame to the wraiths. And as for the rest of the criminals–*cadre*, she corrected herself–she hadn't seen them at all.

It was as if they disappeared.

Or, more likely, moved about the ship so perfectly, they avoided both knights altogether.

It didn't offend her that she wasn't invited to their conversations, she'd been on the outs more times than one and considering who they were and who she was, it only made sense to be wary of each other. But even if it didn't bother her, it did concern her.

When darkness blotted out the sun and the sound of Birdie scuffling about on deck quieted, she crept out of her room, leaving Nora snoring in her bunk. This time, she didn't head for the familiar ladder, she headed straight for the starboard quarters, where she suspected Stone to be.

The narrow hallway was almost completely dark save for the light seeping from the bottom of the door at the end. Aesira ran her fingers down the wooden panels that lined the walls but froze halfway when the door at the end burst open.

"Commander!" Patch waved her forward, a wide smile stretching across his lips. His dark hair fell loose near his shoulders and the crooked smile only made him more handsome. "Join us for a drink!"

Aesira took a tentative step. Her aim was to speak to Stone alone, question him using her training in the hopes of getting the truth out of what he'd been doing all day, see what his motives really were, but from the sounds coming from the doorway, it was unlikely that was going to happen.

Patch patted her back as she joined them around a small table in the room. Why they chose here and not the crew mess to gather was beyond her, but she squeezed in next to Birdie.

The table was quiet, only the faint pelt of sand against the window. She'd always kept her circle small. Nev, Nora, and Kamari. The only people she could truly rely on. If someone had asked her if she ever imagined sharing a table with four Odega's, she would have told them they were out of their mind.

"A drink?" Stone broke the silence, sliding a heavy, empty glass toward her before popping open the cork from a slender brown bottle.

"No thanks." Aesira slid the glass back. She needed her head clear.

You need to stay in control.

Stone watched her long enough that heat crept over her skin but to her relief, he said nothing else before taking a long drink straight from the bottle. He grimaced, his face puckering before handing it off to the woman to his left. She had a warm face and bright, round eyes. "Don't hog it," she said with a smile.

Stone cleared his throat, drawing her attention back to him. "To what do we owe the pleasure, Commander?"

"Couldn't sleep." She shrugged. "Didn't realize there was a party I was missing."

"Hardly a party." Birdie snatched the bottle from the other woman. "Anyone willingly heading to the Outpost deserves a drink." The crew laughed darkly and raised their glasses.

"We're..." She pushed the stray curls back from her face. "Tonight? We enter the Outpost tonight?"

"Our course is set to dock in the next few hours," Stone said. She flicked her eyes back to him. "Nervous?"

"Why would I be?" She crossed her arms. Around the table, the rest of the crew sat relaxed, their faces and bodies giving away nothing about their day. No tremor in their hands. No sweat on their brow. No shifting of their eyes.

They weren't nervous and truthfully, she wasn't nervous either, but she couldn't imagine a well-received welcome for two knights of the Order in a place that thrived without law.

She glanced back at Stone. He kept his eyes on her as he took a deep drink from the bottle. Her gaze snagged on the ink marked on the side of his neck, peeking out from under the collar of his white shirt. The outline of two stars. Two, not three, like Celestria's symbol.

"If I interrupted something," Aesira said, "by all means let me leave you." She tried to slide off the bench but Stone's hand gripped around her forearm causing her to pause.

"You didn't," he said. "Stay."

His hand lingered on her arm as she relaxed back into her seat and when he finally removed it, it was as if she'd been branded, seared by him. The warmth traveled up her arm and to her cheeks.

"Stone was just going off on one of his tangents," the woman next to Birdie said. Her wide grin dimpled either side of her brown, plump cheeks. "Honestly we're happy you found us, he would have talked us all to death."

"It wasn't a tangent, Bee." Stone swirled the empty glass meant for Aesira, back and forth between his hands. A light pink swept across his cheeks and Aesira followed it as it trailed down his neck. Blushing? Was Stone Odega blushing? "It was the truth."

"Here we go," Patch said under his breath, running a hand across his jaw.

Stone shook his head. "I mean how is it that we were gifted galaxies and instead of spending our time celebrating the infinite and impossible nature of the stars, we've become too busy, too focused on the ground we can conquer and the people we can control." Stone's fingers tapped the edge of the table and Aesira had a good suspicion that if she glanced underneath his leg would be bouncing as well.

"It's a waste to see such miracles fade to the background in lieu of power," he said, his dark blue eyes shot to hers, pinning her in place. A heaviness crept into her chest, pressing like a weight on her lungs.

She was in a position of power.

She was in charge of order.

Discipline.

Punishment.

"Wow," Birdie muttered. "Nothing truly gets you worked up like the stars does it?"

"Maybe a woman," Patch said through a laugh. "If he ever landed one."

Aesira's eyes darted to Birdie, then to Stone. That night at the Phoenix she'd seen Birdie and Stone together. They'd sat so close, touched each other with more familiarity than two people on a crew together. But as she watched them now, Birdie was more interested in Bee. Holding her hand, the back of her neck. Kissing her cheek and whispering in her ear. Aesira hated the relief that spread like warm water spilled onto a tabletop through her chest. Why did she care?

She didn't, she decided. She wouldn't care if Stone Odega slept with a hundred people, it wasn't her business or her problem.

"Harsh," Stone mumbled before taking another long pull from the bottle. The pink staining his cheeks deepened making his eyes look that much bluer.

"He could land any girl he wanted." Bee reached over and ruffled his already unruly, auburn hair. "Thanks, Bee."

"If he put in any effort," she said.

"Again, harsh." He shot her a glare which quickly dissolved when she kissed his cheek. Were they all so close as to touch each other?

"We're just looking out for you Stoney," Birdie chimed in. "Not natural for someone to go that long without–"

"And with that, I say it's time for bed." Stone shoved his glasses to the top of his head and pressed his palms into his eyes and she couldn't help it, Aesira smiled. Each time she'd run into the smuggler it was nothing but sarcastic quips. It was nice to see him on the receiving end for once.

"Boo," Bee and Birdie said in unison.

"Log a few hours before we dock, you deviants," Stone said. The crew filed out, Aesira following behind Patch when Stone tapped her shoulder.

"Commander, a word?"

His blush hadn't faded but he didn't shy away when she met his gaze. "Yes?" she asked, retaking her seat.

"I figured it would be good if we discussed..." He gestured between them. "Before we get to the Outpost."

"Discuss what exactly?" Sleep was beginning to weigh on her, her eyes scratchy and limbs heavy. If they were to dock at the Outpost within the next few hours, she'd need some semblance of rest.

"You know," Stone said. "Discuss what happened between us."

Aesira's laugh was so jarring it made Stone jump from across the table. "Us? There is no us, Odega."

He watched her, his eyes tracing her face from her brows to her lips. "I know that," he said. "I just meant maybe we should clear the air. Lessen the awkwardness a bit."

Now it was Aesira's turn to blush. Heat scorched the tips of her ears down to her chest. "There's nothing to talk about." All humor was drained from her tone. She stood from the bench, a new determination to get as far away from Stone as possible fueling her steps.

"Right," Stone said. "I guess it's easier to ignore the fact that you kissed an Odega than accept it."

She crossed her arms over her chest, wishing she couldn't feel the hammering of her heart. "You're right, I'd rather ignore the fact that it happened altogether."

He took a ragged breath and downed what was left in the bottle. "You want to know what I think?"

"No. You're reading too far into it." She stood and turned for the door, ready to leave Stone and the memory of them in the Phoenix together behind her.

"I think you're ashamed of what happened."

Aesira spun around, mouth popped open but when Stone held up a hand, she closed it. "I think you're angry, too," he said. "And not at me." He took a step closer and she wanted to move back, but didn't. She stayed rooted in place, seeing what he would do. "I think you're angry at yourself for letting it go as far as it did." He brushed a piece of hair from her shoulder. "And ashamed of how badly you liked it. Kissing someone like me. *Wanting* someone like me."

Her teeth ground together, flames licking the tips of her ears and cheeks. "Like I said, you're reading too far into what happened." She took a step backward, letting a cool draft pool between them. "Don't give it a second thought, I sure haven't."

"Fair enough. We agree then, it was nothing. Wouldn't want to tarnish that Zeliath reputation." Stone dusted her shoulder and smiled but something sharp pierced her chest again.

Her *reputation*.

How could he know it was her very reputation that she loathed? It made people see her differently. Treat her like she was on a pedestal or fear her when they had no reason to. It made it difficult to make genuine friends and absolutely impossible to find a partner which is exactly what the Order wanted. To keep their knights loyal only to them, with no room for any outside distractions, but she *was* distracted and had been for some time now.

"Anyway," Stone said, drawing out the word, "Let's forget it ever happened. Agreed?" He stuck out his hand but she kept her arms crossed.

The night could have easily been with anyone else, but when she walked into the Phoenix, it was only him that she saw. He was the only one in the tavern who didn't look her way. He didn't offer to buy her a drink or sweet talk her ear because of her stature. And so she made her move and then he ended up rejecting her.

She had no real reason to be angry. She'd done to others the same thing he'd done to her countless times, but being on the other side of his dismissal stung more than she cared to admit.

Normally, there wasn't a grudge in the world that Aesira couldn't hold onto for as long as possible. She'd let it fester out of control until her mind warped what actually happened, making it seem that much worse. But this time, she thought of Kamari. What she might do. Rightfully born first, her sister was full of grace and patience. Two things Aesira could use a dose of.

"Commander?" Stone still had his hand suspended in the air. "Are you okay?"

"Agreed." She gripped his hand in hers giving it a firm shake. "Let's move on."

It's what Kamari would do.

Let it go.

Nine

Stone

The desert thrummed with life as Aquila docked at the only port in the Outpost. Stone relished the liveliness of the desert-dwellers, even if he despised the Outpost itself. With temperatures too hot during the day, the small colony came to life at nightfall. It was well after midnight, but music clung to the sticky air as Stone led the crew to the tavern.

"So this is the Outpost?" Aesira joined his side, her eyes wide and drinking in the surroundings. Tents spanned either side of them, a few that could afford *astra* had lights strung from their ceilings showcasing various goods for sale. Music and dancing, singing, and laughter spilled into the alleyway as Stone took a hard left turn.

"Is it what you expected?"

"Not really," Aesira said. He glanced at her just in time to see a smile retreating from her lips. "Middle of the desert, no resources for days, I didn't expect so much—"

"Joy? Life?"

She looked up at him. "Yes."

"People make do." He took another turn before stopping at a small doorway attached to an ancient limestone building. "Here we are."

Aesira's brows bunched as if she were about to ask a question, but Birdie and Bee pushed in front of them and swung the door open. Soft, sensual music spilled out from the open door.

Aesira and Nora took a step forward but Stone blocked them, clicking it shut.

"What are you doing?" Aesira asked, hand resting on the pommel of her sword. His eyes drifted over her armor, the cuffs hanging at her hip. He should have told her to change, but he had a sneaky suspicion that if he'd suggested it, she would have told him to fuck off.

"We have a long way to go, if we're to find the king. The crew needs a night off from flying. And if there's anything that's universally true, it's that people who drink also like to talk. If the king stopped at the Outpost on his way to Ravki, someone in there would have seen him. Might have answers."

She relaxed her grip on the handle of her sword. "Okay, then why isn't Patch here?"

"Someone has to stay with the ship."

"Fine," Aesira said, "well let's go in."

"We're not going in there." Stone blocked their path again. "Birdie and Bee will question any one they can. If you go in dressed like that"— He scanned Aesira's armor—"No one will talk." He sunk his hands in his pockets and nodded over their shoulders. "So we're going there instead."

"And there is?" Nora asked as they both turned.

"The Apothecary," he said. He knew what they'd see. An unimpressive building that looked worse for wear, free from any signs, but like most of the Outpost, its beauty was hidden. Tucked away from undeserving eyes. "If finding Desmond is what you wish most—"

"Of course it is," Aesira said.

"Okay." Stone studied her face as she studied the small stone building across from them. Her dark hair was still windswept, the curls falling freely down her back, a few tiny freckles dotted over the bridge of her nose. She looked so different from the times he saw her in Vargah. More relaxed with her hair down. He liked it, more than he expected. Her posture, however, reminded him that she was not relaxed at all. Just as rigid as usual. "*There*"— he pointed— "is a way for us to narrow down our search. Let's go."

"Wait," Aesira said. She pulled Nora close and whispered something in her ear. The knight nodded once, her bright red locks catching in the dull *astra* lamps that lined the streets, and turned back for the dock.

"And where is she going?"

"Back to the ship to change so she can question people on her own," Aesira said.

Stone shook his head. "You don't trust my crew to get information?"

Aesira ignored him, taking the lead to cross the street. "I thought you knew where Ravki was?"

"You're really good at changing the subject."

She glanced at him over her shoulder. "You're really good at not answering my questions."

"Fine," Stone said. "The truth is no one really knows where Ravki is." *Or if it exists.* "Who's to say the king didn't wander here, realize he was over his head, and stay hidden somewhere?"

He caught up to her side and could see enough of her face to see she was frowning again. "But the maps—"

"You mean the maps the king decimated with scribbles and notes and tragically bad folding?" They reached the Apothecary but Stone blocked the door before Aesira could open it. "We don't know how viable they are. We don't even know if they're real. So in here"— he tapped the door three times—"if finding the king is your utmost desire, there's a way." The *astra* lamp outside of the Apothecary winked on, the light catching on her armor. "Also, you really should change out of that."

"Trying to undress me, Odega?"

He grinned, readying his next remark, but the door creaked open behind him.

"It's late," a voice growled from the darkness. "Go away."

"Apologies, Soo. It's Stone Odega and I've brought a friend." He glanced over his shoulder and urged Aesira to join his side. "Can we come in for a tea?"

The door slid open another inch, a tiny slice of candlelight leaking out. "Did someone say tea?" the ancient woman asked through a soft chuckle. "Well you should have started with that." She pushed the door wide open and a waft of sage and mint burned in his nose. "There's always time for tea."

Soo, a tiny woman with a severe hunch Stone couldn't remember her ever not having led them inside. Her short cropped hair shone silver in the candlelight and her narrow eyes and deeply wrinkled skin stood out against the overflowing life that was tucked into every corner of the small space.

Aesira ran her fingertips along the green vines that stretched from floor to ceiling, eyes wide and curious.

Stone traced her movements and he couldn't blame her for being so enamored. Each wall of the Apothecary was lined with wooden shelves and on top of each shelf was cacti, shrubs, dried herbs in tiny jars, skulls of various animals, and even a tortoise shell. The Apothecary was always this way. Stuffed to the brim with oddities. Plants. Warmth.

He'd found Soo shortly after Patch dragged him in from the open desert. She was just as much family as the cadre was, even if she was the most stubborn.

"What kind of tea can I make for you this time, Stone?" Soo stood behind a small counter, hands resting on top of each other, silver and gemstone rings adorning each knobby finger.

"Same as last time," he said. "We're looking for some-thing–*someone*. Did you happen to see anyone out of the ordinary pass through?"

Soo laughed. "I'm an old lady. I don't get out much let alone participate in gossip."

Stone pushed his glasses up so they sat more firmly on his nose. He knew for a fact that wasn't true. Old, yes. Not a fan of gossip? Hardly. If there was gossip, Soo was either starting it or feeding it. "Only a question, Soo. Which you didn't answer by the way."

Soo grunted. "You know where you need to go if you want answers in the Outpost." She leaned closer, propping her elbows on the counter. "You know who keeps the desert's secrets." She leaned close, pulling him down so she could speak softly into his ear. "What are you really doing here? Looking for something you shouldn't?"

He straightened, clearing his throat. The light in the Apothecary was dim and Stone wondered if Aesira could see his jaw clench at the mention of the desert's secrets, or where to go to find them. He needed to keep his composure. To make sure she didn't see the rising panic in his chest. "Just looking for someone who's lost."

Soo grunted and he knew she didn't believe him. He'd tell her his plans, later, as he always did. "Then you know where to go, Stone."

"The last time I checked, he wasn't pleased with me," he said, choosing his words wisely. Vaguely. "Plus you know his general disdain for outsiders."

Soo grabbed a glass jar from the nearest shelf, a moth with thick, furry wings fluttered inside. She reached in and pulled it out, letting it sit atop her hand. "Mmm," she said, stroking the moth's wings. "I'm sure for someone so pretty"— she leaned around Stone and smiled at Aesira— "he'd make an exception."

"She isn't a bargaining chip." Stone's voice dropped low.

Soo laughed again. "Defensive." Stone's mouth dropped open but she shook her head. "You mentioned tea. Now do you want some, or did you truly wake me up to ask me unnecessary questions?"

"Fine, if you haven't seen anyone unusual," Stone said, "you must at least have a remedy to help point us in the right direction."

Soo chuckled then immediately got to work. She shuffled about the small room with bare feet and brightly colored chiffon robes that draped onto the ground. She pulled vials from shelves, snipped flowers and leaves, humming quietly to herself, the moth perched on her shoulder.

"Wait here," she said before disappearing behind a curtain of tiny bells and beads.

After a few moments of silence, Aesira cleared her throat. "How is tea going to help us find Desmond?"

Stone picked up a crystal from one of the shelves, examining it through his glasses. "Soo is a mage." He set the crystal back down, leaned against the shelf, and crossed his arms across his chest.

"A mage? There haven't been mages in..." Aesira's eyes went distant, like she was trying to make sense of what he'd said.

Stone laughed. "Centuries. She looks good for her age. Or maybe she has a tea for that too."

"I do." Soo rounded the corner, the peal of bells following in her wake. "I have a tea for everything." It was impossible to tell with the heavy weight of wrinkles around her eyes but Stone thought he saw the woman wink. "Here." She handed Stone a satchel stuffed to the brim. "Make sure your water is hot, let it steep for three minutes." She held up a finger, pointing it at his face. "Not two minutes, not four minutes. Three minutes. Understood?"

"Understood." Stone slipped a few coins into her hand and turned away before she could tell him his money was no good to her.

Aesira snatched the satchel from Stone, holding it to her nose and taking a deep inhale. "What's in it?"

Soo plucked a dry, yellow flower from her wall and began to grind it with a heavy mortal and pestle. "Who are you, girl? You come to the Outpost, a place for miscreants and drifters dressed like a woman of the law." Soo's eyes burned a trail from Aesira's chestplate down to her boots.

That cursed fucking armor. He wanted to rip it off her. Not just because he liked her better without it, but because it would get them in trouble and trouble was the last thing they needed.

"Are you? A woman of the law?" Soo pressed, adding another flower to her mortar.

"I am." Aesira tossed the tea back to Stone. "Commander Zeliath." She held out her hand but Soo busied herself, grabbing more leaves and flowers, grinding them to dust. The moth on her shoulder stretched its wings but made no attempt to fly away.

"And it's you who seeks this drifter?"

"Yes," Aesira said. "He's my brother-in-law. My sister is worried about him."

Soo huffed a laugh before wiping her hands on her robes and pouring the dust into another satchel. "And finding him is what you seek the most?" She didn't look up as she spoke. She kept her eyes down, drawing shapes and letters into the flower dust that had spilled onto the countertop. A riddle, Stone guessed, that would leave them more questions than answers. That's how it went with Soo. Her guidance was a broken mirror and she held the missing pieces, but still somehow expected you to fill in the empty shards on your own.

"I wish to find him more than anything else," Aesira said and for some reason Stone believed her. She said it with her chest out, her chin high. He respected her dedication. Her loyalty. Even if it was toward the crown, the same people who put him in prison.

"Good." Soo glanced at her now. "Drink the tea. If finding him is what you want most in your heart, it should lend you some answers. Take this. I have a feeling you might need it." She tossed another satchel to Aesira before turning to Stone. "Three minutes." Then, she was gone, back behind the curtain of bells.

"You heard her," Stone said. "Let's go."

Another bell chimed as Stone pushed open the door but Aesira took a step toward the counter. "What is it?" He rejoined her in the back of the store and mapped her gaze to where Soo had drawn in the flower dust.

There was a single word in the center of a set of peculiar drawings.

Lost.

Ten

Aesira

After a few dizzying twists and turns from the Apothecary, Stone stopped in front of a ram-shackled building with darkened windows and a red painted door. "Here we are," he said, "the one and only Outpost Inn."

"What a unique name."

"Thought you might like it." They ushered inside, paid the surly woman behind the counter, and took the three flights of narrow stairs until they reached the door to Aesira's room. "I'll be back with your water." Stone handed Aesira the satchel before trotting back down the stairs.

Inside was sweltering but simple; a mattress on the floor with worn but seemingly fresh linens. A window which overlooked the docks that Aesira immediately opened, hoping for a hint of a breeze to cool down the space.

The Aquila loomed in the distance, hovering several feet above the bank of sand. There was a small bathroom with a single *astra* sconce, a basin for washing and a bar of yellow soap which smelled similarly to the flower Soo had turned to dust.

Aesira tore off her armor, replacing it with a long shirt and leggings, then she stripped her boots and sank onto the mattress. It was larger than the one back on the ship, but thinner. Either way, she was glad to be on land for the night. From her pocket, she pulled the extra tea from Soo. Its sweet smell hit her first, but there was something there at the end she couldn't place. Something sharp. Medicinal.

She tossed the satchel aside, landing next to her armor that was piled on the floor. She stared at it, resenting it, but before her mind could drift to that dark place, a knock at the door had her jumping to her feet. "Come in."

Stone joined her with a small iron kettle and two porcelain mugs. "Was able to find water, didn't come cheap though, bastards." He set the kettle down on the countertop near the bathroom. "Do you have the tea?"

Aesira set aside the sweet tea and pulled the second satchel from her pocket and tossed it to him. "Are you sure this is safe?"

Stone set to work, heaping a spoonful of loose leaves into one of the mugs and topping it with steaming water. "Soo has been making tea longer than we've been alive. If she says it's safe, it's safe." He handed her the mug and a pungent waft of sewage hit her. She wrinkled her nose at the brown water. "Not a fan?" Stone asked through a laugh.

"Can't say that I am." Aesira sniffed the tea again and then regretted it. "So all I have to do is wait three minutes then drink and it'll show me where Desmond is?" She looked up from the muddy water to see Stone readying a second cup. "What are you doing?"

"Joining you," he said. He held the mug to his nose and took a deep inhale, the steam fogging over his spectacles. "Better we both drink, double up our chances of it working."

"I have a hard time believing finding King Desmond is what you desire most."

Stone froze, his hand clamped around his mug. "If I do my job correctly, Birdie, Bee, and Patch are free. We all are. So, in a way, yes. I wish to find him as much as you do."

In all of the excitement the last few days, she'd forgotten the deal he made with Kamari. She cleared her throat, eyeing the murky tea again. "Nora will need to know where I am."

"I've already taken care of it," Stone said. "You underestimate me, Commander." He shot her a look. "She has a room down the hall." Aesira's mouth hung open and Stone laughed. "Time's up." He nodded to her tea. "You're first, I still have another minute."

Aesira studied the tea again, the color dark enough she could see the mismatched reflection of her eyes staring back at her. She decided it would likely go down better if her eyes were closed so she pinched them shut and downed the dreadful liquid in a single gulp. When she finished, she wiped her mouth with the back of her hand.

Stone chuckled. "That bad?"

"Dreadful as expected. Your turn."

Stone sniffed his tea, made a face Aesira completely understood—disgust—then drank. "Wow," he said through a cough.

"I told you." Aesira smiled, unsure what came next. "So, does it just…"

"Tonight when you sleep," he said. "It'll show us what we most desire." His eyes flicked to hers. "It should show us where to find King Desmond, I mean." Stone's stare stayed pinned on her even as he set his mug on the countertop. "It could be a place or even words, I'm not really sure, but tomorrow we'll reconvene and map out our plan."

"You talk like you've drunk this before?"

A hint of a smile tugged at the corner of his scarred lip. "Maybe once." He shrugged. "Maybe twice." Aesira's brows leaped to her forehead which made Stone laugh, a deep rumbling sound tied to that memory that made her skin heat.

"And did it work for you? Did you find what you desired most?" It was an innocent question, but for whatever reason she could feel the tension between them growing with the silence, stretching and pulling until it ran taut.

He ran his tongue over his bottom lip then smiled, a true smile this time. "In its own way, yes," he said. The tea sat like poison in her stomach, heavy and unsettling. "I should get back to Aquila."

"What about seeing that man Soo suggested?" Aesira asked. Stone's grip around the tea kettle tightened. "She said there was a man who kept the desert's secrets. Maybe he might have answers. Might be able to tell us if Desmond's been seen."

He relaxed his grip and smoothed his hair back. "Like I said at Soo's, he isn't fond of outsiders."

"Or is it that *you* don't want to see him?" She crossed her arms and waited.

"Vic and I have a history, he'd speak with me even if he was reluctant to. I can go–"

"I'm going too, then." She wanted to trust Stone, but there was a larger part of her that knew deep down she couldn't trust anyone. Not really. And there was too much at stake here to leave everything in his hands.

Stone ground his teeth, his eyes veering past her, settling on her pile of discarded armor in the corner. "There are certain measures we'd need to take to make that happen," Stone said. "Give me until morning to think of a plan and see if I can arrange a meeting."

She nodded, satisfied that he hadn't completely shut down the idea. Any bit of information regarding the king was vital. She wasn't willing to pass up a lead just because it might be difficult.

"Birdie and Bee will be just down the hall from you if you need anything." Stone opened the door and stepped out. "Though I'd say it's wise to let them have their privacy. And Nora is just one door past them. Patch and I will be on the ship. Goodnight, Commander."

Music from the Phoenix filtered into the washroom, muffled by the thick iron door. Hands grazed Aesira's waist, lifting her shirt just enough so that a slice of skin peeked through. Lips pressed against her

neck, raising the hair on her arms. "You taste so good," the voice said. She tilted her head back, giving him a better angle on her neck. His tongue slid against her hot skin before pressing another kiss to her throat.

"Aesira." Stone's eyes met hers, lids heavy, lips parted. "I'm going to kiss you now." She nodded, giving him her full permission. Then his lips were on hers, his hands gripping onto her hips. His teeth sank into her bottom lip and when she pressed her hips forward he rewarded her with a pleasant hiss. "You're going to need to stop that."

"Why?" Her words came out breathless. She grabbed his shirt, pinning him between her thighs. "Kiss me again." He didn't hesitate. His mouth was bruising against hers, his hands no longer just curious, but ravenous. On her hips, her back. Between her legs.

She moaned and threw her head back, pushing her hips forward again. "Keep doing that," she breathed. His fingers pressed between her thighs and she wished now more than ever that she had worn a dress and not pants.

Curse the fabric between them.

She reached for him too but he pulled away.

She needed more. She wanted—

Aesira jolted up from her bed, skin slick with sweat, hair a nest of curls. Her breaths were heavy as she rubbed the remaining sleep from her eyes.

Only a dream.

She relaxed back onto her pillow, urging her heart to slow with deep, intentional breaths when the memories of last night slammed into her.

Stone.

The tea.

Her deepest desires.

No, no, no.

Groaning, she pressed her face into her palms. The tea was meant to give her a clue to find Desmond and she had wasted it dreaming about Stone Odega.

The bottom level of the inn had been shrouded in darkness when they arrived, but in the full morning sun Aesira appreciated the cleverness of the space. The sandstone was bright against the sunlight dripping through the open windows. There were old wooden hubs placed atop metal barrels being used as tables, mismatched chairs stuffed around them filled with people of all sorts. Gears hung from invisible strings from the ceiling, swaying in the small breeze, ringing out a soft clinking sound.

She heard them before she saw them. Stone sat with Birdie, Bee, Nora, and Patch around a small barrel table.

"You really have lost it, haven't you?" Birdie chided. Aesira managed to find an open chair and pulled it over, settling next to Nora. Stone's eyes shot to hers briefly before he went back to pointing at a map he had sprawled out on the tabletop.

"I promise I'm just as sane now as I was when you trusted me last." There wasn't an ounce of arrogance in his voice, it was as if he was reading something already written. Factual. Calm. Aesira tore her eyes away from his face, for more reasons than one, and found on the map where his finger was pointing.

"Ravki?" Four very pointed "shh" sounds were directed her way. She mouthed sorry then glanced back to Stone. "I thought you said the maps were fake."

"They are," Bee said. "Fakes. Or ancient. Or fake *and* ancient." She glared at Stone but he missed it because his eyes were on Aesira.

He studied her from brow to lip and she studied him back, not wanting to be the first to break away. Even if all she saw when she looked at him was images from her dream last night and heated moments from the tavern, she didn't want him to know just how much he affected her.

"I know it's a risk," Stone said, finally looking away. "But Soo said the tea never fails, and if that's true, this is the path we need to take."

Against her control, Aesira's stomach plummeted.

He drank the tea with her last night in a moment of solidarity. Only hers betrayed her and his seemed to work. "What about you, Commander? Did the tea give any direction on where to find King Desmond?"

"It showed me ruins," she lied, remembering the note from Desmond's journal he'd written next to Ravki. "But other than that, no."

Stone squinted a moment before he rolled up the map. "Likely Ravki as well, it's rumored to have been destroyed in the first war."

"By Vargah," Patch finished for him between bites of his breakfast. "Making us an enemy to any remaining Ravkian."

"There are no remaining Ravkians." Again with the sure, factual, tone. Stone reclined in his chair, the rolled map clutched in his hand. He used his other to push his glasses up on the bridge of his nose. "The war was a long time ago. *Everything* was destroyed. Ravki would have been no exception. As well as—" He caught himself, his mouth frozen around the word none of them dared to speak aloud.

Dragons.

"The king had maps that shouldn't exist," he continued. "Even if they aren't accurate, he had to have gotten the information from somewhere." Stone propped his elbows on the table and glanced at each of them, lingering a moment too long when he got to Aesira. "He had notes about a country that hadn't existed long before his time." He let out a long breath before draining his mug, which only reminded Aesira of how dry her throat was.

"We'll do another sweep around the Outpost, make sure he isn't here and if he isn't, there's nowhere else he would have headed." Stone set his mug down, his eyes bouncing between each of them. "We have enough *astra* to get us to the Whispering Mountains and back. Enough food provided by the queen. With everything the king had written in his journals, with the maps he kept locked inside them, it only makes sense it was where he was headed."

"How do you know his notes are true? Wasn't the king..." Bee's thoughts died in the air around them. She didn't need to clarify, because everyone at the table already knew.

Wasn't the king mad?

The cadre chattered quietly amongst each other, Patch leaning over to whisper to Bee, Bee leaning back to whisper to Birdie. Even Nora joined in, like she was an Odega herself. Leaving Aesira and

Stone to stare at each other. The corner of his mouth quipped up, a half smile, pulling taut on the scar that spanned the entire left side of his face.

She helped herself to a cup of tea, plopping a cube of sweetener in and watching it dissolve completely before adding another.

"Are you going to have any tea with your sweetener, Commander?"

She picked up a third cube, held Stone's eye as she dropped it in. "Want some?" She smirked before taking a sip; sweet, just how she liked it.

Stone reeled back. "I'd rather choke."

She laughed into her mug. "We can make that happen."

"Oh?" Stone leaned forward. "Is that a promise or a threat, Commander?"

"Would you two shut up?" Birdie snapped. "Some of us are trying to think."

Stone tsked. "So unprofessional."

Aesira scoffed. "But you're the one–"

"I have a question," Nora interjected. They all paused and for a moment it seemed the entire place silenced. Nothing but the soft clinking of the hanging gears above them. "If there is nothing left of Ravki, why is it so dangerous? You make it seem forbidden." Like an exercise they'd practiced a dozen times before, the three Odega's turned to Stone and waited for his answer.

He chewed his bottom lip for a moment, glanced beyond Aesira, then settled his gaze on Nora. "The journey can't be an easy one," he said, much quieter than before. "If it truly lies where the maps indicate, whose to say what kinds of beast might be roaming."

"Then why would anyone travel there?" Aesira pressed.

"Because there are other rumors as well. Not just of beasts." Stone settled back in his chair. "Rumors of magical blades left untouched from the war a century ago. Rumors of plants that only seem to grow there–some say they contain cures for certain diseases. Other rumors say they give magic, even to humans. And then, of course, rumors that dragons still thrive there. Hidden in the mountains."

"What good would finding one of those be?" Nora asked between mouthfuls of fruit.

"Save some for the rest of us, sweetheart." Patch snatched the bowl from Nora, popping a piece of dried stone-fruit in his mouth.

"No." She stole the bowl back but didn't hide the smile twitching at the corner of her mouth.

Bee snatched the bowl from Nora and ending her and Patch's back and forth game. "Finding one of *those*," she said, "wouldn't bring us any good. If something like that exists and hasn't been seen for centuries, there's a damn good reason for it."

Aesira could admit she hadn't taken the time to know Desmond well. They only spoke on a few occasions but her sister had told her more than enough. Desmond was kind and thoughtful. He doted on Kamari's every step and never once pushed or pressured her.

They fell in love as naturally as two people could, according to her sister. She couldn't connect the missing pieces. Why would Desmond leave on some ridiculous quest to find magic or dragons? Why would he leave Kamari to fend for their country alone? Especially this close to Naming Day. Why wouldn't he tell her or bring a crew of his own?

The more she thought about it, the angrier she became. It didn't make sense, and she loathed the fact that she'd been handed a riddle she couldn't solve.

Birdie sighed. "Some people who still believe in the old ways believe *you know what's* to be healers. Life-givers. They believe their presence is what made the world."

"That's absurd," Aesira said, shaking her head. "Celestria would smite you if she heard that."

"Celestria doesn't give two shits about us," Birdie said, her eyes narrowing. "She's proven that all our lives."

Bee wrapped her arm around Birdie's. "The rumors I've heard are that the world we know wasn't always this way," Bee said. "According to some, there were places where water ran freely. Where trees grew to the heavens and food from the ground. There was even something called *seasons*. Periods of time when the weather would change. The sun would trade for rain. The rain would trade for *snow*."

"Snow?" Nora cocked her head to the side.

"Like water, but colder," Patch said through a grin.

"I've never heard of such a thing," Nora said.

"Well you wouldn't have," Stone said, standing from the table. "It's not taught and any textbook with the mention of"—he mouthed the word dragon again—"has long been burned. Except, it would seem, for the one your brother-in-law was hiding. He had to get this imagery from somewhere. Maybe he was made of more secrets than the queen realizes."

Nora leaned around Aesira to get a better look at Birdie and Bee. "And how do you know all of this?"

Bee shrugged. "I don't *know* for sure," she said. "When you run in the desert, you meet all kinds of people. Scammers, drifters, even royals want their fill of drugs." She smiled behind her mug. "Anyway, they liked to tell stories and I liked to listen."

"The point is," Stone continued, "we have a direction. A path. My dream last night showed me a route that would get us to Ravki in just over a week." He pointed to the map again. "If you're with me," he said to Aesira, "the queen will want an update."

Bring him home, at any cost.

"I'll send a hawk," Aesira said. "To let her know."

The heat of the desert reached the inn, the small room now stifling. Aesira brushed out her hair before pulling it back into a tight braid. Her armor was constricting but she was used to its weight.

"Do you need me to take that?" Nora asked, pointing to the letter Aesira had penned for Kamari.

"We can take it together."

Nora shook her head. "Let me. After last night, I'll admit I could use some time alone to think about my life choices."

"Oh?" Aesira grinned. "Do tell."

Nora's dimples deepened on either side of her freckled cheeks. "There's a chance I never made it back to the tavern after going to change."

Aesira shot her a look. "Now you definitely owe me the details."

Nora scrunched her nose. "Might have stayed on the ship. Might have done something I shouldn't have."

Aesira's laugh tumbled out of her. "Patch?" Nora buried her face behind her hands before smoothing her red hair out of her face.

"Like I said, I need fresh air and a long walk in silence to think about where my life is going." Aesira signed her name on the parchment before sealing it with wax. She would give Kamari the details as vaguely as possible, just to be safe in case anyone intercepted the hawk. It would be enough to put her sister at ease, knowing she was safe, and knowing there was still hope Desmond could be out there.

"Then by all means," Aesira said, passing the scroll to Nora, "your walk awaits."

With Nora gone, Aesira clasped the last hook on her chest plate, examining herself in the small washroom mirror. The bronze glared at her in her reflection. She thought twice about peeling it off and throwing it out the window, but she was nothing if not loyal. So she brushed off a speck of dust and straightened her shoulders.

"Can I come in?"

Aesira peeked out of the washroom and as expected, Stone stood with his hands in his pockets, the map from earlier and a few books tucked under his arm.

"Come in."

Stone set his pile of books and papers on the small counter, the same one he brewed the tea on last night. "You left breakfast early," he said, turning to face her. "Thought you might want to know the plan." He was right, which annoyed her.

"I needed to send a message to Vargah, remember?" She sat on the end of the bed, regretting the full armor she'd donned. "Better to send the hawks before it gets too late in the day."

Stone nodded, which made his glasses slide down his nose a fracture, forcing him to push them back up with his index finger. Aesira would have chastised herself for noticing such a detail but decided it was her training that made her so observant.

"What's the rest of the plan?"

"Right," Stone said. "The plan was to leave today for the Whispering Mountains, there's a small village there where we can dock the Aquila."

"*Was* the plan?" Aesira's brows pinched together.

Stone cleared his throat and picked up a box on the counter that was hidden under the books. "You asked last night about the man who Soo said we should see. I've arranged for a meeting but that'll set us back."

"It would be worth it, wouldn't it? Shouldn't we exercise every lead before we leave?" she asked. "What if Desmond didn't leave the Outpost? What if someone saw him and he headed east?"

Stone nodded again. His glasses slid down. He pushed them back up. It was almost mechanical, his movements. She wondered if he realized the habit as he was doing it, or if it was so second nature he didn't notice at all. She noticed, though. Even if she had no reason to.

"I do agree he's worth talking to." Stone handed her the small, plain box.

"What is—"

"He's not an easy man to deal with," Stone said. "But he's agreed to see us both together."

Aesira ran her fingers over the edges of the box. "I thought you said he doesn't like outsiders."

Stone shrugged. "He doesn't, but he made an exception."

"Why?"

Color rushed to his cheeks and neck and he cleared his throat again. "He's an old colleague, and I told them you were part of my crew, that he didn't need to worry about you."

She squinted, like if she narrowed her eyes she could focus better, see all the details he was leaving out. "Easy as that? So Birdie and Bee and Patch have all met him?" She tilted her head to the side to study Stone. He ran a hand across the back of his neck, averting his eyes. He was nervous, but she couldn't pin why.

"Oh they've met him."

"What did you really tell him?"

"Shit," he muttered. "They're overprotective of the Outpost. They think it's their territory."

"It is the kingdom's."

Stone held up a hand. "I know, but they think it's theirs since no one from Vargah has ever deigned to visit." He let out a long breath. "I told him you were with me, that we were together, and that I trust you."

A prickle of nervousness shot down Aesira's spine. "What do you mean you told him we were together? As in *together*, together?" He nodded, his face reddening. She glanced at the box and considered throwing it at him but decided since she didn't know what was in it, she couldn't risk it breaking. "You should have run this by me first."

"This was the only way to get him to believe you weren't a threat." Stone pulled his glasses off and pinched the bridge of his nose. "You can go back to bossing everyone around tomorrow, but for tonight you'll have to trust me."

"That sounds like a terrible idea."

"Do you have a better one, Commander?"

She bit the tip of her thumb. "Unfortunately not."

Stone sighed, slipping his glasses back on. "Our meeting is in two hours." He pointed to the box he'd handed her that she was still gripping like her life depended on it. "Wear that."

Eleven

Kamari

Kamari drifted through the Citadel like a ghost, a beaten down apparition of her former self. She used to be fun, she recalled. She used to enjoy life and all it had to offer.

She used to have hope. Hope for the changes she and Desmond would make. Hope for a future full of love and passion. Her mother always said she was her romantic child. Daydreaming of a world that knew peace before war and for a long time, she thought it was a complement. To find beauty in the midst of pain. Find hope despite despair.

Now, it seemed the well of hope she thought once to be endless had dried up.

Meetings with the council, preparations for Naming Day, all loomed over her shoulder like a rising storm. She could only stall for so long before she'd need to address Desmond's disappearance. She just needed more time to find something, anything, to give her hope, to give the *people* hope.

She flipped aimlessly through one of Desmond's journals, pausing on a page to trace her finger over his handwriting. The swoopy 'y's and short 't's.

Words were scribbled at the edge of the page. Some circled several times. Others underlined so hard he broke through the paper. She still had no idea what most of them meant, but every time her eye caught a particular word, her stomach plummeted.

Dragon.

She circled the word with her finger. This time, the passage was written so small she had to squint to make it out.

"...to find where they dwell would be our refuge, a way to reconcile the marks we've left on our country. Our world. They are not bringers of doom, but the hope of life."

Passage after passage was more of the same. Dragons. Ravki. And with each entry she read, she knew she would have to keep the journals hidden. Away from any wandering eyes. To speak of dragons as the creators of life, and not Celestria, was a crime fit for death. "What were you up to, Desmond?"

She thought she'd come to know her husband well over the last year, but if he was able to keep his belief in dragons a secret, what else was he hiding?

A knock at the door had her slamming the journal shut. "Shit," she cursed under her breath. She had made a mess of Desmond's office. Journals, ripped parchment, old cups of tea, all scattered about his desk.

"Your Majesty?"

"Just a moment." Kamari shoved the journals into the desk and slammed the drawer shut. Sliding off her necklace, she locked each drawer with the tiny key before placing it back around her neck. "Come in."

"Sorry, Majesty." Nev stepped in, her eyes instinctively scanning the space. "I know you don't like being interrupted when you're in here." There was a twinge of sorrow in Nev's voice, maybe pity, but Kamari pushed it aside. "Lord Raffe has requested to see you."

"Oh?" Kamari sat at Desmond's desk, hiding the tremble of her hands by placing them in her lap. "Did he say what was so important?"

Nev shook her head. "He's in the temple, but I can tell him now isn't a good time."

Kamari had dismissed Raffe the last several days. She had no interest in seeing him, no interest in pretending there would ever be a future with him on the throne by her side.

But even if she wanted nothing more than to pack his bags and throw him over the wall, leaving him for the monsters in the desert, there was the small issue of appearance. And of all the things Kamari had been taught growing up; language, arts, perfecting a proper curtsey, maintaining appearance was favored above all else.

"I'll see him," she said, unclenching her fingers from her lap. *It's what a queen should do*, she thought to herself.

Nev gave her a pointed look. Her dark red hair was styled tightly in a braid, her onyx armor seemed to be glued to her body, though when she moved it was fluid and with grace. "I'll escort you."

"I think I can find my way to the temple alone."

"You could." Nev held out her arm. "But then I would be disobeying my Commander's orders." She leaned in close. "And I'm not sure if you've noticed, but it's a rather distasteful thing to be on her bad side."

Kamari snickered a laugh and took Nev's arm. It felt ridiculous being escorted in her own home, but with the uncertainty surrounding Desmond's disappearance, she couldn't be too careful.

As promised, Raffe was waiting in the temple. He stood with his hands in his pockets, leaning against one of the columns that lined the massive room. "I'll be right outside," Nev said.

Kamari nodded before she bowed at the temple's entrance. The long skirts of her rich brown chiffon dress pooled around her. She placed her hands on the stone floor, the gold cuffs on her wrists clinking together, as she closed her eyes and offered a prayer.

"Celestria, Goddess of All," she whispered, "I enter your temple as your servant. May you continue to bless Vargah"— She paused, flipping her eyes up to see Raffe watching her—"*and* Novaria with your generosity." When she rose to her feet, she adjusted the slender gold crown that sat across her hairline and smoothed her dress. "Lord Raffe."

"My queen." He bent his middle, offering a deep bow. "Walk with me." He held out his arm and, with appearances in mind, Kamari took it.

Other than the library, the temple was Kamari's favorite place in Vargah. Though, it'd been some time since she visited.

The large bronze columns and grand arched doorways were a perfect structure for the seemingly endless, domed roof. Pillars were adorned with stars and crescent moons to honor Celestria. Intricate filigree was etched around every arch, every paver they walked on.

No expense was spared by past rulers, Desmond had told her once, to create a place of worship for the Goddess of All.

"I wanted to apologize," Raffe said. Kamari's eyes must have bulged because when he glanced at her, he laughed. "Not what you were expecting?"

They strode down the center of the temple, passing a few abandoned altars with half melted candles and dried flowers. "I didn't know what to expect," she answered honestly.

"With my cousin's disappearance, tensions are high, as you already know. My family insisted I come immediately when we heard that Desmond left and it was their pressure that drove me to be so…"

"Brash?"

Raffe glanced at her and smiled. "Exactly. I didn't go about this the right way, and I'm sorry."

An inkling of warmth spread through Kamari's chest. She still had no intentions of marrying Raffe, but if they could co-exist for the next few weeks until Aesira and Stone returned with Desmond, life would be much simpler. An apology on his part was a start.

"I appreciate the apology."

They stopped at the back of the temple where an intricately painted mural spanned the entirety of the wall. This one portrayed Celestria as a woman, her deep red hair was fanned around her, tiny stars dotted into the loose waves. Droplets of water were painted falling over her, dripping down her face and bare chest. Her eyes and lips were closed, hands held up, palms open. Inside one palm rested the moon and the other—a bright, purple flower.

Astra.

The life-blood of their kingdom.

The most powerful gift a goddess could give and the Goddess chose to give it to them. It struck her then the severity of Desmond's journals. Of his claims that dragons were a refuge and *not* Celestria. Her stomach clenched and without thinking, she gripped Raffe's arm tighter. His hand slid across the top of hers and the sudden contact of the warmth took her breath away.

"There are two ways we can go about this," Raffe said. "We continue as we are, despising the situation we've been put in. Or..." His fingers wrapped around hers and the grief she'd buried deep about Desmond leaving came rushing up her throat. It ached and burned when she swallowed. "We can come to an agreement together."

"What kind of agreement?" Kamari worked the words around the knot in her throat.

Raffe slid his hand from hers. "The council has given you a month," he said. "After that, the treaty will be nullified and Novaria and Vargah will be right back where they were a year ago. At war. I don't know you well, Your Majesty, but I can't imagine that's a future you want to see."

She shook her head, glancing again at the mural of Celestria.

The Goddess had blessed Vargah with so much and left places like Novaria and the Outpost behind. If it weren't for Piscis Spring, Novaria would cease to exist. The water the spring provided had kept their small kingdom alive and running but it also brought them so much death.

Greed would do that, she supposed. It could make men like Desmond's father turn a blind eye on what is right and only see what they want to see. What they think is theirs.

"So, I have a new proposal," Raffe said. "One that involves just you and me."

She tore her eyes away from the mural and looked up at him. "And that is?"

Raffe ran a hand through his dark hair. His linen pants and matching red tunic were bold against the muted bronze of the temple and when he turned his head to a certain angle, she could see the similarities he shared with Desmond. The dark hair and brows. The strong nose. "After a month, if Desmond doesn't how, you accept my marriage proposal–"

"I–"

"Let me finish." His hand found hers again, smooth and gentle. "You accept my proposal, but you continue your search. We make the council see that Vargah and Novaria are still aligned, the treaty is still intact, that war is unnecessary. But between you and I, that's all it will be. A show."

"An appearance of unity," she said under her breath.

"Exactly."

She let the thought mull over as they walked back through the temple. The stained glass of the domed room cut distorted shadows across the stone floor. "And what if Desmond shows? What if he comes home?"

Raffe slid his hand to her back and escorted her through the arched doorways, where Nev was still waiting. "Then we void our marriage. I step down, step back. As long as a Vargahian heir is on the throne alongside you, the council will not question it."

It wasn't a perfect plan, there were so many unknowns and moving parts, but it was *something*. The bit of hope she'd been searching for.

It would keep the council off her back and give more time to find Desmond. "Thank you, Lord Raffe." She dipped her chin. "I'll consider your offer."

"That's all I ask."

Kamari flicked on the *astra* lamp on her side table and cracked open Desmond's journal. She scanned the page, finding where she left off earlier but the words blurred together. She was too distracted by her encounter with Raffe. His sudden change in demeanor was certainly unexpected and it swirled in her head all day.

A fake marriage, essentially, to hold the treaty together until Desmond came home. But what was in it for Raffe? Appeasing his family and keeping war from Vargah, she supposed. She snapped the journal shut. She was too tired, too confused, to try and decipher any more of Desmond's notes.

Darkness settled over her room as she switched the lamp off. Sleep hadn't come easily since Desmond left but with how overwhelmed her head was feeling, it was the only thing she thought she could actually do.

Besides, when she slept, she dreamt of him.

She sank into bed and closed her eyes. She could feel his hands on hers. The warmth of his breath on the back of her neck. She imagined the outline of his dark eyes and the thickness of his black hair as it ran between her fingers. She could see the markings that lined his forearms. She remembered tracing each one with the tip of her tongue.

She rolled onto her back, her fingers gripping the sheets, as she pictured him again. She could see him kissing her neck, her chest. Could feel his lips brush against her pulse and then her ear. Heat pooled in her stomach, her fingers tightening around the silk sheets. She pressed her eyes shut tighter, focusing her energy on the only thing she still had control of. Her own body. She trailed her fingers over her nightgown, lifting the soft fabric until it pooled around her middle and she thought of him. Her skin heated, her legs rubbed together.

Desmond.

Desmond.

Desmond.

Her eyes flew open as six bells chimed from the port in quick, succinct bursts.

Six chimes.

Something was approaching the wall.

Before she could fully cover herself, Nev was in her room. "Your Majesty, you need to get to the keep." Nev's gaze dipped to where Kamari was still sprawled atop her blanket, nightgown bunch, cheeks flushed. She quickly looked away.

There wasn't any time for embarrassment as Kamari sprinted from the bed and threw on her silk robe. "What's on the other side of the wall?"

Nev escorted her from her room and into the hall where three other knights were waiting. "We aren't sure yet," she said. "Only whatever it is, it's moving fast. As must you."

She gently pushed Kamari's back, leading her down the winding staircases where they'd eventually follow the narrow path to the keep.

"Wait!" Kamari stopped. "Where is my handmaid, Hanna? If she's still asleep–"

"I will go to her next." Nev pushed Kamari forward.

The bells chimed again. Six sharp rungs that pierced her ears. "Nev, we can't leave her up there."

"You are my priority." But as she said the words, a muscle in her jaw flexed. She was just as worried about Hanna.

"Let the other knights take me the rest of the way," Kamari insisted. "Go to her. Make sure she joins me."

Nev paused and glanced at one of the women at her side and with some unspoken command, she took her place by Kamari's side. "No one enters the keep without the password," she said, a sharp edge to her voice that raised the hairs on Kamari's neck.

Six more chimes.

"Go!"

Nev didn't hesitate again. She spun on the heel of her boot and ran back toward Hanna's room.

The *astra* sconces lit a path as the three knights escorted Kamari into the keep. The rough, stone walls felt more like a cell than a room and even though Kamari knew it was protocol, panic clawed at her chest. "How long will I be down here?"

"Until the lieutenant gives us the clear," one of the women said. Her skin was dark, eyes a hazel that reminded her of Aesira. "We'll be right outside."

"But–"

They shut the door.

Six more chimes.

The *astra* flickered, creating dancing shadows across the jagged walls.

She'd only been in the keep once before, but with Desmond, when a lone snake-like creature slithered over the wall, large enough to swallow several guards whole. She'd never been so afraid. The screeching and screaming and horrible crunch of a massive jaw. The sounds were embedded in her memory, and now, alone in the same keep, the memories rushed forth, drowning her in fear.

"Breathe, Kamari," she said to herself. "Breathe." The air was stale underground and her mind knew there wasn't enough of it to last forever.

If something happened outside, would she have a way out?

That thought had her on her feet in seconds, cracking open the keep door. She fully expected it to be locked, but to her surprise, it slid open with ease. Relief unclenched her shoulders.

Six more chimes, this time accompanied by various shouting.

No screams yet.

She peeked through the door, expecting to see the figures of the knights Nev had left for her but the small corridor was empty.

She was alone.

Over her shoulder, she looked into the keep. The *astra* flickered once before snuffing out, leaving an unending pit of darkness. Her fingers gripped tighter to the door when the dark shifted, snaking from one side of the room to the next.

"Nev!" She backed her way out of the door. The darkness slithered further, spilling over the floor in inky tendrils, reaching, reaching. Just like the serpent from last time.

"It's just the shadows," she said aloud. "Just the shadows." Weakness spread through her legs, her arms holding her up against the wood door. More shouting rose outside but she couldn't tear her eyes away from the darkness that seemed to rise and fall, move and shift as though it had lungs to breathe.

A clatter sounded behind her, drawing her attention and in the instant her head was turned, the shadows swept around her ankle, moving up her leg. She stumbled backwards, nails clawing into the ground as she pulled herself farther and farther away.

"Your Majesty!" a voice from behind her made her jump. "You need to come with me." The knight grabbed Kamari's arm, pulling her to her feet, leading her away from the keep. Over her shoulder, Kamari watched the darkness retreat, slithering back into the keep like a serpent and the *astra* light flickered back on.

She shuddered, facing away. "Where are we going?" More shouting and screams sounded outside. Whatever was approaching the wall had arrived. When the knight said nothing, Kamari studied the woman.

Her face was concealed with half a mask, a few bits of dark hair escaping around her nape. She didn't look like one of the knights Nev had left her with, but she wore the same armor, same boots.

"Just come with me." Her grip tightened around Kamari's arm, sending warning bells to her brain.

"Where is Lieutenant Nev?" The woman said nothing, pulling Kamari along through the Citadel. More screams rose outside, louder now that they were back above ground. "I really don't think Nev would have–"

The woman yanked her arm forward. "You're coming with me," she said again, her voice severe, her fingers crushing around Kamari's arm. Her eyes were frantic as she scanned the corridor. Like she was waiting for someone–something. Kamari wriggled her arm, trying to free herself.

"Unhand me," she said but the woman's grip only tightened. "Nev! Rahashi!" Her shouts were drowned out behind the screaming outside. Gusts of wind blew bits of dust into the open windows of the corridor.

"Stop making a fuss," the woman hissed but Kamari fought back. Scratching at her with her free hand, putting all of her weight into her feet, planting them into the ground. "I didn't want to have to do this," the woman said as she pulled a small knife from her side. "You will come with me and you will not fight me any further." The blade was sharp as she angled it under Kamari's chin. "Do you understand?"

Kamari did her best to nod without the blade pricking her. The woman moved behind her, walking so the blade was tucked into Kamari's side. There was no one in the corridors. No one in the halls as they moved their way through the Citadel. Everyone would be in their respective hiding places or fighting at the wall. A tiny spark of relief lit inside Kamari's chest.

Hanna.

Nev went to get Hanna and when they returned to the keep to see Kamari was missing, they'd look for her. The woman led her down the final steps that would take them outside the Citadel.

Metal clashed together, smoke and flame filled the air from the torches that lined the wall. A group of soldiers breezed past Kamari but when she opened her mouth to scream, the blade dug into her side. She jolted at the sharp pierce of pain, her eyes burning from the smoke in the air. They wove through the crowd, hysteria sweeping over the courtyard. Kamari glanced up, to where dozens of monsters flew overhead, sharp teeth illuminated by light of the torches.

Muscular bodies and wide-spread feathered wings soared over the flames, their sharp teeth painted red. Kamari knew these beasts. Knew them from a rogue encounter in Novaria.

They were more bird than cat but the way they dove and struck their prey was predator nonetheless.

Kamari's heart raced. The armada moved through the court-yard, shields positioned over them like a tight shell. They stopped, bodies going completely still. Waiting, Kamari realized, for an-other beast. The flap of many wings tore through the courtyard then they were there. Feathered and furred and screeching, they swooped over the wall.

The shell of shields shifted, giving enough open space for a single flame-tipped arrow to pierce the air and land in the beast's chest.

Horror seized Kamari but the woman dragged her forward. Bodies pressed against them as they pushed their way through the crowd all the while the blade in Kamari's side dug further in, warm liquid pooling against her silk robe.

"Almost there," the woman's voice was against her ear, her arm tight around Kamari's middle. They slipped through the last of the crowd, finally an open space, just before the massive iron gates that would open up to the desert.

Kamari took a deep breath, smoke and iron filling her lungs, then she spun, the blade twisting between her ribs. She grit her teeth through the pain, elbowing the woman in the nose. Hot, bloody spurts poured down her face. The woman dropped her grip on the blade, her eyes going wide. "Wait–"

"Your Majesty!" Nev's voice filtered through the chaos. The woman scrambled for Kamari again but missed, falling to her knees. "Arrest that woman!" Nev's voice was closer now.

The gleam of the blade caught Kamari's eye as it lay abandoned on the ground. She reached for it, but it was too late. The woman snatched it before Kamari could take another breath and disappeared into the crowd, her hair and mask fading into the crowd of people and beasts. "Forgive me Your Majesty," she said. "I came for you but–"

"I need a healer," Kamari managed, then the world spun and she was on her knees.

TWELVE

AESIRA

Aesira tightened the blade around her thigh one more time for good measure. The dress Stone gave her hugged her chest but flowed loosely from her hips to the ground. Beads and charms were woven into the smooth, red fabric and loose sleeves hung slightly off her shoulders.

She let her hair down, shaking it out to give the curls some volume, frowning at her reflection in the small washroom mirror. If she'd known going as Stone's partner was the only way to see this mysterious man of the desert, she would have thought twice.

It was too late now, he was already outside knocking on her door.

"Wow," he said. "The dress fits." She smoothed out her skirt then pulled the door closed behind her.

"Wow yourself." His normally slightly worn shirt and pants were replaced by a pristine black shirt, buttoned to his throat with pants to match. His hair was slicked back, glasses tucked into his shirt pocket.

She followed Stone's lead down the hallway, where the several flights of stairs would be waiting for them.

"Just something I had lying around," he said over his shoulder and Aesira couldn't help a small laugh. She hadn't seen Stone in anything other than well worn mechanic pants, but the effort he went through to garner their outfits for this meeting sparked a flame of curiosity in her.

"I know it's a fuss but the Den isn't somewhere you go in knight's armor." They wound down the several staircases. "They're not fans of the law or anyone who might–"

"Uphold it?" she fathomed a guess.

When they reached the bottom, she adjusted her hair again, silently chastising herself for not bringing something to tie it up. She wasn't used to wearing it down and the heat of the desert was making sweat collect on the back of her neck.

"Exactly," Stone said. "I know it's not ideal, but this was the best way to get you in with me."

They passed Soo's Apothecary where it was dark inside, much like it was last night. She followed Stone, squeezing behind him between two tall, limestone buildings, until he reached the end of the narrow alley and came to a stop at a metal door.

"We're here." He straightened his collar then turned to her. "Let's make this quick. They'll offer you a drink. Take it but don't drink it. When they ask you who you are–"

"I remember," she said, twisting her hair off her neck again.

They'd discussed it earlier that day. Aesira was to be an artist, a sculptor who was passing through Vargah when she met Stone, fell in love and then stayed. It was absurd, as he said before, but if going along with the lie meant finding more about Desmond, she'd do it. And she'd do it well, she decided. It was a job, just like leading her knights, and Kamari was depending on her.

"Here we go, then." Stone took a deep breath, then knocked on the door. Once, at first, then a pause and another three quick knocks.

He took a step back and slid his hand onto Aesira's lower back. "Just for show, remember." The deep timbre of his voice ghosted over her skin, now sticky from the mix of heat and the cold. The weight of his hand felt reassuring when the door opened and a man stepped out.

He was taller than Stone, with eyes so dark Aesira wondered if they contained any color at all. His deep brown skin stood out against the bright pink scar that stretched across his left cheekbone. "State your name."

"Stone Odega."

The man scratched his bald head and squinted. "Stone?" There was something softer in his voice now as he stepped out of the doorway. "Holy shit," he said, "it is you." The man moved to wrap Stone in a hug and the absence of his hand on Aesira's back was like a cold slap. "What are you doing back here?"

Stone whispered something Aesira didn't quite catch but both the men turned to her at the same time. "My wife," Stone said, "Lucy Odega." Stone cast her a small, apologetic smile. "Lucy, this is Doc. He's been a friend for a long time."

Aesira took Doc's hand in hers, introduced herself again, then followed the two of them inside the building. They spoke low and tilted their heads together, laughing occasionally, like true friends separated for a long time, but she was so distracted by the inside of the Den she hardly heard a word they said.

"...flew in on Aquila."

"Royal money's that good, then?"

The hallway was narrow enough Aesira's shoulders almost brushed either side, she had no idea how Doc could possibly fit. Despite there being no windows, the glow from the lights that lined the floor of the entryway were enough that she could see everything clearly. Massive portraits hung from the walls, their eyes watching her as she slithered her way out of the tight space.

When it finally opened up, light spilled into a wide room with lavish crimson carpet and gold details at every corner. Stone continued making small talk with his friend, stealing a look her way every few seconds. Maybe making sure she was okay. More likely making sure she stayed in character.

Lucy.

A free spirited artist.

The opposition was almost enough to make her snort. Aesira couldn't remember the last time she felt free. Maybe when she was younger, before the Order stripped her bare.

A woman dressed similarly to her passed by with a tray of drinks, tall slender glasses with a bubbling clear liquid inside. Stone grabbed two and handed one to her.

"I'll get Vic," Doc said. "He'll be pleased you're here."

When it was just the two of them, Aesira let herself really take in the room. The extravagant chandelier. The tufted chairs. The portraits of different men who somehow all resembled each other. Family, she guessed. A few other women breezed by to attend a few other patrons sitting distantly around similar tables and chairs, their long skirts swayed lightly and their cropped tops revealed slices of soft skin.

"What is the Den, exactly?"

"A meeting place for Vic's most esteemed customers." Stone sniffed his drink, but didn't take a sip. "They drink. Gamble. Generally do things they shouldn't."

What could there possibly be to gamble on this deep in the desert, she thought. Her throat was hoarse from the heat and she knew not to drink the drink but if only a tiny sip to satiate—

"Stone the viper." Aesira whipped her head up to where a handsome, older man wearing a suit similar to Stone's stood. His hair was dark and neatly cropped with thick bands of silver around his temples, his beard close shaven and sharp at the edges.

"It's Stone Odega, now."

Vic tilted his head back and laughed. "Odega. Leave it to the royals to brand you all the same." He slapped Stone's shoulder. "It's been awhile." When Vic smiled, it didn't warm his face, it somehow hardened it. He had a strong nose chiseled from stone. A perfectly arched brow made of granite. His gaze slid to hers. He studied her from her feet to her hips, then to her eyes, burning a trail that made her skin crawl. "And who do we have here?"

"My wife, Lucy." Stone said as he squeezed Aesira's hand. Vic's brows shot up. "She's one of us."

One of us.

"Stone the viper, a husband?" Vic took one of the bubbling drinks from a tray and swallowed it back. "You must be a special woman to get this man to settle down." He snapped his fingers and a fresh drink replaced his empty one. "And what do you do, Lucy?"

This was the test and she was ready for it. She slipped her hand from Stone's and tucked a curl behind her ear.

Feign innocence. Politeness. Make him think you're anyone but you.

"I'm an artist," she said, her voice higher than usual. Sweeter, too. She knew how to play this game. Knew when to soften her edges to give the illusion that a man was in charge. "Sculpting, most recently, has been my muse. Though I couldn't help but admire the oil paintings."

She pointed to the ghastly row of portraits lining the wall. All men and their secrets and gazes full of hunger. "They're so well done." This earned her a smile from Vic, but more rewarding, Stone's hand slid around her, squeezing her hip just once.

Vic moved to one of the tufted chairs, they joined him. The bubbles in her glass had stopped popping, teasing her to take a drink.

"Thank you for allowing me in. My husband was very excited to see you." She placed her hand on Stone's knee. It was subtle, the way he jerked under her touch, but he corrected himself and snaked his fingers with hers.

Cords of gray smoke encircled Vic's face as he took a deep puff from a cigar and reclined into the chair. "Stone has been a friend for a long time." Smoke billowed from his mouth as he spoke, distorting his face. "I'll be honest though," he said, "I was surprised to hear it was you at my door. Especially how things ended the last time I saw you."

"Just been busy since I got out," Stone said. His voice was hard, his eyes sharp behind his glasses.

Vic snubbed out his cigar in the thick glass bowl on the table. "What are you doing here, Stone? Looking to get your old job back?" Vic's laugh was not humorous, but cold and deep and filled with threat. "Not getting paid enough with that royal money?"

"We're only visiting–"

"Bull shit, viper." Vic leaned forward, his brows bunching together like a fissure in the granite he was carved from. "You haven't been back to the Outpost in years. You took off with half my crew, left us high and dry with routes to be worked and no smugglers to work them and now you show up with this little number out of the blue." He nodded at Aesira, his lip snarling. "What do you want?"

"I don't want my job back." Stone's voice remained steady, unnerved, but the hand that was still holding Aesira squeezed tighter. "I don't need it anymore. I'm a free man."

"The brilliant Stone Odega. Always so fucking arrogant." Vic laughed, snapping his fingers for another drink. "I wasn't offering."

"We're just visiting." Stone slid his hand from hers and emptied his entire drink. He grimaced before slamming the glass down on the table. "You're being rude to my wife," he said. "Now drink with me, celebrate like old times, stop acting like a fucking prick."

Aesira's heart galloped in her chest. What was he doing? No drinking was the first and most absolute rule he gave her. Stone waved one of the women down with the flowing skirts and grabbed another glass.

"There he is." Vic laughed and grabbed a glass of his own. "Welcome back, viper." They clinked their glasses together and drank.

You could tell a lot about a person by the way they acted when they were drunk. It started with a shift in body language.

Stone, who typically held his shoulders high and his jaw tight, now lounged in the chair with a broad smile spread over his face. His hands, which were taking turns grabbing another glass and resting on Aesira's knee, were now enthusiastically swiping through the air as he told Vic the story of the sandstorm they flew through on the way here.

"Gusts so big they sent swells of sand clear up to the masts."

Aesira didn't know Stone well, but she liked to think she knew him enough to know that if he were sober, this story would be a lot more dry. So while she was entertained to see him so relaxed, she was also doubling up her guard. She would need to be alert for the both of them, now. She would also, it seemed, need to somehow remind her *partner* of the reason they came here tonight. To find information about Desmond.

"Stone," she said as his story dwindled and Vic rose to use the restroom. His glasses were off, tucked into the front pocket of his shirt. His eyes were glassy as he tried to find focus on her face. "What happened to not drinking?"

He shrugged. "Need to make him believe we're only here to celebrate. Figured this was the best way to put him at ease." He wrapped a finger around one of her curls. "You're very pretty," he said through a lazy smile. "But I'm going to be sick."

"Oh no you're not," she warned. "Pull it together." She clipped the last word short as Vic returned with a fresh round of drinks. He handed one to Stone, then the other to Aesira. Stone had somehow managed to polish off her drinks while Vic wasn't looking before, but as he raised his glass for a toast, she knew she'd have to partake.

"To the happy couple." Vic's gaze slid to Aesira's dipping to her chest briefly. She clenched her jaw. "May your love be endless." Stone mumbled a garbled 'here, here,' before tossing his drink back. Vic took a slow sip, keeping his eyes on her.

Damnit.

She pressed the glass to her lips. The sweet bubbles popped when they hit her tongue, but burned as she swallowed. She looked at Vic again, who wore a smile like he'd just won first place in some sick race.

"How long will you be in the Outpost?" Vic asked.

Stone hiccupped and Aesira clenched her fists to keep from shaking him. "We're only passing through on our way–" the words were out of her mouth before she could think any better. Vic's brows raised and damnit, how was she the one to let such a detail slip?

Stone had been drinking all night and yet she was the one who jeopardized their story.

"Passing through to *where*?" Vic set his glass down, still full.

"The Isles." Stone sat up, pulling his glasses from his pocket and slipping them on. "Lucy's never been. Thought I'd show her something other than the desert."

The lie wasn't totally unbelievable. Except that the Isles were in the opposite direction of the Outpost and months away by ship and required an exorbitant amount of money.

Vic's dark eyes bounced between them. As if he was waiting for another slip up. Waiting to pounce on one of them for lying. "You're lucky to have found each other."

Stone shifted beside her, close enough she could smell the drink still on his lips, feel the heat of his skin. His eyes met hers, wide and somehow clearer than before and without saying it, she knew what he was asking.

Make him believe us. Make him trust us.

She closed the final gap between them, pressing her lips to his in a brief, barely-there kiss that lit her up from her stomach to her toes.

Stone was still close enough to her that if she shifted at all, her nose would brush his. "Very lucky," he whispered but Vic paid no mind, talking as if they weren't even there.

"Isles are beautiful this time of year," Vic said but Aesira barely heard him. Her mind was stuck on Stone's lips. On the sweetness of his breath and the gentleness of his fingers as they tangled with hers. "Your timing is interesting. Not long ago we had another visitor passing through. So rare to have outsiders here at the Outpost and now we've had two in a span of a week." Vic picked up his glass from earlier and took a sip. "Must be the eclipse, making people anxious for change."

There it was.

Their opening.

Panic surged in her chest as she waited for Stone to say something. To do something. *Forget the kiss,* she thought, *if he doesn't get the information we need–*

"Another visitor?" Stone sat forward, bracing his elbows on his knees. "How peculiar."

Vic grunted. He pulled a fresh cigar from his pocket and soon the room smelt of smoke and sweet from the drinks. "Seemed harmless, albeit not totally sane. Kept mumbling to himself. Scribbling shit on parchment. We saw to it he didn't stay long."

Desmond.

It had to be Desmond.

Blood rushed to Aesira's cheeks. "How did he find his way here?"

Vic shrugged, another ring of smoke floating between them. "Desert brings all sorts of people. Drifters. Madmen." He watched her through the twisting bands of smoke. "Sculptors."

Aesira's head was fuzzy, a mix of the alcohol and information and Stone's kiss made it impossible for her to concentrate. "It's getting late. Should we head back to the inn?" She squeezed Stone's hand.

"You're probably right, as usual." He shot her a wink. "Vic," he said as he stood, "thank you for the celebratory drinks. I'm glad we could make amends." Stone extended his hand, but when Vic took it he pulled Stone forward, slamming him into his chest.

"Did you think you could really come into my house and lie to me?"

"We aren't–" He pushed Stone away.

"Tell me where you're going." Vic snapped his fingers, sending two men rushing from the corners of the room, like spiders descending from their webs.

Aesira chastised herself for not spotting them earlier. But she saw them now, and now would have to be enough. Vic's attention was honed in on Stone, grabbing him by the collar.

"I know Stone Odega didn't come all the way to the Outpost to show this bitch the sights." A glint struck from his gold tooth as he smiled.

Stone sighed and shook his head. "I really wish you didn't just say that." Stone reared back, his forehead colliding with Vic's nose, spurts of blood dripping down his manicured face.

The men closed in around them, various weapons in their palms; knives, a club, a heavy ball and chain. Aesira's brain went to work, categorizing the best way to escape while Stone and Vic had it out with each other.

The blade holstered to her thigh was in her hand and slashing through one of Vic's men before she took another breath. She cast a quick glance at Stone, still brawling with Vic, before she moved onto the next man. He was larger than the first, but that made him slower.

She ducked around a punch, dropping to her knees and slashing her blade on the back of his thigh. He screamed out, then swung for her again, but she was already on her way to Stone. Both men were bloodied and she could hardly tell who had the upper hand but Aesira's blade tucked under Vic's chin, freezing his next move.

"I wouldn't," she said, kicking his legs from under him. She dug the knife deeper as he fell to his knees, a few droplets of warm blood ran down the blade, pooling onto her hand.

Stone used his sleeve to wipe the blood from his face, crouching to meet Vic's eye. "Thanks for the drinks." His fist collided with Vic's jaw and when he fell to the ground, they bolted for the door.

The wind ripped through her thin dress as she and Stone ran through the Outpost. Aquila was hovering in the distance, shouting growing closer behind them with every step.

"I suppose I owe you." Stone pulled her hand, guiding her down a small alley which ended up being a shortcut to the docks.

"Yes," Aesira said, "I suppose you do."

"What the hell happened?" Nora was the first to greet them as they stumbled aboard.

"No time." Stone brushed her off. "We need to move. Now." He barked a few orders at Birdie and Bee and then the Aquila lifted off the ground with a rough shake. The sand below them skirted out in all directions, limiting their visibility.

"You need to let her warm!" Birdie shouted against the roaring wind.

"Again, no time." Stone cranked the wheel and yelled for Patch to set the main sails. Aesira's heart raced, blood from Vic's men still staining her fingers. She pulled her goggles over her eyes and her mask over her mouth. Through the grit of the sand-festered wind, she could make out the outline of another ship. Its black sails tattered but strong.

"Vic's on us!" Bee shouted.

Stone cursed then cranked the wheel harder than before, sending her and the rest of the cadre sliding across the deck. Wood splintered under her nails as she clung to a beam, her chest burning from exertion. The ship surged in the opposite direction, flinging her body like a ragdoll. The wind and sand pelted the air, leaving tiny abrasions on her exposed cheeks, over her bare arms and legs.

Stone clenched the wheel until his knuckles turned white, his body craning to the left.

He needed help turning the ship.

Legs shaking, Aesira pulled herself to her feet. Patch, Birdie, and Bee remained tethered to the ship's bow. "Commander!" Nora's voice was faint in the wind but Aesira trudged forward. Gravity worked against her, pushing her back, forcing her legs to work past their limit.

When she reached Stone's side, she clutched the handle and pressed all of her weight into him, forcing the wheel as far left as it could go. With the added weight of Aesira's body, the ship craned a hard left, sending barrels and loose cargo sliding across the deck. Her eyes shot to the bow, but the cadre stayed low, their tethers keeping them safely in place, Nora included.

"It's slipping," Stone ground out. She refocused and wrapped her hands tighter around his on the handle, then pushed again. The ship turned, battling against a massive dust cloud. A screeching then snapping sound cut through the air. Through her dusty goggles, Aesira could see the stern of Vic's ship.

They were heading back to the Outpost.

They'd done it.

After several more excruciating moments, the ship pushed her way through the storm. Aesira's gaze searched the ship for damage. Some broken crates, a few loose lines, but overall—they'd made it.

"Thanks for your help, Commander."

Her focus landed on Stone. Blood stained his nose, his knuckles. Their bodies were still pressed tight, her hands wrapped around his on the wheel. She peeled herself away.

"Just doing my job." The goggles scraped against her skin as she pulled them off. Sand filled her hair, her cleavage, and she wondered if she'd ever get used to the grainy feeling. She needed to change, immediately.

"Everyone alive?" Stone shouted. The crew untethered themselves and joined them at the wheel.

"That was a stupid move," Birdie hissed at Aesira. "You should have tethered."

"She saved our asses." Stone swapped his goggles for his glasses, polishing them on his undershirt before sliding them on his nose. "I wouldn't have been able to work against the wind if she hadn't been there." His finger slid under the strap of her dress, situating it back on top of her shoulder. "I believe thanks are in order." She swallowed hard, then turned to the crew.

"Thank you," Birdie said through gritted teeth.

"It's nothing," Aesira said. She didn't do anything other than her job. She didn't need thanks for it, she needed a moment alone and a hot bath and the memory of Stone's kiss erased.

"So, Vic knows we're going to Ravki?" Patch's deep voice cut through the silence.

"He doesn't know it's Ravki we're after, only that we're after something which for him would be enough." Stone steered the wheel to the right before propping it. "Do a sweep," he said to Patch. "Make sure everything's in order."

"On it, boss," Patch said before disappearing under the ship.

"Why the hell were you at the Den, anyway?" Birdie peeled off her jacket, emptying sand out of her pockets and goggles.

"We needed to follow through with a lead about the king." Stone found an empty crate and sat down, pulling his boots off. "King Desmond was here a week ago," he said. "Which means we're not far behind. If we sail through the night–"

"And what about Vic?" Bee joined him on the crate. "The storm won't set him back far. If he thinks we're after something of value, he'll be back on us by morning."

"Aquila can out fly him," Stone said. He rested his head back and pushed his glasses up. "We have more than enough *astra* from the queen to sail straight through. We've already gained enough of a gap. I'm confident we can lose him."

"And if we can't?" Nora asked. "If he follows us? Finds Ravki?"

Stone's eyes shot open. He looked exhausted. His skin was pale, eyes bloodshot. She imagined she didn't look much better. "He doesn't know where Ravki is."

"Neither do we," Birdie huffed.

Stone sighed then stood. "Why does everyone have so little faith?" He dug into his jacket and pulled out a scroll. He pushed them into Birdie's hands. "One trip to an old friend who confirmed they're real. And *original*. I'd say we're better equipped than anyone else foolish enough to try and find Ravki."

Knots formed in Aesira's stomach. If the maps were real, why would Desmond leave without them?

Birdie's brows shot to her hairline. "When did you see the cartographer?"

Stone's lip quirked up. "You all sleep too much," he said. "While you need eight hours, I thrive on five."

Birdie unrolled the map, her eyes darting over the parchment. "Real maps of Ravki," she said under her breath.

Bee peered over her shoulder. "Holy shit."

"Holy shit is right." Stone stood and stretched his arms above his head. "We have a week's worth of catching up to do," he said. "Once we make it to the base of the Whispering Mountains, we'll dock Aquila and head out by foot. It's too unpredictable for her to fly." Birdie and Bee nodded, muttering curses of disbelief under their breath.

Aesira couldn't believe it either and one glance at Nora confirmed she was stunned too. They were certain the maps were a farce and even more certain Desmond had ruined them enough to be worthless.

She was wrong and something about that fact stung more than the granules of sand wedged under her fingernails.

"If we're lucky, the king is holed up at the small outpost there called Dire. Best case scenario, we find him early and send him home."

"And what about Vic?" Aesira took Stone's seat on the crate. "If he manages to follow us and finds Ravki? You said yourself if Ravki is real and still exists, there are things there that could be dangerous. Is he really someone we should allow to get his hands on them?"

Stone chewed his bottom lip. "It's unlikely he'd catch up. As long as we fly straight through, we'll lose him." He rolled his shoulders. "We'll fly in shifts. Patch will be first. Birdie and Bee, sort it out who's next. Nora, you'll team up with one of them. Aesira, you'll take the last shift. With me."

Patch rejoined them on deck, rubbing a hand across the back of his neck. "We got a problem, boss. The supply cabinet's been raided. Food's low." He winced before letting out a long breath. "They siphoned the *astra* tanks."

"How much?" Stone asked, a firm edge lining his voice.

"This is my fault," Patch said, running a hand across the back of his neck. "I was distracted last night, I should have noticed–"

"How much *astra* did they take, Patch?"

Patch stole a glance at Nora, then quickly back to Stone. "We'll be lucky if we make it to Dire at all."

THIRTEEN

AESIRA

Aesira stood outside Stone's cabin.

Nora had gone to bed, riddled with guilt from her and Patch's fuck up, which meant it was Stone and Aesira's turn to be on watch. She raised her hand again. This time she would knock. She would not be a coward and she would–

The door flew open and her fist collided with Stone's chest.

"Ouch." He laughed, rubbing his chest.

"Sorry." She drew her hand away and tucked it behind her back.

"Commander," he said, opening the door wider. "Did you want to come in?"

Did she?

No.

Of course not.

"It's our turn on deck," she said. Simple. To the point. Stone nodded, slipping on his worn, leather flight jacket and joined her in the hall. "I meant to thank you earlier," Aesira said.

Stone's gaze shifted to her as they made their way above deck. He pulled his goggles from his back pocket and slipped them around his neck.

"For what?"

Aesira wasn't one to admit she was wrong. In fact, it was her biggest vice according to her siblings. Pride, she argued it was. Ego, more likely. "I wanted to thank you for letting me join you with Vic, and for getting the maps verified." It was a detail she hadn't thought of and as much as it ate her up, she was grateful for Stone's quick thinking.

Stone shrugged. "Han owed me a favor, so really it was nothing."

She puffed her cheeks then let out a long breath. "Are you always so nice? It makes not liking you very difficult."

Stone flashed her a quick grin which made his scar tighten. He gripped the wheel, turning them slightly left as she found an empty crate to sit on. "Would you prefer I be mean?" He shot her a look before focusing again on the horizon. "I thought we were friends, Commander."

She could feel his grin without looking at him, feel how his eyes watched her, burning an outline of her face. "I'm not as gracious as you, but I'm trying."

Stone laughed, steering them to the left. "Maybe don't try so hard." She turned to him then, because he had no idea what he'd said to her.

Don't try so hard.

As if she had any other way of existing.

Try harder.

Work faster.

Be better.

Words of her childhood etched into her like they were carved in stone.

Permanent.

When she arrived at the Order, she was twelve years old. Her father had had enough of her animated spirit. Her sharp tongue and restless limbs.

"Sit still, Aesira."

"Try harder."

"Why aren't you more like your sister? A princess should be poised on a chair, not dirty and perched in a tree."

They sent her away to break her spirit, to eliminate all the untamed energy that was constantly bubbling up inside of her. They cut the wildness out of her chest, where it grew like thorny vines, and replaced it with heavy rock. Something to hold her steady. Keep her still. Keep her theirs. So she couldn't do anything *but* try hard, because anything less than perfection was met with punishment.

Under the light of the moon, Stone's eyes glistened. Like water from Piscis Spring. Blue and endless. "How long until the next outpost?"

Stone rubbed a hand over his jaw. "Two days if we don't stop."

"And Dire will have *astra* reservoirs?" Aesira pulled the small blade from Kamari from her pocket and used the edge to pick sand from under her nails. The ship sailed smoothly above the desert, the light from the moon and stars guiding their way. She ignored the distant screeching. The faint sound of her name being called. If the crawlers wanted to come back for her, this time she'd be more than ready.

"Not much," Stone said, "but they'll have enough to get us home. Plus, this close to Naming Day, their reservoirs will be refilled in a few weeks." His fingers tightened around the wheel. "So, if we don't run into any more problems, it should be smooth sailing."

Aesira tucked the knife away. "More problems like running out of fuel before we get there? Because it seems like a big one to risk."

"It'll be close," Stone said. "But what choice do we have?"

To that, she couldn't argue. Her name drifted on the wind again like phantom nails raking down her spine. "And what about crawlers?"

Stone propped the wheel, dragging a hand through his auburn hair. "Crawlers are always a possibility. Serpents, storms, Vic, all things we'll need to be ready for."

"I thought you said Vic couldn't catch up?"

"I said it was unlikely, not impossible."

Aesira was learning that Stone spoke in such a calculated way that oftentimes his version of the truth was a stretched one. She was torn between being annoyed and impressed with his ability to skirt around the truth. He pushed his glasses up onto his nose and she smiled. "You do that a lot."

"Hm?"

"Push your glasses up."

He tipped his head down, smiling at her. "I'm flattered, you noticed, Commander."

"I didn't–" She shook her head. "My job is in the details. I get paid to notice things."

"I see." He adjusted the prop to keep them flying straight then joined her on the crate. "Is that why you came? To make sure I'm doing what I'm meant to?"

She straightened to match his posture. "Yes." There was no sense in lying. Not when they'd come this far with so much farther to go. She didn't care if he knew she and Nora were here to oversee him and the rest of the Odegas. To ensure they weren't planning to steal her sister's money and run.

She and Stone had been in more than one unfortunate situation since they left Vargah. First with the crawlers, then with Vic. He was starting to prove his loyalty to the job and so she wanted to prove hers back by telling him why she really came.

"I appreciate your directness," he said through a laugh. "Do you want a drink?" He stood and went to a small crate tethered to the ship. Unlatching it with a key he pulled out a small bottle and two cups.

"I shouldn't, the Order doesn't allow it."

"The Order isn't here," he said over his shoulder, holding up a glass. "I'm asking you, not them."

Her breath caught in her throat. It would be easy to say no and let that be it, but something about having the choice, about someone asking her what she wanted made a light spark in her stomach. So she simply nodded and he got busy preparing their drinks. "You're not upset that my sister doesn't trust you?"

That I don't trust you.

He laughed again, the deep rumble filling the open air between them. "She is the queen and I am a reformed criminal. I would expect nothing less." He popped the cork off the bottle and filled two cups until they were each half full. "Here." He handed one to Aesira. "Now that we're being honest with each other, a drink."

She tapped her glass with his and took a sip. It burned down her throat and sat warm in her belly. The taste not nearly as good as the satisfaction that she made the decision to defy an ironclad rule she typically swore by.

"Drug smuggling isn't the worst of things." Aesira took another sip. "I've met far more deranged criminals."

"In the honor of transparency and honesty," he said raising his glass as if to toast, "you should know I didn't just smuggle *durgi*." He tipped his glass back and emptied it. "I helped make it."

Realization sunk its teeth into Aesira's chest making it difficult to breathe. "That would mean you're–"

"A chemist," Stone finished for her. She slammed her mouth shut. "So maybe I *am* just as bad as the other delinquents you've arrested." He tipped back his cup, only to realize it was empty. When he stood to pour more, Aesira turned her focus to the moon and to the inky dark that had swept over the desert. She focused on the slight movement of the ship. Focused anywhere but on him.

A chemist.

To smuggle drugs was one thing, to *make* it was a crime that was tried on the same parallel as murder and somehow, Stone had managed to pull off the facade that he was just a smuggler. Maybe he was a better liar than she thought.

"I'm not proud of the work I did for Vic, if that helps," he said, retaking his seat next to her. "I've spent a long time hating myself for what I created." He held his cup to his lips but didn't take a sip. "I wish I could say I'm different now but that doesn't seem fair. Besides, I think no matter how much we change there are parts of our pasts we can't escape." He swirled the drink in his cup. "Maybe I don't want to. Maybe I keep the reminders of who I was as punishment for being able to move on when so many can't."

He took another sip but grimaced as he swallowed. Like it was difficult to enjoy now that the truth was out there. Despite their differences, she could understand what it meant to live with shame. The feeling of despair that your life could keep moving even when someone else's ends. "Do we still get to be friends?"

Aesira swallowed hard, then finished her drink. "I don't..." She set her cup down. Other than Nora and Nev, she didn't have friends. Kamari, she supposed. But making friends while in the Order was almost impossible. She and her squadron were reassigned to different areas of the country every few months. There was never time for any sort of relationships to take root. Never time for somewhere to feel like home.

She glanced at him and in the rigidness of his shoulders and pinch of his mouth. Maybe he wasn't proud of his past either, and that was something she could relate to.

"I don't like what you *did*," she said, "but it seems like you don't like what you did either and that matters."

His shoulders relaxed, like he had been holding his breath waiting for her answer. She had seen firsthand the lasting effects of all manner of drugs created by chemists. Had seen how they ravaged Novaria like a plague. Seen them change people into unrecognizable versions of themselves. Destroy lives. Reputations. Families.

She also arrested many smugglers of the drug who showed very little remorse. They were nothing like Stone. They wouldn't sit here with bated breath confessing their sins. "Does you being a chemist have something to do with why Vic was so angry with you?"

"Ah, that." He smiled over the top of his glass. "Birdie, Bee, and Patch had been running under Vic for a few years before I showed up. They took me under their wing, made sure I had a place to stay, food to eat. I was ten, I think." He frowned into his cup. "Anyway, we ran together for two decades and Vic would keep us running until there was nothing left of us, if we didn't get out. We saved up, stole a ship, and took off, leaving his well-oiled drug routes suddenly without four runners. That's why he's pissed at me."

She swallowed the last dregs of her wine, savoring the sour taste on her tongue. "Yet you took a chance to meet with him knowing how angry he'd be."

"I wasn't worried about Vic. He puts on a good show, but he's an old man. I knew we'd be fine."

"Your confidence precedes you, Odega."

"Something else you've noticed about me, Commander?"

She didn't hide her smile this time. "Anyway," she said in an attempt to steer the conversation away from the list of things she'd noticed about Stone Odega. She watched Stone, his eyes shining from the moonlight or the drink. His flushed cheeks and clenched hands. The scar that ran alongside his face. The cluster of stars inked on the side of his neck.

The alcohol numbed her fingertips and the tip of her tongue. She forced a smile before glancing back to the desert as the ship sailed silently above the ground. "I'm not perfect either, you know."

Stone gasped. "The great Commander Zeliath has flaws?" He bumped her shoulder with his and all of the blood in her body came rushing to her cheeks. "I'm not convinced."

Was that a compliment? More likely the alcohol.

"I'm not so great, as you put it." The crawler's dead eyes and haunting words flashed behind her eyes. "I've hurt people in ways I'll never forget." She could hear them now, their screeching voices tugging at her ears, but Stone sat unphased and she ignored them the best she could.

"Maybe the two of us," Stone said, bumping her shoulder again, "have more in common than we thought."

There was something comforting about that. About finding someone who could not be more opposite from her; in their upbringing, in their professions, and still finding commonality. It made the world seem less big. Less overwhelming.

"We're human, after all," he said. "We're made of mistakes and regrets and even if there's nothing else about us that's the same, it's a relief knowing that at the end of the day, we as humans bear the same burden."

She tilted her head to the side and pretended not to study the lines of his face or the way his scar traveled to his lips. "What burden?"

He smiled and she would later blame the wine but in that moment Aesira could admit to herself that maybe Stone Odega was a little bit handsome and maybe he'd gotten under her skin more than she liked to admit.

"The burden of maintaining our humanity when the world makes it so easy not to."

Fourteen

Aesira

Days of endless desert traded with jagged red rocks. A heavy mist clung to the craggy mountain peaks, offering limited visibility to the outpost below them.

Aesira cupped her hands and blew into them, warming the frost from her fingertips. In Novaria, the elevation was higher but the land was still temperate. No extreme drops or spikes in temperature. Nothing like the heat of Vargah or now the frigid air of the Whispering Mountains.

"If those crawlers don't kill us, surely this cold will." Nora wrapped her hands around a steaming cup of tea.

"Once we're on the ground, we'll warm up." Aesira rubbed her hands together. They sailed straight through the day and now the moon was lighting the way for Aquila to dock at the next stop.

Dire, Stone had called it. A tiny speck on the map, and the last known civilization in the west.

Aesira's armor held in her body heat well enough that she waved off a cloak from Bee. Deciding it would only get in her way should a need for her weapons arise.

"Almost there," Stone said from behind her. They spent their rotations together the last two nights, just as he'd said.

He was patient, teaching her how to fly while they made simple conversation. The weather, Vargah, finding Desmond. She was finding his company more and more comfortable. Actual friendship, as Stone liked to remind her. Except when his hands met hers on the wheel of the ship, his callouses scraping against her skin, sending tiny thrills down her spine. Or when he laughed at his own stories and Aesira caught herself leaning into the sound, savoring it.

She'd chastise herself in her room later for being so easily distracted.

Aesira left Nora to warm with her tea and joined Stone at the helm. "What's the plan?" His goggles sat snug on the top of his head, his hair tousled from the wind.

"We dock. Ask around." He spun the wheel slightly to the left, angling them toward Dire. "We hope King Desmond is holed up here and if not, we prepare."

Hope.

Aesira had done her fair share of hoping in her younger days. Hoping her father would change his mind about sending her off to train with the Order. Hoping Kamari would not be sent away to a foreign kingdom. Hoping her brother had found peace in the afterlife. Hoping her mother would intervene and protect her children.

She's outgrown the notion that hoping for things meant anything.

Over the edge of the ship, red rocky earth stretched beneath them. The crawlers had been mostly quiet all night, but every now and then her name drifted on the wind. Her secrets and shames.

The dock was in sight now. It was worse for wear, broken planks and missing hinges. Stone managed to land with grace, only knocking a few planks loose in the process.

He led them off the Aquila and into Dire, checking over his shoulder three times that the ship was tethered.

The wind tugged at Aesira's hair, biting at her chapped lips and cheeks. The moon and stars twinkled through the growing clouds, but other than their light, the rest of the small encampment was dark. No music like in the Outpost. No *astra* lamps or sounds from the small cluster of buildings. She imagined the rations of *astra* were minimal out here, but still, shouldn't there be some evidence of life?

"It can't be that late," Nora whispered at her side. "Where is everyone?"

Stone finished wiping the condensation from his glasses and slid them back on. Together, the six of them scanned the meager outpost.

A set of crumbling buildings sat vacant to their right. The windows had been shattered, the door barely hanging from its hinges. On the other side was another set of buildings. They glowed blue in the moonlight but through the broken windows, Aesira could see nothing but darkness.

"Shouldn't there be *someone* here?" Bee asked, coiling her arm around Birdie's. Dread snaked in Aesira's stomach. She knew it was a small outpost, one that didn't garner many visitors. But it shouldn't be completely vacant. Holding her breath, she scanned the ghost-like town before her.

"We'll go in teams of two," Aesira said. "Nora and Patch take the northernmost building. Birdie and Bee, head to the eastern cluster." She nodded at Stone. "You and I take these." She pointed to the set of dilapidated buildings in front of them.

They divided the torches they brought from the ship between them before they split up. Nora's sword glinted under the moonlight as she and Patch trudged through the desolate outpost.

The building in front of Stone and Aesira was drowning in darkness, the shattered windows giving a distorted view to the empty void inside. "Hello?" she called out, her own voice echoing back to her. Her sword felt heavy in her hands after a week without use, but her muscles were quick to remember their training as she raised it higher, tighter. "Hello?" She took a step into the building when something crunched under her boot.

Broken glass.

"Here." Stone lit the torch. Flickers of firelight cut through the room, illuminating shards of glass that littered the floor in every direction. Tables were overturned, a few chairs still sat in place, deep scratches carved through the backs and bottoms. Curtains hung in tatters on the ground.

"What happened here?" She sheathed her sword, broken glass crunching under her boots. "Rebels?"

"I don't know," Stone said, angling the torch to light the way in front of them.

The drifters of the desert had been quiet as of late. They had no real home, no ties to either of the kingdoms, coming and going as they pleased, usually bringing a torrent of crime with them. Theft, mostly, of resources like *astra* and water. Sometimes more violent, like the time they invaded Novaria. They'd held a woman hostage and demanded medicine from their healers.

The room before them was destroyed, pillaged. There were little resources here to begin with, but she couldn't imagine that would stop the rebels from taking their fill anyway.

Stone pointed the flame toward the back of the room, where another dark doorway sat. A thread of instinct pulled taut in Aesira's chest. She moved through the room until she stood in the doorframe.

The light from the torch flickered from side to side as Stone joined her. The dread that was in her stomach crept its way up through her chest before clenching around her throat. "Stone." She swallowed past a scream. "Stone."

"What is it?"

Something dark slid from the wall, falling to the floor.

Drip.

Drip.

Drip.

Aesira took a step closer but recoiled when the odor hit her.

Tangy and pungent.

Blood.

It dripped from the ceiling, pooling on the edges of the broken glass. Aesira covered her mouth with her sleeve.

Movement in the corner caught her eye, too far back for the flame to reach. She pulled her sword again and took a step forward. Stone's free hand clenched around her arm. "What are you doing?"

She shrugged him off. Another shift in movement, another crunching sound from the glass beneath her feet. She took a tentative step, the heat from the torch touched her cheeks as Stone followed closely behind.

"Is someone there?" Her grip tightened around the pommel of her sword, the shadowy movement from the back corner froze.

"Aesira," Stone warned but she raised a hand to silence him. She could appreciate his caution, she understood it. But this was more her element than tending a ship or overlooking a wall. She knew what she was doing and when she looked at him over her shoulder, the quick dip of his chin told her he knew as well.

There was another sound. Not the bite of glass under their boots. Not the crackling of the flame from the torch. She craned her ear and held her breath, honing in on the instincts she'd sharpened since she was twelve.

Singing.

From the farthest room, a woman's voice faintly drifted through the open doorway. "Do you hear that?" Aesira kept her voice low but with how close Stone was pressed to her body, she knew he heard her. His fingers gripped her arm like a vice.

The singing continued, high pitches and coos. Bird-like. Soft. Sweet.

"Who's there? Do you need help?" Anticipation churned in Aesira's stomach as she thought of the blood coating the ceiling and floor, the destruction of the building itself. The singing grew louder, a chirping melody that rang in her ears. She took a step forward. "We're coming in."

Another step and a high pitched note rang through the building. *"What if we all fell down, down, down."*

Despite the cold, sweat pooled in Aesira's palms and on her brow, clinging to the thick dark hairs around her nape. *"What if we all fell down,"* the voice sang again and then all at once, nothing. A wave of silence settled into each nook and crevice of the vacant building, like calm skies before a sand storm. The odor of the room was strong enough to spring tears from her eyes, burning her nostrils.

Aesira thought of herself as a brave woman. A noble knight and fearless on the battlefront. But when Stone raised the torch and lit up the room, a fear so deep cut through her, her sword trembled in her hand.

A woman's face was illuminated in the flame. She threw her head back, hissing at the light. A pale face with large, yellow eyes, a chin stained crimson with blood dripping from her needle-like teeth. Dark, stringy hair clung to her scalp, falling well below–

Aesira reared back, bumping into Stone's chest. He dropped the torch and pulled her so tightly into him she could feel the erratic beating of his heart.

From the neck down, the woman morphed into feathers and rippling muscle, all held up by powerful legs and sharp talons. Aesira's pulse hammered in her chest. Her sword slipping, slipping from her grip until it clattered against the glass on the floor.

The woman rose, tilting her head to the side at an unnatural angle, her yellow eyes narrowing to slits. The light from the torch on the ground flickered once, twice, the flame dwindling to almost nothing. There was a scrape of talons against the floor. Then another.

Aesira's breaths were short, her hands empty and useless without her sword. Another scrape. A flutter of feathered wings. "Stone..."

"Strix," Stone said in her ear, his hands clutched around her shoulders.

Strix.

The word evoked a memory in Aesira's brain, but it was muddled and locked away.

Strix.

Strix.

How did she know that word?

Stone scrambled to pick up the torch, blowing softly until the fire roared again. The Strix screeched, hiding her face behind massive wings. Aesira and Stone took a step backward, on their way she picked up her sword, the weight giving her a false semblance of strength.

"Move slowly," Stone said, his lips pressed to the shell of her ear. "It doesn't like the light. As long as we keep calm. Keep the torch lit..." Something bumped into the back of her calf. Aesira looked down. Dozens of limbs scattered throughout the room. Veins sucked dry, sinew stretched and discarded. Bodies left to rot and decay. Bile rose in her throat.

"Stone—" A flap of wings sounded behind them, then a shriek so loud she was sure her ears would bleed.

"Forget what I said," he yelled, "run." Stone's hand tightened in hers pulling her through the rooms, their lone torch leading the way through the tomb of broken bodies and glass. She gripped her sword in her free hand and didn't dare look behind her.

Another flap of wings.

A closer shriek.

They followed the light of the moon, beaming through the doorway.

"Faster, Commander!"

But she was already running as fast as she could. Wind gusted at her back, blowing her hair in her face, wrapping her spine in cold, sharp fear.

The fresh air outside the building filled her lungs but it was no reprieve. Stone tripped, landing on his knees and because he kept her hand in his, she went down with him.

Turning on her heel, she pressed her back into Stone, pinning him to the ground and raising her sword. The Strix shrieked, its wings beating, ruffling the sand below. It darted but Aesira rolled to her side. Its talons dug into the sand, marring the earth, barely missing her and Stone. It righted itself, then launched forward, snapping its teeth and flapping its wings.

"Stone!"

Bee.

Or maybe Birdie. Nora? Aesira wasn't sure. All of her effort, all of her focus was on avoiding the Strix' talons and teeth. Keeping herself between it and Stone.

The torch snuffed out in the sand, no fire to ward it off.

Over and over it attacked, quickly darting in then flying away but not before leaving a deep cut on Aesira's thigh. Searing pain rolled through her leg, burrowing deep in her bones. Through gritted teeth, she slashed her sword, nicking the Strix's middle, then on another down swing, its wing.

"We need to get back to the ship." Stone's arms were there, pulling her away.

Not yet.

She thought of the bodies in the building.

The broken glass.

The sounds of singing and a memory buried deep, rousing itself awake, clawing its way to the surface.

Not now, she thought. *I don't have time for this now.*

"Go!" she shouted over her shoulder. She swung her sword, moved her feet swiftly in the sand, waiting, waiting. The Strix flew higher, its feathers blending into the night. The only tell was its yellow eyes so she honed in on them, pushed that dark memory away.

Watched those eyes like they watched her.

There was no prey here, only two predators, one aground, the other in flight.

"Commander!" Nora was at her side, sword drawn, red hair swaying under the wind of the Strix's wings. Warmth from the other torches hit her cheeks and the Strix screeched high then hissed, darting behind a building.

"Protect them." Aesira nodded toward the others and Nora angled her body without question, putting herself between the Strix and the cadre.

Another screech, a dash of movement, and it reappeared, shooting downward, talons first, aiming for Aesira's throat. She swung her sword, the crunch of metal on bone followed by a cry–this time human. Black blood sputtered from the wound on its leg, leaving a trail in the sand as it darted behind a building, away from Aesira's sword, away from the flame of the torches.

"Fuck." Bee gripped Aesira's shoulder. "Commander Zeliath. Now I see where your title comes from." Aesira's mind was fogged over, trying to make sense of what her eyes were telling her. The memory from before, scraping and clawing, begging to get out.

Not here.

Not in front of them.

Her breathing shallowed, pain lancing up her leg, through her chest. "Come on." Stone took Bee's place by her side, his hand wrapping around her middle. "Let's get you back to the ship." It was only when she warmed from his touch that the searing pain enveloped her and her knees gave out and that memory, the one she'd tried to drown long ago, rose to the surface.

FIFTEEN

STONE

Stone pulled off his glasses and pressed his fingers into the bridge of his nose. A headache had started earlier that day but now it spread across his face like a boulder plundering down a mountain.

"She still asleep?" Birdie sat in the chair next to him.

He nodded and looked at Aesira, sprawled across his bed, leg wrapped in a fresh bandage. "She's been mumbling, but none of it makes sense."

"I'm amazed she remained conscious as long as she did after the beast ripped her thigh open. The talons of a Strix contain enough venom to knock someone out almost instantly. Must have been motivated." Birdie cut him a glance. "Are you alright?"

"Fine," he said. "I imagine it'll be at least a few more hours before she wakes up." Birdie sighed, a note too long and he already knew what she wanted to say.

"The Strix could have solved our problem."

There it was. The ugly truth. The bold reminder of who they all were.

Odegas.

Criminals.

"You would have preferred me to leave her paralyzed in Dire?" Stone shook his head. "Deranged, even for you."

Bird smiled, her sharp eyes narrowing. "I'm just saying, if we wanted to run away with the queen's loot without harming the Commander ourselves, nature gave us a way."

"You're sick."

She laughed and Stone knew her well enough that she wasn't serious about leaving Aesira in Dire to fend for herself. "We can continue to look through Dire, but the chances that we find—"

"We can't turn back now, Bird." He kept his eyes pinned to Aesira, monitoring the pinch of her brows and twitch of her lips. "Not when we're so close."

"Are we close?" She shot him a glare. "You're not the only one who can read a map, you know."

He did know that. He knew that if there was anyone to stand over his shoulder, fact checking along the way, it would be her.

"Six days," Stone said. "It'll take roughly six days to get to where Ravki is located on the map." He turned to face her, keeping Aesira and the door to his room in his line of sight. Nora had checked on her every few minutes, she was due to be back any moment. "We can't turn back when we're less than a week away."

"Bee and I found no survivors." She cast her narrow eyes down to her feet. "No evidence of supplies that haven't spoiled. The reservoirs were empty. There's no *astra* to fuel the ship." She shook her head and sighed that long, telling sigh. "If one Strix could do that much damage, just imagine what might be waiting for us in the Whispering Mountains." She blew out another long breath and tucked her short, blonde hair behind her ears. "There's a little *astra* left, it would give us a small start for Vargah."

Stone chewed his bottom lip, eyes darting between the door and Aesira.

"Not everything lost is meant to be found, Stone." Birdie stood and took a few steps to the door.

No, he thought. He knew that. But Ravki held so many promises and they were just outside his reach. Everything in his life, it seemed, was always just outside his reach. His eyes flicked back to Aesira. "The Commander won't turn back easily," he said. "She'll insist we persist to find the king."

Birdie's laugh cut through the small room like a razor blade, jagged and deadly. "If she wakes and really thinks the king could have survived the Strix on his own, she's more delusional than you."

Stone had already thought of this, of course. It was one thing for the king to survive the storms and make it to the Outpost, it was another to survive a Strix. They were solitary creatures who hunted only at night, but they made crawlers look like children. If the king made it as far as Dire, Stone had very little faith that he made it out.

"We'll need to vote," Birdie said, pulling him from his thoughts. "Rule number one." Stone nodded and stood to join her.

A swift knock at the door drew their attention. "Still asleep?" Nora poked her head inside. Dark purple lined around her eyes, her freckled cheeks more sunken than usual.

"Likely will be for a while longer," Birdie said as Nora settled in beside Aesira. "Looks like you've got it from here, we'll be back."

The walk from his room where Aesira slept to the crew quarters felt ten miles long. When Birdie opened the door to the mess, Bee and Patch were waiting. Relief unclenched his shoulders as he slid into the booth.

"You okay, boss?" Patch asked, pouring four cups of tea. Stone watched the hot water melt into the loose leaves but bit his tongue from mentioning their lack of rations.

How did everything go to shit so fast? That was life in the Outpost, and he chastised himself for believing things could be better somewhere else.

"Fine," he said.

Bee slid her hand across the table and Birdie met her halfway, giving it a squeeze. "Been a long time since I've been that scared." Stone could feel the heat of Birdie's stare burning into his face, so he focused on his tea. If Bee wanted to turn back, Birdie wouldn't hesitate.

"We need to vote," Birdie said. "We knew it was a risk coming here, but with the lack of supplies and the Strix, we have to be practical about moving forward."

"You're suggesting we turn back?" Patch reclined in his chair, scrubbing a hand down his stubbled jaw. "What do you say, boss?"

Stone's glasses fogged over from the heat of the tea. He wondered how long he could say nothing until Birdie punched his leg.

A minute, he guessed. "I won't ask you to continue if you're not comfortable," he said. "The Strix poses a real threat as well as Vic."

Heat scorched Stone's cheeks. It shouldn't bother him so much that Vic found a way to sabotage his plans, but the fact was, it did bother him. Even years away from the Outpost couldn't change the fact that he was always on the losing end when it came to Vic.

"We don't have enough *astra* to make it to Vargah." Birdie filled the silence for him. "But we can at least use what we have to head that way and hope we pass a cargo ship or a hauler."

There was very little Stone hated more than failing. Which was why being a smuggler appealed to him so much. It was something he knew he'd succeed at. Something that challenged him and pushed him and gave him a false sense of pride. Like he actually accomplished something with his life. Until, of course, he was caught.

Birdie leaned forward, her elbows braced on the table. "If there are no supplies left in Dire, the sensible thing to do is turn around. The queen will understand, Stone."

"And abandon our mission? Our king?" Nora's voice came from the doorway.

Shit.

"So much for rule number three," Birdie mumbled. Stone shut his eyes. He was tired. His bones ached and worry for Aesira chewed away at his middle.

But Ravki was days away. *Days.* If they could only push a little farther.

"We're going back?" Her voice came from behind him. Stone's eyes shot open and when he turned, Aesira was in the doorway next to Nora. Her eyes were bloodshot, her skin pallid, but she was awake. Breathing. Standing. His eyes trailed to her leg where the bandage was still wrapped tight, a hint of pink scattered across the white cloth. "Is that what you've all decided?" she asked. "We're turning around?"

Stone clamped his mouth shut and to his surprise, so did Birdie.

"We're not sure," Bee said.

"Sit, Commander." Nora squeezed her arm. "I'll get you something to eat." The rest of them shuffled in their seats. Birdie switched sides, leaving a space for Aesira to sit next to Stone.

"I'm surprised you're up," Bee said. "Strix venom is potent."

Birdie shot Stone a look from across the table but he focused on his tea again. *Strix venom is potent,* he thought to himself, *if left unattended.* The small satchel of tea from Soo sat in his pocket like a secret.

"I'm still a bit lightheaded," Aesira said, "but it's lifting." She bit into a dry biscuit. "Back to the issue at hand. Are we leaving?"

Five sets of eyes landed on Stone and he knew his stalling had run out. "It's sensible to turn back while we can," he said, locking eyes with Birdie. "We need water. *Astra.* The food we have left will cut it close." Birdie shook her head but he could tell from her eyes, she knew he wasn't going to budge. Because while Stone knew her better than himself, Birdie knew him just as well. "But I believe there's still value in finding Ravki."

"Finding Desmond, you mean." Nora cocked her head to the side. "We're here to find the king, not just some ancient city."

"Of course." Stone's skin itched. He wasn't lying, not exactly. He had every intention of bringing the king back to Vargah should he find him, at least now he did, he just also happened to have other interests in pursuing Ravki. Other interests that sat like a nagging fly in the back of his mind buzz, buzz, buzzing until it was all he could think about.

"I won't ask any of you to continue." He reached for Bee's hand. "You and Bird can head back. The Outpost isn't far. Aquila will get you as far as she can. You'll be safer."

"Right," Birdie interjected, "and if we run into Vic along the way? We need to avoid the Outpost altogether. Our best bet is heading straight for Vargah and the only chance at survival is sticking together."

"It's too far, Bird." Stone rubbed his temples. "There isn't enough *astra* to make it even a quarter of the way."

Nora cleared her throat. "Celestria is always listening. Maybe if we pray, we'll be blessed?"

Patch clucked his tongue and shook his head, a lock of dark hair falling across his forehead. "If you think prayer will help, you haven't been paying attention," he said. "There are no gods out here. Only monsters and men." A flush of red swept over the knight's cheeks.

"Is that right?" Nora leaned forward. "And which one are you?"

A smile stretched over Patch's lips as he mirrored her pose, propping his elbows on the table. "Which one do you want me to be, sweetheart?"

Aesira sucked in a breath next to Stone, like she was waiting for Nora to lash out or pull her sword but instead, the knight smiled, dimpling her freckled cheeks.

"We can't just sit here," Birdie said. "We need to leave. Now."

"We aren't abandoning our post." Nora and Birdie threw a slough of curses at each other, arguing about leaving or staying and all the while Stone's head pounded harder and harder. The pain would take his entire head soon, behind his eyes, down his neck.

"We can make it," Birdie said. "We'll push the Aquila as far as we can."

Stone shook his head. "I already told you there isn't enough *astra*."

She slammed her fists on the tabletop, hard enough to rattle his mug. "Then do you suggest we go and *find* some?"

Silence stretched across the table, digging into Stone's sides, making it difficult for him to breathe. He ran an unsteady hand through his hair, pushing it off his forehead. "Bird–"

"Hold on." Aesira grabbed his arm and he felt it clear down to his toes. Where her fingers dug in. Where their bodies connected. "What do you mean, find *astra*?"

Stone's nails drew lines down the tops of his legs. "Nothing," he said, keeping his eyes trained on Birdie. "She misspoke."

Aesira's hand was still wrapped around his arm and he wondered if she realized she was still touching him. Maybe if he didn't move, she wouldn't either, so he held his breath and stayed put.

Birdie's eyes pinned him like cornered prey. "Bullshit," she hissed before facing Aesira. "Of all the rumors of Ravki, Commander, I'm shocked you haven't heard the most famous one."

"Birdie," Stone warned but she blazed on, ignoring him and everyone else in the room.

"There's an old drifter story of a place where *astra* grows from the ground. Where it blooms on petals and through the spines of trees." Birdie's smile tightened. "That place, of course, is Ravki."

"This is blasphemy," Nora said under her breath, standing from the table. She frowned, all cheekiness, gone. "*Astra* is a gift from

Celestria." She turned to face Patch. "I hope you're right about prayer not reaching the gods out here, maybe your words won't reach Her, either." The door slammed behind her and the remaining cadre cast a few wavering glances.

"*Astra...*" Aesira stretched the word out, her brows furrowed, fingers still wrapped around Stone's arm, searing through his shirt and leaving a mark on his skin. "You believe *astra* grows from the earth?"

Stone shook his head. "No, we don't." Birdie's boot collided with Stone's shin under the table but he dropped his voice low and when Aesira's gaze met his, frightened and wide, it was like they were alone in the room. He rested his hand atop hers which seemed to snap her from her daze. She pulled away, leaving the warm spot on his arm to run cold. "It's just another rumor."

She frowned. "A rumor that would entice a smuggler to take a job." His stomach tightened. They spent the last few days being honest with each other. Learning bits about each other. Becoming friends. He could have told her at any moment his real motive behind finding Ravki was not just to find the king, but to see if the story was true. If *astra* did grow from the earth. If there were more bodies of water like Piscis Spring. But he didn't because he knew how it would change the way she looked at him, like it just had.

Patch's fingers strummed against the tabletop, his eye watching the doorway as if he could conjure Nora back by staring hard enough. Stone could see Aesira watching him from the corner of his eye. His heart pumped faster knowing she was looking at him, but he couldn't find it in himself to look back. "We vote, then," Patch said. "All in favor of turning back, say 'aye'."

"Aye." Birdie raised her hand.

Silence.

Painful, uncomfortable, stretching silence.

"Bee," Birdie snapped.

"I'm sorry," she said. "I love you Bird, but we've made it this far and the idea of getting stranded in the desert during stormy season doesn't sound at all appealing." She turned her attention to Stone. "What are the chances *astra* grows in Ravki? What are the chances there's enough there to fuel the ship all the way to Vargah without issue?"

Birdie laughed. "Slim to none. They're just stories, Bee."

"And what about the Strix?" Aesira asked. "What if that kills us instead?" There was something cold in her voice, something detached.

"We'll be smart," Stone said. "The people here were unprepared for the attack because they didn't know it was coming. We have that to our advantage. We travel during the day when it sleeps, and hide at night. If by some chance the story is true," he said, "there would be enough *astra* to get us safely home. It's our best option."

Stone had never begged for anything in his life, mostly because there was never anything to beg for, but the thought of dropping to his knees and asking them to trust him was right on the tip of his tongue.

"Again, all in favor of moving forward, say 'aye," Patch said, locking his gaze with Stone's. An understanding. "Aye."

"Aye." Bee gave Stone a slight nod, but her wide, honey eyes gave her away.

"Aye," Aesira said to his right, relief pumping through his veins.

Birdie's black eyes narrowed and he could hear everything she wanted to say in them, but didn't. *You're being reckless. Chasing a myth you have no business chasing.* But she raised her hand because rule number two was never something any of them could get around and never wanted to—*we always have each other's backs*—and said, "Aye."

Sixteen

Kamari

The stars were fading, each one twinkling out in the sky leaving only a few moments of tolerable heat before the sun would rise and take claim to the city. Pain bloomed on Kamari's side as she rolled over, reading the note from Aesira again.

We haven't found him, but we have a lead.

I can't say for sure but there are reasons to believe he was here, in the Outpost.

If I don't write, don't worry.

Hawks won't fly in the Whispering Mountains but know that I'm fine.

That we are still looking for him.

The maps are what they claim to be so we have a way to find him, Kam.

We just need time.

Be strong,

Aesira

She rolled the note and tucked it safely into her pocket. They'd found a lead. A clue. Proof that Desmond was out there. *Alive.*

An oil painting of her and Desmond that took up nearly the entire eastern wall, watched her, taunted her, as she changed out of her robe and into a light dress. It reminded her of a life that now felt so far away.

The painting was done before their wedding as a gift from her parents. She remembered the nerves she felt. The uncertainty of the entire arrangement. But that moment, posing for the painting, was the first time she realized Desmond was nothing like she'd expected. He had made a joke, though she couldn't recall what he'd said, the memory of her nerves settling was something she couldn't forget.

Desmond's dark curls were thick and wild. Her hands twitched, remembering how soft they were when she dug her fingers into them. She gazed into his eyes. She loved his eyes. They were lighter than his hair but deep like the sky just after sunset.

Her gaze drifted to his full lips and she had to fight the urge to walk to the painting and trace them with her fingers. Her gaze snagged on his arms, to the markings and symbols that lined his skin. "A king's marks," Desmond had told her, though she couldn't recall his father bearing them.

She squeezed her eyes tight and turned away, gripping her side as she found her adornments for the day. She was still healing from the night of the attack, but it was embarrassment that hurt more than anything else. Willingly, she'd walked with a complete stranger. Believed that woman was helping her, just to end up with a blade in her side. The other knights on watch were found tied and bound, unconscious and drugged according to Nev.

But even so, Kamari couldn't help but feel as though she was useless. Blind to what was right in front of her.

"The council is waiting, Your Majesty," Nev said from beyond the door.

Kamari adjusted the thin, silver crown on her brow and met her in the hall.

The walk was quiet as they passed a row of stained-glass windows, intricate stars and moons poured light of all colors onto the stone floor.

Since the attack on the wall and the attempted kidnapping, the council had increased security, assigning twice the amount of sentries to the Citadel. The extra bodies did nothing to make Kamari feel more safe. The night that woman tried to take her, she was surrounded by people, and yet totally alone.

Another storm churned outside the wall, pelting the windows with harsh winds and bits of rock. The markets were closed today and the day prior, everyone sheltering from the massive sand swells that loomed over the city.

Nev opened the door to the meeting room and Kam stepped in. "Thank you."

"My daughter." Kamari's heart froze as her father rose from the end of the table. "You look well."

"Father, I–"

"Kamari." There was a warning in her mother's tone. She stood, her dark hair bound tight on the top of her head, a thin, silver crown resting on her forehead. Her eyes were the same mismatched as Aesira's, one green, one hazel, and it made Kamari's stomach drop when they narrowed on her. Her mother didn't need to speak to make her point clear.

Remember your manners. Remember who I raised you to be.

"I'm so happy to see you." Kamari switched on a smile like an *astra* lamp, rehearsed and polished, and her mother's eyes softened as she retook her seat. "To what do we owe the pleasure of your visit, during a storm season no less?"

Nev's eyes bore into her, like she was trying to read through the forced politeness. Trepidation rose in the room like a wave of sand during a storm, burying her, clawing up her throat, suffocating her.

"We were sent word on your husband's disappearance," her father said, breaking the silence. "Albeit, we were a bit surprised the word didn't come directly from *you*."

Tea was brought to the table and poured. A scattering of puffed pastries and dried fruit that neither she nor her parents reached for.

It was true, she hadn't sent word to her parents of Desmond's disappearance. How would it look to them, she wondered, if they realized the one duty she was bred and raised for, she'd failed at?

"I'm sorry I didn't write," she said. "I've been busy. There's been so much going on the closer we get to Naming Day, it slipped my mind." Truthfully because of the attack on the wall and the attempted kidnapping, she hadn't thought of Naming Day much at all and now that the words were out of her mouth, they tasted like ash.

If Desmond didn't return, she would be forced to partake in the ceremony alone. Watch as one of her own people was chosen to give their life to Celestria. To fill their wells of *astra* and water.

She waited for them to ask how she was handling Desmond's disappearance, how she was handling the move to Vargah.

But her father's dark eyes studied her from across the room. A stare she knew well. A stare that told her, he was not here for a visit out of concern for his daughter. Wordlessly, her father waved a hand forward and Raffe joined them, taking a seat to Kamari's right, as if he conjured himself straight from the shadows.

"King Godrick, Queen Marta," he said, helping himself to a powdered pastry before directing his attention to her parents. "My parents will be pleased you got their letter."

Kamari's eyes widened, her gaze darting between her parents and Raffe. He shot her a pained look, as if he was also a subject of his parents control. *Make them believe we're cordial,* "he'd whispered before they left the temple that day. *"Make them believe there's nothing to worry about."*

She could do that.

She could pretend, even now with her parents a few feet away.

She'd done it before, made people see what they wanted. In fact, she could be so convincing that nothing was wrong that oftentimes no one ever asked. Because they believed they already knew how she was.

Kamari, the bright star.

So polite compared to your sister.

So well mannered.

So happy.

"There are plans in place for the unfortunate circumstance that King Desmond doesn't find his way home." Raffe's words broke Kamari out of her fog.

"There's still a few weeks left," she said. "The council allowed a month for His Majesty's return."

Flames rose to her father's cheeks, his thick graying brows furrowing above deep, green eyes. "Even a week without a Vargahian heir on the throne is a week too long. Do you have any idea what the people of Novaria would do if they knew the king has left you?" The words lashed against Kamari's already raw skin.

Left you.

"They would tear the treaty in two. Another war would be on our doorstep before you could finish lunch."

"Godrick—" Her father waved her mother off, silencing her.

"Enough, Marta." He turned his attention back to Kamari. "I hear Raffe has offered a solution to our problem. To *your* problem." He pointed a thick, ringed finger at her. "You will accept and I'll hear nothing else of it."

She fought a flinch against his tone, moments of her childhood flashed behind her eyes like lightning striking the sky. Quick and then gone. Though her father's anger was typically pointed at Aesira, none of the Zeliath children grew up unmarked by his unattainable standard of perfection and the wrath that came with not achieving it.

"There are traditions." Her heart was a needle in her chest, stitching and stabbing against her ribs, but she thought of the painting in her room. The weeks it took to marry Desmond. At the time, she wanted to discard the customs and take him there in the temple, but now... She reached for her teacup and took a long sip. Now, she could use these traditions to her advantage, buying her the extra time Aesira would need to get Desmond home.

"Correct me if I'm wrong, Lord Raffe," she said, "but aren't marriage customs in Vargah quite sacred? I'm sure your parents would not be pleased to see them brushed aside as their eldest son inherits a throne."

Raffe dabbed his moustache, his eyes caught between her and her father. "There are traditions," he said after a thick swallow. "Public appearances, sometimes counseling with the High Priestess."

Her father's sigh filled the room. "Fine," he said. "Whatever must be carried through to see to it you're rightfully wed, do them." He pointed that same finger at Kamari again, his cheeks still tinged red. "It starts now and I won't hear a word about it."

She slid her smile back on, gave her father just what he needed to see, complete complacency. "Yes, Father."

"Where is your sister?" Her mother snapped her fingers before Hanna scurried over to pour more tea.

Kamari's nails dug into the wooden arms of the chair. How had she not thought of a lie sooner? It was one thing to send a crew looking for Desmond, another to send her sister, especially without consulting the Order first.

"She's at the wall." Kamari cut a glance to Raffe who seemed more interested in another pastry. "I'm sure she's busy with the recent attacks." Her mother's face distorted with unease. *Good*, Kamari thought. *Make her uncomfortable enough to leave.*

Kamari cradled her side as she sat in Desmond's office, her mind circling on all the ways she could make her parents leave. She'd never wished for an attack on the wall before, but now she wouldn't mind if a herd of bloodsuckers showed up.

One of Desmond's journals sat open on the desk. Every page was marked. Half sentences, drawings, languages she couldn't decipher. She flipped the page again and it was more of the same. Words written atop one another, leaving very little that were actually legible. Angry lines dug deep into the paper, black swirls drawn in the corners and menacing eyes that made her shudder.

In the weeks before Desmond left, he had grown more and more distant from her. A truth she hadn't let herself accept until now. Maybe he was losing his mind. Maybe he was as mad as the council and Raffe said.

But it didn't take away from the truth. That he was her husband and he loved her and she loved him. He was hers and he would never just leave her.

Except, he did.

She wiped her eyes and flipped to the back of the journal. The last page was dissimilar to the rest. It was written neatly, the penmanship consistent and steady.

It was a letter. A letter to Kamari. Like a rabbit scurrying from prey, her heart bounced in her chest. Her eyes shot to the date. Four months ago. She racked her brain. Four months ago she was visiting her family in Novaria. It was the first time she and Desmond had been apart since their wedding.

She took a deep breath, sent a silent prayer for strength to Celestria, and read the letter.

My sweet, Kamari~

I feel a bit ridiculous writing to you only days after you left and surely if you were here, you'd laugh at the pathetic state of me. I am a king and yet I am a fool. I should have come with you to Novaria. I couldn't leave the Citadel, ~~*they would never let me and*~~ *for that I'm sorry.*

I'm sorry I'm not a stronger man for you. A better husband. I promise to try. I promise I'll find a way.

Nevertheless, my love, I long for you in a way I've never felt.

So fiercely I'm beginning to scare myself.

Scared of the things I might do just to see you.

Touch you.

Taste you.

The clock is ticking and the sun is setting but time is not moving fast enough.

Never fast enough when we are apart.

How is it that I ever breathed, ever lived, without you by my side? It has not yet been a year of you and yet it feels like a lifetime.

I miss you. I love you.

Until I see you, I'll dream of you.

Always,

Desmond

She read the letter three times. She studied the cadence of his lettering. Pictured him sitting at his desk in his study, beating himself up for not joining her. She was angry at the time. Disappointed that he chose not to travel with her to see her birthplace. See her parents and sister. It all seemed frivolous now. She knew Desmond had a difficult time leaving the Citadel, let alone Vargah. But still, she remembered the disappointment she felt as the ship flew north. The questioning glances her parents gave her when she arrived alone.

She reread the letter one last time.

"I couldn't leave the Citadel, they would never let me..." The passage was crossed out with a thick black line and she couldn't help but wonder, who?

Kamari's fingers shook as she closed the journal. He'd written to her while she was away but never sent the letter. Maybe it was shame that held him back, maybe it was something outside of his control. Tears burned her cheeks, a vice around her heart tightening until the ache spread across her chest.

She focused on her breathing, inhaling the lingering scent of tobacco and leather before yanking open the single drawer in the desk. She was missing something.

Surely there was something.

She pushed aside a few loose papers, tossed out a handful of pens.

Nothing.

There was nothing else here. She sighed and reclined in her chair. Helpless.

She felt helpless.

But beneath the helplessness, she felt *angry*. Blood rushed to her cheeks, a storm brewing in her chest, ripping through her veins and taking hold of her heart. *He left me*, she thought. *He left me and now I'm backed into a corner. Alone.*

Kamari was never one to show her anger. Not like Aesira who forced it out during training or her father who let it flow through his voice. Kamari was best at swallowing it down or pretending it didn't exist. It was not queen-like to be angry. It was not lady-like to show any emotion other than complete contentment and appreciation.

But there was no one here and she was sick and tired of pretending to be complacent when the truth was, she was burning up from the inside out. She was alone and she was angry and it spilled out of her like a jar of honey, sticky and thick.

She threw the lamp from Desmond's desk, shattering the porcelain shade as it hit the ground. Pushed the papers off the sides. Took the few pencils he had tucked into a jar and broke each one in half.

He left me.

He left me.

She fisted the clay mug, then threw it against the wall, its broken pieces scattering about the floor. Nev would hear that and soon she'd come rushing in. She'd see the mess Kamari had become.

Breathing heavy, hair unkempt, she stood over the desk, looking down at it like it was an unwanted spider, then she kicked it, as hard as she could. She hissed through gritted teeth, pain piercing her side where her stitches were too tight. Then she kicked it again before slamming her fists onto the top.

She hit it again and again until her hands felt bruised, a few splits opening on her knuckles. Her side ached, a pool of warmth soaking through her silk robe.

Sweating and exhausted, she slumped back in Desmond's chair. A laugh rose in her throat as she glanced around the horrendous mess she'd made. Papers and broken pencils and porcelain littered the floor.

Boots sounded outside but she made no move to pick anything up, including herself.

She laughed again, at the absurdity of her outburst. What would the council think of their queen if they saw her this way? What would her father think? The thought of her father only made her laugh harder. He would be ashamed. Embarrassed. Disappointed that the entirety of her youth was spent learning to be a disciple of Celestria and a doting wife and here she was, just as mad as the king.

She pulled herself up from the chair before Nev could find her, but a glint inside the now broken drawer caught her eye.

Bending down so she was eye level, the drawer hung loose from its hinges and there, under what she thought was the bottom of the drawer, sat another journal.

Seventeen

Aesira

The wound on Aesira's leg still throbbed and the cabin air in her room was stale and heavy but she breathed in and closed her eyes. Flashes of wings and teeth, torn limbs and veins and that memory—the one she forced herself to forget—flooded her vision. She snapped her eyes open. It'd be easier to never sleep again, she decided.

A knock at the door had her pulling herself to her feet. She and Nora had switched bunks, making it easier for her to get in and out of bed but the pressure from moving still stung. Stone was on the other side when she opened it, casually leaning against the wall across from her room.

"Hey," he said, a soft smile turning up his lips.

"Hey." She clicked the door softly shut behind her, joining him in the hall.

"Wanted to check on your wound. Is Nora asleep?"

"Yes." Truthfully she wasn't sure if Nora was asleep or pretending to be. The conversation surrounding the idea that *astra* could be something other than a direct gift from Celestria had rattled her to her core. Moreso, it had pissed her off and Aesira knew better than to press her on the subject.

"I have supplies in my room," Stone said. "If you want me to take another look."

She followed him down the hall until they came to his cabin. Stone's room was similar to hers, only slightly larger and with a single bed, not a bunk. She'd woken up in that exact bed earlier, head foggy, leg throbbing. "Sit," he said, pointing to the end of the bed. He busied himself, rifling through a small trunk as she made herself comfortable.

Hands full, he dropped to his knees before her, setting his supplies out next to him.

She squirmed as he began to unwrap the bandage. "Still hurts?"

"Only a little," she lied. His fingers worked deftly, peeling the sticky bandage off with little contact. He balled the old cloth up and set it aside then pulled out a fresh one from his pile along with a small tub.

"This might sting."

"What is it?" she hissed through her teeth as Stone's fingers pressed into her wound, layering on a thick salve that smelled both sweet and medicinal.

"Just something to quicken the healing, fight off infection." His fingers were gentle as he spread the salve across the wound on her thigh, his free hand bracing the back of her calf. As he massaged it in, the throbbing ceased and eventually, when his fingers swept over her leg again, it stopped entirely.

"Did you make this?" She picked up the tub, holding it to her nose. There was something she couldn't place but through it all, a faint whiff of floral. The yellow flower Soo was crushing at the Apothecary, she realized.

"Just something I threw together before we left." He tightened the bandage around her leg, much slower and more gently than probably necessary.

"You really are something of a genius aren't you?" His laugh caught her by surprise. He smiled up at her from where he still knelt, his hands wrapped around her leg, his broad shoulders taking up most of the space between her thighs. "Where did you find the supplies?"

"Soo," he said, just as she'd suspected. He stood and pulled a towel from the floor, using it to wipe his hands. "We won't have to change it again until tomorrow."

"Thank you."

His eyes met hers and she hated the tiny dip it caused in her stomach. "You really okay? You were out for a while and you were..." He tossed the towel aside.

"I was what?" Aesira tried to stand but the salve only did so much, her leg was sore and her body tired so she sank back onto the foot of the bed.

"You were saying some things in your sleep." He bent down and collected the supplies from the floor. "A name I think. Eldrin?"

A sweep of dark curly hair flashed behind her eyes, then crimson and teeth. She stood up, putting her full weight on her leg, wobbling, hands searching for purchase.

"Don't go too fast," Stone said, his hands finding her waist. "Sit back down, take a minute." He guided her back on the bed, her heart beating against her ribs so quickly she hardly noticed the pain in her leg. Stone lingered next to her but when she nodded up at him, giving him reassurance that she was fine, he went back to organizing the supplies.

"Eldrin was my brother," she said, looking at the freshly wrapped bandage on her leg. The throbbing had disappeared and she was up and talking. Moving. When Strix venom should have taken her out for days. She knew that, because she'd run into one before. Had fought one before. Had lost to one before. "He died," she said. "I must have been dreaming of him."

She wouldn't say how or that it was her fault. She wouldn't say she was not brave or noble or fearless like all the knights that looked to her for guidance were. She wouldn't say how long she pushed that memory of him away and how strongly she'd built the walls in her mind to keep that night out. How easily they came crumbling down.

"I'm sorry you lost him," Stone said. She gazed up at him, arms full of bandages and ointments, glasses slipping down his nose. Brick by brick that wall in her mind went back up, layer by layer she buried her mistakes.

"Is the reason you took this job because you think *astra* grows in Ravki?" she asked, changing the subject before her emotions could slip out. Stone set the rest of the supplies in a drawer then ran a hand across the back of his neck, his muscles bunching under his shirt as he took a seat on a stool across from her.

"When I was fifteen, I had already been working for Vic for years. Smuggling drugs and tinkering during any free time I had. There was a man in the Outpost, a regular who bought weekly. I came to know him well, he was something consistent in a world of chaos."

"I hit all my normal spots that day and Ramses was my last stop. I always saved him for last because he loved to talk and would pin me there until well after sundown." A faint smile slipped across his lips.

"Everything about that day was the same," he said. "I woke up, got my fill from Vic, and made my rounds. Only this time Ramses didn't have the money to pay. He was desperate, begging me for anything I could spare and promised he'd pay me back. Then he offered me something else instead." His eyes flicked to hers. "A book."

"What kind of book?"

He sighed, pulling off his glasses and shoving them in the front pocket of his shirt. "It looked ordinary but Ramses assured me it was worth more than any coin. I gave him just enough to get him through the night and took the book home, decided it wasn't worth showing to Vic in case he wanted it for himself, so I took my beating for showing up with less profit than I sold and that was that." He folded his arms across his chest.

Aesira readjusted, stretching her leg out now that the pain had stopped, grateful for the distraction of Stone's story so her mind could get to work rebuilding the wall around Eldrin she'd worked so hard on. "You didn't tell me what the book was about."

Stone cleared his throat. Everything about the way he was sitting, with his shoulders slouched, the way he avoided looking at her, the way he fidgeted in his chair told Aesira what she needed to know. He didn't want to tell her. He didn't want her to know.

"It was about Ravki." He straightened his shoulders and she couldn't help the shock of surprise that swept across her face. Not just because Stone had a book about Ravki, but because he told her the truth. She expected more of a push and pull with him but he shrugged at her look of surprise and continued. "It spoke of a place where water ran freely. Where trees grew to the stars." He picked at a stray thread on his shirt. "It spoke of *astra* growing in open fields."

Aesira's heart sped up, like she was running for her life and in a way that's how it felt. Like she was being chased by a truth she couldn't accept. "And you believe that's true? That's why you're here?"

"I'm here to find the king."

"Stone." She shook her head. "When you're done lying, let me know."

"Can't both things be true? I want to find King Desmond and I want to see if what I've been reading about for the last fifteen years is true."

He looked tired as he slipped his glasses back on and she didn't blame him. The night was seemingly endless and her body was exhausted from the injury and the adrenaline from the Strix. The sun would be up soon and the idea that *astra* could grow from the earth was something she couldn't wrap her head around. Not with her leg and the memory of her brother being dredged up.

Not with Stone watching her so closely and Nora in the other room questioning her entire existence and everything they served.

She would need to see it first hand. She needed proof. Going off of some book Stone got in a drug deal when he was a teenager seemed impractical at best, so she'd compartmentalize. Put the crew's safety first, finding Desmond second, and then she would deal with *astra*.

"What happened to Ramses?"

Stone cleared his throat again and she thought she saw a flash of hurt behind his eyes.

"He died. Overdose. I read the book from front to back every week for years. Whoever wrote it claimed that *astra* grew wild, a long time ago. The world was overflowing with it. Not to mention the claims that dragons and humans lived in harmony, providing a balance to each other. Soo was the only other person I trusted to show it to. She made me keep it hidden. Keep it safe. So, when the queen brought me those maps and journals from the king claiming the same things, that Ravki was real, there was no question as to whether or not I'd accept."

He watched her through his glasses and she wondered if he could see her entire world shattering behind her eyes. Everything she worked for and trained for and killed for. Celestria and the men who put Her on such a high pedestal.

"So Naming Day..." She bit her lip, cutting off the rest of her question because she wasn't sure she was ready to hear it. If Stone was telling the truth, if *astra* grew from a place and was not a gift from the stars, there was no reason to continue an ancient ceremony that ended in blood. Why would Celestria allow it? Unless the goddess would demand it either way. Would see their lack of sacrifice as rebellion and punish them. Unless...a sick thought twisted in her mind.

Unless there is no Celestria at all.

"Commander." Stone's hand slid into hers and she was so caught up inside her own head she hadn't seen him get up. He squeezed her hand and watched her, like he could see she was slipping deeper and deeper into her thoughts. "I don't have all the answers but I want to find them. *And* find King Desmond."

His thumb swept over the back of her hand, and that tiny movement was enough to raise the hairs on her arms and neck. "Do you think Desmond knew about this? Knew that finding *astra* in Ravki was a possibility?"

Pieces of his disappearance began to click into place. The notes and journals. The obsession with Ravki. The mention of dragons.

"Maybe he left to find Ravki to stop Naming Day. My sister said he had opposed it many times but the council—"

"If the king knew *astra* was something that could be harvested from the ground, and he spoke of it, chances are he never made it out of Vargah. Rulers succeed by holding power over their people, not giving it away. This kind of news would threaten to unravel an ecosystem centuries in the making."

Murdered.

Stone was implying someone may have murdered the king for such knowledge. She couldn't fathom what they would do if they found out someone like her, someone like Stone, knew of it.

She closed her eyes and all she saw was Kamari. Alone and broken in a city that never welcomed her.

Stone's hand slipped from hers, leaving her floundering for a sense of grounding. Her entire world was teetering on an unbalanced scale. Celestria and her blind eye. The men she served and their power-hungry needs. Her sister, in Vargah with no one to lean on.

"I should go." She needed to lie down or to cry or to be pissed off, but mostly she needed to be alone. Her emotions were too big, too raw, and she'd be damned if she let anyone see them take her over.

Stone nodded but said nothing as he helped her to her feet. His hand was warm and even though it wasn't necessary, he wrapped his fingers around hers and led her to the door. "I know it's a lot," he said, pushing the door open. "*Astra*, Ravki, dragons..." He glanced down to where their hands were still knitted together. "I don't know what waits for us on the other side of the mountains, but if there's a chance *astra* is in Ravki, it could get us home safely."

"Goodnight, Stone." She didn't wait for him to reply before she headed down the hall.

Back in her cabin, the window was dark, and Nora's breathing was heavy. Aesira crawled into her bunk but kept her eyes open. She was afraid to close them. Afraid of what waited for her when she did.

She didn't know what was worse, the memory of her brother and the Strix or the fact that her entire world may have revolved around a lie. She wouldn't know until they got to Ravki but the pit in her stomach told her what she couldn't admit to out loud.

That it all made too much sense.

That Vargah was lying to their people about *astra*, forcing a sacrifice, holding power over their heads, and in turn, so was Novaria.

"If there's no *astra* in Ravki, we're fucked." Birdie tapped her pencil rhythmically along the table as she spoke. Aesira had come to learn that Birdie was definitely a morning person. Not in a positive, slow start kind of way, but in the *"let's get our asses on the move the sun has been up for five minutes already"* way.

"Bird." Stone tsked. "Have faith."

Birdie crossed her arms, her sleek hair tied back tight in a low ponytail. "In *what*?"

Stone rubbed the sleep from his eyes. "I don't know. How much do we need to find to fly home?"

Aesira was a fly on the wall this morning. She had woke to a sore leg but the pain was manageable and now she perched silently and watched as the three Odega's went about their tasks like nothing out of the ordinary happened last night.

She could see Stone out of the corner of her eye, but he still had his eyes pressed closed. Nora had slipped past her in the hall, without so much as a hello, and joined Patch on deck to man the wheel so it was just Stone, Birdie, and Bee and the three of them bickered back and forth over the same topic.

"We need at least a six *astra* flowers," Birdie continued, "and if we don't find them in Ravki, we are well and truly fucked."

"How many more times are you going to say that? We hear you, Bird." Bee squeezed Birdie's shoulders, placing a kiss to her cheek. "Not everything bad that could happen, will happen. Now, a storm's coming in," she said. "If we want to miss it, better get a move on."

"Pack whatever we can carry comfortably on our backs," Stone said. "We have a long trek ahead."

"About that," Patch said as he and Nora descended the stairs. Patch's dark hair was pulled back, his jaw unshaven and rough. Nora stood next to him, freckled face unnaturally stern. "I'm thinking it's best if I stay behind with Aquila." He held up a hand, presumably to stop Stone from speaking, then laid it on Stone's shoulder.

"I fucked up, Stone. I should have paid better attention in the Outpost. Let me amend it by protecting the ship now, like I should have done then. If Vic comes, he won't leave a trace of the ship for us to come back to."

"He's too much of a coward," Birdie said. "He won't come."

"He very well might," Patch interjected. "Coward, maybe. Spiteful, certainly. You caused a scene back there, Stone. Made him look like a fool in front of his crew. You know sure as I do that he's coming after us and if Aquila is here, unattended, he'll take her or worse, burn her. Then we'll truly be fucked, as our weapons master so gracefully said."

Birdie and Bee exchanged glances. The looks in their eyes made Aesira believe they were inclined to agree with Patch. That he should stay behind. "Alone?" Aesira asked. "You think you're able to ward off his entire crew yourself?" She glanced at the rest of the cadre, waiting for someone to look remotely on her side, but to her surprise none of them did.

"I've had worse odds." Patch grinned. "Plus, this one here"— he bumped Birdie's arm—"has made more weapons than Vic's entire slew of delinquents."

"You realize you're also a delinquent," Stone said.

"I know," Patch said through a grin. "But I'm a delinquent with better weapons and more to lose." It was quick, the way his eye darted to Nora then faster away.

Birdie hauled a large bag onto the table and opened it. Inside were more weapons any one person should ever have access to. Bows, arrows, swords, knives, more of the fire-shooting mechanism she'd used on the crawlers.

"What is this?" Nora picked up a metal cylindrical ball.

"Be careful," Birdie snapped, grabbing it slowly from her hands. "One wrong move and you'll kill us all." She buttoned the bag back up and handed it to Patch.

"And yet you've been carrying it in...a canvas bag?" Nora crossed her arms but Birdie just smiled. "I'll stay too." Nora glanced at Aesira. "If that's okay with you, Commander. Patch could use an extra set of eyes."

"Ouch." Patch laughed. "Eye jokes, this early?"

Nora smiled. "You know what I mean." She turned her attention back to Aesira, positioning her hands behind her back. "Commander?"

Words were lost on her. The last thing she wanted was to be separated from her only knight but Nora had a point. Her staying behind would help Patch keep the ship safe and it would also ensure Aesira had someone she could trust guarding their only way home. She nodded and Nora relaxed her arms, busying herself with breakfast.

Within the next hour, Birdie, Bee, Stone, and Aesira were set to leave the ship, Patch, and Nora behind. The pack on Aesira's back wasn't any heavier than the armor she was used to, the minimal supplies inside would hopefully be enough to make it the two week trip.

Patch took his time saying goodbye to Birdie and Bee. He was even polite enough to offer Aesira a handshake though she couldn't really call them friends. When he got to Stone, the two leaned close and whispered something she couldn't make out.

"See you soon, boss."

"Keep the torches lit," Stone said. "Never let it go dark."

"Of course." Patch grinned. "Never let it go dark."

Stone, Birdie, and Bee trudged ahead, giving Aesira and Nora some space. "I expect you to keep things in order," Aesira said. "Keep an eye on Patch and if anything feels off, you have my full permission–"

"Patch is a good person." She reached for Aesira's arm and gave it a squeeze. "It's our fault the ship was ransacked, let us make it right. And whatever you find, whether it be the king or..." She sighed and closed her eyes.

"Hey," Aesira said, "whatever we find out there won't change anything. We're still servants of Celestria." She grabbed the back of Nora's arm, right where she knew her matching "C" would be and gave it a squeeze.

Nora's brows furrowed. "And if you find *astra*? Water?" She bit her bottom lip and shook her head. "We've done terrible things to claim them, Commander. If *astra* and water are out there, there's no going back."

Aesira opened her mouth, then quickly clamped it shut because Nora was right. If *astra* grew and water was accessible, how could they ever return to Vargah and pretend it wasn't?

Eighteen

Aesira

Stone led the way through what was left of Dire. Aesira avoided the building from last night the best she could and despite knowing the Strix was holed up somewhere away from the daylight, she couldn't help the uneasy feeling that they were being watched.

A few sparse trees lined a path up the mountain and rocky ground churned under her boots, so different from the grainy sand she was accustomed to. The lights of the torches on Aquila eventually disappeared and when the first star shone in the dusty pink sky, Stone made the announcement they were going to stop for the night. He led them to a small cave that would provide some protection and with enough torches to surround them while they slept in shifts.

"I'll take the first watch," he said. Birdie and Bee busied them-selves by pulling some pre-packaged food from their bags while Aesira tossed her pack aside and helped Stone with the torches.

"You really think these will be enough to keep the Strix away?" She pressed the torch into the dirt, twisting until it felt stable.

"We're far enough outside of town, I don't think it will be a problem." He tossed her another unlit torch. "They have one goal and that's to feed as much as they can in order to breed. Judging by the number it did on Dire, the Strix we ran into likely had its fill and will leave to find a mate."

Aesira could only hope that would be the case. Still, she made sure the torches were secure and completely surrounding the out-side of the cave. "And Patch and Nora..."

Stone lit the last torch, warm flames tangling with the darkness. "I can't speak for Nora, but Patch can hold his own. If he isn't scared of taking on Vic, we shouldn't be either."

After a quick dinner of preserved meats and a few precious sips of water, Stone took first watch like he said he would. Aesira tossed and turned on her thin bedroll. She had so many questions that didn't have definitive answers so instead of continuing to stew over them, she decided to put herself to work elsewhere.

"I'll take it from here." She sat down next to Stone, who had one of Desmond's journals opened in his lap.

"You should be sleeping, Commander."

She shrugged and peered through the line of torches, out to the jagged peaks tinted blue from the moon. "Sleep and I don't get along these days." Her gaze drifted upward, to the stars twinkling like millions of eyes watching in the dark sky. The eyes of Celestria, they were told as children. *She's always watching. Always sees.*

"What do you believe in, Stone?"

She glanced at him. He closed the journal but kept it clutched in his fist. "I believe in a lot of things."

"Celestria?" The name felt bitter on Aesira's tongue. She spent her life devout to the goddess of the stars.

As a child, it was drilled into her that everything they have was because the goddess allowed them to have it. As a girl forced to join the Order her reverence in Celestria was made permanent. She could still smell the sting of burnt flesh when her commander touched the white-hot iron brand to the back of her arm. The "C" forever marking her skin. Proving her loyalty.

"There was a time I believed in the goddess," Stone said. "I thought she might save me from the Outpost. Save me from Vic."

"And now?" She was grasping for something, she just wasn't sure what. Even after what she'd learned, that *astra* may be something organic, a part of her needed to believe in Celestria. Needed to know that all the years of her life spent on her knees was for a greater good. She needed it to be real.

Stone sighed and pulled his glasses off to clean them with his shirt. A sliver of skin exposed when he pulled the material up. Thick scars ran over his ridged muscles and Aesira had the fleeting thought to run her finger over them and ask him where they came from.

"Now," he said, "I've learned the only one that's going to save me is myself." He slid his glasses back on. "I believe in the practical. I believe what I can see and hear"— his eyes slid to hers—"taste and touch." His eyes dipped to her mouth briefly before darting away. "I believe in what's reliable. What's always been there to get me out of a bind." He nodded over his shoulder, where Birdie and Bee slept curled around each other. "Them. Patch. They're the only ones I pledge my loyalty to."

Her throat burned as she swallowed back the memories from all the years of servitude and dedication. The punishments for saying her prayers wrong. The crack of a whip against her back. The piercing of sharp splinters under her nails for singing the wrong key at temple. The sting of a needle to her neck when she refused to obey.

All in the name of Celestria.

"That doesn't mean miracles don't exist," Stone said. She snapped her gaze to his. "*Astra* exists and that's a miracle on its own." He gave her a smile and some of the frayed edges inside her began to soothe.

A crack sounded from beyond the torches, loud enough to make Aesira jump.

"Just the wind," Stone said. He slid closer so their shoulders pressed together.

"What are you reading?"

He handed her a book, it was worn, the spine frayed and barely held together. "It's my favorite. About an empress who defied her father to free her lover from his oppression."

She studied the book, like she could find something in the pages that would stop her from spiraling. "Stone Odega, a romantic?"

He laughed and snatched the book back. "We all need to find joy somehow."

Her cheeks warmed from the torches, the anxious thoughts that kept her awake settling in the back of her mind as she and Stone sat comfortably together. "I just can't wrap my head around what

Desmond wanted when he left. What he was thinking he'd do if he found Ravki."

"Haven't you ever wanted something so badly you'd betray anything, even yourself, just to get it?" Stone was still pressed close, the heat from his body spreading to hers. He rested his hands on his knees and her fingers drifted to them, tracing a scar on his knuckles.

"No," she answered honestly. "To want is a vice, it only sets you up for disappointment. Just look at my sister." She pulled her hand away and placed it safely in her lap.

Stone smiled. "I guess that's fair. Even still, there are plenty of things I want, but I suppose I'm not naive enough to think I'll get them."

"Do you think my sister is naive for wanting us to find Desmond? For believing he's still alive?"

Stone stretched his legs out, lining them with hers so they sat side by side. "No," he said. "I just think she's in love and people in love tend to do desperate things."

"And you know this first hand? Or was it from one of your books?"

"Not me," he said through a smile. "But them." He gestured over his shoulder to where Birdie and Bee slept in the back corner of the cave. "I've watched them do enough careless, desperate things for each other, it's easy to spot when I see it in someone else."

A bright star shot across the night sky, leaving a trail of blazing dust in its wake. Kamari could find love in everything. Even when they were children and they'd found an injured bird, she refused to let Aesira put it out of its misery. She kept it alive, cared for it, named it, helped it. Aesira was a hammer and Kamari was a feather, soft and light and now she was pinned in a corner with very little room to escape.

"I don't know of love," she said, "but I know my sister is overflowing with it. She carries enough for the both of us." She yawned, her body betraying her. "I should actually try to sleep." She made to move but Stone caught her arm.

"Maybe you could lay down here," he said, pushing his jacket toward her on the ground. "Let me read to you."

Their eyes met through the firelight and a flurry swirled in her stomach. Before her mind had the time to go over why it was wrong, she found herself settling her head on his jacket, closing her eyes.

Stone cleared his throat, the spine of his book creaking open. "Every great story starts the same. With a time and a place and a hero or heroine desperate for change. This story is no different." His voice poured over her, velvet smooth, as he continued reading and the more Stone spoke, the more ease Aesira felt in her muscles.

In her mind.

The soothing cadence of his voice settled over her like a blanket and the nightmare she'd been dreading was nowhere to be found. Her body melded into the ground, the scent of his flight jacket wrapping around her as it acted as a cushion under her.

Stone flipped a page, cleared his throat, before starting a new chapter when another crack sounded beyond the torches. Aesira's eyes popped open.

"The wind again?" she asked before sitting up.

Stone closed the book and set it aside. "I don't know."

They both stood, Aesira drawing her sword, all thoughts of sleep abandoned. Blurry shapes of a few naked trees and rocks but otherwise, she couldn't see anything.

Another crack.

She raised her sword.

"I thought you said the Strix doesn't like the light."

"It doesn't," Stone said.

"What is it?" Bee asked, joining her side.

"Quiet," Stone whispered and took a step back from the wall of flames they'd barricaded themselves behind.

Another crack followed by a deep rumble that traveled through the soles of Aesira's boots up to her teeth.

Aesira continued backward until her back hit the wall of the cave. Another rumble, another crack. "What is that?"

The four of them stood shoulder to shoulder, their breaths syncing together. One of the torches flickered to Aesira's right, then another to her left. The low rumbling increased. It sounded just like–

"Holy shit, it's raining!" Bee slapped her hands over her mouth.

Rain.

Aesira took a deep breath, the scent of wet earth filling her. She hadn't seen rain in almost two years, since the last time Celestria blessed the desert with a wet storm.

"Let's go," Bee said, pulling off her shirt.

"No way." Birdie shook her head. "Mountain temperatures drop at night, you'll freeze."

Bee tossed her shirt at Birdie who of course caught it seamlessly. "It's *raining*, Bird. Rain! I'll keep you warm, I promise." She winked then peeled off her pants until she was just in her under clothes and snuck out through the torches. Her happy squeals echoed through the torrent and Aesira couldn't help but smile.

"If I'm going in, so are you," Birdie said, tossing Stone a playful smile. She stripped off her clothes and ran through the gap in the torches. Another clap of thunder rattled the cave and Aesira sheathed her sword. "Get your ass out here, Stone!" Birdie's shouts were followed by Bee's laughter and for a moment Aesira's racing thoughts slowed.

She honed in on the steady beat of rain on rock. The high pitches of Bee's laugh and the low rumble of thunder in the distance. She could feel the anxious flow of her blood slow and the tightness in her chest loosen.

"Are you coming?"

Aesira was so wrapped up in the sounds around her, she'd forgotten Stone was standing so close. Except now he'd stripped down to just his pants, his chest bare. His muscles were lean, his arms toned. The same scarring on his face ran down his chest and over his arms. When he cleared his throat, she snapped her mouth shut. "I can turn around, if you'd like," he said. "If you need privacy."

"Oh." She glanced down at herself, still fully clothed. "You go ahead, I'll be right there." Stone gave her a half smile, then left her to undress in the cave.

After meticulously folding and piling her clothes on the cave floor, she took a timid step out.

The rain bit against her warm skin. She flexed her fingers as the water seeped through her under clothes. She untied her hair, letting her dark curls spill over her bare shoulders, droplets of water clinging to each ringlet. Bee and Birdie were still laughing and dancing, though the rain was so heavy now she could hardly make them out through the sheets of water.

"Pretty amazing," Stone shouted, his voice fuzzy.

"It is."

And it was. There was something so healing about it. She closed her eyes and held her hands out, letting the rain soak her through, down to her bones.

Drip.

Drip.

Drip.

The sound soothed her. It washed away the swirling thoughts in her head. The constant noise.

Drip.

Drip.

Drip.

Her eyes flew open, the Strix and the blood and her brother forced their way behind her eyes. Stone's fingers brushed hers. Her arms were still outstretched, rain dripping from her fingertips.

Just rain.

Not blood.

Her heart slammed in her chest when his hand closed around hers. Birdie and Bee laughed from somewhere behind them but Aesira honed in on the blurry shape of Stone's face through the rain. On the heat of his hand in hers. On the weight of his other hand as it wrapped around her waist and pulled her into him.

"Is this okay?" His breath brushed against her ear. He was warm, despite the chill in the air, and she found herself resting her cheek against his chest. The bumps and grooves of his scars were rough against her skin but she closed her eyes and studied the beat of his heart.

Fast.

His heart was beating so fast and so was hers and she wondered what it would be like to kiss him again. Not like in the Phoenix when they'd both had too much to drink and she had something to prove. Not like in the Den when they were both pretending. She wondered what it would be like to kiss him for real. "Your hair is beautiful when it's down."

His large hands splayed across her back, pinning her close to his chest. He wanted to kiss her, too. There was no other reason he was always seeking her out. Grabbing her hand. Holding her close. Whatever this attraction was would never become more than that, but what would it hurt to seek some comfort amidst pain?

"Stone?"

"Yes?"

She leaned away and looked up at him when another drip landed on her lips. When she wiped her mouth with the back of her hand, it came away stained crimson.

Blood.

"Stone..." Her hands trembled.

"What is it?" The rain was still heavy, impairing her vision but through the heavy pelts she could hear Bee's laugh. She peered past Stone.

"Bee?" Another drop of blood landed on her cheek, then another. She looked up, the laughing she thought she heard, she realized, was screaming.

The Strix hovered several feet above her, its wings strong against the wind and the rain. Its yellow eyes, wide and haunting. Blood dripped from its mouth, tinting its chin and white feathers of its chest. It dripped down to where a body lay motionless in its clutches. Dark brown curls stood stark against its light talons and Aesira's head spun.

Eldrin.

Aesira reached for her sword only to remember she'd left it in the cave.

Shit.

The Strix's piercing shrieks hammered against her ears as she ran for her sword, then another sound.

Another scream.

"Commander!" Birdie was there pulling something from her bag. "Commander, let me help."

Aesira brushed her off, her sword now eager and hungry in her hands. The Strix's large wings beat against the heavy rain and thunder, then, all at once, it opened its talons and there was Eldrin, falling from the sky. Dying all over again.

"No!" Aesira lunged, keeping her swords tight in her palms. The body slammed into the ground with a sickening crunch but when Aesira rolled it, it wasn't her brother's face that greeted her. The boy's hair had once been blonde, now soaked in old, putrid blood. Still, the curls were the same. The age. Her heart sped, mind racing through the memories she'd pushed away for so long.

The boy's head was heavy as Aesira brought it to her lap, her sword laying useless at her side.

A roll of thunder clapped in the distance followed by a beat of wings.

"Wake up." Aesira shook his shoulders. She couldn't save her brother but maybe she could save him. She just had to try harder. Be better.

Blood caked his mouth and nose, his body rigid. Someone screamed behind her, maybe Birdie, followed by another shriek from the Strix.

"Commander," Stone's voice drifted to her through the heavy rain. "Aesira!" Aesira whipped her head up just in time to dodge the Strix's talons. She screamed, then drew her weapons from the ground. "We can help–"

"No," she ground out. The Strix hovered above them, its pallid skin now kissed pink with blood, its moonlit eyes wide and watchful. Aesira held her breath, let her lungs burn and scream, and only when the Strix dove towards her did she let it out. Rain pelted her skin. Her lashes. It mixed with the blood left on her from the boy.

Not Eldrin, she reminded herself.

It isn't him.

She tasted salt and iron and water and rage. The world stilled until it was nothing but the *drip, drip, drip,* of the rain and the flap of wings and the hammering in her chest and only when it was close enough for Aesira to smell the decay on its breath did she strike, piercing straight through the heart.

NINETEEN

KAMARI

Kamari traced her fingers along the words etched into the parchment as she read them again and again.

"My name is Desmond Orathka. My story is not a happy one, but I hope you will listen to it anyway. The voices have told me never to write these thoughts down. Never to tell anyone what they've told me but I fear I can't hold it in any longer. My mind is slipping faster and faster and if the only way to"

There was a quick tap on the door. Kamari's stomach sank and she slid the journal under her pillow.

"Are you ready for me, Majesty?"

Just Hanna.

Kamari blew out a puff of air. How bad would it be if she just denied the Naming Day Banquet and stayed in bed?

Well, they'd call you a traitor for one, she thought.

And then there was the matter of her parents and Raffe. Everyone's eyes, always watching her and now with the wedding customs to begin, she supposed there truly was no more hiding.

"Your Majesty?"

"Yes," she said, smoothing her nightgown. "Come in, Hanna."

There was no way out of it. She was going to put on her best queen's smile and dance and shake hands with the priestesses and the lords and ladies and praise Celestria for her upcoming gifts. She would have ceremonial tea with Raffe the following day and she would take his hand and she would be what they needed her to be.

Even if all she wanted to do was hide under a blanket and read Desmond's hidden journal over and over again.

"The storms have finally settled," Hanna said as she swept through the room, tidying things. "Markets have reopened. Should be a beautiful evening."

Kamari chewed her nail, sitting perched on the end of the bed like a child, her mind filled with Desmond and his journals. The key to finding him was in that journal she found locked away, she knew it. If only she could just finish reading it.

"Are you thinking the purple or the red?" Hanna held two gowns up for selection.

"Hm?" Kamari looked up at the streams of fabric. One, a deep purple with intricate gold beading, delicate moons and stars dangling from the sleeves. The other was red, a silky fabric with a deep cut down the chest and tiny dazzling stars stitched into the hemline. Both were beautiful, both made her feel sick.

Celebrating a day that would steal someone's life didn't sit right with her and dancing while Desmond was missing, felt disloyal.

Her eyes snagged on the red dress, the color filling her chest with longing. She ached at the memory of wearing it the first time, only to make sure it fit. Desmond's fingers traced the stars at the edges, the plunging neckline. He'd moved her in front of the mirror, made her watch everything he did to her. Asked her to say all the things she wanted him to do. She'd never felt so vulnerable. So open. So raw.

And she loved every second. Loved being in control. Loved passing that control onto Desmond and him picking up her cues seamlessly. He took his time learning her body, her wants, her needs.

Her throat tightened. "The purple," she said before closing her eyes and sinking lower into bed, pushing the memory away.

"You'll look radiant."

She could hear Hanna hang the dresses up, and tinker around on her vanity. Likely pulling jewelry and other accessories. She chirped on about matching with Raffe and how lovely the menu sounded and whether or not there might be a new painting of Celestria revealed.

Hanna deserved a gift, Kamari thought. Or a large increase in pay. Anyone who could remain so bright under the oppressive cloud of sand they lived in, she thought, deserves to be able to indulge themselves.

The banquet hall was located in the very center of the Citadel. The enormity of the space was overwhelming. Extravagant chandeliers brightly lit with *astra* hung from the ornate mosaic ceiling. Huge tiles etched with Celestria's stars led to a vast dance floor, shining and waiting to be used. A band was perched on a dais, string instruments and flutes drifting through the open space.

It was beautiful and expensive and yet all Kamari could think about were how many places someone could be hiding. Nev and her knights escorted her, staying dutifully behind her as she shook hands with various lords and ladies, the council, her parents, then finally, Raffe. He wore a similar deep purple tunic, lined with thick gold and small stars adoring his shoulders. Several long necklaces hung down his chest, all layered on top of each other, each of them representing the different phases of the moon. "Your Majesty." He dropped in a deep bow to which she curtsied in return.

Please don't ask me to dance.

Please.

Please.

"May I have this dance?" Resolve settled between her shoulders. With her parents, the council and half of Vargah watching, she couldn't get away with saying no.

"Of course, Lord Raffe." She held out her hand. The long, delicate chains attached from the rings on her fingers, wound around her wrist and twinkled in the *astra* light. Raffe's fingers wrapped around hers, his other hand landing lightly on her back. The music was a soft tempo as she and Raffe swept through the ballroom. His movements were confident, assured.

"They're all watching," he whispered against her ear.

Kamari drew her eyes from where she'd fixed them on the farthest walls of the room and met the crowd. Dozens of people stood, frozen, watching the enemy queen dance with someone who was not their king. "And what do you think they see?"

He spun them, following the sway of the string instruments. Her parents' faces flashed briefly before Raffe spun her again and pulled her flush with his chest.

"A queen that's trying," he said. "Your efforts haven't gone unnoticed, Kamari." His hand slid down her back, burning a line every place they touched. She didn't mean for her fingers to flex around his, didn't mean for that to signal that he should pull her closer.

"I'm sorry about my parents," he said. "By the time I realized they'd sent a letter to Novaria, there was nothing I could do."

The music grew louder, switching to something more upbeat. More couples joined them, the *astra* lights flickered, Raffe's hands tightened around her, trapping her in place against his body and her lungs tightened.

She was suffocating and no one noticed.

Her skin became hot and sticky under the lights and under everyone's gaze. Under Raffe's unwelcome touch. Couples danced around them, laughing, drinking. Life continued on and all the while Desmond was missing and a sacrifice loomed in the near future. She should not be here. They should not be here. Celestria—

She cut her thoughts short. Her anger with the goddess was something she hadn't admitted to out loud, only in her weakest moments when night was thin and dawn was swiftly approaching, when sleep and hope were lost, did she allow herself to truly feel.

After all their sacrifice, the least the goddess could do, she thought, was offer a semblance of hope. A moment of peace or knowing that Desmond was safe somewhere under Her watch but the goddess had given her nothing, even after Kamari had given Her everything.

The music began to fade so Kamari took advantage of the shift in songs to peel herself from Raffe.

"Thank you for the dance." She dipped her chin and Raffe's face morphed from bewildered to calm and collected in an instant. He was almost better at playing this role than her.

"The pleasure was mine." He bowed again and over his lowered back she caught the reddened face of her father. The disappointing shake of her mother's head. The sneering glances of several lords and ladies.

She spun on her heel and wove her way through the crowd, smiling and being cordial when she needed to all the while her heart raced, her stomach sick and filled with disgust. She was almost out, almost to the hall when the High Priestess made her way toward Kamari, purple silk robes dragging behind her, face hidden beneath a veil of moons and stars.

Not now, Kamari thought. *Please, not now.*

"Your Majesty." The priestess' voice was honey smooth, her pale hands stretching out from beneath the draped fabric, reaching for Kamari.

"High Priestess." Kamari dipped her head, felt her father's eyes bore into her from across the room. "Thank you for attending. Your presence has put the people at ease."

The priestess slipped her hand around Kamari's. It was cold, hard. She fought the urge to wriggle free from her grip. "I am told I'll be seeing you soon," she said. "Counseling?"

Right. Counseling with Raffe.

"Yes," Kamari said. "In a few weeks. After Naming Day, when *astra* and water are restored." *Hopefully, never,* she thought. "I appreciate you being here, Priestess, but I was just heading for the washroom." She pulled her hand free but the Priestess snagged it back, gripping it tight, the cool metal of her rings biting into Kamari's skin.

"Be cautious, daughter of Celestria. She is always watching, always *listening*. Even to the things you do not say." Her grip tightened around Kamari's hand. "Doubt would be an awful thing for the Goddess to hear this close to Naming Day, wouldn't you agree?" Kamari's fingers shook but she forced a smile and nodded. With that, the Priestess let her go, slipping into the crowd, her purple robes long and flowing like water.

Kamari hurried away, disappearing into the small corridor used mainly by the attendants, before anyone else could grab her attention.

The music from the hall hummed through the narrow walkway, trickling into the dark corner where Kamari tucked herself. An ache grew in her chest, dense and smothering. She smoothed her hand over her heart, urging it to find a normal rhythm.

A familiar voice rose above the music, edging down the walk-way. "I want each of you at every exit. I want eyes on everyone coming and going."

Kamari peeked around the corner just enough to see Nev's black boots. She pressed herself tighter into the corner, stifling her panting breaths with the back of her hand. Nev barked her orders again, boots scuffled, likely sending the other knights on their way.

When she only heard the music again, Kamari stole another glance to see Nev still waiting, lips fused together and face hard as granite. Her red hair was slicked back, her bold brows furrowed.

Her gaze dipped right to where Kamari was hiding. She slunk back into the corner and pressed her eyes tight.

Minutes passed and there were no other noises than the music. No heavy boots. No orders being called.

Nev had given her the gift of privacy, albeit she would wager a large sum of money that the knight was at the entrance of the corridor, hand on her sword, ready to stave off anyone who deigned to enter.

Still, Kamari slunk all the way to the floor, waves of purple silk pooling around her. She pressed her hands against her chest, as if the pressure would be enough to soothe the deep ache that ripped through her since Desmond's disappearance.

She closed her eyes, focusing on her heartbeat, trying her best to drown out the revelry happening just on the other side of the corridor.

You're celebrating someone's death, she wanted to shout.

You're celebrating while my husband is missing.

While your king *is missing.*

She hated them. All of them. Her parents, the council, Raffe. Hated them for their apathy. Hated them for assuming the worst and moving on. Hated that she was playing a part instead of helping Stone and Aesira find Desmond.

She rose to her feet, ready to confront Nev only she couldn't before a hand closed around her mouth and she was dragged backward through the dark corridor, the flowing panels of her dress slipping beneath her, the music from the hall fading until it was only the sound of her struggled breathing.

TWENTY

NEV

Nev stood with her back to the corridor, sword hanging at her side, eyes alert, scanning the ballroom. Raffe was smiling, talking with the King and Queen of Novaria, a few lords and ladies lingering next to him. Nev didn't trust Raffe's too smooth smile. The way he entered the kingdom as if it were already his own. Her back stiffened, a soft cry coming from the hallway behind her.

She didn't mean to catch the queen crying, which is why she turned as quietly as she could. Offering her a moment of privacy in a world that typically gave her none. It was the least Nev could do, as her protector. She stood firm like a wall, turning away even the Citadel attendants.

Then, the faint crying stopped.

A shuffle behind her.

Nev drew her sword, the sharp slice of metal scraping against the sheath was swallowed by the music. "Your Majesty?" She crept forward, toes pressing lightly into the tile floor. Her eyes darted to the small wedge of darkness where she'd seen Kamari sink into.

Gone.

Her hand tightened around her sword, her boots now flying against the floor. She would have worried, would have felt the smallest tingling of fear, had she had time for it. The smallest glimpse of deep purple silk floated through the back door as she neared the end of the corridor.

"Your Majesty!" She tore down the rest of the hall, her armor clinking, boots thudding. The door was open when she reached it, leading to a narrow, spiraling staircase.

Nev didn't remember this door. Aesira had assigned she and Nora to scan every surface of the Citadel upon their arrival. Every service entry, every tunnel, every dark corner that may be used as a place for an unwanted visitor to hide.

This door, she did not remember.

She pounded down the stairs, her armor echoing off the narrow stone walls. The tip of her sword caught on a loose stone, tripping her up for a moment. She pulled it higher. Moonlight spilled across the stone tile at the bottom.

Panic fanned in her chest like a moth opening its wings. She would not let harm come to Kamari again. She would not fail her only duty to protect her, again.

The warm, dry air of the desert slapped her cheeks as she plundered out of the doorway. The moon was new, hanging in the sky like a slice of silver. The granite wall of Vargah loomed before her, the flickering of torches kissing the deep, night sky.

The door had led her straight out of the Citadel.

"Your Majesty!" Her voice echoed back to her, bouncing off the wall. Biting her tongue, she forced her lungs to slow, her breathing to steady, so she could focus on the sounds around her.

A crackle of flame.

In the distance, music from the party.

A bell from a cart in the main square.

And there—stuck on the breeze—a scream.

Nev's boots dug into the sand as she abandoned the doorway in a sprint. She focused on the wind, hoping it would bring her another trace of Kamari's voice. The breeze curled around her neck, her ears, and there it was again.

Another scream.

Her boots skidded in the sand as she reached another door along the wall, small and inconspicuous. It pushed open with easy effort from the sole of her boot, and when she stepped through, a gasp caught in her throat.

A woman held Kamari by her shoulders, arms pinned behind her back. "You!" A scream rushed from her throat, deep and menacing, a warriors-cry, as she took off through the sand, sword in hand.

The woman holding Kamari wore a mask, concealing the lower part of her face, but her eyes were exposed and went wide as saucers. "Stand down!" her voice wavered, a thin knife wobbled as she pointed it under Kamari's chin. "She's coming with me."

Kamari thrashed in her grip, black smudged around her eyes, but there was a fierceness there that Nev recognized from Aesira. The queen was not losing this fight.

"Put your knife down," Nev called, lowering her own sword. "I only want the queen to be let go." She put her hands in the air, palms out. "I'll do you no harm. Just let her go." She met Kamari's eyes and gave the slightest dip of her chin.

I have you, she wanted to say. Nev had distracted the woman enough for Kamari to wriggle slightly from her grip to clamp down on her hand with her teeth. "Shit!" the woman reeled back, giving Nev just enough space to swoop in and pull the queen free.

The woman scrambled backward, abandoning her knife in the sand. The wind picked up, sand churning in the distance, a new storm brewing on the horizon. Then, the woman was on her feet, darting straight for the storm.

"Go back to the Citadel, Your Majesty! Get Rahashi, tell her what happened." She glanced to her right, where Kamari was still panting on the ground. "Go, Your Majesty!" There was no time for politeness and she would apologize later but right now, she needed the queen on her feet and back to safety. "Kamari!" Her eyes snapped to Nev's, the use of her name seeming to wake her up. She jumped to her feet and darted toward the small doorway hidden in the wall.

Nev returned her attention to the woman. She'd made it halfway from the wall to the growing storm. Determination guided her boots as they dug into the sand. She set an unrelenting pace, her sword long forgotten behind her. It would only weigh her down, when her bare hands would do the job.

Lungs burning, eyes stinging from the sand that whipped around her, she reached the woman with more ease than she anticipated. She hurtled forward, pinning her to the ground and pushing her face into the sand. A muffled scream, maybe a plea, Nev wasn't sure, nor did she care. Sand flew around them and Nev knew the patterns of the storm well enough to know that they had only a minute before they'd be completely engulfed.

"Let me free!" the woman shrieked as Nev pulled her to her feet, pinning her arms behind her back. She shouted and pleaded and perhaps at one point started crying but Nev trudged forward. Through the sand, through the wind, through the door, until Rahashi was there, her dark skin and white hair, like a beacon of hope in the midst of the storm.

"Take her below the city," Nev said, pushing the woman forward into Rahashi's arms. "I'll deal with her later."

Without a word, Rahashi spun, the now prisoner in her grip, still pleading and crying that it was all a misunderstanding. Nev slammed the door shut, sand and wind pelting the other side.

She took only a moment to close her eyes, thanking Celestria for the speed at which she was able to run. For sparing Kamari's life not once, but twice. Then she wiped the sand from her face, plucked it out of her ears, and headed straight for the temple, where she knew her punishments would be waiting for her.

Twenty-One

Aesira

Aesira cupped the boy's cold cheek and brushed the stiff hair from his face. "Celestria be with you," she whispered, then gently laid his head on the ground.

There was nothing but the quiet drum of rain against rock as Stone and Birdie worked together to get the torches relit. It seemed overly cautious since the Strix was dead, but she also understood the need to be busy at a time like this. She wished she could keep busy too. She glanced down at the boy again and her stomach lurched.

For a sick moment, she thought it was Eldrin in the Strix's clutches. But it couldn't be. That nightmare had already happened. Eldrin was dead. The pain of that memory overtook her like a storm, swelling in her chest until her lungs were too full to work.

"Hey." Bee crouched next to her. "Are you okay?" She tugged Aesira close, her arm tight around her shoulders. "You were brave," she said.

"I was careless." Aesira stood, brushing Bee off. "We all were." She cut a glance at Stone, who was already watching her over the flickering of the freshly lit torches. She'd let herself get distracted. Let her guard fall and if she hadn't been so quick, it could have been any one of them lying dead on the ground.

"We should sleep," Aesira said, trudging back into the cave. "It's almost dawn and we have a long trek tomorrow." She dressed in everything but her armor and found a spot away from the group to settle.

The ground was cold but she pressed her body tighter into it, letting the rocks tear into her skin. She'd do this. Find punishments where she could. Sometimes small. Other times, more devastating. She deserved it, she thought. To be uncomfortable and in pain. To be sick with guilt and shame for being so distracted. For ignoring her duties even for a moment.

Sleep did not come easy, just as it hadn't the last few nights, but this time when she dreamt of the Strix, it wasn't her it was after. It was after Eldrin again.

The sun exposed the extent of last night's storm as they packed and ate a ration of dried meat and fruit each. The few bare trees that lined the mountains had lost limbs, branches broken and scattered. But none of the carnage was as bad as what lay before the cave.

The Strix, with its awful stench and razor teeth.

And the boy, with his sunken face and pale cheeks. Stone helped Aesira wrap him the best they could with her blanket. Aesira withdrew a small piece of charred wood from her pocket, one that had broken off from one of the torches last night and with it, drew a small 'C' on the center of the boy's forehead.

C, for Celestria.

She pressed her fingers to her lips, then touched his forehead before joining the others. It wasn't a proper burial, but it would be enough to get him through Celestria's gates.

"We'll walk all day," Stone said. "The incline is steep but if we keep a consistent pace we should make good headway."

She let the others lead the way, lingering behind for a few extra moments to create some space between them. She needed the silence. Needed to breathe the fresh air of the open mountains. Needed to clear her head before the weight of her mistakes came crashing down again. Not just last night, but all the others that festered inside of her like a plague.

Her brother, being the worst of them.

The sun reached mid-sky before they stopped for a break. They each had their own canteens which they refilled during last night's rain storm.

Aesira made herself comfortable under a mature olive tree, finding relief beneath its thick branches. She sipped her water in silence, counting the seconds until it was time to move again.

Move.

That was the key.

She needed to keep her body moving. Keep her mind going, otherwise—

A tall figure eclipsed the sun. "Can I sit with you?" Stone crouched next to Aesira and pulled out a piece of dried fruit. "Here," he said. "In case you're still hungry."

"I'm not," she lied.

Stone kept the fruit hung between them and her face burned where his eyes met her skin. "Aesira," he said softly. She whipped her face toward him. "It wasn't your fault, what happened." He tucked the fruit back into his bag. "We couldn't have known the Strix was that far in the mountains."

"You said the Strix left." Her throat burned. "You said it was likely full and off to find a mate."

Stone pushed his glasses up and it was such a small, insignificant movement, something she'd seen him do over and over again, but it enraged her. A movement so normal and routine as if they didn't almost die hours ago. As if that boy didn't die hours ago.

It wasn't Eldrin.

She wanted to rip them off his face and toss them in the dirt.

"I did say that because I thought it was true," Stone said. "I was wrong." He shook his head. "I'm sorry. But it wasn't your fault. That boy was dead long before the Strix found us." He pulled out one of the Ravki maps, unrolling it between them. "We need to keep moving." He pointed to a spot on the map, a tiny insignificant set of hills that could also be easily an ink blot from one of Desmond's quills. "We're here," he said, "but we need to at least crest this ridge by nightfall."

Aesira took her time studying the map. The locations were in a language she couldn't read. All but the one word she'd come to know well over the last two weeks.

Ravki.

The ridge Stone pointed to looked roughly a half mile past a perfectly flat base.

"What difference does it make if we crest the ridge tonight?" She handed back the map. "We should save the incline for when we're fresh in the morning. Sleep somewhere flat and protected by the base of the ridge."

He shook his head. "Tonight," he said. She was too tired to argue.

"Fine." She pointed to the map in his hand. "Is this something you learned in one of your books? To read maps and this–language–whatever it is?"

Stone rolled the map and placed it back in his pack. "Yes," he said. "Though it's easier to learn than it looks." He stood and offered his hand, which Aesira took.

Lightning buzzed in her fingertips and for a brief moment, she forgot her promise to herself. That she was here to find Desmond and that was it. For a moment, she was back at the tavern or on the ship or in the rain but when Stone squeezed her hand, everything came crashing back.

"Commander…" She pulled her hand away and brushed it off on her pants.

"Easier than it looks?" She drew the conversation back to safety. Not of Stone or her and how often they found themselves entwined.

The map. The mission. Desmond.

Stone cleared his throat. "Our language is a direct derivative of Ravkian, it seems. Or vice-versa, I'm not sure which language came first. The patterns are all there and once you recognize one, it's easy to decipher the rest."

Aesira didn't believe that anything about learning a dead language was easy, but for Stone it might be. She envied his mind. She had the ability to make calculations on the fly. To anticipate her enemy's move. To avoid a strike. But it was never a skill that came easy to her. She had to make a conscious effort in training and even now, years after her schooling was complete, it was active resolve, not instinct.

Every so often she felt herself slipping, making decisions with her heart instead of her head. Like last night.

It was precisely what her father would scorn her for when she was younger. The same reckless behavior that got her thrown into the Order in the first place. That got Eldrin killed. But Stone, he was smart. Brilliant maybe, and she could see the gears in his mind turning when he spoke. Could see how easily he made a decision. How self assured he was.

Her life would be so much easier if she could turn her conscience off. Turn her heart off. It was exactly what the Order wanted from its knights. Cold, calculated. But she failed, even to do that.

The sun faded and the sky turned a cool shade of violet as they reached the ridge. The steep incline of the trek only progressed throughout the day and despite the years of sweat and endurance, Aesira's legs were burning when they stopped to make camp.

Other than a run in with a few too large scorpions, the day had mostly been uneventful and Aesira counted that as a blessing. Perhaps Celestria was watching after all. "You need a hand with that?" Birdie asked between mouthfuls of canned soup.

Aesira shook out her bed-roll. "No, I've got it."

"You haven't eaten."

"I'm not hungry."

Bee sighed then knelt beside her. "You need to eat. You're a soldier, you know best how important it is to preserve your strength and energy." Shame burned through Aesira, hot and nauseating. "Here." Bee handed her a small square wrapped in a white cloth. "They're lemon squares," she said. "Birdie paid a shitload of money for them from Soo, so don't waste them. They're packed with nutrients and don't taste like shit," she said, gesturing to Birdie's canned soup.

"I can't take these from you—" Bee and Birdie were already walking away, leaving Aesira with the food she didn't deserve.

The stars from the mountain peak were brighter than in Vargah, no *astra* lights to dilute their beauty and even though she complained about making the extra half mile of steep terrain, the view was worth it.

The moon crested over the mountain top, thin and sharp. She stared at it and wondered if Kamari was looking at it too. She missed her so much and yet a part of her dreaded going back. Dreaded what they'd find in Ravki. Dreaded what they wouldn't.

"You weren't lying when you said you don't sleep." Stone slid onto the ground next to her, perching his back against the same tree trunk.

"You don't either it seems," she said. Warmth encompassed her as he angled his body closer.

"Why waste time sleeping when you could be reading." He pulled out a map and unrolled it. "According to this, we're on the Polaris Ridge." He tapped the map, where some words were scribbled in Ravkian.

"And?"

"And," Stone said, "the Polaris Ridge is a special place. In the book I got from Ramses, there's a legend that only here can you find the Lunaris moths. They supposedly breed in the crooks and hollows of the ridge and are born under the new moon."

She peeked at the sky again, to the nearly nonexistent sliver of light hanging in a bed of inky darkness. "Tonight is a new moon."

A smile spread across Stone's face, stretching his scar and brightening his eyes. "Exactly."

Aesira matched his smile. It was infectious, the way he looked at things. Found beauty in them. "Is that why you were so insistent we make it here tonight?"

"Maybe."

Aesira couldn't help it, she laughed and Stone did too and in that small moment, she forgot her anger and her disappointment in herself and for a moment she was not a knight of the Order, she was just a person sitting alongside another person.

And it felt good.

"You're something else, Stone Odega."

He shrugged, eyes focused on the edge of the ridge.

"How can you believe anything in that old book?"

He scooted closer, so their shoulders were touching. His breath was warm and sweet on her cheeks. "Isn't that all faith is?" he whispered against the shell of her ear, the warmth of his breath cascading down her spine. "Believing?"

The reminder of Celestria, the Order, all their rules and devotion, burned in her mind and that brief moment where she was someone else, vanished.

"Over there," Stone said, "do you see?"

The moon loomed over the mountain ridge, so thin and close, Aesira wondered if she reached her arm out, if she'd be able to grab hold of one of the sharpened points and climb on. Silvery light spread over the mountain top, then dripped down the ridge, until it reached where they sat. It lit up Stone's face, highlighting his blue eyes and wide smile. His knuckle was warm as it tucked under her chin, pointing her attention back to the ridge.

"There," he whispered again and sure enough, twinkling orbs of light began to ascend from hidden spots in the rocks. The orbs danced, their light pulsing silver and gold.

"It's amazing."

"Wait," Stone said, his hand sliding to rest on the back of her neck, like he wanted to make sure she didn't look away. Didn't miss whatever it was they were about to witness.

The orbs flickered, bouncing higher and higher in the air, spreading their dazzling wings, light reflecting off their tiny antennas. Dozens of them rose from the ridge, dancing and flying under the light of the moon and stars. Their wings sparkling, their bodies glowing. In a world that seemed so destined to destroy them, this kind of beauty was unknown.

Unreal.

The moths drifted closer, the light from their tiny bodies illuminating the night sky.

They are real, she reminded herself. Her heart pressed firm against her ribs, like it was reminding her to breathe.

"Isn't this the most beautiful thing you've ever seen?"

When Stone didn't answer, she turned to him, a flush rising to her cheeks when his eyes were already on her.

"It's a very close second," he said. His hand tightened on the back of her neck, a gentle squeeze that traveled clear down her spine.

The light from the moon and the moths danced over his face, but when it caught his eyes again, her thoughts disappeared. All she could see was him and all of the reasons she'd told herself to stay away from him didn't matter. He was distracting. An Odega.

He was also handsome and smart and—

"Can I kiss you, Aesira?" He leaned closer, his forehead resting on hers. His breath was sweet, like the lemon squares Bee had given her earlier. "I know that I shouldn't. That we'd forget anything ever happened..." His fingers flexed on the back of her neck again. So tentative. Like he was unsure if he should be touching her at all. She liked that he was nervous. It made her feel like she was still somewhat in control.

She tried to remember her plan. Tried to think of how he was nothing more than a distraction for her. Tried to scream at herself that getting tangled up with someone, an Odega no less, was the absolute last thing she needed to do right now.

But her traitorous heart pounded in her chest and her stomach flipped and even if she could lie to herself most of the time, she didn't want to tonight. Not when he was so close and the Lunaris moths were dancing and the new moon brought so much hope and his hands touching her was the only thing that seemed to keep her head on her shoulders.

She closed the gap between them, her lips closing in on his. Her hands moved over his chest, his muscles tensing under her touch, then relaxing before he kissed her back. Still gentle, but he moved with a purpose. His fingers slid up from her neck and buried in her hair, nails scraping lightly against her scalp.

He kissed her again, firmer now and Aesira couldn't stop her body from leaning into his touch, couldn't stop her lips from parting and her hands finding their way to the nape of his neck. He pulled her tighter, kissing her harder.

Perhaps he needed the distraction as much as she did, or maybe it was something else, but it didn't matter because all there was to do on this mountain, on this journey was overthink and Stone was giving her a few minutes of relief from being inside her own head. Her fingers ran lightly over the back of his neck, down to his chest, catching on one of his scars peeking out from the top of his shirt.

She leaned forward and kissed it. "Did somebody do this to you?" Stone tensed again and she leaned back to see his face. "I'm sorry, I shouldn't have asked."

"It's okay," he said through a smile. His hands slid down her body until they anchored at her waist. "I've had the scars for as long as I can remember." She frowned and he must have seen because he pressed his knuckles under her chin again and tilted her head up. "They don't hurt. Not anymore."

She breathed a sigh of relief and leaned forward to kiss him again when something soft tickled her hand; a tiny moth had perched there, its furry legs stretched out beneath its body. She held it between them, the bright light of the Lunaris moth tinted Stone's face a light purple.

"We've made a friend," Stone said. Aesira raised her hand, urging the moth to fly away but it stayed anchored to the back of her hand, its light growing dim. "I think you're putting it to sleep."

"Sleep?" Aesira stroked the back of the moth, admiring the softness in its scales.

Then it hit her.

All at once, a heavy sense of familiarity rushed her, like walking into a room you've never been in but recognizing the layout, the curtains, the scent.

"I've seen these before," she said. "These moths."

Stone shook his head, stroking a gentle finger down one of the moth's wings. "It's unlikely. They only breed and live here. On this ridge. So sacred to the mountain my book didn't even have drawings of them, only where to find them."

Aesira glanced at the sleeping moth again. The large expanse of its wings. The markings adorned on them, like tiny crescent moons. As if Celestria created them herself. But it was in the markings that she knew what she'd seen.

"No, I've seen this before, Stone. Not in person, but in one of Desmond's journals. Kamari showed it to me the day we came to see you. He'd drawn at least a dozen of them on a single page."

Stone's brows pinched together. "Maybe," he said. "It's possible he could have seen them in a book. Vargah does have a much more expansive library than the Outpost." The moth fluttered on Aesira's hand then took off through the air, a dizzying orb of silvery light.

It was entirely possible that Desmond had seen a Lunaris moth in a book and became fascinated with them. Maybe he knew they'd be here, on his way to Ravki. Which only meant he'd planned his journey ahead of time. For months, maybe, without Kamari knowing.

Stone's fingers drifted up her back, bringing her thoughts shooting straight to where all the places their bodies were still connected. Bee's distant laugh sounded behind them, echoing off the ridge.

"We should get back to the others," she said.

"Right." Stone nodded and her eyes dipped to his mouth. Still pink from their kiss, still parted like he was waiting for another one. Would it be so bad to kiss him again?

Yes. It would be bad, she decided. Because if she kissed Stone again, it wouldn't stop there. She would keep going and she would use him just as she'd used all her past lovers and she didn't want to do that with him.

And the realization struck her through the chest.

Maybe Stone Odega was her friend, after all.

"We should go," she said, moving to stand. "It would be the responsible thing to do."

"You're right." He stood, dusting dirt from his pants, straightening his shirt. "I know how much being responsible pleases you."

Twenty-Two

Stone

The question was on the tip of Stone's tongue as he and Aesira joined Birdie and Bee around the fire.

Why me that night?

So often he'd wondered what brought Aesira's attention to him at the Phoenix. In a room full of suitors, she could have easily gone home with anyone. Not only because of her name but because she was beautiful.

He flicked his eyes to her as she settled in around the fire. Her dark hair was looser than she normally wore in Vargah. Curls hanging down her back and framing her face.

Then there was the matter of her eyes. One green. One hazel. Both mesmerizing. Freckles danced across her broad nose and dark, full brows that seemed to permanently be furrowed but it didn't take away from the unique beauty of her. Bee said something and Aesira smiled and Stone's heart leaped to his throat.

No, Aesira Zeliath was not just beautiful. She was unholy.

He stole a drink from Birdie's canteen and savored the coolness as it reached his belly.

He doubted Aesira even realized how beautiful she was. Otherwise, there was no logical reason for her to approach him that night *or* tonight. Maybe she thought it would be casual. Wild and fevered and thoughtless.

He could be those things, if that's what she needed.

But truthfully, Stone had never done anything casually in his life. When he met Vic and became a drug runner, he had to be the best in the Outpost. Even at twelve years old, he was bringing in more coin and regular business than some of the most seasoned smugglers.

Not because the drugs he was running were better, but because Stone had figured out the best routes. Had studied the corners and knew just the right time to hit them. Figured out what customers wanted and catered to them.

Then, when Vic realized Stone had more brains than an average runner, he became a chemist, finding solutions for their drugs' weak potency and introducing new forms of it.

So, no, Stone Odega did not possess a casual bone in his body. He tried, when he was younger, to be like the other runners in the Outpost. To meet a woman, sleep with them and move on.

He got good at pretending because even with something he hated, he couldn't fathom doing it half-heartedly. So he learned to be someone else when he needed to be. He'd figured out a way to switch off his brain. He learned he could do this not just with women, but with work. With anything.

That's when his reputation began to precede him. He would make more potent products. Would demand they be sold for double, triple, what they were used to. He carved out new routes for his own pack of runners, establishing connections with the eastern kingdom of Novaria, bringing them new drugs, expanding his region ten-fold.

Building his own empire right under Vic's nose.

The boy with a heart of stone, they'd called him when he made these demands. When he began edging Vic out. The name stuck and he didn't care. He forgot who he was before he became Stone, because whoever he was before, wasn't the *best*.

He could be cold, if that's what he excelled at. He could be empty and ruthless, if that was what others needed from him.

Living a lie was easier than living with the truth that when he took away all the faces he wore, he wasn't sure who he really was. Wasn't sure what his birth name even meant, if it meant anything at all.

He was Stone the viper and now, Stone Odega, and he was the best at being nothing and being everything and even when he got caught, even when everything he'd built crumbled around him, he didn't bat an eye because he knew if a criminal was what he'd be branded, he'd find a way to be the best at it.

Which is how he got here, flying a ship with the queen's money and his crew huddled around a fire.

Bee was singing, an old tune from the Outpost that made Birdie laugh. Aesira smiled, sipping quietly from her canteen, her bronze skin lit up from the light of the flames. He traced the ridge of her nose, the shape of her lips. Envied the freckles inked on her skin because they were close to her and he was not.

When Aesira approached him that night in the Phoenix he figured he would do what he did for so many years in the Outpost.

Switch off the part of his brain that held any kind of empathy or attachment and switch on the part that knew how to make a calculated decision despite any risk.

Then her lips met his, stalling his heart, pulling his skin taut, and he knew that even though he *could* pretend with her, he didn't want to, which is why he walked away.

Now they'd kissed again. Once at Vic's, which even though he knew didn't mean anything, kept him up the entire night, tossing and turning, replaying the touch of her soft lips against his until there was nothing left he could do but drop his hand and find release.

And then there was tonight, and it was tonight's kiss that woke a hunger inside of him. A feeling he'd buried deep and tossed a torch to. That had him fidgeting and skin burning and fingers aching just to touch her again.

Why me?

But he knew the likely reason was because she needed a distraction. And if that's all it was, he'd be the best distraction he could be, because he did not do things casually.

Aesira laughed, drawing his attention and he swore, as her eyes watched him through the flames, he felt that hunger broaden in his chest. Despite the impossibility of it, his heart made of stone began to beat.

"So they aren't your real names, then?" Aesira glanced at Stone, then back to Birdie and Bee

"Technically no," Bee said, stoking the fire. "But I've been called Bee for so long, I can't imagine going by anything else."

"Same," Birdie said. "When we were dragged into Vic's, a new name was the first thing we were given. Make us understand that we were his. Melt us down to nothing and re-sculpt us."

Aesira frowned. "Oh trust me, I know how that goes."

Stone watched her over the fire. He wanted to dissect that sentence. Tear it apart, dig through the words until he could see everything in between that she wasn't saying aloud.

See if the lies she told herself matched his own.

"But wouldn't you want to take your old name back?" Aesira tossed a stick into the flames. "You know, now that you're away from him."

"For some of us," Stone said, pulling Aesira's attention to him, "there's no going back to who we were. There's no remembering a life that wasn't the Outpost."

Her brows pinched together again. "You don't remember your name?"

Stone shrugged. Whether or not he remembered his name didn't matter. He was Stone now and he'd been Stone for more than half his life. He remembered very little about his childhood before finding the Outpost, before finding Patch and Vic.

But what he could remember—being alone, dying of thirst in the desert—wasn't anything happy. His scars itched as he ran a hand down his face, exhaustion seeping into him like water over sand. "Some things aren't worth remembering."

A bone-shattering chill ran down Stone's spine, jolting him awake. He pulled his glasses from his pocket, wiping them on his shirt before slipping them on.

Bee and Birdie slept tangled together, the last remnants of the fire still smoldering, sending plumes of smoke into the night sky. He glanced to his right where Aesira was curled up under his jacket he'd laid on her after she'd fallen asleep.

A frigid breeze stung the few errant tears on his cheeks. He stood, dusting off his pants and peered over the ridge. The Lunaris moths were gone, likely hiding in the rocks to protect themselves from the cold.

More wind rippled through the air carrying a tune of soft chimes. The high peals reminded him of Soo's bells. Then, a flurry of whispers danced around him, snaking in his ears.

"What is that?" Bee was up. Birdie, right behind her. Another gust of wind and the chimes sounded again, their high pitches growing closer. More whispers, more voices.

"Music?" Aesira joined Stone's side. He hadn't heard her get up, too focused on the unnatural wind and the sound of chimes and the voices he wasn't sure anyone else could hear. "Is there a settlement on the Whispering Mountains?"

"It's possible, but I don't know for sure," he answered truthfully. He wasn't keen on not having answers, but he figured better to be honest than get them into trouble. He couldn't recall any settlements being noted on the Whispering Mountains. As far as the maps went, it should be barren until they eventually descended on the other side, which would bring them to Ravki.

The chimes rang again, then the whispers, closer this time, swirling around them from all sides.

"Maybe a drifter," Bee said. "Or rebels."

"Maybe it's the king." Birdie smirked but a small stroke of worry landed in Stone's stomach. Could it be King Desmond? A better person would hope it was Desmond so they could turn around and get him home safely but that would mean not reaching Ravki.

Not finding out if fields of *astra* really existed.

More wind, more chimes, more voices that said nothing, another chill down his spine.

"I'm going out." Aesira marched past him. He caught her arm before she could make it to the mouth of the cave.

"We don't know what's out there," he said. "Think of the Strix. Of her song."

"It could be Desmond." There was a pleading looking in her eye, only for a second before she shifted and her gaze turned cold. Calculated. "I need to check."

"We live in a land of monsters, Commander," Stone said. "Don't let hope blind you."

She hesitated a moment before wriggling free of his grip and drawing her sword from the ground. "There," she said, "now I'm going out."

Stone could admit he was smart but he wasn't necessarily brave and damn, if seeing Aesira march out of the cave, weapon drawn, didn't bolster his courage.

"You two stay back," he said to Birdie and Bee. "If you hear anything, head down the ridge."

"And leave you?" Birdie shook her head. "Fuck off, we're coming."

Bee lit a torch and handed it to Stone. "Never let it go dark." She cast him a smile before she and Birdie took the lead out of the cave.

Vicious gusts pulled at their skin, their clothes. Chimes drifted on the wind, filling his head. Debris flew in the air, but through it he could make out the shape of Aesira near the ridge.

"Commander!" He charged forward, shielding his eyes from the branches and leaves caught in the wind until he reached her side. "Aesira." He took hold of her shoulder but she was rooted in place, her body stiff. The tip of her black boot slid over the edge of the ridge but he wrapped his arms around her middle before she could fall.

Her head rolled back, her eyes glazed and distant. "Aesira." He shook her but she didn't move. He pushed his fingers to her neck, checking her pulse.

She was breathing.

Alive.

Though her eyes were open, she seemed to be rendered unconscious.

"Wake up, Commander," he said against her ear. The chimes grew louder, more and more wind tore through the ridge, making him lose his balance. He fell backwards, keeping his grip on Aesira's waist, making sure he took the brunt of the fall. "Wake up, Aesira," he demanded again but a voice slithered into his mind.

Sleep, it insisted.

The sudden urge to close his eyes was irresistible but he fought against it, keeping them peeled.

Sleep, the voice whispered again and his eyes grew itchy and heavy. The ridge faded, his grip on Aesira's waist loosening.

Sleep.

Maybe just for a moment, he thought. *I'll close my eyes just for a moment.*

Darkness unfurled behind his vision and he could no longer feel Aesira in his arms.

TWENTY-THREE

AESIRA

Salt and decay filled Aesira's nose and when she opened her eyes a beam of light washed over her.

"Stone?" She glanced to either side of her, but she was alone atop a hill, the warmth of the sun and soft breeze running over her bare arms. Her hand flew to her side where she found her sword missing. As was her armor, she realized.

The gauzy fabric of her dress floated behind her in the breeze as she pulled herself to her feet. "Stone? Birdie?" Another gust of wind drew the scent of decay closer. She covered her mouth with the back of her hand.

Tall flowers swayed in the wind, their petals tickling her arms and fingertips. She knew this meadow. Knew the sounds of the breeze playing between the thin leaves on the sparse trees.

Novaria.

Her pulse hammered in her chest, her mind fuzzy and memories diluted.

She couldn't be home, could she?

She remembered the ridge.

The Lunaris moths and Stone's lips on hers.

The unexpected warmth of Stone's jacket and then the chimes.

Then, she was here. How was she here? A sharp pain erupted behind her eyes then a trickle of warmth ran down to her lips. She wiped the blood from her nose.

Blood.

The boy.

The Strix.

"Aesira," a voice called, one she knew she recognized but couldn't quite place. She scanned the meadow, keeping her feet planted in the cold dirt. "Aesira," the same voice called. "It's time to come home, Aesira."

Home.

No. She couldn't be home, when the last place she stood was the ridge.

"We live in a land of monsters." Stone's voice washed over her.

"This is a dream." A breeze lifted the ends of her hair and a bright, purple moth drifted past. "This is a dream," she said louder now. Convincing herself and anyone–anything–else that might be lurking.

A few loose leaves rustled up from the ground. Then a distant *drip, drip, drip.*

The sound filled her with memories of her childhood. Of Kamari and Eldrin. A life that was now so far away.

Drip, drip, drip.

Blood, from the Strix. From the boy.

Drip, drip, drip.

Piscis Spring. The sound was Piscis Spring.

Drip, drip, drip.

The voice, the voice was—

"Come home, Aesira."

Eldrin.

Another jolt of pain burst behind her eyes, white and blinding. All of the memories she'd suppressed, all of the moments of her childhood she hid away crashed through her like a hammer through glass, the jagged edges cutting and slicing and letting out all the things she did not want to remember.

Her brother and the Strix and the way he fell down, down, down.

She snapped her eyes open and watched the water ripple over a few large rocks in the spring. She needed to move. Find a way out. Find the others.

Her dress dragged behind her as she climbed down the hill, grounding herself in the grit of the rocks and sound of the water lapping the shore. It splashed against her bare feet, cool and bitter. She stared out at the horizon.

A flurry of blue pulled her attention as another Lunaris moth fluttered by.

"Only a dream," she said again.

There wouldn't be moths here. I wouldn't hear Eldrin's voice. This is only a dream.

"Now how do I wake up?" She took a tentative step into the water and the bright sunlight grayed out, flashes of teeth and blood coming from every angle. She tumbled backwards, out of the water, and the sun returned. The faint sound of birdsong and the meadow were untouched. Breathing heavily, Aesira stood and dusted off her dress.

"Aesira." The same voice from before called to her. She closed her eyes, teeth biting into her tongue. *Only a dream.*

"*Aesira.*" The voice nipped at her ears and another memory sprang forth. The crawlers from the desert. This was similar and all she had to do to break from their spell was keep control of her mind.

Only she hadn't done it alone.

Stone had been there. He'd woken her up. Saved her.

She squared her shoulders and lifted her chin. There was no one here to save her. Her mind was the weakest weapon in her arsenal but right now it was all she had. Ghost-like fingers ran up her arms, sending a chill down her spine. *"Aesira, come."*

She scurried from the phantom touch, toward the water, digging her toes into the rocks, the sharp points pressing under her toenails.

It's only a dream.

One foot submerged and the sun flickered. Flashes of gray and wings and death spewed across the sky. Aesira bit her tongue harder, this time to stop a scream. A push came from her back and the whispering voices were like leeches in her ears, teeth taking hold of her heart, her head. *"Come home."* Another foot hit the water and then there was no sun left. Darkness stretched across the sky, blacking out the meadow and silencing the birds.

Water lodged in her throat as she was pushed under, eyes bulging and arms and legs pumping as she flailed for a way out.

Swim, a distant voice in the back of her mind called.

Fight.

She willed herself to calm, smoothing her arms and legs around her. She knew how to swim. She'd done it a few times in the spring with her siblings when they were children. Before she was sent to the Order. She just needed to remember.

Her legs stretched behind her, her arms in front and she propelled forward.

Shadows darted beside her, inky and fluid like the water. She focused in front of her, her lungs on fire, when a tug pulled on her leg. She flipped to her back, a dark shadow wrapped around her leg, then the other, tying her down. Kicking, she fought until her muscles burned and head grew dizzy. The shadows wrapped tighter, squeezing and pulling her down.

This is only a dream.

A dream.

Aesira's training kicked in and she decided to test her theory. If this really was a dream, perhaps she couldn't die.

Her body went slack, preserving her energy, as the dark shadows ran up her legs, around her middle, over her neck, into her mouth. They wrapped her completely, her body encased in darkness. Only when her back hit the ground beneath, did she wriggle her fingers, loosening a sharp rock embedded in the bottom of the spring.

The shadows held her tight, moving around her body like a serpent. But her lungs, while frantic, *worked.*

Just a dream.

She angled the small rock between her knuckles, sharp edge pointed out, and when the shadows slithered across her body again, she punched as deeply as she could into one of them. A wretched, gurgled screech burst in her ear, but she did it again and again, jabbing any shadow she could reach. She nicked her own leg in the process, hints of blood floating in the water around her. But she didn't stop. The shadows screeched, still squeezing her body, but with every slice of the rock, their grip loosened more and more.

"Aesira, don't fight."

She ignored the familiar voice, fighting the shadows wrapped around her legs until she was free of them. The one in her mouth shriveled away, leaving her exposed, nothing to keep her lungs from filling with water. Fire engulfed her lungs as she shot toward the hazy surface.

Almost there.

She was almost there.

An achy gasp leeched from her throat as she emerged from the water. Lungs heaving, she tore at her chest, pulling off dark tendrils of the shadowy figures that still clung to her like vines. The gauzy dress from the dream was gone, she was back in her black armor, boots tied to her feet. The sun began to rise, bleeding into the sky, turning it a dusty pink.

She was on the ridge.

Relief and exhaustion crashed into her when a noise came from her right.

Bee.

Aesira stood on unsteady legs and ran to her. She was still asleep, whimpering, her brows bunched tightly together. "Bee," Aesira said, grabbing hold of her shoulders. "Bee it's just a dream, wake up." She shook her again, harder this time until her eyelids fluttered open.

"What happened," Bee said through a sob. "Where are we?"

"On the ridge." Aesira helped her sit, pulling a few loose twigs and leaves from her hair. "You're safe now, the sun's up." She looked past Bee's shoulders, finding solace in the warmth of the sun, but her face hardened when in the distance she could hear the faint sound of chimes. "Where's Birdie? Stone?"

"I don't know." Bee rubbed her temples. "The last thing I remember was the beautiful music and then–" Bee pressed her fingers to her temples. "I thought we were back in the Outpost. Bird was there too but it was different." She shook her head and stood. "We have to find them. I could feel those things draining me. Like they were reaching into my soul." She took Aesira's hand. "I'm not sure I would have woken up if you didn't help me," she said. "I owe you."

"Let's find the other two."

Before it's too late.

Bee and Aesira split up. Aesira checked the camp first.

Empty.

Then she remembered the edge of the ridge where she nearly fell. Stone had come to her. Even in the dreamy vision she could remember his warmth around her. She sprinted toward the cliff. His jacket was discarded a few feet from the edge and then–there–one leg dangled over the cliff, he laid on his back, his eyes closed and face smooth.

Her hands shook as she knelt beside him and pressed her ear to his chest.

Don't be gone. Not yet.

It was faint, but his heartbeat sent a surge of hope through her, blossoming like a flower in her chest. She pushed his hair back from his forehead and whispered against his ear.

"Wake up, Stone." She gripped his shoulders and shook. "Wake up!"

He didn't move.

Was she too late? Had those creatures sunk their teeth into his soul and leeched every drop? She shook him again. "Stone, you have to wake up." He frowned, his lips twitching. She gripped his face in her palms. "Wake up, Stone. It's time to wake up."

Wake up, wake up, wake up.

He didn't move.

Defeat slumped Aesira's shoulders so she laid her head on his chest. There was still the faintest movement, but it brought her more dread than hope. Whatever they were putting him through, she couldn't imagine. If it was even a fraction of what she'd seen in her dream...

"Commander." Stone's hand cupped the back of her head.

"You're okay?" She sat up. Her hands went to his face, searching for any marks that may have been left on him.

He sat up and she pulled her hands away. "I'm okay. Dreamweavers," he said. "Fuck, I should have seen that coming." He sat up and ran a hand across the back of his neck.

She handed him his jacket which he reluctantly took. "This is the west, remember. The land of monsters. In fact," she said, helping Stone to his feet. "It was your reminder that got me out of my dream. Trust nothing, right?"

"Trust nothing," he repeated. "I suppose here there are dreams and there are nightmares and somehow we are living through both."

"Holy shit," Bee shouted. "You're okay?" She and Birdie joined them on the cliff's edge.

"Barely," Stone said.

"I know we all need sleep," Birdie said, a scowl deepening between her brows, "but I'd like to get off this ridge immediately."

TWENTY-FOUR

AESIRA

The terrain evolved from sand, to red rock, to dense woods–something Aesira wasn't accustomed to but she couldn't complain about the shade the expansive trees offered. They were lovely and massive, with their thick trunks and spindly green leaves.

"Over here," Bee called, pointing to a small thicket of trees. "This should give us some coverage for the night." The four of them discarded their packs before Bee and Birdie set off to look for any food the new terrain might offer.

The air was damp, springing Aesira's curls tighter than usual. She struggled to pin them back and eventually gave up, letting the ringlets fall around her face in frizzy clusters. Her muscles spasmed as she stretched her arms above her head. Stone settled in across from her, pulling out his maps and a few journals from his pack.

"Anything useful in there?" She nodded to the journals. Kamari had only shown her a few pages, most of them full of nonsense, but she wondered how valuable they must be for Stone to continue to pack them around. The extra weight couldn't be doing anything good for his back.

"I'm not sure." Stone opened the map and laid it on the ground. "This, though"— he tapped the map's center—"is proving extremely valuable. I still can't believe we have a real map of Ravki." His voice lit up.

Aesira's eyes drifted from the map to Stone and she found herself studying him instead. The curve of his mouth, the way he ran his finger softly against the worn parchment. Then, as he traced a long line down the map's center, she tore her eyes away. The way the veins in his hands worked as he moved them and the softness in which he traced the paper made her cheeks flush.

"Why wouldn't Desmond take it?" she asked, forcing herself to focus on anything but Stone.

"Take what?" Stone didn't look up.

"The map." She stood and peered over his shoulder, getting a closer look. "It's authentic, right?" she asked.

Stone nodded, running a hand across his jaw.

"And it gives us a direct path to one of the most fabled cities in the world. If Ravki is where Desmond was headed, why wouldn't he take the map with him?" Adrenaline and exhaustion warred with each other as more and more questions rose in her mind.

Stone frowned and tucked his pencil behind his ear. "Maybe he didn't know it was authentic. Maybe he was just adding it to his collection."

"Desmond went so far as to write about Ravki in not one, but several journals," she said. "He drew pictures of Lunaris moths, of dragons. Things no one alive should have any reference to. It doesn't make sense. If he thought that this map would lead him to Ravki, he wouldn't have left it behind."

Stone sat silent, his eyes still roaming the map, his brows pinched together. "I can't believe I haven't thought of that before."

Pride surged through Aesira's chest. That she had thought of something Stone hadn't. "Well, maybe you're not as smart as you think."

He laughed. "Definitely not." Their eyes met and warmth kissed Aesira's cheeks. The last few rays of sunlight fought through the trees, just enough to highlight Stone's eyes. The scar running down his cheek. The shape of his lips. "Birdie and Bee will be gone for a while," he said.

"You don't know that."

"I'm willing to bet after last night, they're more than ready for some time alone." He shrugged. "You know, after nearly dying and all."

Aesira didn't want to think about that.

About the Dreamweavers and how close they came—how close Stone came—to not waking up. She wondered what he dreamt about. What kept him pulled under so long. If it was anything as terrifying as what they showed her.

"Are you hungry?" It seemed like a safe question, a way to steer the conversation away from her thoughts of Stone and his lips and his implications. Until those lips tilted up and his head cocked to the side.

"Starving, actually."

Her stomach erupted, like a million Lunaris moths fluttering inside of her, trying to get out. She didn't know why she'd let him kiss her last night. Didn't know why she kissed him back. But as he scooted closer, as he attempted to tuck her untamable hair behind her ear, she found it more and more difficult to care. Because it felt good to be looked at and it felt good to be wanted and the chances of them even making it back to Vargah seemed less and less likely so what did it matter?

"Commander–" Stone started but she didn't let him finish, running her fingers through his hair and pulling him in until his mouth was close enough to hers that she could almost taste him.

"Yes?" Her lips brushed his with her question, brief enough to send a wave of anticipation through her.

"What happened to forgetting the night at the Phoenix?"

She pulled away enough to see his face. "Maybe something has changed." She nipped at Stone's bottom lip, coaxing a groan from him while his hands found their way to her waist. "Or maybe we have cheated death twice and I need a distraction."

His lips brushed against her jaw. "I could do that," he said against the soft skin of her neck. "If that's what you wanted." His hands ran up her spine, then back down again.

There was no future for Aesira Zeliath and Stone Odega and before, she was fine with that. But now, they were friends, weren't they? She hadn't considered what their friendship might look like if they took things further. Truthfully she hadn't considered their friendship past this journey to Ravki.

Perhaps she should have thought about it before kissing him again, but she'd never had a partner who lasted more than a few lust-filled nights. Never bothered to know someone on a level as deep as she now knew Stone. Her thoughts must have played across her face because Stone bumped her arm with his shoulder.

"What did I say? Did I mess this up?"

Aesira stood and grabbed his arm, pulling him up. "No. I'm just not good at this even though I try to be." She let out a nervous laugh in an attempt to cover up all the things she didn't want to say out loud.

My job would never allow me to be with you, she wanted to say. *My family would never allow it.*

I would never allow it.

His blush deepened, bringing out all the hues of his eyes. "What did I tell you about trying so hard?" His hands found her waist again, pulling her flush with his body. "Out here, you're not Commander Zeliath." His fingers twisted around a loose curl. "I'm not an Odega." His breath ghosted across her skin. "We could be anyone." His hand wrapped around her waist, pulling her flush to his chest.

The sun was mostly dappled out behind the trees, but her body felt like she was in the training pit. Hot and achy and needing a release. "What do you say?" He pressed a soft kiss to her jaw. "Should we pretend? Like we did at Vic's?"

Yes, she wanted to say.

That's exactly it. Pretend. Be someone else with me.

One hand snaked up the back of her neck, getting lost in her hair, while the other cupped her jaw so her mouth was angled perfectly to his. "Tell me what you want."

Her throat was tight when she swallowed. All the places Stone and her body connected, a blaze of heat and want. "I want to pretend."

A quick smile slashed across his mouth, then he kissed her. It wasn't gentle like last night, but firm. Like it was the most sure thing he'd ever done. Her hands grabbed at him, greedy for more and he kissed her deeper, his teeth grazing her bottom lip. His mouth was hot against her neck, one hand still tangled in her hair and the other holding firm at her waist.

He whispered her name between kisses, alternating from sweet to demanding and she wanted to get lost in that feeling. The feeling of being someone else, just for a little while. *Keep doing that,* she almost said out loud. *Keep kissing me and touching me and making me forget who I am and what I've done.* His tongue slid up her throat making her moan until a twig broke under his foot and they both jumped. Stone laughed first, then Aesira. "Sorry," he said.

Aesira's mind was still racing. Stuck on a loop of Stone's hands and mouth.

"We found water!" Bee's voice doused the fire between her and Stone, chilling her down to her toes. It took a moment for her heart to slow and her lungs to even out but when they did, her eyes shot to Bee.

"Water?" She smoothed her shirt, pushing her curls from her face.

"Can you believe it? There's a small spring just around the corner." Bee was either oblivious to the state of them or she was decent enough to pretend she saw nothing.

Birdie on the other hand. "Looks like you two found something to kill the time." A slick grin split across Birdie's sharp face. Her hand hung loosely at her sides, dripping wet.

"You really found water?" Aesira asked again, hope and something darker swirling in her gut. "Like a pool from the rain?"

Birdie shook her head. "This is more than collected rainfall. It's a whole fucking spring."

Aesira's mind wavered between amazement and disbelief. If Piscis Spring wasn't the only natural water source in the country...the war had been for nothing. The treaty had been for nothing. Celestria's demands of sacrifice...

They would have to tell the kingdoms. Would have to find a way to transport the water back to Vargah. Her militant brain switched on, silencing the part of her that for only a moment could pretend she was something else, anyone else.

"A miracle isn't it," Bee said. "It's small, but it's clean." Beads of water dripped down her dark brows, landing on her full lips.

"How is that possible?" Stone pushed his glasses up, the Ravki map already out and flattened against the ground. "There's no mention of a spring."

"Maybe whoever made that map didn't want anyone to know about it," Birdie said. "Check it out after we eat. See for yourself."

"Sure," Stone said, his voice still a bit breathless.

"I'm going to clean up first," Aesira said but what she meant was she needed to see it with her own eyes. Water. Water freely flowing from somewhere that wasn't Piscis Spring. That wasn't a gift from Celestria.

"Just around that group of trees," Bee said, "down the hill."

Stone crouched to start a fire, but turned and smiled at her over his shoulder, sending a shiver down her spine and Aesira considered the very real possibility that even though she thought she was in charge here, maybe he had more power over her than she liked to admit.

There was water.

Actual, free-flowing from the earth, ready to cup in your hand and drink *water.*

Aesira slid her boots off, toeing the waters edge. It was freezing but it felt too good to have the fresh water trickling over her bare feet to care.

She cupped her hands full and splashed her face. Large trees bracketed each side of the pool and beyond that, red, jagged rocks were illuminated by the setting sun.

Novaria had trees, but nothing like the ones here. Here, they stretched to the skies, the bark as rich as the dirt and the leaves pointy and deep green. She laid back on the rock and watched through an opening in the canopy as stars began to dot the newly night sky.

Kamari would love this.

The trees and the sky and the bubbling sound of the brook.

Guilt cramped her stomach so Aesira sat up and braided her hair, giving her hands and mind a purpose. If Stone was right, they were only two days from Ravki. Two days from getting answers and then they'd be heading home where she would have to face Kamari and all the truths about their journey. About the possibility of *astra*. About the water.

About how she'd been reassigned and she hadn't told her.

And more than anything, if they didn't find Desmond, she would have to lay out all her failures for everyone to chastise.

Again.

Footsteps through the forest grabbed her attention. Stone stepped through the small clearing as she finished tying off her braid.

"Did you get lost?" she teased. He tossed her one of the dry meals they'd packed.

She picked at the stale bread and dates while she and Stone watched the moon rise. The trees groaned as a breeze struck, their branches swaying, cutting sharp shadows over the water's surface. "I didn't think you'd come," she said.

Stone's glasses were off, tucked in his front pocket. He rubbed his eyes. "I wanted to come, Bee just wouldn't shut up. And I could never tell her to."

Aesira smiled. Of all the cadre, Bee was the most suited to her name. She was sweet, like honey, but could sting when necessary. She couldn't picture how Stone had gotten his name. Nothing he'd done or said had proven him to be hardened, but she supposed she didn't know him well enough. At least not yet.

Yet.

A tiny word that held such power. Like there would ever be a *yet*. They were pretending, she reminded herself. Only for now they were just two people who had the option to kiss freely and not think of the consequences.

Stone walked to the water's edge and she traced his body in the moonlight. Broad shoulders and lean frame. Corded muscles flexed in his forearms as he pushed up his sleeves and scrubbed his hands and face. "It's fucking freezing." He glanced at her over his shoulder. "Are you coming in?"

"What?"

"Coming in," he said, peeling off his shirt, then his pants. "I don't know about you, but four days of travel and I could use a bath." He tossed his clothes in a messy pile then dove into the water.

"Stone!" She sat up, watching the water's surface. He popped up less than a minute later, his hair swept back, water dripping from his brows and nose.

"Well?" There was a challenge in his voice, a dare. She weighed the consequences of joining Stone in the water, especially with how they left things earlier.

Do you want to pretend?

The night air nipped at her bare skin as she peeled her clothes off, layer by layer. Stone tried and failed to keep his eyes anywhere but on her, but when she tossed the final layer on the ground and stood in just her underclothes, he didn't try to hide his face anymore. He drank in every inch as she stepped into the water, moonlight rippling around them. Her face bunched, the water numbing her toes and then her hips but eventually her body adjusted and then it felt refreshing.

Divine.

Sinful.

People at home would be rationing water by now, waiting for Celestria to fill the wells after Naming Day. And here they were, bathing in it, treating it like excess.

"Can you swim?" she asked, inching closer, making sure to not go farther than waist deep.

"No," he said. "Are you offering to teach me?" He drifted closer, not quite touching, but close enough for her body to steal some of his heat.

"I hardly know how, myself." She looked up. The moon was still a sliver in the sky, perched right in the center of the canopy opening. "I've never seen trees like this," she said. "I've seen paintings. Read about them. But this is..."

"Beautiful." She didn't look at him, didn't need to because she could feel him looking at her. He closed the small gap between them. "*You* are beautiful." Her legs wrapped around his waist, his hands immediately finding the deep curve of her hips.

Pretending, she reminded herself.

They were just pretending.

"Can I tell you something?" he asked.

"Hm?"

"I lied to you before." Stone's hands traced her back, her hips.

"About what?" She leaned back so she could see his face. He looked pained, like whatever he was about to tell her would shatter their facade, would destroy their new pretend personalities. "What, Stone?"

He licked his lips, his eyes darting to her mouth for a moment before he looked at her again. "I dreamt of you."

Twenty-Five

Stone

Stone was fucked.

Moonlight spilled over Aesira's skin, highlighting the water droplets that clung to her hair and lashes. He didn't mean to tell her he'd dreamt of her, but with the moon and her eyes...

He knew they were pretending for the sake of the trip, but he was so enraptured by her that the truth slipped out.

"You dreamt of me when we drank the tea?" She frowned, a tiny crease forming between her brows.

"Yes," he said. Her legs were still wrapped around his waist, so he anchored his hands on her hips hoping she'd stay put. "I didn't know how to tell you, so I made up the Ravki–"

"I dreamt of you too." A smile crept over her lips and he wasn't sure if she meant to, but her legs tightened around his middle.

She desired him and the thought alone had his skin scorching.

Was it reckless that they'd both lied about seeing visions of Ravki in their dreams? Maybe. Did it make his heart race and his stomach tighten knowing that she'd thought of him, possibly in the same depraved way he'd thought of her? Absolutely.

There was more he wasn't saying. He wanted to tell her of *all* the times he'd dreamt of her, but he couldn't find any words that didn't make him sound so desperate.

"So who will we pretend to be tonight?" His fingers drifted over her skin, pebbled from the cold of the spring. Maybe he'd tell her one day, of all the dreams he'd had, but tonight this was enough. The fact that she was even in his arms, was enough.

"Hm." Aesira scrunched her nose. "Maybe tonight I'm a free spirit. A drifter." She laced her fingers behind his neck. "Wouldn't it be easier to erase our last names?" she said. "Scratch them from the parchment. Start over. Be nobody."

"Is that what you wish to be? No one?"

"Sometimes," she said through a sigh. "Sometimes I wish I was brave enough to run away from the Order. I wish I never became the person they wanted me to be."

He stroked a piece of hair from her face. "And what is wrong with this person? I see someone who is brave and cunning. Respected by her knights. Loved by her family." He kissed the tip of her nose. "Someone who is insanely beautiful."

He'd hoped she'd smile but instead she frowned and a pit of worry grew in stomach, unfurling like a fresh sprout. "This person," she said, "has made one too many mistakes. If I were no one, I could erase them."

She couldn't know it, but that was all Stone wanted too. It's why he was here. Why he was determined to find Ravki–find *astra*. It was why he made the terms to get the others out of prison before they came. All they wanted was to be somebody forgotten, erased from memory, so they could finally have a fresh start.

"So what do you say, tonight we're no one?"

"Sure." He stroked his hand down her back, settling on the crook of her hip. "I could be nobody with you," he said.

She smiled then and his heart, a wild thing he'd kept caged for a very long time, threatened to escape. Her eyes traced his lips, before she leaned in and met him with a soft kiss. It was brief, barely-there, but he felt it in every ounce of blood flowing in his body, electric.

Pretend with me. Lie to me. Let this desire consume us both.

She kissed him again, stealing his breath. She tasted sweet like dates, her lips were cold, her tongue warm, her body still tangled around his. He could get lost in this–in her. In the past, kissing and intimacy were simply nothing more than a task to be marked done but with Aesira, his heart raced and his overly loud mind quieted and it didn't feel like something he had to do, but *wanted* to do.

Needed to do.

He cupped the back of her head, holding her tightly to him so he could kiss her deeper. Her fingers tangled in his hair, her legs still around his middle. A small voice in the back of his mind reminded him that they were pretending. That she was somebody so far out of his reach. That this wasn't real.

Then her lips met his neck and that voice inside his head went completely quiet and he focused on all the ways her lips moved against his skin, all the things her simple touch did to his body. How it made him feel alive.

There was movement under the water, rippling the surface and brushing against his leg, making him jolt away. "What happened?" Aesira's eyes went wide and then without any warning, she was pulled under the water.

"Aesira!" Stone dropped below the surface, the icy spring water burning his eyes and nose. The dark was endless, only a few shards of moonlight piercing through the water's surface.

Another slither against his leg. He spun, arms fanning around him. Searching and failing. His lungs burned as he broke through the surface, took another large inhale, then dove back under where a serpentine body darted around him. He planted his feet firmly to the bottom of the spring, mud and rocks scraping against his toes.

Thick scales were rough against his chest as the beast circled tighter and tighter. He thrashed in the water, kicking his feet up, up, letting his instincts take hold, until his face breached the surface, just long enough to take a precious inhale, before the monster yanked him back down.

Its snake-like body wrapped around him, its long, dark tongue darting out, pressing against his face, his neck. His head dizzied, his vision blurred. He wouldn't last more than a few minutes, and Aesira...

He fought against the massive beast, finding its gills and punching straight into them, clawing with his nails at the tender flesh of its underbelly. All he needed to do was get away from the beast and stand, break through the surface, fill his lungs. Find her.

Move faster, Stone.

Hit harder.

Never let it go dark.

Dark.

It was so fucking dark, but through the murk and the pain of the water snake tightening around him, he could make out the blurry shape of the moon.

Stand up, Stone.

With new determination, his nails dug deeper until the beast thrashed around him, a gurgled screech leeching from its maw.

He gathered the last of his strength and when the beast opened its mouth, black tongue darting out, he caught it with his hand. Stone twisted the tongue around and around until the screeching bled into his ears and the beast let him go.

He crashed through the surface, a gnawing, endless pain spreading through his chest.

"Aesira!" He scanned the pool, it was eerily still. Calm. As if the water didn't realize what it housed below its depths. The thought had him flying for the shore.

Clawing his way through the rocks, he laid on his back, steadying his breathing enough to jump to his feet. "Aesira!"

The trees groaned, wind curling through their branches, rippling the water across the spring.

"Stone!" His name caught on the wind, but it wasn't her voice. Birdie.

"Stone!" His bare feet slammed against the rocks, but he ran through the pain until he saw her on the distant shore. Aesira laid half in the water, half out, Birdie and Bee clutching her shoulders. Blood dripped from her nose, her curly hair spread out beneath her in a tangled mess.

He pulled her out of the water and wrapped her in his arms, covering her as best he could, rubbing his hands over her arms to warm her.

"Fuck." He examined her face, her arms and legs. "Is she alive?" His pulse pounded up his throat, in his ears.

"Somehow, yes," Bee said. "We heard you scream." She tossed him Aesira's shirt and he placed it over her.

"Aesira," he whispered against her ear.

"She's unconscious." Birdie stood and toed the edge of the water. Stone nearly ripped her back in case the beast was lurking just beneath but Aesira coughed and grabbed all of their attention.

"Commander." He pushed her hair from her forehead. "A rough go?"

A half-hearted smile split across her lips, then she held up a tiny blade, vile green ooze dripping from its edge. "Good thing I had Kamari's pathetic blade."

"Where were you possibly hiding that?" Bee scanned over Aesira's almost naked body, save for her undergarments.

She shrugged then sat up with another wet cough. "Always be prepared."

"I wasn't." Stone's body ached, his lungs still reeling from exertion.

"But you're both alive, that's what matters." Bee offered her jacket to Aesira which she took and draped over her shoulders.

She closed her eyes, her breathing deep so Stone guided her back down until her head rested in his lap. He brushed her hair from her face. "Hey," she said. "Looks like us nobodies have cheated death, again."

Aesira was still asleep as the first beams of sunlight bled through the treetops. Stone was grateful he'd woken up early enough to start packing the camp and still get to steal a few minutes of unbridled staring. Orange light kissed her skin, highlighting the shape of her strong nose and full lips. Small bits of dried blood still lined her nose, making his stomach wretch.

Fuck.

Last night.

They'd been so close to doing something that they'd never be able to take back. If they hadn't been interrupted, who knows how far things would have gone. Who knows how it would have changed things between them.

He'd walked away from her once before, before he really knew her because even then he knew there could never be a future between someone like him and someone like her. She came from a family of power. Royalty. Money.

And he was a rat on the street people like her family were constantly attempting to get rid of.

An insect under pristine boots.

"Good morning," Aesira groaned, rubbing the sleep from her eyes.

"Morning."

She sat up and stretched. Stone joined her. His muscles were stiff from the last several days of travel but the ache reminded him of how far they'd come, how little time they had left until they found Ravki.

"I'm starving." Aesira smiled as Stone handed her a few handfuls of dried meat. "Where are Birdie and Bee?"

"Back at the spring." Aesira stopped mid-bite. "Just filling canteens," he said. "Under no circumstance are they to go in the water." Her shoulders relaxed and she finished her breakfast in silence.

After Birdie and Bee returned, they packed up the rest of the camp and continued on, following the map.

The sun was warm as they set out again and while they hadn't seen any birds, their song drifted on the breeze as it rustled the trees. If he closed his eyes, it'd almost be a perfect day.

Almost.

If it wasn't for the suffocating thoughts swirling in his head.

Stone dragged his feet, buying himself a few minutes alone under the broad span of trees while the other three took the lead.

He believed the map. Believed in the books he'd studied, but a small voice inside of him questioned the practicality of Ravki still being there after all this time. The journey had not been an easy one by any means. The monsters that lived beyond the wall of Vargah seem to thrive in the uncharted west—the Strix, the Dreamweavers, whatever that was last night—but the trek wasn't *impossible*.

With the right resources, an armada could easily conquer the area. Could find the remains of the magical city. The question that infected Stone's mind—as he ate breakfast that morning, as he packed his bag, as he set forth down the other side of the mountains—was why?

Why, if Ravki was real, had it been left unattended all these years?

If the rumors of the magic that dwelled there—the dragons—were real, surely someone would have made this attempt sooner. Certainly someone other than a lone king with a decaying mind.

Why would the king go looking for it now?

It was a parasite burrowing in his brain. *Why, why, why,* it gnawed and chewed and spat and the only way to kill the questions were the answers he didn't have.

No one has attempted to find Ravki, he thought, *because maybe it truly does not exist.*

The terrain changed again, the further they descended from the mountains and away from the desert. The red rocks and trees remained but it was the over abundance of life that stole Stone's breath away. Green-ladden rocks and tree trunks. Green on the ground, soft and spongy. Green in the trees. And not just that—there was more water.

Everywhere they turned, there was water. Flowing freely from the mountainside. In small lakes nestled between the trees. In a bubbling brook that was too reminiscent of the spring with the beast for him to dare to go near it.

They stopped to fill their canteens from a small waterfall off a cliffside, the cool, crisp taste coated his tongue and he thought for a moment what they would have done had they not been so fortunate to find all of this.

Even if it was a miracle that the water existed, it felt wrong to use it. To drink freely from it. To bathe in it.

It was excessive, considering water back home was so rare it brought on war. But here, everything was different. As if this was truly how they were meant to live. Surrounded by birdsong and green trees with heavy leaves that offered shade and shelter and of course, *water*.

Despite the monsters and the freezing nightly temperatures, the world here seemed so far from Vargah. So different from the dry and the dust and the storms.

Stone pulled out his map, sweat beading on his dark brows. He pushed his hair back out of his face, glasses sitting snugly on his nose. "This says we're here."

"What?" Birdie peered at the map over his shoulder. "This is Ravki?" She gestured to the large, open field they were currently standing in, where blades of green rose from the earth in an endless blanket. "Shouldn't there be..." She looked around. "Something here?"

Stone rolled the map and tucked it in his back pocket. He'd checked the map every day since they departed the ship. He calculated the exact time they'd need to spend sleeping and the amount of miles they'd need to walk.

It should be right here, he thought.

It should be here and it isn't.

"Let's keep walking," he said, determination and a stubborn sense of hope fueling his steps. "We've got a few hours left of daylight, we may as well make good use of them."

Even Birdie couldn't argue with that.

The grass, as Stone recalled from one of his books–swayed in the breeze as they trudged through the open field.

As far as they could see, it was nothing but flat, green earth. No ruins like they'd read in Desmond's journal. No semblance of a city whatsoever.

As they walked, Stone realized that the field was not flat like he originally thought. In fact, they were on what seemed to be on the top of a very steep hill. Aesira joined his side and peered down, the wind rustling her dark curls free from her braid, and there at the bottom he could see–

"Ruins," Stone said. "Those are ruins." He looked at Aesira, a grin split across her face that matched his own. "Just like in the king's journal."

"Holy shit." Birdie and Bee joined their side. "They're large enough to swallow the Aquila," Bee said.

Even from where they stood at the top of the hill, Bee was right, the structures were massive. Tall, wide columns surrounded by vines. Domed roofs with broken glass ceilings. Arched windows, overrun with nature.

"Let's go down." Birdie tightened the straps on her backpack. "The sun's getting low." The four of them slid carefully down the hill, the grass acting as a soft landing. The closer they got to the ruins, the thicker Stone's fear felt in his throat, making it more difficult to breathe.

How could the king have known the ruins were here?

And it wasn't just the ruins. It was the moths and the detailed descriptions of the landscape. Everything Stone had read from Desmond's journals matched and that parasite in his mind burrowed further with each unanswered question that presented itself.

When they reached the bottom of the hill, a few stars speckled the sky but Stone hardly noticed them, too distracted with what lay in front of him. It wasn't just one ruin, but dozens, all laid out in a grid-like pattern.

"It looks like a base we have at the Order," Aesira said at his side. "Militant. Looks like every building has a purpose."

Ornate spires, crafted of stone shot from the ground, into the sky. Arches paved the way for what once used to be openings. The crumbling evidence of a city that once was.

Ravki.

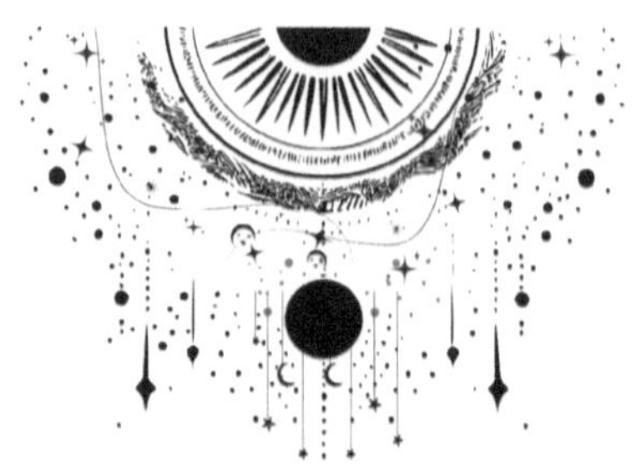

TWENTY-SIX

KAMARI

Naming Day was approaching swiftly and without any more word from Aesira since she and the crew departed the Outpost, Kamari had begun to prepare to face the ceremony alone.

Well, almost alone.

Unfortunately her parents were still there and Raffe and after two attempts to kidnap her, the rotation of knights outside her door was endless. She thought her lack of privacy was a problem before, but now it was nonexistent, giving her hardly any time to read the journals at all.

Hanna handed Kamari her tea then resumed braiding her hair. "I hate to say it, Your Majesty," she said through a sigh, "but your mother has asked me to inform you that Lord Raffe will be joining us this morning."

The tea lingering in Kamari's mouth turned sour.

Of course he would be joining her for breakfast.

Raffe was everywhere. At most of her meals. Sneaking up on her in the library. Waiting for her in the garden. He showed great concern when that woman almost took her from the party and even though they'd made a pact to keep things cordial between them, he'd become too comfortable. Moving about the Citadel like it was already his. Conversing with her parents at such ease she wondered if he forgot they were royalty.

"How is Nev?" Kamari stood and slid into her gown; the violet gauze lightweight in the blooming heat.

"She's..." Hanna's fingers paused on the buttons at Kamari's back. "She's okay."

Nev found Kamari, took that woman into custody, and then swiftly found her way to the temple where she exacted her punishment for failing her post. The thick bands of red across her knuckles proved how severe the Order took failure and whenever Kamari caught a glimpse of the knight, the words *"I'm sorry"* gathered on her tongue, but before she could say them Nev walked away or spoke first or Kamari had a meeting to run off to.

The timing was never right but she needed to say it, should say it, because it was her fault for leaving the party. For not telling Nev where she was.

"Is she on patrol at the wall?" Kamari plucked a pair of jade earrings from the bowl on her vanity and put them on.

"Yes." Hanna busied herself about the room. Tidying and propping up pillows. "She's finally stopped physically punishing herself but I think inside she can't get over the fact that she failed you. Twice. She hasn't laughed in days."

"I can hardly recall her ever laughing at all," Kamari said with a thin smile, hoping to break some of the tension rising in the room.

"She did." Hanna's eyes met hers through the mirror. Her normally joyous face was stern. Unrecognizable. "Only now she's so guarded and I don't know how to help her." She frowned, her full lips hiding a quiver.

The words begged to spill out of Kamari again. *This is my fault,* she wanted to say. Not just because she hid from Nev at the party but because when the woman took her, she didn't fight.

Not at first, anyway.

There was a fleeting moment when she was dragged down the hallway that maybe this was for the best. To be stolen away from her responsibilities. Forget Naming Day and the treaty and her missing husband. Let the sand drown out her demons.

"If I'm being honest everyone seems different now." Hanna smiled tightly, her bright eyes anchoring on the floor.

"Fear always heightens close to Naming Day," Kamari said. She squeezed Hanna's arm, hoping to offer some comfort. "Once it's over, I'm sure everyone and everything will be back to normal." The lie stuck to the back of her throat as she made her way out of the room.

The dining hall was dripping in warmth from the massive windows that framed the room. The long table was already set and the king and queen of Novaria were in their places when Kamari arrived.

"Daughter." Her mother's smile warmed her otherwise stoic face and Kamari forced herself to smile back. The double doors to her right swung open and by the heavy footfalls she had come to recognize, she didn't need to turn to know it was Raffe who joined them.

"You're looking lovely, Your Majesty." He reached for her hand but Kamari slid it into her lap and offered him a smile instead. Raffe smirked and helped himself to the various plates of fruit and pastries that sat on the table.

"If my math is correct," Raffe whispered, piling his plate, "there are two weeks left of your little bargain with the council." He took a bite out of a custard filled pastry, the powdery sugar getting caught in his mustache. Kamari's stomach roiled. She hid her disgust behind her teacup.

"Have you considered my offer?" He gestured between them and the thought of even pretending to be Raffe's wife no longer gave her comfort, but instead gave her a bout of nausea.

"Two weeks is a long time," she whispered, shooting a glance at her parents who were blindly chatting amongst themselves at the opposite end of the table. "I have faith."

Raffe's smile widened but he raised his cup of tea in a sort of cheers before turning and discussing Naming Day with her father.

The conversation around Kamari pulsed in and out.

Naming Day.

Astra.

Desmond.

Her kidnappers.

All topics she wished not to discuss, especially with the people around her. The food on her plate made her stomach clench. When was the last time she'd eaten? She pushed it away and focused on her tea. Closing her eyes, the warmth of the sun settled on her cheeks and the tension in her shoulders relaxed.

"Isn't that right, Your Majesty?" Her eyes snapped open. Raffe's hand was wrapped around her arm so she tugged it free.

"What?"

"That Commander Zeliath won't be joining us for Naming Day." Raffe shot her a pained look.

"Is that true, daughter?" Her father was far enough away his voice was small but she felt his question rake over her skin as if he'd taken claws to her bare arms.

"Kamari," her mother warned. "Where is Aesira?"

Kamari glanced around the table, catching Hanna's eye for a moment as she refilled water glasses. "She's tending to the southern end of the wall."

"Oh bullshit." Her father slammed his glass down, making Kamari jump. "Is that really the best lie you could come up with?" He shook his reddened face. "Lord Raffe, where is my second daughter?"

Other than the soft pelt of sand against the glass windows, silence flooded the room. Kamari's chest burned, her fingers clenching in her lap.

Don't tell them, Raffe.

Don't tell them.

"Commander Zeliath has left Vargah. She and a cadre of criminals headed west to look for King Desmond."

Damn him.

She knew her lies to her parents would only stretch so far, but Raffe had crossed a line.

"West?" Her mother's eyes blew wide, making her look like one of the porcelain dolls she and Aesira played with when they were younger. She wasn't sure if she was scared for Aesira or generally frightened of what might lie in the west.

Likely the latter.

"How dare you send your sister away," her father snapped. "Wait until the General finds out about this."

"She won't find out," Kamari said, "she'll be back in just a few weeks." Her father raged on, ignoring her, chastising her, reprimanding her like she was a child.

They were still acting as though Kamari wasn't there when she stood and slammed her hands against the tabletop.

"Just because my voice is quiet," she said, "does not mean what I have to say isn't important." She glared at her father from across the table. "Lord Raffe, your visit to Vargah has been a pleasant surprise, but you've overstayed your welcome."

Raffe's brows shot up, her father's face burned in her periphery but she poured all of her focus, her unrelenting rage toward Raffe. "When my husband returns, I don't believe he'll be pleased to see his seat taken." She nodded to the chair Raffe had claimed as his own the last few weeks.

"Now if you'll excuse me," she said, smoothing the loose hairs from her face. "I have an address before Naming Day." She turned and spoke only to her parents, ignoring the burning stare from

Raffe. "I'll admit there's much to tell you both," she said, "but now is not the time. If you wish to leave, I will have your things packed at once."

"We're staying." Her father rose from his seat and joined her on the other side of the room.

She couldn't look at his face, didn't care to see this broken version of herself reflected back at her through his eyes. She focused instead on a brooch of the Novarian crest, a waterfall to mimic Piscis Spring, pinned to his left lapel.

"Whatever is going on with your husband," he whispered so only she could hear, "I will get to the bottom of it. This treaty will not dissolve simply because you are incapable of doing your job."

Admittedly, confronting her parents and Raffe right before the public address was not Kamari's finest idea.

Her nerves were rattled, leaving her open and exposed as she stepped onto the balcony that overlooked the square where hundreds of Vargahians waited for her. Some cheered as she waved, a soft smile fixed on her lips, most others booed or shouted profanities.

"Where is King Desmond?"

"Traitor queen!"

Being called an enemy queen was not uncommon in the year she'd been here, but traitor was new and for some reason the word pricked her skin and left her heart bleeding.

She inhaled a deep, dry, breath and braced her hands on the iron railing of the balcony. "Naming Day is almost upon us." Her knuckles ached around the hot metal. "Let us pray together." She lowered her head, beads of sweat dripping down her spine. "Celestria, Goddess of All, we call upon you to hear our prayers—"

A loud crack against the railing startled her. She looked down to see a rock the size of her fist had flown from the crowd, rattling the iron bars. Kamari's head whipped up and Nev was there, just in time, before another rock pelted through a window, shards of glass spewing onto the tile floor.

"Murderer!" several people shouted as more rocks flew onto the balcony. Nev blocked her body, shielding her own head with her arm. "You killed King Desmond!"

"The treaty is broken!"

"They want our *astra*! Our water!"

"Death to Novaria!"

Nev escorted Kamari inside as dozens of stones flew onto the balcony, some crashing through the window, others making it all the way into the foyer. With wide eyes Kamari stared and listened as the people of Vargah—*her* people—turned on her.

"Let's get you out of here." Raffe slid his hand around her waist and led her through the Citadel. Kamari's mind was blank, her body numb.

Voices echoed through the Citadel. Voices of Desmond's people, her people. Now they wanted her dead.

Did they not see how she missed Desmond, how she longed for his homecoming? Raffe's hand tightened around her as they descended the stairs and the weight of him, the pressure of his hand burned through her gauzy dress. She wriggled free from his grip. "I thought I told you to leave."

Raffe opened his mouth, but Rahashi and Nev stepped forward and escorted Kamari the rest of the way to her room.

Of course they see me as a traitor, she thought. She'd been walking with Raffe. Dancing with him. Dining with him. She thought she was doing good for the treaty, making it appear things were running smoothly by keeping a Vargahian heir close.

She was doing her best not to raise panic and all the while, she was undermining her own standing.

The people saw her unaffected by Desmond's disappearance because she thought that was better than to see a queen panicked.

She was wrong.

Hanna was waiting outside her door, waving her inside.

She slid out of her dress and into her pants and long tunic. The open curtains gave her a view of the heated crowd and the mass of knights and sentries that were making arrests and ushering the rest away. She could hear them still, all the things they claimed her to be.

An enemy queen.

A murderer.

A *traitor.*

The bell in the square chimed again, signaling a storm approaching and Kamari wanted to claw at her ears. Bury her face under a pillow and hold her breath. Anything to make that damn noise and the sounds of the people below chanting their hatred for her, stop.

She slammed her window shut and when she spun back around, the journal she was reading earlier was opened to where she'd left off. She swallowed her tears and flipped to the last passage.

"Finding it will eliminate the need for the sacrifice. Will give power back to the people. All of these years, I believed the voices in my head to be a burden but now I see them for what they are. A gift, perhaps from Celestria herself, guiding me to the truth of astra. The truth that was meant to burn in the great fire of Vargah. The truth that was eliminated in the Great War. The truth, that Ravki is real."

The words became rushed together, messily scratched onto the parchment.

"I don't have much time to get my thoughts out. I have been advised to not seek that which has been buried. I don't know what I will do, but I know that I have to do something. Kamari, know that I love you. Know that I am doing this"

The rest of the page and journal were blank.

Kamari's head swam with a million thoughts. Desmond truly believed *astra* was something that grew from the earth? And he believed it to be in Ravki, which explained the maps she found and hundreds of notes. Why wouldn't he tell her where he was going? Why wouldn't he tell the council–

Her eyes darted to the top of the page, where he always wrote the date of his entries.

This one was marked the day before he disappeared. The night she'd found him yelling in his study. The night he had kissed her then left her.

I have been advised to not seek that which has been buried.

Advised by *who?*

"Nev," she yelled and her knight came bounding through the door.

"Are you alright?"

"What if I told you *astra* was something that..." She threw the journal across the room where Nev caught it. "What if it grew from the earth? That it wasn't a gift from Celestria." Kamari clutched her chest, the rapid rising and falling bringing her a constant to focus on. "Would you believe me?"

Nev flipped through the journal and Kamari knew what the knight saw. The ramblings of a mad man. The drawings and scribbles and nonsense, but hidden beneath there was so much more than that.

"I would say that's heresy, Your Majesty." Nev's eyes were cautious as they watched her, a dark look sweeping over her face.

"Yes." Kamari snapped her fingers. "Exactly."

Nev shook her head and tossed her back the journal. "I don't understand."

"Heresy. Blasphemy." She took in a large breath, opening the journal again to Desmond's last entry. "All punishable by death."

I have been advised to not seek that which has been buried.

Death.

Kamari's throat wrapped around the word until she felt like she might choke.

If Desmond told someone about his suspicions, if he told the council what he believed to be true...

"Desmond did not leave me to find Ravki," she said. "Because"—she crossed the room and slammed the journal into Nev's chest—"he did not *leave* at all."

The adrenaline of realizing that Desmond didn't leave her on a some perilous quest was quickly drowned by the fact that if Desmond told anyone about what he thought about Ravki and *astra*, then he was, in fact, dead.

Twenty-Seven

Aesira

Massive columns framed crippling stone steps that led inside one of the abandoned buildings. Aesira squinted, daylight was being chased away by night, but with what was left of it she could see an engraving, Ravkian words carved between the two columns.

"What does it say?" she asked Stone.

"Heed this warning," he read aloud, "those who enter uninvited shall bear death's wish, a burden of unimaginable things, for in you'll find the–" He let out a shaky breath and threaded his hands through his hair. "For in you'll find the heart of the city of lost kings." He shot her a look and she knew he felt it too, the power that emanated from those words. The realization and meaning etched into the stone.

City of lost kings.

Desmond sought a place of lost kings. Her head spun but Stone's gentle graze of his finger on hers anchored her to the present. "You found it," she whispered.

"We all did."

"Well fuck," Birdie said. "And we have to go in there?" They peered into the dark opening of the largest ruin. "How important is *this* lost king, anyway?"

"Bird," Bee warned but the look on her face proved she was just as nervous as Birdie. "What do we do, Stone?"

Aesira peered through the doorway of the ruin again, the Strix and the water beast flashing behind her eyes. She leaned closer, listening for any sign of movement. Singing. Voices. Scuffling from the wind. It was silent save for their own breathing. Even the birdsong they'd become accustomed to was gone.

The dark was endless inside the ruin, pulling her in. Luring her.

"Commander?" Stone's finger brushed against hers again.

Her vision focused, like a band snapping, as she came back to the present. "Birdie and Bee, stay back and make camp," she said. "There's no sense in all of us going in tonight." She bumped Stone's arm. "You and I will go in, and tomorrow at daybreak we'll explore the rest." He nodded, his eyes tracing back to the doorway.

"Uninvited?" Birdie shook her head with a laugh. "You're going to ignore that message?"

"It's ancient, likely meant to scare off thieves." Stone slid off his pack and handed it to Bee. "It doesn't mean anything."

Birdie let out a low whistle. "Suit yourself."

"Take a quick glance around the area then make a fire and stay put." Aesira slid her pack off as well and dropped it on the ground.

"We'll go in, look for any signs of Desmond, and be back out in an hour."

"One hour," Stone mimicked.

Green, serpent-like vines wrapped around the columns, tangling over the steps. Aesira was careful where she placed her boot, trying her best not to disturb the life growing there. It was so precious, to see so much growing from the ground, when back home was so barren.

She and Stone tip-toed into the building, a single torch in Stone's hand lighting their way. Inside, more vines swept across the walls, wrapping around the columns that held the ancient building up. Pebbles and loose rocks kicked under their feet, echoing through the vast room.

"Where did the birds go?" She clutched Stone's arm.

"The birds?" He held the flame higher. "I haven't seen any."

"But you heard them? All day yesterday and even today. And now they're just...silent?"

Something crunched under Aesira's boot and the sound and feeling was so painfully familiar, flashes of the Strix in Dire blurred her vision, she was afraid to look down.

"It's after sunset," Stone said. "The birds are asleep."

Aesira pointed toward the back of the building where another large arch opened up into a small room. "Let's try this way." Moonlight crept over the walls and onto the floor from a huge crack in the ceiling. More crunching under their boots and when Aesira braved a look she was relieved to see, it was a mix of broken glass and dead twigs.

No bones.

No discarded limbs.

The torch filled the small room with warm light but it was more of the same. Crumbling ruins. Leafy vines. Broken glass. But there, in the center, was a lone short column with a glass case on top and inside the case, sat a single, glowing gold flower.

Stone propped the torch against the wall and the two of them together circled the small, domed case. "What is it?" she asked. The flower glowed faintly, pulsing every now and then, reminding her of the Lunaris moths and their wings.

"I think it's *astra*." Stone knelt on the ground, putting his face as close to the glass case as he could without touching it.

Aesira's brows pinched. "*Astra* isn't gold. It's purple."

"How can you be sure?" Stone looked up at her from where he knelt.

She'd only seen *astra* once, when she first was stationed in Vargah.

There was an incident with one of the water workers and Aesira was called in to manage the situation. He had been attempting to steal extra water for himself. He was so desperate, she remembered, he pleaded with her that he needed it for his family, to get through the next few days until Naming Day, but she had arrested him anyway. Threw him in jail and handed off the key like it was as normal as reading the morning parchment. The water reservoirs were kept in the same vicinity as the *astra* reservoirs, and because she was curious, she peeked.

The *astra* flowers were similar to the one in the case, only the ones in Vargah shone purple, not gold. Which is why, she assumed, Vargah had chosen purple as their city colors centuries ago. To match the magical flower from Celestria.

"I saw it once in Vargah when I first arrived." Skipping the details of how. How heartless she had been to that man who was only trying to save his children. "There's a mural in the temple, it shows Celestria balancing the moon and *astra* as well. It's purple."

Stone shrugged. "Only one way to find out." He moved to lift the case but Aesira slapped his hand.

"Don't! What about the warning outside? Surely this isn't sitting here just for us."

Stone glanced around the vacant, decrepit room. "Who is it for then?"

The light of the glowing flower flickered, drawing both of their attention. "Someone put this here for a reason is all I'm saying," she said. "It feels wrong to disturb it."

"Fair enough," Stone said, grabbing the torch. "Let's keep walking then."

As wrong as it felt to disturb the flower, it felt more wrong to leave it. She could admit that while the color was not the same as the *astra* she saw in Vargah, the flower was unsettlingly similar. A taut line pulled at Aesira's middle, drawing her back to the golden flower, but Stone trudged forward with the torch so she ignored the tightness in her stomach and followed him into the dark.

TWENTY-EIGHT

STONE

Stone and Aesira's boots crunched against more dead twigs and glass and bits of stone from the crumbling pillars. Green vines and plants grew through every tiny crevice, small slivers of light seeping in through the cracks in the walls. There was so much to see. So much to study. All of the plants and the flowers and ruins, Stone could stay perched here all day with his notebook.

But, with everything they'd seen, there was no sign of the king.

"We've been walking for almost thirty minutes," Stone said, "which tells me this building stretches farther back than I anticipated. We should start heading back before Birdie and Bee begin to worry."

Aesira's face scrunched. She did not like the sound of that, Stone gathered, but he could tell in the deep sigh she released and the resolve of her shoulders that she agreed with him.

"You're right," she said. "By the time we make it back, our hour will be up."

He followed behind Aesira, using the torch to find their way toward the entrance all the while he couldn't stop fixating on the details in the ways she moved.

The breaths she took, the faces she made and the observations surprised him. Not because they were unpredictable, but because he had learned so much about her in such a short time. It surprised him that he cared to learn so much about her.

He was so wrapped up in his own thoughts, he failed to see a large crack in the floor. He tripped, sending himself and the torch flat against the hard ground.

"Are you alright?" Aesira pulled him up.

"Just wasn't paying attention." She still clung to his shoulders and the weight of her hands on him was another thing that surprised him. How much he liked it. Craved it. He opened his mouth, no plan as to what to say, but knowing that he wanted to say *something* when she turned abruptly and bent to grab the torch from the ground.

Stone's stomach dropped. What was his problem? He had never let anyone get this close before, why the hell would he think it was a good idea now?

"Stone." Even that, her saying his name, was enough to send a lightning strike through his chest. "Look at this." Aesira was still kneeling on the ground, holding the torch outwards.

Rocks bit through Stone's pants as he kneeled beside her. Aesira swept away the loose vines that were shriveled and brown and underneath, there was—

"It's a hatch." Aesira ran her fingers over a bronze, circular handle. The metal was worn in places, likely from use, and attached to it was a wooden hatch. "Where do you think this goes?"

Stone surveyed the room, something prickled at the back of his neck. Like he was being watched. "I don't know," he said. "But we should keep moving. We can come back tomorrow."

"Stone, we're right here." She pulled on the handle. It didn't budge. "We have to check it out. What if there's a clue about Desmond inside? What if *Desmond* is inside? An underground hatch would be the perfect place to hide, don't you think?"

Hide from what?

Stone's stomach knotted. Any other place, he would have said fuck it and threw the hatch open himself. But a sharp feeling, with teeth and watchful eyes, tore at his middle. "What happened to 'it's not here for us'. We should leave it alone just like we left the flower alone."

"That was different," she said. "Desmond wasn't going to be hiding under that glass case." She tapped the door again. "But he could be in here." His mind flashed to the spring, to the black water and to Aesira on the shore.

"I don't want you to get hurt again." He grabbed Aesira's arm and tugged her closer. He hadn't admitted how much it bothered him that night, thinking he might have lost her but he couldn't stand the thought of anything happening to her.

She cocked her head to the side, her smile illuminated by the warm light of the torch. "You worried about me, smuggler?"

"Something like that."

Her arms wrapped tighter around his middle. "I'll make you a deal. We'll just take a peek at the bottom, if nothing's there, we turn around. Save any further exploration for tomorrow. Deal?"

He didn't like it, but he knew her well enough to know she wasn't going to change her mind and the alternative was her going in alone, which absolutely wasn't going to happen. "Fine," he said. "Deal."

She handed him the torch and knelt before the hatch. The handle released a loud groaning sound that echoed through the empty chambers of the ruins.

Dust and moths fluttered up from a deep, inky chasm in the ground.

"I need the torch." He stepped closer and angled it over her shoulder, the pathetic flame barely lighting enough to see the rickety ladder bolstered to the inside of the hole. The bottom was nowhere in sight, the darkness was seemingly endless and that feeling in his gut, the one that was hungry enough to eat him from the inside, began gnawing at his sides.

Aesira tied off her hair at the nape of her neck. "I'll go down first."

"You can't be serious."

"Stay here then," she said. "Be the lookout. I need to check for Desmond."

Fuck that.

If she was going, so was he. Stone angled the torch in a way that she could better find her footing. On the first step, the ladder creaked, more moths scattered through the opening. "Just go slow."

She smiled up at him, half her body now inside the hatch. "Yes, darling."

Stone groaned. "Commander, if you're going to call me pretty names can you at least save it for when you're in my bed and not climbing to your certain death?"

Her faint laugh echoed up the hatch. "Sorry, *darling*."

"I'm serious," he said, heat rising to his cheeks, the back of his neck. "Pay attention to your footing, you don't know how old that ladder is."

Her sigh drifted up through the hatch and settled around him. "Scared of a little adventure, Odega?" Another step down. Another damning creak.

Scared of whatever is sure to be lurking at the bottom, he thought. *Scared of the teeth ripping through my stomach.*

Once Aesira was fully on the ladder, he handed her the torch and began his descent. Slowly, one unstable rung at a time, they made it to the bottom. The light from the torch flickered across cracked walls. Dead vines wove through the room, tangling with forgotten webs. More moths fluttered in the air, circling around the light of the torch. Stone covered his mouth with the back of his hand as dirt kicked up beneath their boots.

"Over here," Aesira whispered but her voice carried through the chamber as if she were yelling.

That's what they were in.

A chamber.

Every which way they turned was a different tunnel. Each one full of shadows and a promise of a disastrous end. The tunnels were wide, easily enough space for the entire crew to walk shoulder to shoulder, proving the expanse of not just this ruin, but of Ravki.

If the king was hiding here, it would be almost impossible to find him.

"Stone, look." Aesira held the torch to a wall where symbols were etched into the granite. "What does it say?"

He wiped the dust off his glasses and stole the torch from Aesira so he could hold it closer and get a better look. The symbols were carved deep. Large swirls followed by small triangles.

Runes.

"This is ancient Ravkian," he said, sweeping his finger over a large rune. "Protection." He swept his hand across the ancient wall, scattering a few loose pebbles to the ground. "And this"— his fingertips brushed against the largest rune—"is for light."

"Protection and light."

He nodded. "Protection, light"—his fingers were frenzied, running across the wall—"Harmony, peace, balance. Magic." His eyes darted to hers for a moment before he moved to the last rune where his fingers stilled, ice splintering through his veins, that monster in his gut opening its maw and ripping at his middle.

"What is it?" Aesira traced the rune in front of them. "Stone?"

"*Drako.*" The Ravkian word rolled off his tongue, lit a fire to something deep in his belly. "Dragon."

Aesira stiffened next to him, lacing her fingers with his. "We should look a little further." She made to walk away but he pulled her back.

"Something isn't right here. It doesn't look like anyone's been here in years. It's unlikely Desmond—"

She pulled her hand away. "I just need a few more minutes," she said. "I have to be sure he's not here."

She grabbed the torch and spun toward one of the hallways.

"Aesira, you're wasting your time."

She stopped, her boots digging into the ground, dust and dirt billowing out from beneath them.

"There are no boot prints other than our own," Stone said. "The dust on the ladder was inches thick." He took a tentative step toward her. "I'm not saying he isn't in Ravki, I'm just saying he isn't *here*. There are dozens of other buildings, Aesira. He could be in any one of them."

She spun so quickly the fire on the torch flickered, nearly going out. "He has to be," she said, "and I have to find him."

She closed her eyes, her shoulders slumping forward. "I can't go back without him. I can't fail again." She bit her lip on the last word, like she didn't mean to say it. "We don't have time to comb through each building. It would take weeks." She threw her arms wide and spun around. "Look at them! They're massive, Stone. The search would be endless."

"Then we return to Vargah and have your sister send a larger crew."

Her laugh was humorless. An empty, cold, sound that raised the hair on his arms. "You don't know anything, Odega."

Stone gently grabbed her hand, untangling it from where she gripped her hair. "So then tell me."

She shook her head and spun back toward the tunnel. "If I return to Vargah empty handed, my father will disown me. More than he already has."

"I don't understand."

"I made a mistake," she said so quietly Stone almost missed it. "When we were all children. I made a mistake and it ruined my family. It ruined me." Aesira lowered the torch and faced Stone. "I can't afford to keep making mistakes. To keep disappointing and hurting people. I have to find Desmond. I have to get this right. Kamari will be out of time. The treaty will be abolished. War will be back in Vargah and Novaria before we know it." Hurt flashed across her face, in her eyes, in the tightness of her mouth.

Stone wouldn't have that.

"The very fabric of my being is stitched together by my mistakes," he said. "It doesn't mean I don't deserve a chance at a future. It doesn't mean you don't either."

Silence hung around them as she watched him. Her face morphing between sadness and resolve. Then, she stepped forward, her arms snaking around his middle, her face pressed against his chest. "Thank you."

His hand found its way to the back of her head where he anchored her in place. "For what?"

She looked up and he had to fight against the urge to thread his fingers through her hair and keep her close.

"I just think I've needed to hear that for a very long time," she said. To his pleasure, she pressed her cheek back into his chest, her voice muffled through the fabric of his shirt. "Eldrin was only nine when he died. We were huddled together in our safe room. Kamari, Eldrin, and I. We were meant to stay put. Stay quiet. He heard the singing first and wanted to follow it. Kamari tried to stop him, but I let him go. I opened the door. I dared him to look."

The beating in his chest slammed against his ribs and he wondered if Aesira could feel the way his heart overworked when she was close to him.

"The Strix was waiting on the other side. It flew so fast, he was gone before I could even scream." She pressed her face deeper into his chest, so he held her closer, one hand around her waist and the other against the back of her head.

"I was sent to the Order that same year and if I fail this, I'm done," she said. She peeled herself away, letting the spot against his heart grow cold. "The Order has already stationed me elsewhere but if I don't make this right, I'll be forced to hang up my armor. Forced to join the temple. Live a life of solitude." A broken smile spread across her lips. "Pathetic, right. The great Aesira Zeliath."

Her dry laugh rang down the cavernous tunnels. "I'm a fraud. My reputation is built on desperately trying to please others in the hopes of burying my own mistakes. I thought coming here I'd be able to find a part of myself worth saving. Be this great person so many others see but the truth of who I am—a reckless, broken girl with horrible habits of hurting those she cares about—can't be outrun."

He swallowed hard against the lump in his throat. "If you are a fraud, then we are the same." Her face twisted, then a deep, nefarious growl cut through one of the tunnels, splintering the stone in the wall of runes.

"What was that?" Aesira clutched his arm.

Another growl shook the ground beneath their boots, vines quaking on the walls.

"Run." Stone grabbed her hand as she ditched the torch. The ladder creaked and wobbled.

Another low growl from the hallway. Closer. Louder. "Quickly," he said, pushing Aesira up, the ladder shaking beneath the weight of them.

The ceiling shook, rocks tumbling to the ground, slicing into their arms and legs on the way.

"Almost there," Aesira said.

She reached the top, pulled herself up. Stone was a few rungs behind, another ear-splitting roar reverberated up the tunnel. Stone's hands gripped the opening, Aesira's fingers pulling at his shirt, when the last rung gave way, making him slip farther down. "Stone!"

He caught himself, pulled himself up and out of the opening just before one of the rungs on the ladder snapped and they slammed the hatch shut.

"A dragon?" Bee's honey eyes were wide as they sat around a campfire. "A real dragon?"

"We don't know if it was a dragon." Stone tossed a stick into the fire. Another headache was brewing behind his eyes but he was thankful that whatever feeling had gnawed at his stomach in the tunnels had disappeared. "We didn't actually see anything but whatever it was, it was not happy we disrupted it," he said. Aesira glanced at Stone through the flames. The firelight mixed with her eyes, kissing her skin in warmth.

They hadn't talked since they fled the hatch, hurriedly told Birdie and Bee to find a campsite as far from the ruins as possible, and now they were here. Not saying what they should be saying.

We almost died, again. You told me your secrets now let me tell you mine.

"I guess we can rule out that the king is not anywhere underground." Birdie wrapped her arm around Bee's shoulder. "A small blessing."

"I'll take the first shift," Aesira said. Birdie and Bee found a place to curl up and Stone should have left too, should have found somewhere quiet to close his eyes until it was his shift, but he couldn't find the strength to leave her alone. Not after what she told him underground. When she noticed he was still next to her, she sighed and bumped his shoulder. "Go to bed," she said. "I have this."

"I'm not tired." It was a lie. He was exhausted but he wrapped his fingers around hers and held her hand tightly. "I wanted to tell you something, before..." He shook his head. "Well before whatever that was, interrupted us." She stroked her thumb along the back of his hand, he savored the gentle notion. "I've seen Ravki before."

Aesira studied his face and he wanted to shrink against her burning eyes. She was so beautiful. Powerful. Leagues above him, but she was also right here, still holding his hand, and maybe that meant more than he would allow himself to believe.

"What do you mean?"

He was grateful for the crackling fire and the hooting of what he assumed to be owls in the background. All the noises covered up the unnatural pounding of his heart. "About ten years ago, I was desperate to get away from Vic. To get the cadre out. So I went to Soo and drank her tea." Their eyes met and something quiet like hope blossomed in his chest. "The same one we drank before."

"And it showed you Ravki?"

"It showed me a woman with dark curly hair. Mismatched eyes." He ran a hand down his face. "You were standing in an open field of endless green and all around you were golden flowers. I didn't know what the dream meant at the time. Didn't know you even existed. I figured her tea didn't work." He took in a labored breath. "Then I saw you at the Phoenix." He stole a glance her way but she was watching the fire, brows pinched. "There wasn't any mistaking who you were."

"But the tea points you to what you desire most..." Her voice faded, as if she had answered the question before she even asked it. "If you didn't even know me, how could you dream of me?"

"I don't know. It's why I pulled away at the Phoenix, why I left. I didn't know if what was happening was real or a dream but I want to make one thing clear." He gripped her chin, softly pulling her toward him until their eyes met. "I didn't walk away because I didn't desire you, I walked away because of how badly I *did*." His eyes dipped to her mouth and his body remembered just what it was like to have those lips on his skin.

He'd learned it was a dangerous thing to want, to desire things that were too good for him. Which is exactly how Stone found himself, still. Both wanting and desiring a woman who was too far out of reach. A dangerous game, one that he knew he'd never win, but that wouldn't stop him from trying. If there were odds to beat, he'd find a way. "I still do," he said. "Desire you."

He dropped his hand from her chin but she didn't pull away from his gaze. "And the golden flowers from your dream? Did you know what they were?"

A log popped in the fire, sending embers of light into the air. "I had a good idea of what I thought it could be," he said.

A beat of silence save for the crackling of the fire and the pounding of Stone's heart. "This has never been about finding Desmond for you, has it?"

"No." He turned so their faces were close. Noses nearly brushing. "I mean, not at first, but I care about it now. About finding him."

"Why?"

He assumed she already knew, but it was like she wanted to hear him say it. Needed to hear him say it. He wrapped his finger around a loose spiral curl.

"I care because *you* care."

Twenty-Nine

Aesira

The fire burned and the wind groaned through the trees, but she couldn't take her eyes off of him.

He reached out, drawing a line down her jaw, tracing her lips with his fingertips. She shuddered. "I'm sorry I didn't tell you about finding *astra*," he said.

She reared back and the curl that was wrapped around his finger sprang free.

"You don't owe me anything." The truth doused her heated skin. "We hardly know each other." There, she said it. The words built a new wall between them, taking the place of the others that had been shattered over the last few weeks.

It was better this way, she reminded herself. Her time in Vargah would be over the moment they returned. She would go wherever the Order deemed fit. Whether that be the temple or a new station. She would bury the truth about Ravki and Celestria and she would live the remainder of her life stuck in a loop of constant regret.

"I don't think that's true," Stone said, interrupting her thoughts. He flicked a loose leaf into the fire. "I know that you take your duties seriously." Aesira snorted. Anyone who was a knight took their duties seriously, she wanted to say but didn't have a chance, because Stone kept talking. "I know that pride and family mean more to you than anything. I know you like your tea ungodly sweet–" She shot him a glare which made him smile. His hands drifted back to hers. "I know you have many regrets and you never let yourself forget them."

He leaned forward and pressed his forehead to hers. "I know the way your lips feel against mine and the noises you make when my hands are on you." Her stomach dipped. Skin heated. "I know the way you frown when you sleep and smile when you wake. Like you're relieved to realize you were only dreaming." He leaned back just far enough so he could see her face, using his thumb to tilt her chin up. "I know you like it when you catch me staring at you. I know you like when I touch you."

A broken smile slashed across her face when she thought of all the ways she knew him too, then it quickly disappeared when she remembered who she was. Who he was. "There's nothing wrong with a bit of sweetener in tea." Stone's laugh rumbled deep in his chest and Aesira felt it travel across her skin and down to her toes.

"Perhaps our biggest disagreement, Commander."

A silence fell between them; just the flames and the wind and the noises Aesira was sure would keep her up the whole night. There were so many things she could say to Stone. So many things maybe she should say, but the only words she could think of were, "I do like you." A blush crept across Stone's cheeks, a small smile begging to unfurl across his lips. "But that scares me."

The smile vanished and his shoulders sank and Aesira wondered if she had ever said anything right in her entire life.

"I know." Stone's hand was still wrapped in hers, their bodies still pressed tight. "But there aren't any rules out here, remember?"

"I suppose you would like that." He laughed again and Aesira committed the sound to memory.

"I like that here I'm not an Odega," he admitted. "I'm just someone passing through." Aesira sat up straight and stared at him.

"I like that out here I don't have to be tame," she admitted. "I can just *be*." Aesira nestled into Stone's shoulder. It was a nice thought, imagining a world without walls. Without sacrifices. Without punishments.

"I have to ask you something," Stone said. Aesira peeled herself away from him so she could see his face. "If you had known who I was that night at the tavern..." He watched her and through his glasses, she could see the worry in his eye. "If you knew I was an Odega, would you have let me kiss you?"

Her heart sped up, the guise of who she pretended to be was slipping, slipping. Noble. Fair. Just. But she was none of those things, not really.

"You know what"— he shook his head at her silence—"don't answer that. It was an unfair question and I shouldn't have asked."

"I knew who you were," she blurted out. "That's why I..." She bit her tongue. How could she explain that she pursued him that night because he was just a rebellious itch to be scratched? A way to lash out from the strict demands of the Order constantly pulling her in whatever direction it pleased. Stone was a distraction. A way to push back against the rules that defined her.

"I see." A muscle flexed in his jaw as he focused his attention on the fire.

Did he see? Was he now realizing there wasn't much good left in her? That she was something rotten masquerading as something noble? "I was using you," she said. "I was upset that the Order sent me a new station. Upset that every moment of my life was—*is*—dictated by someone else." Stone sat silent next to her but his eyes softened and he leaned closer.

"I'm sorry," she said. "I just wanted to make a choice that was completely my own and I saw you sitting there. With your goggles pushed up in your hair and the grease on your hands and you were laughing at something someone said. Then, you looked right at me and then immediately away and I knew you must be trouble."

He smiled, the light returning to his eyes.

She didn't want the new wall between them to grow any stronger. Not when they were just admitting to each other how they felt. Not when she was just admitting to herself how she felt.

She wanted to tear the whole fucking wall down until there was nothing between them at all, but she couldn't lie to him. She didn't *want* to lie to him. Whatever this was growing between them, she didn't want to ruin it like she had ruined everything else in her life, even if all they had was this trip. Even if they had to pretend.

He pulled her hand, urging her into his lap. Her legs straddled either side of him, chills snaking down her spine as his hands worked their way under her shirt, ghosting across the bare skin of her back. "Commander," he said, "if there's anyone I wouldn't mind being used by, it's you." He kissed one side of her neck. Then the other.

"And for what it's worth, I don't want you tame," he said. "I want you wild and fierce and terrifying." He punctuated each word with a kiss and her heart leapt to her throat as his hands slid lower, wrapping around her hips and pushing her tighter to him until their bodies melded together. "I'm at your mercy." A small scrape of teeth against her throat followed by another kiss. "So use me. Lie to me. Break my fucking heart. I should be so lucky." He kissed her lips before pulling back. Giving her a chance to say no. To walk away.

"Who will we be tonight?" She smiled, lacing her finger around the back of his neck. "A painter, a sculptor, a rogue debutante?"

Anyone but Commander, anyone but Odega.

"I'll be whoever you want me to be, Aesira."

She ran her fingers through his hair. "Tonight, I am a runaway and you are my bounty hunter."

"Oh?" His arms tightened around her. "Does that mean I finally get to use those?" He tapped the restraints on her hip.

"If you can catch me."

She jumped out of his lap and sprinted away, making sure to head in the opposite direction of the ruins. She could hear him behind her, the fire in the background fading as she wove around a group of trees, finding one to hide behind.

Anticipation curled in her stomach as Stone's boots crunched through the fallen twigs on the ground. His breathing was heavy and she wondered if it was because of the run or the reward that'd be waiting if he caught her. He took another step, inches away, before she bolted again.

Darting around another tree, Stone's footsteps faded behind her. She slowed her pace, giving her lungs a break, when a large hand wrapped around her wrist, pulling her to the ground.

Stone fell on top of her, his chest heaving, pushing into hers. "Caught you." He slid her other arm up, pinning both wrists above her head. "Awfully pretty for a runaway."

Her lips crashed into his, a new fierceness blooming in her chest. He loosened his grip on her wrists so she could pull her hands free. She snaked them through his hair, holding him as close to her as she could. Stone's lips were demanding. Desperate. His hands grabbed at her, the rough calluses scraping across her skin. She rolled her hips forward, looking for any kind of friction, any way to be closer to him. He cupped the back of her neck and kissed her again.

His lips trailed over her neck, her chest, her mouth. She rocked her hips up again and Stone moaned, like he was in agony. But she was too. Agony that there were too many barriers between them. Clothes and layers and weapons. Duties and demands and stations. Pleasure and need pulsed between her legs as Stone rocked against her and she against him.

"Stone," she whispered against his ear and she felt his body shake. He climbed off of her so they were side by side. Then, slowly, his fingers trailed down the front of her shirt.

"Do you like when I kiss you here?" He kissed a line down her throat, coaxing a moan out of her. "What about here?" He pulled her shirt down just enough to kiss over her chest.

"What else happened in your dream?" His lips paused against her skin, his hands tensing around her hips.

"How about I make you a promise," he said, sliding his hand lower, lower, her breath hitched when he stopped right at the edge of her pants. "When we get back to the ship, I'll show you everything that happened in my dream."

The need for him to touch her was growing so desperate, she clawed her nails into his arm just to keep from touching herself. He kissed her pulse then his fingers dipped below her pants and she closed her eyes.

More, she heard herself saying. She needed more. More time. More of him. More everything.

He slid his fingers slowly, circling, building her up. It was more than they'd ever touched before, and still it wasn't enough. "When was the last time someone made you feel good?" His whispered words were warm against her chilled skin.

Right now, she wanted to say because truthfully she couldn't remember. All other thoughts flew right out of her head, all she could focus on was his hand, right now.

She sucked in a sharp breath as Stone dipped his fingers into her, his lips pressing against her neck. "A long time," she admitted, then he kissed her again, hard enough that when they broke apart she gasped for air. His lips tipped up, his scar pulling taut.

"I want to touch you," she said but Stone was busy, his fingers moving and lips kissing, the weight of his body pinning her to the ground. In this game, he was in control.

A distraction, she once thought of Stone. Just a distraction. Then his fingers circled that spot that made her see stars and he whispered all the things he wanted to do to her, all the ways he pictured having her and she knew there was no going back after this.

They had been through so much in so little time and even though she wanted to, she couldn't deny how she felt. Couldn't deny that when he kissed her, it felt *right*. She'd show him the broken parts of her, all of her ugly truths, and he desired her anyway. Even if it would never end well, even if their lives were more opposite than night and day, even if they had to pretend to be other people, at least they had right now.

"*Yes*," she gasped, which earned a moan from Stone, his teeth sinking into her neck, the sound vibrating through her.

She moved her hips in time with the thrust of his fingers, and then she was crashing over the edge. Her breathing came in desperate, heavy pants. When she came back down, he kissed her shoulder, her throat. She smiled and Stone kissed her again, softly, slowly. Like they had all the time in the world. "Not bad, bounty hunter, but you didn't even use the restraints."

A pained look crossed Stone's face. "Oh, fuck," he said through a laugh. "I was too distracted by the beautiful woman underneath me." He moved to button her pants then pulled her to her feet, sweeping her hair from her face, smoothing her shirt. "Don't think I'll forget you giving me permission to tie you up."

"Don't think I won't ask you to." She nipped at his bottom lip.

He smiled and tucked her under his arm. "Where did you come from, Aesira Zeliath, and how do I keep you?"

Her heart skipped as the implication of his words settled around them.

How do I keep you?

She wished she knew the answer.

Stone kept his hand in hers as they walked back to camp and for whatever reason, that felt more intimate than what they'd just done.

Stone stroked her hair and pecked a kiss to the top of her head as she settled in his lap. She knew by the creaking spine that he'd flipped open his book and when he began to read aloud her shoulders relaxed and her mind drifted to some faraway place.

Her eyes grew heavy but when she was about to close them and let Stone's voice lull her to sleep, there was a flicker of light in her periphery. It was bright, luminous. She sat up and rubbed her eyes. Then she saw it. A ball of glowing light floating out of the ruins. Then another. And another. "Do you see that?"

"What is it?" He traced where she pointed across the darkness.

"Are those Lunaris moths?" It couldn't be. They only hatched on the Polaris Ridge, according to Stone. One of the balls of light floated closer, the purple pulsing in the darkness.

"I think it is." Stone held out his hand, a safe landing for one of the tiny moths.

Aesira's eyes went wide. "How are they here?" The tiny moth drifted off of Stone's hand and Aesira followed its path back to the ruins. Her stomach dropped and her breath caught in her throat.

Hundreds.

There were hundreds of them glowing and ascending from the ruins. They floated in swarms, all moving together like a solid beam of light over the open field. Aesira trailed their movements, and when there were enough of them to light up what she thought was an empty field, her mouth fell open. In the distance a deep roar echoed up from the ruins. She gripped Stone's arm, eyes transfixed on the field.

It had transformed under the glow of the purple light from the moths and the moon, highlighting rows and rows of glowing, golden flowers. Just like the one in the ruins.

Astra.

THIRTY

AESIRA

Aesira woke with Stone's arm draped around her middle, his other arm tucked under her head like a pillow.

Birdie and Bee were chatting in the distance–possibly bickering–about how much food they had left. The sun was less intense on this side of the Whispering Mountains, the thick trees acting as a blanket, keeping the bulk of the heat at bay. The air was warm, but not stifling as she peeled herself away from Stone. He was still asleep, his face smooth and brows relaxed. She stood and dusted the dirt from her pants and shirt and joined Bee and Birdie.

"Good morning." Birdie tossed her one of the ration packs. "We only have a few left each which means our stay here can't be long. If we're going to make it back Aquila, we have to save some." She rolled her eyes. "Can thank Vic for that."

"We haven't explored much." Aesira ripped open the bag, wincing at the smell of dried meat. "There's water which means there could be food here."

"I don't trust anything in this place, especially to eat," Bee said.

"It seems to be a pattern," Birdie said, "you, not trusting things." Her eyes narrowed at Birdie as she sipped from her canteen.

"I'm just saying, nothing about it feels natural." Birdie scoffed and Aesira couldn't help but feel there was a large piece of the conversation she was missing. She took her ration pack and found somewhere quiet, under a large tree with thin green leaves and cracked white bark. The wind twisted through her hair, kissing her cheeks. In the distance she could hear the faint bubble of water, from a spring they found.

Aesira couldn't disagree with Bee more. Everything about Ravki felt natural, wonderful. The trees and the green and the abundance of water. Foreign, yes, but not unnatural. Like this was how life was supposed to be and somewhere along the way, they'd messed it all up.

She tore into a piece of the dried meat and rested her back against the tree trunk. The field across from her appeared plain, just as it had yesterday afternoon when they arrived. But last night she and Stone had seen with their own eyes how Ravki transformed under the moonlight, with the Lunaris moths.

They were barely noticeable, balled up so small they looked like seeds, but the *astra* flowers covered every inch of the field. Easily mistaken for grass at first glance.

She couldn't wrap her head around the color though. In Vargah the *astra* reservoirs were purple. She knew she was remembering correctly because she told Kamari they matched her dress perfect-ly.

"Can I sit here?" The deep timbre of Stone's voice startled her, but she made room for him to sit. "It's amazing how different it looks in the daylight." He gestured to the field but she wondered if anything else looked different under the sun instead of the faint light of the moon.

Her, for example. Their choices last night.

"Birdie and Bee said we can't stay long." She forced her mind in a different, safer direction. "I don't know where to start looking for Desmond." She glanced over her shoulder, to the looming ruins behind them. "I certainly don't want to go in there again."

Stone chewed his food in silence, his eyes fixated on the field of *astra*. "We split up. Look for any tracks or traces of someone being here. If we find nothing by nightfall..." He took another bite so she finished the thought for him.

"If we find nothing by nightfall, we leave, with or without Desmond."

He nodded and swallowed down the last bites of his food. "I'm sorry," he said. "Unless we find a reliable food source, we can't burn much time waiting."

Vic and his crew had plundered most of their supplies, including their ration packs, leaving them with the bare minimum. She knew they wouldn't have much time to explore Ravki but it still left a disappointed taste in her mouth.

"And what do we do about that?" She nodded to the field of *astra*.

Stone licked his lips. "We take what we need to get the Aquila back to Vargah without stopping, as planned."

"And nothing else?" It was a cheap, baited question, but she wanted to know the answer.

Stone's very reason for coming on this mission was to see if Ravki was real. See if *astra* grew here, and it did, in abundance, straight from the earth just like he thought. Would he take it, she wondered, and fly out of Vargah for good? With the pardon from Kamari, it would be easy to leave and never look back. To find his way here again and pillage the flower for himself.

"Nothing else." His eyes were still on the *astra*.

A more forceful breeze kicked up, sending a pile of fallen leaves swirling through the air. "What do I tell Kamari?" Stone glanced at her. "About the *astra*, I mean. About Ravki?"

A muscle clenched in Stone's jaw. "What do you want to tell her?"

The golden buds were closed tight, tucked away until they would open under the moon, but the image of them glowing in the field last night hadn't left her mind. How beautiful they were. How much power they held. The last thing she wanted was to risk this place being attacked by the kingdoms–both Vargah and Novaria–which is exactly what would happen. They were two kingdoms starved for power and a discovery like this would bring another war. Peace treaty or not.

"We don't tell her everything," she said, "at least, not right away. Until we can figure out what's best."

Stone bumped her side. "We?" He smiled.

"Yeah." She bumped him back. "We. Unless you don't plan on staying in Vargah." Another cheap question, it burned the tips of her ears, making her feel like a fool.

Stone studied her face, eyes dipping to her mouth.

"If you two are done confessing your love, can we get the hell on with it?"

"Coming, Bird." Stone's eyes stayed glued to Aesira's, that small smile still slashed across his mouth. He leaned in and kissed her temple. "Ready?"

"I'm with you, Stoney," Birdie said.

So much of Ravki was like walking through a dream. The clouds were perfectly puffed and white. The sun was warm but not sweltering. The trees swayed, their green leaves sparkling. The water trickled down the rockfaces, landing in pools of vibrant blues.

There were more ruins than the ones they saw yesterday. Several were smaller, but just as crumbling with vines coiling through the cracks. A few had fallen completely, leaving nothing but piles of rubble.

It was easy to see how the city was laid out before. The main ruins were likely similar to the Citadel, the smaller ruins, where civilians lived. It was a painful dichotomy, seeing the beautiful skies and trees next to collapsed buildings that once housed life. People. But that was war. It was life and it was death and whatever happened to Ravki, it was clear now, it was not a natural extinction.

Aesira and Bee walked for what felt like hours. Through meadows, careful not to disturb the sleeping *astra*, around the ruins, up and over several hills. Everything seemed untouched. No trails or recent tracks. No sign of life, outside of them.

No signs of Desmond.

Her mind bounced between the Strix and the Dreamweavers. Maybe Stone was right, maybe there was a chance Desmond never made it this far. Defeat threatened to swallow Aesira whole, casting her body and mind in a blanket of darkness, when Bee shouted, startling a flock of bright orange birds from a nearby tree.

"Commander! I found something!"

Aesira trotted ahead and met Bee under a massive tree, its branches jutting out in all directions, its leaves large enough to cover her face.

"What?" Aesira followed the line of Bee's finger as she pointed under the expansive tree. Remnants of a camp lay scattered under its wide branches. Old canteens, a ratty blanket, a broken compass. "These are Vargahian steel." Aesira ran her finger along the hilt of one of the blades. It was small enough to fit in the palm of her hand, but the steel she recognized from the weapons room in Vargah. A deep 'V' was engraved right in the center.

Bee picked up another similar blade. "Not Ravkian?"

"No." Aesira pointed to the engraving, despite its age, was clear as day. "These weapons are from Vargah."

"Desmond?"

Aesira pocketed the knife and riffled through the rest of the camp. There was no recent fire or food. The maps were worn and illegible, most of them torn through with age or weather. Even the weapons, including the pocket knives, were dated. "No knight or soldier would carry a weapon like this anymore."

Bee picked up the blanket, sniffed it once, then tossed it back down. "Maybe it's all Desmond could find."

"The king couldn't sport for better survival tools?" Aesira shook her head. "Whoever these belonged to, they've been here for a long time."

Bee's eyes went wide, realization playing across her round face. "Like how long?"

Aesira pulled out the small knife again. The ornate handle was carved, intricate moons and stars etched around the entire hilt. Weapons were not made with so many details, anymore. Artistry had been lost by way of convenience. This was not a new knife, not by years.

"Decades, at least." Something sour spun in her gut. The breeze had stopped and the stillness of the trees and the old abandoned camp now seemed an omen of a different kind. "I don't get it," Aesira said. "How could there have been Vargahian soldiers stationed here?" She handed Bee the canteen.

"Beats me," she said before taking a slow drink. "You're sure the king didn't just swipe some old shit from the armory? Maybe he didn't want anyone to notice anything missing."

"Maybe..." Aesira bit the tip of her thumb, glancing around the camp again. It didn't make any sense. It wasn't just the weapons that were dated, it was *everything*. The maps. The discarded uniform. The compass.

"Or maybe Vargah has been here before." Bee glanced around. "Maybe they're watching us right now." Aesira's lungs froze and the fear must have shown on her face because Bee laughed. "I'm kidding, Commander. If anyone from Vargah had been here recently, this place would have been run dry."

"What makes you say that?"

"The *astra*," Bee said. "Once the word gets out it's here, it'll be a fucking bloodbath."

"And who do you plan to tell?" Aesira straightened, tossing the canteen to the ground. "Because Stone and I decided it was best to keep the *astra* a secret."

"Of course," she said. "We won't tell a soul. Let's walk, I need some air."

"You're outside, Bee." It was no use, Bee trudged ahead, a new determination in her steps.

"First Birdie is pissed at me because I told her we couldn't look in the tunnels." She stomped forward, her boots crushing a cluster of tiny yellow flowers. "Now, you and Stone are making decisions without us? Seems as though our rules mean nothing anymore."

Aesira froze. "What?"

Bee turned to her and what Aesira thought was anger before she realized was maybe more akin to hurt. "I said our rules mean nothing."

"Not that," Aesira said. "Why does Birdie want to look in the tunnels?" Stopping short at the shore of another glassy pool. The reflection of the sun and sky bounced off the lake's surface, casting shards of light across Bee's face. Her sweet, honey eyes narrowed.

"She thinks whatever you and Stone saw might be a clue." She shook her head. "I told her it was insane."

"A clue to what? Whatever's down there, it certainly wasn't Desmond."

Bee picked up a rock and chucked it at the water's surface. Aesira fought the urge to flinch as the still water was disrupted, rippling with the weight of the stone. "A clue to where the dragons went. Where they might be now."

"Why does she want to know that?"

Bee shrugged. "I don't know. She has a weird infatuation with them I guess. Either way, I told her no and now she's pissed."

"And now she's with Stone," Aesira snapped. "We need to go back to the ruins."

"We still have more perimeter."

"Now, Bee!"

Aesira didn't wait for Bee to catch up before she was running as fast as her legs could take her back to the ruins. She didn't stop to catch her breath. Didn't stop to see if Bee had followed. She ran as fast as she could, back to the ruins, because whatever lay beneath them was not meant to be disturbed. Not meant to be awoken.

Thirty-One

Stone

"It's not a good idea, Birdie." Stone gripped the torch, high-lighting the building he and Aesira were in yesterday. The sun was high in the sky but with the thick coverings of moss and vines, it was mostly dark inside the ruins.

"You didn't even go in the tunnels," she said. "You could have missed something." Birdie scoured the floor, wiping away dust and dead vines until she found it.

The hatch.

"We didn't have time to go in the tunnels before whatever was down there tried to kill us." He reached for her arm and tugged it away from the hatch. "Bird, don't."

"What if it is a dragon, Stone. You, of all people, are going to leave without knowing for certain? It could be the discovery of a lifetime."

"We won't have a lifetime if there's a dragon down there. Let go of the handle." Her dark eyes flicked to Stone's then back to the hatch. She was hesitant, which was good, Stone figured. It meant she didn't think it was the best idea either. "Bird, let's go back."

Her fingers tightened around the handle, indecision weighing on her face. He set the torch down and crouched next to her. "Come on, let's go back." He slid his hand atop hers.

She whipped her head towards his and narrowed her eyes. "You don't always get to decide." Hurt slashed across her face then the hatch flew open.

"Shit." Stone stumbled backward and reached for the torch. She peered down the hatch, the rickety ladder barely hanging on after he and Aesira fled up it yesterday.

"I'm going down," she said. She stepped onto the ladder which released a loud creak through the empty room.

"One of the rungs broke," Stone said. "You need to be careful."

She nodded, then stepped down another rung. Then another.

Soon, Stone couldn't see the top of her head at all. Soon, he couldn't hear the creaking of the ladder. Soon, he found himself doing the same thing he did yesterday, taking the ladder one step at a time.

Fear coiled in his stomach like a snake cornered, that monstrous feeling rising up his spine, wrapping around his throat, but he couldn't let Birdie go alone.

Rule number two, we always have each other's backs.

Even when it's a stupid fucking idea, and it *was* a stupid fucking idea.

His feet hit the dirt.

"You came?" Birdie smirked, arms crossed.

"Did you really think I wouldn't?" Stone held the torch to the wall with the runes and old Ravkian text. A shudder ran down his spine, that snake in his stomach coiling tighter, those teeth growing sharper and sharper, scraping against his insides. "Let's make this quick."

"This way?" She pointed to one of the long, endlessly dark chambers.

"Unfortunately, yes."

Their steps echoed through the chamber, the weak flame of the torch doing little to light their way. Birdie was silent next to Stone's side, other than her occasional curse when she tripped over a rock or bumped into the chamber wall.

"I thought you said there was a beast down here," she asked after they'd been walking for a while.

"There was. Is. Forgive me for not knowing its schedule." This earned him a dramatic sigh and it was almost enough to make him smile and forget they were walking toward their certain death. "Bird, I know this is important—"

"Did you hear that?" She gripped his arm.

Stone held his breath.

A deep scratching sound came from the back of the chamber. Like nails on rock. "We need to go."

"Not yet." Her grip was firm on Stone's arm but he could feel her tremble. "When you and Aesira came, it was nightfall," she said as they took a tentative step. "Maybe they sleep during the day and it was simply waking up when you were here."

"Even if that's true, what are you going to do if we get to the end of this chamber and there's a dragon there?"

"I don't know." The words came out fast, all running together. "We came all this way, it feels wasteful not to at least look for the most powerful creature in the world."

"We came to find the king, Birdie."

"He's not our king."

Stone stopped, forcing her to stop too. "We have a job to do."

"Oh please." She shook her head. "You don't give two shits about the king of Vargah. What, because he gave you a job after years in that underground prison? You care about the pay. The adventure. It's not like you to be so..." She shook her head again.

"To be so what?" He wanted her to finish the sentence. Say what she—and likely Bee—were thinking as well.

Her dark eyes glowered in the light of the torch. "It's not like you to be so obedient."

Stone reared back. "I'm not obedient. I accepted a job that would change our lives, and I'm trying to do just that."

She sighed again then took the torch. "The old Stone would be exploring every chamber here without question. He'd be figuring out a way to capitalize on whatever we find."

They continued down the tunnel, it grew wider the farther they walked. Their voices felt too loud, their boots too loud. He tried to hold his breath, slow his breathing, steady his heart, but the further they walked, the more Birdie talked, the more that serpent in his stomach tightened and hissed.

"The old Stone would have ditched the king and the commander and taken the Aquila as far as it could fly."

The old Stone, he thought. The one that broke the law. The one that was miserable and desperate for a way out. Was that who they wished he was, still? A runner with no future in sight?

He took a chance before, getting them out of Vic's empire and succeeded in keeping them safe for a long time. If it wasn't for Vargah and their flying ships, they wouldn't have been caught on their last run. Wouldn't have ended up in Vargah's prison.

He owed it to them to try again and this trip gave a real chance to get him and the cadre out of Vargah. He was trying, for once in his life, to do the right thing. Then there was the matter of Aesira. They'd found her to be an unexpected obstacle but she wasn't an obstacle at all.

She was trying to find herself, just as he was. Just as they all were.

Another deep scratch came from the end of the chamber, stirring and rousing the monster in his chest, but Birdie pressed on, taking the torch with her. Stone followed behind, keeping his distance, thoughts of who he was and who he wanted to be muddying his mind.

"*Shit,*" Birdie gasped. "Stone..."

Stone took one, two, three, dreadful steps until he was caught up with her. The tunnel had come to an abrupt end with nothing but a steep drop off. They were hundreds of feet above the bottom of a cliff and there, nestled at the bottom, was what Stone could only believe to be one of the beasts that were erased from history.

Black scales and expansive wings. Talons that stretched out in its sleep, scraping against the walls, leaving thick lines in the stone, massive horns jutting from its forehead.

A dragon.

Stone's mouth hung open as he watched the beast sleep. It was enormous. Larger than any animal he'd ever seen. Maybe even larger than the Aquila. "See!" Birdie squealed. "If we hadn't come, you wouldn't have seen this. A real dragon." Her face beamed as she peered farther over the edge.

"It's incredible." Stone was at a loss for words. This was the discovery of a lifetime, just like she said. Just as the *astra* and Ravki itself. They had unearthed centuries worth of secrets. They knew the way and yet... "We can never tell anyone about this." He stepped back, away from the ledge.

"What?" Birdie joined him, a deep line creasing between her brows. "And why not? We'll be famous, Stone." She peered back over the ledge. "And filthy rich."

Stone shook his head. Of all the things he wanted in his life, fame was the last of them. "They'll destroy it. The kingdoms. We can't tell anyone Ravki is here. We certainly can't tell them a real fucking dragon exists."

The fear in his stomach had uncoiled at some point, and had been replaced with deep, deep dread. If anyone in Vargah or Novaria or even the Outpost knew this was here—everything preserved in Ravki would be threatened. They would use every last drop of resource until there was nothing left, then blame the world for not providing, rather than facing their own greed.

"We need to go." He reached for Birdie's hand but she shrugged away.

"Not yet," she said. "If you're making me keep this a secret for the rest of my life, at least let me look a little longer."

He peered back over the ledge. The dragon was incredible. Powerful, even from the distance at the top of the chamber. He couldn't imagine the things it could do–would do–when it surfaced.

"How long do you think it's been here?"

Stone shrugged. "I have no idea," he said. Its wings were tucked tight and hundreds of lines marred the wall where its talons scraped as it stretched. "My guess is a very long time." He and Birdie stood for a while, watching the sleeping beast. Memorizing the shape of its wings and massive head and deadly talons. "We really should go." He expected another protest but to his surprise, she nodded and turned back toward the chamber.

"Thank you for coming down here with me," she said. "Bee couldn't understand why it was important."

"I'm not sure I understand either," he said as they walked back down the long chamber to the entrance.

"I just wanted something for myself, you know. Something I can look back on and say, 'I really did that.'"

"You've done so many things. Remember the time you and Bee stole Vic's ship and sailed halfway to the Isles." A smile stretched across her face. "He was so pissed when he found you."

"Yeah but if it wasn't for you and Patch, he would have killed us." Birdie snaked her arm through his. "This was just for me, but I'm glad you're here."

Despite still thinking it was a shit idea, Stone was glad he was there too, but they had wasted almost an entire day, leaving little time to do what they actually needed to. Look for the king. "We need to–"

A deep roar echoed through the chamber, cementing them in their steps. Stone's heart thundered in his chest, setting a bruising pace against his ribs. Another roar and scrape of talons against rock. "Stone..." Birdie's grip tightened around his arm.

He dropped the torch and the light blotted out, leaving them in nothing but darkness.

THIRTY-TWO

AESIRA

"What was that?" Bee asked as another piercing sound shot through the air.

"The dragon, or whatever that was, Stone and I heard last night." Fire spread through Aesira's chest, her legs trembling. "We need to get them out." Another roar tore through the ruins as they pushed their way in, weaving around vines and debris. "Stone!" Her voice echoed back to her, a pit of unease sinking in her stomach. "Birdie!"

The hatch.

She had to find the hatch. A root caught her boots, sending her toppling to the ground. Scrambling to her feet, she crawled the rest of the way to where she remembered the hatch was. The door was thrown open, the weak ladder trembling with the power of another roar. "Stone!" She couldn't hear anything but the heavy beating of her heart in her ears and the roar of the beast.

Bee pushed her aside. "I'm going down."

Aesira gripped Bee's arm and yanked her back. "And get yourself killed?"

"Birdie is down there!" The next roar shattered one of the only windows left, shards of glass cutting through the room. "Birdie!" Bee's voice cracked as she reached for the hatch again.

"Bee?"

A brief pulse of relief pushed through Aesira's chest as Birdie's voice drifted up the hatch.

"We're almost there!" Aesira wasn't sure there was anything better than the sound of Stone's voice right then. Nothing sweeter, nothing more full of promise. "You need to get out!" he called, his voice drifting closer.

Bee and Aesira shared a glance. There was no way they were leaving them now. They watched the hatch, waited for some semblance of light or life all the while more deep bellows filled the room, loud enough for them both to cover their ears to dull some of the pain. Other than the deep, deep rumblings of a beast that should not exist, no other sounds drifted up the tunnel.

"We have to go in." Bee was frantic, biting her lip and pacing next to Aesira.

"Just give them a minute." *Please, let it only be one minute.* Aesira watched the darkness at the bottom of the hatch like it was her job and then, through the inky black, a flicker of movement.

"Stone," she whispered, not entirely sure if her eyes were deceiving her. Then the ladder shook and Stone and Birdie emerged one at a time. Sweat beaded across their brows, dirt splayed across their cheeks and face.

"I told you to go," he said, cupping Aesira's face in his hands. Bee and Birdie were already wrapped up in each other, whispering things Aesira couldn't make out, nor cared to. All she wanted to do was look at Stone. Drink him in.

"And leave you here?"

A smile slashed across his lips. "You worried about me, Commander?"

Another roar echoed up the chamber, bleeding into her ears, and the reality of their situation came crashing down. "Something like that," she said. "Let's go."

The four of them ran for the entrance of the ruins. Dusk had settled across Ravki, the luminous moths starting to emerge from their cracks, making their way to the fields of *astra*. Behind them the earth shuddered, more and more bellows shook the ground and pierced their ears. They tumbled through the opening of the ruins in a giant heap, panting and sweating.

Stone was on his feet first, pulling Aesira to hers. They ran forward, finding coverage behind a group of tall, green trees. Aesira tried to slow her breathing. Tried to calm her heart but when the dragon emerged, not from the opening of the ruins, but from the top, with its glowing orange eyes and black jagged scales, her heart only sped up. The beast shook, its scales rippling down to its long, pointed tail. It fanned its wings, large enough to block the ruin behind it, then spread them wider and took to the sky but then, with a harsh jolt, it was thrown back.

Its roars turned to a broken wail as it tried again to reach the sky. Tethered.

It was tethered to the ruin.

"It can't get free," Stone whispered. Another deep roar bellowed through the air.

Aesira couldn't tear her eyes away. It flew up, over and over without prevailing.

Another roar but this time the sound felt like it had been broken in two. A desperate cry.

A plea.

Stone's hand found hers, their fingers twisting together. He squeezed once and she squeezed back, keeping her eyes on the dragon. "We need to help it."

Stone leaned forward, squinting through his glasses. "And what happens if we let it go?"

"I don't know," she said. She looked back at the dragon as it made a final attempt to break free. "I don't think it's meant to be here."

The dragon retreated back to the ruins and they spared no time gathering their things to leave.

"How much do we need?" Aesira and Stone stood above a row of glowing *astra*.

"At least six," he said. "That should get us back to Vargah."

Aesira crouched and ran her fingers along the glowing petals but reared back when a searing pain shot up her arm. "Shit," she muttered. A deep line bloomed red on her hand, white-hot pain aching through her palm. "How are we going to harvest this?"

Stone frowned then reached out and ran his fingers along the flower. The golden petals opened with his touch, yawning, stretching toward him. She waited for him to revolt back, to hold his hand like she had hers when it burned, only he never did. "I'll do it, you help Birdie and Bee get the rest of the camp packed."

"But how—"

He stroked another petal and the flower shook, golden light bouncing off it like rain drops. "I don't know."

"Stone," she gasped, dropping to her knees beside him. He held the first *astra* flower in his hands, the brilliant light illuminating his face, his arms, but the beauty of the *astra* wasn't what took her breath away. "Your scars." She ran her fingers over the scars on his arms and face. "They're glowing." He placed the *astra* in a bag and studied his arms, now illuminated to match the flowers.

Stone was always attractive, with his dark auburn hair and blue eyes, but with the scars illuminated he looked ethereal. Unreal. Like a painting. She couldn't tear her eyes away.

"Well that's new." Stone held out his arms. She reached out, running her finger along one of his scars. "Must be because I touched the *astra*."

But it burned me, she thought. Maybe it could see how unworthy she was. Maybe it knew if there was anyone here that should be allowed to take the flower, it was Stone.

"What are we going to do about the dragon?" she asked as they made their way back to camp.

"Well, we have two choices," Stone said. "We leave it, pretend it doesn't exist."

Her stomach sank. "Or?"

Stone stopped, adjusted his pack on his shoulder. "Or we let it go. Set it free, somehow."

"Bee will hate that idea."

"But it does feel wrong, doesn't it?" He turned and glanced at the ruins. "The way it cried. Tried to break free." He shook his head. "I can't explain why but I could feel it in my chest."

"Feel what?"

He sighed, pushed his glasses up. "Feel its despair."

She wove her fingers with his and squeezed. "Then we set it free."

His eyes locked with hers. "We set it free."

"We're going to do *what*?" Bee's face scrunched, eyes bouncing between Stone and Aesira.

"It's dying in there," Stone said. "We can't leave it."

Birdie tapped her boot before kneeling and rummaging through her bag. "I've been waiting for this." From her bag she pulled a weapon with a wide, double-edged blade, runes and words etched into the handle that Aesira couldn't decipher.

"All this time, Bird?" Bee shook her head. "What if you tripped and fell with that in your bag? You'd impale yourself."

"It didn't happen so it doesn't matter." Birdie raised the sword, moonlight reflecting off its pointed edges. "Now this is special," she said. "Forged in the Isles with the highest quality steel."

"And how did you afford that?" Bee crossed her arms then rolled her eyes at Birdie's silence. "You stole it?"

"Are you surprised?"

"Not in the least," Stone said.

"If you're all done judging me, you'll see how perfect this blade is." She held it higher. "It would have been a waste to leave it with those stuffy royals." She swiped it through the air then balanced the point of the blade on the tip of her finger. "Surely sharp enough to break through even the toughest of scales," Birdie said through a grin.

"We're not going to hurt it, Birdie," Aesira said. "We're going to help it."

"I know that," Birdie snapped. "I'm saying it's sharp enough to cut through the toughest of scales *or* chains. It'll work. We just have to get close enough."

"And therein lies the real problem," Stone said.

"It's quiet now," Bee said, "maybe it's sleeping."

"The issue is how do we get down." Stone tapped his finger against his lips.

"We can go in through the hatch," Birdie said, polishing the sword with the end of her shirt. "We can use rope to lower us into its den. Cut the tether from there."

"And leave us nowhere to run?" Aesira shook her head. "We have to lure it out the top, the same way it came out earlier." She pointed to the top of the ruins where the dragon had emerged. "There," she said. "That'll get us close enough to strike and leave us plenty of room to escape."

Stone wrapped his arm around her and pulled her close. "A very tactical answer, Commander."

She shrugged. "I'm good at some things," she said.

"Oh I don't doubt there are many things you're good at."

A sharp ping pierced the air pulling their attention. Birdie tossed a stick then sliced it clean in two. "Let's fucking go then." She marched past pulling a wary Bee in tow.

The night air was heavy as they climbed to the top of the ruin and Aesira wondered if it would bring rain. Her heart twitched, thinking about the day only a few weeks ago when she had danced in the rain with Stone. Had watched as the Strix dropped that boy. The sound of his body hitting the hard ground. The memory it tore from her. The memory of Eldrin.

Even if they had not found Desmond, this trip had changed her in so many ways. It had opened her eyes after years of living in the dark. Years, she had done nothing outside of the Order. Years she had spent worshipping a goddess that did not care for her back. Years she had buried the shame of losing her brother, let the mistakes of her childhood dictate her future. What she thought she deserved.

She didn't want to think of what lay ahead. Didn't want to think of Kamari, alone in the Citadel, praying to Celestria. *It will devastate her*, she thought. Everything they'd found on this trip, everything they'd seen.

At the top of the ruin, they peered through an expansive crater where the dragon had risen. "Do we just call it up?" Bee locked her arm with Stone's.

"Oh dragon," Birdie sang, "come out." She laughed and Bee punched her arm.

"Birdie Odega can you take anything seriously, for once?"

"I was serious the day I told you I loved you." Birdie pecked a quick kiss to Bee's cheek. "And not a day since."

From where they stood, Aesira could see the fields of *astra* glowing under the moon. The Lunaris moths circled above the flowers, eliciting more ethereal light. "Stone do you have the *astra*?" He nodded then reached into his bag and pulled a single flower. "Hold it over the edge."

He gave her a puzzled look but did as she said, dangling the flower over the edge. A few moments passed and nothing rose from the ruins. "Why do you think it wants the *astra*?" Stone asked, pulling the flower back.

Aesira's brows bunched, watching the endless dark at the bottom of the ruin. "It seems like everything here revolves around it," she said. "The fields and the moths. The flower we found in the case. The runes. I just thought maybe the dragon was also tied to it somehow."

Stone smiled and held the *astra* back over the edge of the opening. "I love the way your mind works."

Her stomach somersaulted, tripping over a single word, then, he let go.

"Wait!" Bee shot forward. "We need that for the ship."

"We'll get another," he said, eyes pinned on Aesira.

The gleaming glow of the flower faded into the inky black of the pit then, a deep bellow echoed up through the roof.

"Finally," Birdie said, holding the sword higher. "Here we go."

The roof shook but Birdie stood firm, her grip around the sword assured. The ground beneath them quaked and the dark of the pit transformed to white teeth and a flash of orange eyes. A gasp caught in Aesira's throat as the massive dragon tore through the roof and that's when she saw it, a golden chain laced around its neck.

"Bird!" she shouted. "There!" Aesira stepped back into Stone's arms and Birdie stepped forward just as the dragon spread its enormous maw, spittle flying, coating Birdie's face and hair. Its scream wretched through the darkness, bleeding into their ears, trembling their ribs in the chests.

A smile slashed across Birdie's lips as she swung her blade.

One slice.

One sharp, precise slice of the weapon and the chain fell down, down, down until it disappeared into the deep chasm and the dragon soared overhead, dark scales disguising into the night.

Breaths heavy, legs weak, they dropped to their knees. A laugh bubbled in Aesira's chest until she couldn't contain it. It rippled out of her in waves until she was clutching her side and then Bee was laughing too and Stone. Then, Birdie.

"We just freed a dragon," Birdie said and as if on cue the beast roared overhead, sobering their bout of laughter. "Shit, we just freed a fucking dragon." She pulled herself to her feet, grabbing Bee's hand and pulling her too. "We need to get the hell out of here."

They walked straight through the night, found a hidden cave to sleep in during the day and decided it was best to trudge through the Polaris Ridge come nightfall. It wasn't worth the risk sleeping there again, not with the Dreamweavers. They would make the trip through the ridge as quickly as possible, torches lit and wide awake.

The air began to change once over the ridge. Arid and dry. Nothing like the fresh, cool air of Ravki that Aesira found herself missing. She should feel relieved they were almost back to the Aquila but all she felt was sick.

Sick that she'd failed to find Desmond. Sick that the further she walked from Ravki, the more she missed it. She glanced at Stone as he set up camp. A few more days and they would be back to the Aquila, headed back to Vargah, where they would face a hurdle of challenges.

"There has never been a world where you and I feast at the same table."

His words rang in her mind, over and over again. Her father would never accept his daughter to be with an Odega and it didn't matter anyway. She had her orders. She and the rest of her knights would leave Vargah as soon as she arrived, moving on to their next station for several months. At first she was content with the time she and Stone had together but now as he slid next to her and pulled her close, kissing her softly on the lips, she wasn't sure there would ever be enough time with him.

The rest of the trip, save for a bloody run in with a few rogue crawlers, went relatively smooth. Dire came into view as they crested the final hill, desperate for water and ready for sleep on anything other than the ground.

"There she is." Stone squeezed Aesira's shoulders. "Home." He nodded toward the Aquila where it sat still docked and the idea of home roused something deep in her middle.

Nightfall was beginning to settle, turning the sky shades of deep purple. The four of them wove through the remains of Dire, careful not to step on any of the broken fragments left behind from the Strix. When they got to the dock, Aesira dropped her bag.

"Stone…" It was dark. Too dark.

All of the torches on the ship were out.

"Patch!" Stone thundered through the ship, not pausing long enough to notice how disheveled it was. Crates and barrels thrown about. Cut ropes and broken bottles. Aesira's stomach roiled as she approached the hull where a deep, crimson stain smeared across the planks.

"Nora!"

Eerie silence, then, "He's in here!" Aesira, Bee, and Birdie followed Stone's voice until they were in the crew mess. The entire ship had been overturned. Every room in tatters. Their maps torn to bits, their stocks of food and drink completely empty. "He's okay," Stone said, pressing his fingers to Patch's pulse. "Breathing, albeit barely."

Aesira scanned the room again. "Where is Nora?" Stone was at her side, breathing heavy. "Nora!" Aesira tore through the room, her legs bumping into the emptied cargo containers. "Nora!"

No answer.

"I'll check the other cabins," Birdie said.

"I'll find some supplies," Bee said.

"I'll get the *astra* filled." Stone's eyes burned through Aesira, like he was waiting for her permission to go. To leave. She nodded, only once, and the team broke up, doing their assigned jobs with efficiency and ease. All the while Aesira stood there. Her heart slamming in her chest, her breaths coming out short and fast. If she lost Nora–

"Aesira!" She followed Stone's voice until she was on deck and there she was, red hair matted and tangled, body leaning into Stone's.

"Nora." She peeled her from Stone's arms and wrapped her in her own. "Are you hurt?"

"I don't know," she said. "But Patch, he's hurt. He needs–"

"We're on it," Stone said, then disappeared below deck.

"What happened?" Aesira led Nora to a crate where they sat together. Dried blood lined her nose, under her nails.

"Crawlers, I think," she said. "It was hard to tell but they came out of nowhere. Wrecked the ship. Almost took me over." She closed her eyes, a few tears sliding down her cheeks. "Almost got Patch."

"They didn't, though," Aesira said. "You're okay. We're here."

"We're okay," Nora whispered. "We're okay."

Beneath the ship, Stone crouched beside Patch, examining the wound at his side, the bruising along his jaw.

Patch groaned, his eye struggling to open.

His arm was wrapped poorly in a tight make-shift tourniquet. His skin was too pale, his lips dry and cracked. "He needs water." Aesira snagged a canteen from the table and tipped it to his lips and poured. Slowly, he swallowed. Stone unwrapped the bandage on his arm and got to work cleaning the festering wound.

"Where is she?" Patch grumbled. "Nora?"

"I'm here." Nora slid next to him, gently pushing his hair away from a gaping wound on his face. "We're not alone anymore," she said. "We made it."

"We made it." Patch's eye rolled back, head slumping behind him.

Stone gripped either side of his face, giving him a light tap. "You need to wake back up."

"I'm awake, boss." He cracked his eye open. "Glad to see you made it back." His eye quickly fell shut again. Patch hissed as Stone poured something sterile smelling onto his wound. "There was a hive," he said. "More crawlers than I've ever seen." He struggled to sit up then relented when Nora urged him back down. "They were different too."

"Different how?" Aesira's body grew impatient, fingers curling, her teeth digging into her bottom lip. They needed to get out of Dire before whatever tore through here came back.

"Smarter. More alive." Patch closed his eye, his brows knitting together. "We fought them off the best we could, used all of Bird's weapons but they got my arm and Nora–" His eye met Nora's. "We're lucky you showed up before they came back."

"How did you get them to leave?" Stone's voice was rough, his nostrils flaring.

Patch rested his head back against the wall. "Fire," he said. "Whatever the fuck machine Birdie made was our only chance at survival, but even then it was close."

"Let's get you two some food and into bed." Stone and Aesira helped him up and forced him and Nora to eat one of the ration packs they had left.

With the reservoirs filled, the ship fired up with ease and Stone led them away from Dire. Aesira sat alone at the stern, watching as the mountains and the decrepit dock faded from view. She tucked her knees tightly to her chest, the memories of the last few weeks flipping through her mind. The Strix. The Lunaris moths. The Dreamweavers.

Stone.

Ravki and water and the dragon.

She let out a shaky exhale and stretched her legs. Something stabbed her thigh. She pulled out of her pocket the small knife from the abandoned camp she and Bee found in Ravki. She studied it under the light of the moon. The ancient blade, worn and dull. The handle, ornate. Bee thought Desmond brought the blade, thought it was the only explanation for a Vargahian weapon to be in Ravki.

She wasn't so convinced, considering the age of the weapon and all the other pieces of the camp. Which only begged more questions. If Desmond didn't bring it, who did?

THIRTY-THREE

AESIRA

The small cabin underneath the ship welcomed Aesira with open arms. She climbed into the soft bed, burying her face into the pillow before a knock at her door had her sitting up.

Stone popped his head in. "Can I come in?" She nodded, a flurry of butterflies taking flight in her stomach. There was something deeply intimate about being alone, just the two of them, for the first time in weeks.

"It's your room."

Stone sat at the end of the bed and ran a hand down his face. "I like that you're in it." She scooted closer, sitting with her legs crossed.

"Are you okay?"

"Tired," he admitted. "You?" He slid his hand out and found hers without looking, like they were magnetic, drawn to each other by an unseen force.

"I don't know." Aesira stroked her thumb across the back of Stone's hand. "Tired. Worried." Stone's fingers tightened around hers.

He sighed, a deep sound like it fought its way up through his body. "With the *astra*, we'll be in Vargah in just a couple of days." He glanced at her, the dark blue in his eyes catching her breath. "I don't know what awaits us," he said, finding a curl and wrapping it around his finger. He liked to do that, she realized, and she liked when he did it.

"I don't know either," she said, "but we have right now." His gaze darted from her lips to her eyes, the fierceness of his stare melting her. It was just the two of them. No monsters. No Birdie and Bee. Nothing stopping them from being together, if they wanted to. And more than anything, she wanted to. *Only a distraction*, she lied to herself. "Who should we be tonight?"

He leaned closer. "What if I said I just want to be Aesira and Stone." His eyes lingered on her lips. "What if I said fuck all the rest. No thinking about who we are. No worrying about what comes next." His lips brushed hers and she wanted to lean into the touch, get lost in it. "Just be here." A kiss to her lips. "With me." Another to her jaw. "Right now." He pulled back enough so she could see his face.

"It's not that easy," she whispered, their lips still close enough to kiss.

"We know they're lying." His breath was warm against her lips. "We've seen *astra*. Dragons. An abundance of life and water that they've hid from us. Scared us into submission." He leaned away and the space between them grew cold. "Change is possible, Aesira, it's just a matter of how badly you want it."

She knew about wanting things badly.

"You're right," she said. "And when we get to Vargah, I will speak with my sister. I will tell her what she needs to know of Ravki. I will urge for change without risking what we've found. Besides, you'll be a free man, Stone. There is no reason you can't leave Vargah." *No reason you can't go where I go.* "You know, if you want it so badly?"

A grin split across his lips then he was there again, invading her space. "I made you a promise," he said against her ear. The night in Ravki came crashing back into her. Stone's words and hands. His mouth on her and the promises he made.

His eyes dipped to her lips again, then with such gentleness, he used his thumb to open her mouth. He hooked his thumb behind her bottom teeth and guided her forward. "I may be an Odega," he whispered, his breath mingling with hers, "but I do keep my promises." His thumb slipped out, drawing a line across her bottom lip.

Her body was scorching. Everywhere they touched, everywhere they didn't. "Tell me your dream."

"Which one?"

"All of them."

He took a breath and closed his eyes just for a moment. "First, I want you over there." He nodded toward the head of the bed. "On your back with your legs open. In my dream, I tasted you here"—he kissed her on the lips—"and there." He dipped his gaze below her waist. "I want to hear the noises you make when you come. I want your hands on me. Your eyes on me. I want to make you feel good. Better than you ever have before." He leaned in, his lips brushing hers. "That's what I dreamt, Aesira, and that's what I want now."

Her mouth had dropped open and all words escaped her so she stayed quiet and peeled her boots off. Then her shirt, one button at a time. Stone didn't take his eyes off her. Not as she pushed her shirt off completely. Not as she slid out of her pants. Not as she unhooked her underclothes and dropped them to the floor. Color rushed to Stone's cheeks, his pulse racing in his neck.

She turned away from him, crawled to the head of the bed. From behind her she could hear the strain in his breath, a ragged moan. Then the bed dipped with his weight and his fingers ran over the back of her calves.

"You're going to kill me." His voice was deep, rough. When she turned, his eyes were dark, starved, as they drank her in. Her head hit the pillow, her legs making space for him to move between them. She laced her fingers behind his neck, pulling him down so their mouths were even and on their next breath, his lips crashed into hers.

He knotted his fingers around her hair and pulled, forcing her head back so he could kiss her deeper. She moaned into his mouth, her hands grabbing and tugging at his clothes. When she nipped his bottom lip with her teeth he made a deep rumbling noise that Aesira felt from her core to her toes.

"Just so you know," she said between heavy breaths. "What you said back on the ship? That I was ashamed of wanting someone like you. I'm not. I wasn't then, either. I want you, *all* of you, just as you are." It was as if he was still waiting for her to give him permission to let go of any restraint because when she said those words–*I want you*–all timidness fled from his body.

He kissed her mouth, her chest. His tongue was hot on her neck, over her breasts. Then, he slid down until he was on the end of the bed, peeling off his clothes. Her eyes traced every scarred line of his body, every curve of his muscles. They way they flexed when he tossed his shirt to the ground, the broad expanse of his shoulders as he settled between her legs.

He gripped her ankles, his thumb running circles over her skin. "You can still tell me to stop, Aesira."

"Don't you dare."

He smiled wide before he lowered himself and kissed her slowly, starting at her ankles then up to her inner thighs. He looked up at her, pushing his glasses up so they sat more firmly on his nose. "*Fuck.*" His voiced sound pained, like waiting a moment longer might actually kill him. It might kill her too, she thought. He pressed his forehead against her thigh and sighed.

"What's wrong?"

"Nothing," he said. "I'm just praying."

She propped herself on her elbows so she could see him. "You're what?"

He glanced up at her from between her legs, a smile itching at the corner of his mouth. "Praying," he said again. "Praying I can make this last longer than five minutes."

Aesira snorted and threw her head back down. "Been that long, then?"

"It's not that," Stone whispered before planting another kiss against her inner thigh. "It's just you." She didn't have time to reply before the heat of his mouth enveloped her.

The first swipe of his tongue against her had her throwing her head back. The second swipe, her vision blurred. Over and over again he worked his tongue, long, languid strokes that lit a fire in her core.

"Stone," she moaned. "I can't—"

"Not yet. Don't come yet," he said before another swirl of his tongue. Her back arched off the bed, nails clawing and finding their way to his shoulders. He withdrew his mouth then drew a finger down her center, eyes heavy, lips parted. "I dreamt of this, too," he said before lowering his mouth again. "Dreamt of how you'd taste. How you'd sound." His mouth and fingers pressed into her and she gasped. "Even better than in my dream." His teeth dragged across her inner thigh before he positioned himself over her.

She mapped each scar across his chest with her fingers. Kissed the ones she could reach on his face and neck and shoulders. "You're beautiful," she said. "*Darling*." He smiled then responded with another ardent kiss that had her body aching. Desperate. She could taste herself on his tongue and it awoke something feral inside of her. Something made of want and need and all the untamed parts of her she'd stamped out.

"I like when you say that," he said. He urged her legs open and she wrapped them around his hips. His arm snaked beneath her, tilting her hips upwards. Then he stopped moving. Stopped kissing her. Her breathing slowed and only thoughts of doubt rushed her.

"What is it?"

"I just—" He shut his eyes, only for a moment, before they met hers again, his glasses slipping a fraction. "I just want to savor this but I don't know if I'll be able to." He laughed but it was broken, nervous. "You are fucking perfect." Heat coursed through her again, the doubt from before swept away.

She pulled him closer then pushed her hips up so he slid against her. "You can take those off," she said, nodding to his glasses.

"No," he said. "I need to see you." They sucked in a shared breath as he slid against her again and when he pushed inside of her, her eyes rolled back.

So good.

He felt *so* good.

"Aesira." Her name was broken, caught between a moan and a plea. He set the pace, torturously slow at first before whatever control he had been holding on to shattered. He gripped her hair. Bit her neck then kissed where it hurt. Whispered words of praise as he thrust harder and deeper inside her. Her body quaked, nails digging into his back. With each thrust, she pushed against him so there was no space between them. Only their bodies, searing and desperate.

Starved.

She felt herself inch close to the end but just as Stone wanted to savor it, she did too. They would be back in Vargah before they knew it and everything would change. As far as she knew, this night was all they had. So she forced him onto his back, so she was on top of him.

He threw his head back as she circled her hips, a moan tearing from her lips. "You're so pretty like that," he said. "Make that noise again for me."

So she did.

His fingers dug into her hips, words falling from his lips that only spun her higher and higher.

Fuck.

Perfect.

Yes.

Aesira.

Aesira.

Aesira.

Her palms pressed into his chest, her eyes on his and it was like he could read every thought, every worry she had, but he brushed his lips over hers and her thoughts and worries vanished. She slowed her pace before he flipped her again and she was on her back. At some point his glasses must have fallen, or he took them off, she wasn't sure. All she could focus on was his face, scarred and beautiful. His breaths, sweet and heavy.

He drove into her, cupping the back of her neck, kissing her slow and firm between ragged breaths. He used his free hand to hook the back of her leg, opening her up wider, just like he said he would and that was it.

Aesira was falling, falling over the edge. Her body arching into him, molding them together as closely as she could until she was completely undone and all that was left was the beat of her heart in her ears, the rush of blood and the feel of too-hot skin. A moan broke through Stone's lips as he came, following her over that cliff, his teeth finding her shoulder, then kissing where it hurt.

He kissed her deeply before moving away and she had a thought to pull him right back. Start again. Keep him as close to her as possible.

After they cleaned themselves, she tucked herself into his chest, running her fingers along his scars as his ran lazily over her back. "Sleep," he said before pressing a kiss to the top of her head.

She didn't want to close her eyes. She wanted to stay awake. Memorize every scar. Commit every sound Stone made to memory. But as with everything, time moved forward and Stone drifted to sleep, his arms tight around her.

Aesira's mind raced through every moment since they left Vargah. Everything that was to come. And no matter how hard she tried, she couldn't help the sinking feeling that she was losing something.

Losing him.

So, instead of sleeping, she sat up and penned a letter to Kamari.

Stone's breath was warm against her neck as Aesira woke. The light through the porthole was dim, just barely morning. She rolled toward Stone and traced a finger over his bottom lip.

"Mm," he said, cracking an eye open. "Good morning, you're up early."

"Can't sleep." She nudged closer, her nose brushing his. The last two days had flown by and they'd been lucky to only encounter a rogue sandstorm and another hive of crawlers. Nothing they couldn't handle and now, they'd reach Vargah by the end of the day.

"Shall I read to you again, Commander?"

Her lips brushed his. "No," she said. "We should get up. Help out."

"We could do that," he said, "or we could just stay here." He rolled her onto her back so his body caged her beneath him. He was firm on top of her, his lips warm as he found her hand, kissing the inside of her wrist. "I have an idea of what we could do."

He dropped her hand and reached to the small table that sat next to the bed. "What are you doing?" He held up a piece of fabric, one she recognized from flying a few weeks ago. He'd tied it around her mouth before the storm, to keep the sand out.

"Do you trust me, Commander?" His arm bracketed either side of her again, the piece of fabric laid across her bare chest.

Their trust had been tested several times over the last few weeks and even when she felt she could trust him, there was always a small doubt. He was an Odega. The very opposite of what she was trained to be, but he was also now just Stone.

Stone who pushed his glasses up even when they weren't falling. Stone who marveled at waterfalls and moths. Stone who she caught watching her. Stone who tended to her needs as if they were his own. Stone who read to her when she was restless and eased her into a deep sleep.

She did not give her trust easily, always something to be earned. Tested. But more than anything, she wanted to give it to him. He watched her, his question suspended between them.

"I trust you, Stone."

He exhaled, like her words were a relief, then he picked up the fabric. "Good," he said, "because last night I had another dream."

He slipped the fabric over her eyes and tied it gently behind her head. The room went dark, the immediate panic of losing one of her senses sped up her heart. Stone was still on top of her, his hands holding hers. "Trust me." His lips swept past her ear, then pressed into her neck.

"I do. I trust you." The weight of the truth pressed down on her chest, laboring her breathing. She did trust Stone. More than she trusted most people. They'd exposed parts of themselves to each other the last few weeks that no one else had ever seen before. They'd been honest, faced death, found solace in each other's arms and if there was anyone in the world she knew she could trust, it was him.

He let go of her hands and she gripped the sheets, back arching off the bed as his fingers drifted over her heightened skin, feather-light. Over her peaked nipple, down her stomach, between her legs. Barely there touches, alternating between his fingers and lips and tongue, that had her moving and sweating and ready for more.

He teased her right to the edge then moved away, never giving her exactly what she needed. With the blindfold, each touch was a surprise, each kiss from his lips, swipe of his tongue, pushing her closer to the edge.

He was back at her ear again, his body scorching and heavy on top of her. "It's your turn to tell me what you want." Another kiss to her pulse.

"*Please*," she said.

He untied the blindfold, using it instead to tie her hands above her head. She squinted against the light, sunlight now filling the room. She was pleased to see he looked just as worked up as she did, his cheeks flushed and eyes dilated, like touching her was all he needed. "Please just fuck me."

He laughed, then kissed her forehead. "Such good manners," he said, then slid into her, slowly, until she couldn't take anymore, until they were both breathless, both waiting to move. Their eyes caught and she nodded, just once.

I trust you.

He rocked his hips, once, twice, and then they were moving in sync, sharing stolen breaths, bodies hot and aching for each other. There was no savoring it this time, they finished fast and hard, Stone's face buried in her neck, Aesira's legs wrapped around his hips, his name spilling from her lips. She had never felt like this before. Not just the sex but how she felt after. How she felt in his arms. Safe. Content. Like they'd done this a million times before, like they had the time to do it a million more.

Except they didn't.

When he pulled away, he must have seen the worry on her face. He sighed, like he was thinking the same thing, and untied her wrists, taking the time to kiss the inside of each one.

"Are you sure they'll see the ship?" She and Stone stood together on the bow while Birdie manned the wheel. The sun was blotted out by a rising sandstorm and the heat Aesira dreaded returning to was back. Her hair stuck to the nape of her neck, curling tightly at her temples.

"They'll see it." Stone stood behind her, his arms wrapped around her middle. "They're trained just for this. We're close enough to Vargah now they'll know." Through the growing storm, an angry fury of red dust, a hawk took shape. "There." From his pocket Stone drew a small, gold whistle and blew it. The sound was nearly indetectable but the large bird spread its wings and dove for the ship.

The hawk was adorned with light chainmail, several small bells, and two delicate bracelets around its legs—one red and one purple—to signify Novaria and Vargah. "Fly fast, friend." Aesira tied the scroll around the hawk's leg and then it took flight, soaring through the sandstorm with ease. She and Stone set their goggles in place before the storm drew any closer. He pulled her hair back, twisting it into a braid as they watched the hawk, and Aesira's message, disappear from view.

"The goggles suit you." Stone tucked his finger under her chin and kissed her. *You suit me*, she wanted to say. He pulled the fabric mask from his pocket. "You'll need this." He tied it gently around her mouth. "Though I prefer how you wore it this morning." He winked, then tied his own mask on.

How would she ever move on from this, she wondered. How would she ever move on from him?

THIRTY-FOUR

KAMARI

It was Naming Day. Which marked the end of the month.

Kamari's time to find Desmond had run out. She hadn't spoken to the council about her suspicions that Desmond was likely murdered. She didn't trust them for a second, didn't trust anyone.

Her grief and anger warred together, each one battling for dominance before she realized they were one and the same. Her grief *was* her anger. Her husband was gone and they didn't care, because they were the cause.

She clutched the note from Aesira in her dress pocket. Held onto it like it was something to be cherished.

More so, it was something to remain hidden.

They'd found Ravki.

Found something that would change the world, as Aesira put it.

But they had not found Desmond. Not even a single sign of him which, of course, didn't surprise her since learning of his last journal entry. *They didn't find him, because he never made it out.*

The stadium buzzed with nervousness and excitement. People were herded into their seats where they would await their fate. Sentries were stationed on every corner, ready to take the sacrifice to the arena, willing or not.

Kamari fanned herself, her cheeks flushed under the mid-afternoon sun. Hanna sat at her side, Nev and Rahashi in their usual places behind her. Her parents were there too, though they sat further down, the deep red of the Novarian colors a blemish in a sea of purple.

A long horn sounded, making Kamari flinch, before a familiar voice flooded the arena. "In the name of Celestria," the High Priestess called, "a joyous Naming Day is bestowed upon us once again. See our sacrifice, Celestria, and in return fill our reservoirs."

"See our sacrifice," the crowd echoed.

"Bring water to your people who honor you in humble servitude."

Disgust filled Kamari like days old food, rotten and vile, making her stomach dip with unease. She didn't know the whole truth, but if Desmond was correct, *astra* was no gift from the goddess. Her fingers tightened around the scroll from Aesira.

Kam,

It's been awhile since my last letter, but we found it. We found the place we were looking for. We also found something else, Kam. Something that will change everything. We did not find Desmond and I'm so sorry. We'll come home and form a new plan. We'll keep looking. We will find him. Make sure Nev is with you at all times.

Trust no one.

We're coming home. I'm sorry about Desmond. I love you.

~Aesira

It had to be *astra* that Aesira was referring to. What else could she have found that would change the world? Especially when those very words were written in Desmond's journal about his theory. It had to be true and she didn't know whether to be relieved or terrified.

The stadium roared with cries and laughs and prayer, as the anticipation grew for the Naming sacrifice to be chosen.

Three bells chimed from the harbor and the pit in Kamari's stomach unclenched.

Three bells.

A ship was docking.

She turned to Nev whose smile told her she had the same idea. Aesira and Nora were home. "Meet them at the shipyard," Kamari said. "I'll come right after."

The excitement on Nev's face was wiped away with a hardened scowl. "I'm not leaving you again."

Kamari's eyes landed on Nev's knuckles, still pink and puckered from whatever punishment she'd received from the last kidnapping attempt. "I'll go," Rahashi said from Nev's side. "I'll tell them to join you." Nev nodded, dismissing her knight and then she and Kamari shared a small smile. Aesira and Nora were home and even though Desmond wasn't with them, she could at least be glad for her sister's return.

Another three bells chimed, drowning the noise from the stadium.

Hanna squealed next to her, leaned close so she could whisper. "Nev won't admit it," she said, "but she's been anticipating their return. And the king's as well." Kamari's smile faltered. Hanna's smile was so bright, she bit her tongue and kept the truth to herself.

The High Priestess was still prattling on about Celestria, listing all the ways they owed their lives to the goddess. Kamari fought the urge to roll her eyes. If the goddess truly cared about them, she wouldn't force them to kill one of her own every year just so the rest of her people wouldn't die of thirst or heat.

A sudden silence fell over the stadium like a fistful of sand dousing a fire. It was calm. Quiet. It made Kamari's stomach roll.

"This year's Sacrifice—" The High Priestess went quiet, nothing but her breathing sounded over the crowd. She took a large breath, then: "Kamari Orathka."

All eyes burned into the balcony where Kamari sat. She gripped the edge of her seat, sweat dripping down her brow. "Your Majesty," Hanna whispered from her side. "Your Majesty, it can't be."

Two sentries clad in metal armor stepped in front of Kamari. "Stand."

"She'll do no such thing." Nev's tall frame blocked the sentries from Kamari's view, as if hiding her away would somehow change her fate. Her heart raced. Head spun. She gripped the note in her pocket harder, using the only piece of her sister she had to tether her in place.

Three more bells chimed in the harbor.

Hanna's hand flew to Kamari's shoulder. "Surely there's been a mistake." Hanna, sweet Hanna, spoke with such assertiveness even Kamari flinched.

The guards and Nev argued. She could hear them, demanding she stand again, but her mind had slipped away. Back to the first day she'd met Desmond. His dark hair and nervous smile. The markings on his arms glistening in the sun. The way he kept his distance but she always caught him staring and he always blushed like he'd done something wrong. How was that life so far away? How had she gotten *here*?

"We said, *stand*." The sentry's gruff voice snapped her back to the present. To her new reality.

When they reached for her she was ready to fight back. Ready to claw her way out of their arms. Only, they never touched her. Someone mumbled something from behind them and they stepped aside, forcing Nev to step aside too. Relief pulsed through Kamari's veins as Raffe stepped forward in the guard's place.

"Lord Raffe." She put her hand to her chest, willing her heart to slow. "There's been some kind of mistake—"

"Time's up, Your Majesty." His dark eyes were cold, distant, as he looked past her, not at her. "Looks like Celestria has made the decision for you." His smile was all teeth and no feeling when the guards yanked her to her feet.

Nev's sword was drawn, but more sentries filed into her booth. She could hear a cry, Hanna perhaps, but her vision was blurred. Nothing but shapes and distorted sounds pulsed around her.

Fight back, her brain shouted. *Do something.* But fighting and physical strength were never her power. She was not Aesira, she would not win this fight. Not with brute strength, anyway.

Through the million things buzzing in her mind, one word surfaced before the rest.

Treaty.

"You can't do this," she spat. "You need me. If I am sacrificed, the treaty is null. Novaria will attack."

Raffe leaned close, his moustache tickling her ear. She flinched away but he gripped her face, keeping her close. "It's a good thing," he whispered, "there are *two* Novarian princesses."

Kamari's stomach plummeted.

Aesira.

They would use Aesira in her place.

"You did this?"

Raffe smiled and snapped his fingers. The guards closed in. She turned her attention to her parents. "How can you sit by and let this happen!" The guards pinned her arms behind her back, bending them at such an angle a shock of pain shot clear up to her shoulder.

Her mother was half decent enough to at least look grief-stricken that her daughter was about to die but it was her father's cold voice that paralyzed her. "It is the will of the goddess," he said, clenching tightly to the pointed star pendant hanging around his neck.

A goddess that never blessed Novaria. A goddess that bathed in blood.

A goddess that was not real.

A hot tear slid down Kamari's cheek and her lips trembled. "Is it? Or is it the will of men?" Her mother's brows bunched, a befuddled look sweeping across her face but Kamari had no time to explain before the grip from the guards bruised the back of her arms. Nev struggled against several sentries, sword drawn, metal clashing together.

"Please, do something!" Hanna's pleas drifted over the wind like a piece of gossamer, floating and floating, until the breeze swept them away and all that was left were the noises of the crowd.

The sentries pulled her down the steps, through the stands where hundreds of wide eyes bored into her. Some spat, shouting obscenities at her. A queen that was never wanted. Others prayed over her, their greedy hands reaching for any piece of her they could touch.

"Praise Celestria," they said. "Fill the reservoirs. Fill our cups!"

More tears fled from her eyes and when her feet hit the sand of the stadium her legs shook. Somewhere in the distance, through the raucous chatter of the crowd, another three chimes rang, their high pitches getting caught on the wind.

Aesira.

The sentries tied her to the dais, the noose snug around her neck. "Aesira!" she shouted but her voice was lost to the crowd–*her people*–cheering for her death. "Aesira!" she screamed again, this time choking on a sob.

"Screaming will only make it worse," one of the sentries said. His voice was rough, just like his hands, as he bound Kamari's wrists together with thick rope. "Be quiet." He tightened the rope until it bit into her skin.

Tears dripped down her nose, into her mouth as she gazed out at the arena. At the hundreds of people who laughed and clapped and shouted as the noose tightened around her neck. Was this what it was like for all of them? Each name that was drawn? Each sacrifice? The thought of other sacrifices brought forth even more sobs. For decades, Vargah had performed the ritual. For decades, the kings and queens of this country had happily killed one of their own, and it was Desmond who wanted change. Who wrote that he would find a way.

And it was Desmond who was now dead, and Kamari who would die next.

She braved another glance at the crowd. The children that sang and the mothers that prayed. She didn't blame them. They were thirsty beyond reason. Hot and scorching without *astra* to keep them cool. Kamari dying meant they would live and so she would not blame them.

She didn't have all the pieces to the puzzle, but change was coming and her sister would bring it.

"I'm sorry." Her voice went unheard as the High Priestess began a prayer, but her mind was racing through each and every moment in her life up to this one.

Her childhood in Novaria.

Her sister and her brother.

Her husband.

The noose became impossibly tight around her neck and the crowd began chanting.

No, not chanting, counting.

They were counting down until her neck snapped. Counting down until the wells of water would be refilled and *astra* be restored to their parts of the city.

"Five!"

Desmond, she thought.

"Four!"

You were right. I know you were right.

"Three!"

I will find you.

"Two!"

And we will be together again.

"One!"

I love you.

The crowd silenced and Kamari sent one final prayer, not to Celestria, but beyond, to the stars and the moon to welcome her home. The planks beneath Kamari opened up and she took one long, final breath.

Screams erupted from the stands and Kamari opened her eyes to realize her neck had not been snapped.

The sentry that had tied her up was fighting someone, another sentry was beneath her, his back supporting her feet. She balanced on her toes, trying carefully to keep her weight off her neck, the rope tore into her skin, stinging and burning against the tender flesh.

More sentries entered the arena, more fighting and screaming erupted and Kamari didn't know where to look. What to do.

There was little that she *could* do.

Her hands were bound, and if it wasn't for the sentry beneath her, she'd already be dead.

"Get her to the ship!" a sentry screamed but that didn't make any sense. Were they helping her? Denying a sacrifice? "Get ready to catch her!" He pulled out a knife as dozens more sentries filled the arena, headed straight for them. The rope swung as he cut across it and Kamari struggled to keep her balance on the man's shoulders.

"Kill them!" A sentry called out and Kamari could not tell who he was talking to. Kill Kamari? Kill the intruders? Kill the other sentries?

Everything happened so quickly and soon she was falling, tumbling through the bottom of the dais and into the arms of the man whose back had saved her life. Rough hands grabbed her, hauling her over his shoulder before he ran through the arena.

Shouting and screams and the grisly sound of metal on metal sounded behind her but the sentry didn't stop. Kamari closed her eyes, praying, praying, for whatever was to come.

He carried her through the winding tunnels of the Citadel. Through passages that were so void of light, she couldn't understand how he knew the way. He carried her so far, the screaming from the arena began to fade and only when they came out the other side of the tunnel, emerging in the Boneyard District did he set her down.

Her throat burned from the rope, her wrists marked red. He cut the ropes free and she kicked them away as they landed on the ground. The man who'd saved her towered over her, his sentry mask fit snugly over his face.

She opened her mouth, to thank him or to scream at him, she wasn't sure, when voices rose from around the corner. The man grabbed her waist and pinned her to the tunnel wall, his large hand pressed over her mouth, the other firm on her waist. When the voices faded, he slowly peeled his hand away.

"Who are you?" Kamari's voice was hoarse. "What is going on?"

The man stepped back and peered out the tunnel. A flash of light flickered across his mask, once, twice, three times.

A signal.

"It's time to go." The familiar timber of his voice silenced the sounds of the city. She reached for his mask, ran her fingers over it and then under until she could feel the scratch of the hair along his jaw. The curve of his lips. The bend of his nose. She peeled it off, pushing it over dark locks of hair and gasped when she drew her hands away.

"Desmond?"

He stood over her, a deep cut dripping red down his cheek, his nose twisted and bloody. Her knees gave out, sending her plummeting to the ground but those strong arms she knew well wrapped around her waist and pulled her up.

"We have to go." He moved to put his sentry mask over his head but before he covered his face she pressed on the back of his neck until his mouth was aligned with hers.

Then he kissed her. He kissed her until she could not breathe. He kissed her so deeply she forgot, for a moment, where they were or what had happened. For a fraction of time it was just her and him and every ounce of pain and worry and fear washed away like sand adrift in the wind. She was home, in his arms, and he kept kissing her until their souls were threaded, the beat of their hearts syncing together.

Alive, alive, alive, their pulses sang with every press of their lips.

Then, he pulled away and reality came crashing back into her.

The ache from the burns on her neck.

Her wrists.

The fact that Desmond was here, in front of her, when she thought him dead.

Another flash of light cut across his face before he pulled his mask on completely. His arms tightened around her, crushing her into his chest. "Whatever happens, my love, don't let go of me."

THIRTY-FIVE

AESIRA

The Aquila sliced through the red dust that encompassed Vargah as they docked in the Boneyard District. Aesira tightened her armor, straightening her chest plate, positioning her sword at her side.

Feverish air encompassed them as they stepped off the ship but it was nothing compared to the flood of distraught people screaming and shouting.

She leaned into Stone's side to whisper in his ear. "Naming Day?"

"You'd think they'd be cheering."

A woman's toe snagged on Aesira's boot, sending her to the ground. "Are you alright?" Aesira asked, helping the woman to her feet.

"Rebels," the woman managed through a sob. "The rebels are here! They've come to take our water. Our *astra*!" Then she was gone, fleeing into the crowd.

"Rebels?" Stone turned to Aesira, pulling a knife from his boot. "There haven't been rebels in Vargah in years."

Her heart sped up, more shouting and frenzied screaming sounding in all directions. "I need to find my sister."

Stone nodded. "I'll go with you." He turned to face Patch, Bee, and Birdie. "You three stay back. Keep the ship running. We'll need a way out if rebels are truly here."

"We'll need food," Bee said, "and water. We can't make another trip without replenishing."

"Try and find what you can but stay close," Stone said.

Bee nodded then gripped Birdie's hand and dashed through the Boneyard District.

"I'll stay with the Aquila," Patch said.

Stone dropped his bag, his books. "If we're not back by sundown, you'll leave for the Isles. Do you understand?"

Reluctantly, Patch nodded before Stone turned to her. "Ready?"

Aesira waved Nora forward. "Let's go."

"I'm staying, Commander." Nora looped her arm with Patch's.

They'd both blurred the rules between knight and Odega the last few weeks. Choosing desire over duty. Want over sacrifice. But there was nothing blurred about this. This was clear, a sharp line in the sand, and Nora placed herself on the other side, leaving Aesira to choose.

Duty.

Desire.

Her eyes flicked to Stone's. "We don't have to go in there, Aesira," he said.

"My sister is in there."

"And so is mine." Nora stepped forward, letting Patch and Stone fall back. "This doesn't have to be your fight. Doesn't have to be *our* fight." She took Aesira's hand. "Nev is smart, if the rebels are here she'll get Kamari out. When we're safe, we can send word for them to meet us. Think of everything you saw out there, Aesira. Think of what you know is true."

Over Nora's shoulder she could see Stone watching her, waiting to see what she'd do. If she'd cross the line. They'd seen the truth in Ravki. Seen the *astra* and the water and the *life*, but her sister was not on that side of the line.

"Rule number two," Patch said, catching Nora's arm and linking it with his own. "Never leave anyone behind, that goes for you as well now. Find the queen, we'll stay here. Keep things ready just in case."

"Thank you." The words burned up her throat. They'd wait for her because she wasn't just a knight overseeing them, she wasn't someone they feared or hated or resented. She was their friend. *They* were her friends.

The line then didn't seem so hard to cross. She'd tell Kamari everything they'd found. Tell her the truth about *astra*, about what Vargah might be hiding, then they'd flee. They'd sail to the Isles and figure out the rest. "I'll be back as quickly as I can."

"I'm still going." Stone stepped to her side.

"No." Aesira put a hand to his chest to stop him. "I need to go alone." She leaned close, pressing her lips to his ear and whispering so only he could hear. "I will not be able to do my job well if I think you're unsafe and what I might have to do in order to get to Kamari will not be pleasant." When she pulled away, his face was marred with a frown. "Stay here, wait for me, if I'm not back by sundown promise you'll leave as planned."

He tipped her chin up and kissed her and it was almost enough to convince her to stay. "As you wish, Commander."

The looming spires of the Citadel blocked the sun, casting wickedly sharp shadows over the courtyard where even more people ran frantically.

Handmaids and servants darted past her, all flooding for the door. Some crying, most shouting. She worked her way through dozens of people shouting at each other until she broke free from the mayhem and made it to Kamari's rooms.

Hanna was there, tears staining her cheeks. "Commander," she said through a broken cry, wrapping her arms around Aesira's middle.

"Hanna, where is Kamari?"

"She's gone." Hanna cupped a hand over her mouth. "She was the chosen sacrifice but the rebels came and she's gone and there was nothing we could do. Nev tried, she tried to stop them but..." The rest of her words were drowned out by a sob.

Aesira's entire world came crashing down, the walls of the room closing in. She couldn't breathe. Couldn't think. Her knees gave out so she braced herself on the back of the chair.

You couldn't save her just as you couldn't save Eldrin.

"What do you mean she's gone?"

"The rebels!" Hanna shouted. "They took her."

"So she wasn't sacrificed?"

Hanna shook her head. "No," she said. "At least I don't think so. Everything happened so quickly."

"Start from the beginning."

"Her name was called," Hanna said, "but when she got to the dais, something happened. People dressed as sentries ambushed the stadium and then, Kamari disappeared."

"But she isn't dead?" Aesira ran to the window, following the sound of screams, then drew the curtains shut.

"I don't know." Hanna cradled her face in her hands.

"We have to go," Aesira said. "If there are rebels here, it isn't safe. I need to find the others. Nev. Rahashi."

"But you don't understand," Hanna said through a sob, "they're *all* gone."

"Aesira?" A familiar voice called from the doorway, she spun around, her sword tethered in her palm.

"Mother?"

Of all the people Aesira wished to see, her parents were the least of them. "What are we doing in here?" she asked, glancing around the meeting room. "We need to be looking for Kamari."

"Your sister is gone." Her father's voice was flat, emotionless.

"You don't know that," Aesira said. "Did you see her fall? Have the reservoirs been filled?" Her fingers twitched, eager to pull the blade from her side and fight her way through the crowd until she found the rebels. Found Kamari.

Her father shook his head, a thin smile spreading over his lips. "You had no right to leave Vargah."

Aesira reared back in disbelief. "I was obeying the demands of my queen."

He slammed his fist against the table. "And maybe if you were here, your queen would not be gone!"

His words landed like a stake through her heart. She had let Kamari down, just as she had let Eldrin down.

"You were being reckless!" He shook his crowned head, his Celestria pendant swinging from his neck. "Of all my children, you have always been so difficult to tame, Aesira. How is it that I have been left with no heirs except the one that I never wanted." She shrunk back in her chair.

Years and years of her father's scrutiny rushed to the surface, thickening her throat, burning her eyes. "You will do what your sister could not," her father said. "You will marry Lord Raffe. Restore the treaty."

"You do not need *astra* to run Novaria," she spat. "You do not need this treaty other than for your own personal power."

Her father shook his head, the star pendant around his neck swaying. "Piscis Spring is nearly dry," he said, eyes narrowing. "If we do not keep this treaty in tact, if we do not gain water from Vargah, from Celestria, our kingdom will cease to exist." He took a step closer. "You will listen to me. You *will* ensure this treaty remains, or the deaths of thousands will be on your hands."

Aesira curled her lip. "And when Vargah realizes you've lied about the spring? When they see we have nothing to offer?"

"I suppose that will be your problem. Be an asset to your kingdom, to your family, for once in your life." His words were no different from the pain she'd endured in the Order, just as piercing, lashing against her skin until she was raw. The Order had done what he couldn't, which was whittle her down to nothing, and rebuild her into the shape they desired–*he* desired. Something useful. Sharp. All edges and teeth.

Only, she'd let herself slip the last few weeks. She'd let herself remember that she was a person before the Order. That she was human, capable of friendship, companionship. Empathy and love. She was more than just a weapon. More than just a spare.

More than her mistakes.

I don't want you tame. Stone's voice filled her, bolstered her.

Her sword slipped easily from its sheath as she stood.

I want you wild.

It sliced through the air, smooth and effortless, until the very tip pointed at her father's heart.

I want you fierce.

She pressed her sword farther until the pop of fabric sounded. "I will be leaving to find Kamari."

"Aesira, don't."

She dug the blade in, ignoring her mother, smiling as her father's eyes grew wide, panicked. But isn't this what he wanted her to be? Why he sent her away? To become sharp and emotionless and lethal.

I want you terrifying.

The sword dug through his doublet and how easy it would be to pierce his heart and make him bleed.

A bead of sweat rolled down his forehead, collected on his heavy brow. "Please, Aesira."

"You are a coward," she said, lowering her sword.

"Your sister has failed us," he said with a shaky voice. "If the goddess is not pleased with a different sacrifice, she will not fill the wells. People will die of thirst. We'll lose power to the cities. We'll be dried up before the storm season ends. And for what? Because she insisted on finding that madman she claimed to love?" He laughed, a bitter cold sound that pierced Aesira's ears and she had a thought to cut out his tongue for good measure.

"You can spend your life on your knees, Father, praying to a goddess that does not hear you. Or you can be an asset to your kingdom, for once in your life." She spun for the door and there was a sense of satisfaction that pumped through her veins. That she was disobeying him. Disobeying the Order. Disobeying Celestria.

She would find Kamari and leave it all behind, cross the line, and never look back.

The door swung open and the satisfaction that drove her forward vanished. "General?"

The tall, thin woman who Aesira had only known to bring pain, discipline, order, stepped into the room like she owned it. Shoulders back, chiseled face stoic and cold. Her gray hair was tightly wrapped at the nape of her neck and the baton that Aesira knew too well hung from her hip. "Commander Zeliath," she said. "Sit. Down."

Sweat collected on the back of her neck, her temples, the palms of her hands. *Pain*, her body reminded her. *The General means pain. You're not safe.* "No," she ground out. "I'm done." She sheathed her sword and unclasped her breastplate. The first breath of air without it felt weightless. Free. She tossed it to the General's feet. "I resign," she said, stepping forward. "Let me through."

The woman stood firm, her arms tightly positioned behind her back. "You have disobeyed your orders." She took a step forward. "Your station." She pulled the baton from her side, sliding it through her hands. "Do you think you're the first knight to try and leave?"

Her father scoffed from behind her. "You have my full permission but I'll tell you, General, not even the cruelest of punishments seems to get through to her. Unbreakable, this one."

A smile spread over the General's face, grim and thin and amused. "I know better than to try and break her," she said, slipping the baton back into its holster on her hip. "Pain has never been enough."

Aesira's heart sped, racing frantically in her chest. She knew what came next. Knew that if she didn't leave right now, this would be it. Her sword was out of its sheath and in her hands before she could blink but still, it was not fast enough. The General was on her, one hand around her throat, and the other pressing something sharp and familiar into the side of her neck. "You are a disease, Aesira," the General said. "Infecting everyone you love."

Fight.

Fight.

That she could do.

She thrashed, clawing at the General's face but then her arms were restrained, pulled behind her back by two sentries. "I see not much has changed." The needle pricked her skin, a drop of warmth running down her neck. There was no way out. The medicine would enter her blood, render her unconscious and then she'd be done. Lost.

"Mom," she said, finding her mother's face through blurred vision. "Please don't let them do this again."

Maybe it was aimless to believe her mother would finally find her voice and help her children, but her hands were tied and she had nothing left to cling to but to hope that the one person meant to love her most would finally help her.

The last thing she remembered before the needle pressed into her skin was a single nod from her mother and a grin from her father and the General's voice. "Everything you touch, turns to rot."

THIRTY-SIX

AESIRA

The fog that came after a dose was heavy, like seeing through a dust storm, cloudy and blurred. The only bright side to being forced into submission was the others felt she was fine to be alone. Not a threat.

Her head pounded, her pulse beating in her ears. The place where the needle pricked her skin stung. She felt weightless without her sword. Useless without her knights.

Peeling back the curtains, her heart sank as the sun dipped lower into the horizon, casting the city in a rusty glow.

The door behind her creaked open.

"Aesira." She spun around and Stone was there.

"How did you get in here?"

He met her across the room. "I have my ways." He brushed her hair back and Aesira couldn't help but lean into his touch.

"You're supposed to be leaving," she said. "It's almost sunset."

"Do you think I'd really leave without you?" He tilted her chin. "Rule number two, remember?"

A lump grew in Aesira's throat, burning as she swallowed past it. "You have to go."

You are a disease.

"Leave with me." Stone swept the hair from her cheek. "Tonight. We have enough *astra* to make it to the Isles. Maybe further. Nora was right when she said this isn't your fight. You don't know what else they're hiding."

"Stone." She buried her face in his chest, like maybe if she held him close, held him tight, she could pretend her life wasn't falling apart.

"Please," he whispered against her hair and that one single word threatened to unravel her entire being.

All the years of dedication and sweat and tears and blood, all to be destroyed by a single word. But not just a word. A word from *him*.

"Whatever they've asked you to do, you don't have to do it. You know that right?" He cradled her face in his palms. "You can leave with me, with us, right now." He kissed her and she melted into him, clung to his arms, to the dream that they could ever be free from who they really were. "Please come with me, Aesira."

It would be easy to love him, she thought. To leave Vargah and sail through the desert until they reached the promise of freedom in the Isles. It would be easy to forget the life she lived here because it was hardly a life at all.

Everything you touch turns to rot.

Dust churned in her head, an ache pulsing down to the roots of her teeth. "You need to go."

"Aesira," he said her name through a sigh. "We know *astra* is real." He took her hand and kissed the mark where the *astra* flower had burned her. "And they have chosen to ignore it and sacrifice someone anyway. They are serving a goddess who gets satisfaction from seeing one of her disciples slain for no reason. Either way, they are not who they say they are. They don't deserve your loyalty and we cannot stay."

He turned for the door, dragging her by the hand. She wanted to leave. To flee with him and the crew and Nora.

She wanted to stay. To keep him safe from her. To find Kamari.

She wanted both things and when she opened her mouth, her father's voice came out. A soldier's voice. Rigid and authoritative and devoid of emotion, just as she was trained. "I'm not the person you think I am," she said. "I'm not good. I make choices that hurt people. I can't hurt you too."

Stone turned, facing her again. He cupped her face and held it firm. "You're not hearing me when I say that I want you to come with me, so hear this. You can tell me all the terrible things you've done," he said. "Let every horrible thought and memory you have bleed out of you and I would still lap at your confessions like a dog deprived of water." His lips were crushing as they met hers. "It won't change how I see you or that I want you," he said between kisses.

"That's how it feels, Aesira. Like I've been deprived and you are the only thing that has offered me some semblance of life. If you're scared of hurting me, then leave with me and don't."

Her heart cleaved in two, leaving an open chasm in her chest. Stone's eyes pinned her in place. She savored the color of them. The shape of his nose. She memorized the bend right in the middle and the scar that ran down his face, somehow making him more beautiful.

Her body and mind were fighting through the injection, the medicine that dulled her spirit and instincts and she tried, *tried*, to remember that she was more than what her father made her to be. More than the Order made her to be.

More than an infection. A disease to those she loved.

"I'm sorry, Stone." She dug her fingers into her hair, pulling at the roots. "I want to, but—"

"Don't." He shook his head before straightening his jacket, squaring his shoulders. "If your choice is to stay, there's nothing else to say." A muscle feathered in his jaw and then he was stepping toward the door. "We were just pretending anyway, right?" The pounding in her head was drowned out by the agonizing ache spreading through her chest, clenching up her throat.

Every step he took from her, the fog in her mind cleared a little more until he reached the door and it dissipated completely.

She could stay and search for Kamari. Could pretend to be the daughter her father needed her to be until it was just the right time to flay him open–flay them *all* open.

Or she could leave.

She could leave and find Kamari a different way. Trust what Hanna saw.

Find the rebels.

Be with Stone.

When she laid it out in her mind, it was simple. An easy choice.

The line in the sand, just as Nora had drawn, and he was on the other side. "Stone, wait. I'm—"

When he turned from the door, it opened behind him and Lord Raffe stepped in. "Well," Raffe said, smoothing his pristine silk shirt. "Am I interrupting something?"

Stone stepped aside, shaking his head. "I was just leaving."

Raffe's laugh cut through the room. "No you weren't." From beyond the door, another man stepped forward. Stone's body stiffened, his shoulders tight.

"Well, well," Vic said. "Look who it is."

Five sentries filtered into the room behind Vic, still dressed in their Naming Day armor. Three of them circled Stone, the others flanking her sides.

"Stone is a free man, Lord Raffe," she said. "He was heading back to the Boneyard District."

Raffe and Vic shared a look that made Aesira's stomach plummet. "It seems you and my betrothed here have gotten to know each other well the last few weeks, Mr. Stone," Raffe said, "but I'd say it's awfully inappropriate to have you sneaking out of her room."

Stone stole a glance at Aesira over his shoulder. *I told you I'm not good*, she wanted to say. *I told you I'd hurt you.*

"What are you doing here?" Stone's voice had turned cold. Emotionless. The sentries next to him made a move to draw their weapons but Raffe waved them off.

"You of all people should know who holds the desert's secrets," Vic said. "My long time client here"—he slapped Raffe on the shoulder—"told me of a very peculiar group of Odegas traveling to find the king. After your indiscreet visit to the Outpost it didn't take much to piece together where you were headed and why."

Aesira reached for her sides, but all of her weapons were surrendered. No hidden blades. No swords. No knights by her side.

Stone bent his head down, just enough to reach Vic's eyes. "We were sent to look for the king, nothing more."

A cruel smile curled Vic's lips. "Is that so? You know people talk in the Outpost and when they don't, they're forced to. She kept your secrets for a long time and I'll admit she was a tough one," he said. "But with enough persistence, eventually all things break." He pulled a yellow flower from his pocket. "She said you had a plan. A *map*."

Soo.

"If you touched her, I will fucking kill you." Stone lunged, his fist colliding into Vic then Raffe but there were too many sentries. One slammed Stone into the wall while another's fist flew into his cheek with a sick crunch.

"Raffe stop this! There is nothing out there. We found *nothing*!"

Raffe stepped away as the other sentries surrounded Stone, taking their turn beating him. Hitting his face. His stomach. His back. Stone groaned as he dropped to his knees, glasses broken and thrown from his face, eyes clouded and nose bloody.

Vic pulled a scarf from his pocket, wiping his nose until it was clean. "The only one to blame here is *you*." He spat in Stone's direction. "Coming into *my* house, talking to *my* people behind my back." He knelt down and gripped Stone's hair until his head was forced back, whispering something in his ear.

"Take him," Vic said before standing and straightening his shirt.

Aesira tugged free of the sentries grip and ran for Stone. She dropped to the ground, blood on the floor soaking through her night dress. "Stone," she whispered, holding his face in her palms. "I'm so sorry." His eyes were swollen, lip torn open. "I'm sorry—" The sentries from before ripped her backwards, one grabbing each arm.

"Please," Aesira begged. "Please just let him go. I know the way on my own, you don't need him."

Raffe tsked. "But what kind of husband would I be to allow my wife to face such dangers in the west?" Her stomach roiled. "He's going to show us the way." Raffe snapped his fingers again. "Now." The three sentries pulled Stone to his feet and dragged him out of the room, leaving a bloody trail in his wake.

"And don't fuck him up too much more," Vic shouted, "we need his head clear."

Raffe turned to her, a tiny speckle of blood staining his shirt. "And you," he said, "need more taming than I realized."

Everything had gone quiet and dark.

The noises outside. The people scurrying about the Citadel. Her racing heart.

Aesira couldn't get Stone's face out of her head.

Not the broken and bloodied one, but the one just before that. The one where she told him she wasn't going with him.

The General's words rang true, even now.

She could not love someone without hurting them.

She should have left with him the moment he asked. Should have fled this kingdom and this duty and honor without hesitation.

She had been always broken but now Stone was broken too, because of her. Broken and imprisoned when he deserved to be free.

She allowed herself one cry. One moment to sit with her regret before she raised her chin and wiped her cheeks and let out one last wavering breath. She would meet her father in the council room. She would meet Lord Raffe and accept his proposal. She would restore the treaty before anyone noticed it was broken.

She was a weapon, yes. But she was also the spare. Born as a backup in the chance Kamari could not uphold her duties.

What Stone failed to realize earlier when he'd asked her to leave was that there was power in being the spare. No one would expect her to lead, only to be grateful to be given the opportunity so they wouldn't see who she really was, only who they expected her to be.

She was no longer choosing to serve her father or Celestria or the Order. She was choosing, for once, to serve herself, just as Stone begged her to. And she would bring the kingdom down right from the inside, making them pay for his pain.

For Kamari's.

For her own.

And she would do it with a crown on her head and a smile on her face.

She would destroy them, each and every one, and she'd do it as a queen.

THIRTY-SEVEN

STONE

The only godsend of being back in prison was the break from the heat. There was no way to tell what time it was so far underground, but by the meager meal and the absence of *astra* light, he could assume that it was late which meant the Aquila would be sailing straight to the Isles, rule number two be damned.

Something tapped in the cell next to him, through the thick cinder walls.

Tap.

Tap.

Tap.

"Are you going to do that all fucking night?" The tapping stopped and he shut his eyes, leaning his head against the wall. He winced, the pain in his face still pounding, his ribs bruised and broken.

Tap.

Tap.

Tap.

"Sorry," a voice came from the other side of the wall. "I'm going crazy in here."

Stone ran a hand down his face, wincing at the tender flesh. He thought of Aesira, telling him to go, saw how broken she looked, how torn. He struggled to open his eyes and started counting the bricks of his cell, one by one. It was easier, even with the pain, than seeing her face behind his eyes.

The rejection stung more than he thought it would. Birdie, Bee, Patch. They were his friends and his family. He kept his circle small yet he'd invited her in.

He invited her, begged her, and she'd said no.

"What are you in for?" the voice again, too high to be a man, but rough around the edges like whatever she'd been through had destroyed anything soft she might have once been.

He wouldn't tell this woman of Ravki. Wouldn't say that he was supposed to be a free man for the first time in his life. Instead, he sighed, and said, "Smuggling." It wasn't far-fetched, considering that's what all his other citations were for. "You?"

Tap.

Tap.

Tap.

An anxious boot against the stone floor, he decided. *Must be her first time in here.* "I beat the shit out of a sentry." The honesty in her answer made him laugh which turned to a wince when his lungs pressed against his bruised ribs. "Deserved it, though."

"I don't doubt that," he said.

"What's your name?"

"Odega."

The woman's laugh was just as rough as her voice. "We're all Odega's down here. What's your real name?"

Stone slid his tongue across the back of his teeth, eyes searching for an anchor in the dark. He had a real name once. A name that was not tied to smuggling. Not tied to any crimes. A name he was given by someone who loved him, even if that love was brief and eventually abandoned.

He could tell this woman his real name, she was a stranger, no one to him. But when he opened his mouth, the name would not come out. He clamped his mouth shut. He hadn't said his true name aloud in over a decade and for some reason it felt wrong to say it to anyone that wasn't *her*.

Aesira.

Because even though she chose to stay, even though she was to be married to someone else, she still had a claim on him that he couldn't explain. "Just Odega," he said. "That's all I am."

That's all I'll ever be.

Just like Vic said.

"You'll never be more than this, Stone, and she'll never be yours."

His stomach soured. "And you?"

The woman tapped her boot again, rhythmic and calculated, against the stone floor. "Nevani," she said. "But you can call me Nev." He could hear, faintly, as she stood, something metallic bristling, like she was wearing armor. "So, Odega, how the fuck are we going to get out of here?"

Nev had eventually fallen asleep, the cell now eerily still without her anxious tapping and raspy voice.

Stone's body ached, his mind still racing. He carefully moved, lying flat on the ground, one hand resting behind his head, the other placing slight pressure on his stomach. Even if he could sleep, he wasn't sure he wanted to because every time he closed his eyes, he saw her, denying him. Telling him to go.

He'd never wanted much for his life. He wanted to be free from Vic, wanted to see that the cadre found a safe place to land, wanted to fly ships and feel the open air on his face, and now he wanted her. But he wanted her to want him too, which somehow was worse.

He attempted to roll onto his side, immediately regretting it as pain lanced up his middle. Something heavier than exhaustion settled over him, pushing him deeper into the hard floor. His eyes closed and even though the image of her face burned through him, his body relaxed.

"Wake up, Stone."

He shot up, pain tearing through his abdomen. "Fuck." He gripped his side, his lungs working. "Nev?" He pressed his ear to the shared wall of their cell, but there was nothing on the other side. Without his glasses, he couldn't see for shit, and the lack of moonlight or *astra* didn't help, but through the darkness he thought he saw something shift in the corner. He held his breath, waiting for the voice to come again or for whatever it was to move again.

Nothing.

Maybe he was more exhausted than he thought. He sat back down, running a shaky hand through his hair when a swell of darkness caught in the corner of his eye.

Black pooled on the floor of the cell, like ink split in water, rising up the wall, splintering through the cracks in the stone like a spider web. The darkness spread over the wall, down onto the floor, inching its way until it curled around his boot. He sat, eyes wide, pain searing through all the places the men had beat him.

"Oh we know you." Voices from every direction sank their teeth into him, pressing down on his chest until it felt like it was torn wide open. Baring his heart. His soul. His most vulnerable memories all flashing behind his eyes.

His parents.

His scars.

His—

The smoky darkness snaked up his body, settling into the seams of the scars on his arms, his neck, his face. *"Stone, such a shame, to not be called by your true name."*

Epilogue

Kamari

After what felt like days in the dark, a few slivers of sun cut through the overhead planks. The ship Desmond had ushered them to was smaller than those in Vargah but Kamari hadn't had a chance to see much of it since she was immediately stuffed into a tiny cabin.

"Can you at least tell me where we're going?" Desmond shook his head, a lock of dark hair falling into his face, burning a memory behind Kamari's eyes. She could recall his hair falling similarly the first time they kissed. Recalled how it felt to push it back and run her fingers down his face.

In so many ways, he looked the same as when she saw him last. His dark hair, while longer than usual, still fell in waves, barely brushing the top of his shoulders. Hazel eyes, speckled with hints of gold and green, framed around thick dark brows and lashes. The patterns that marked his bronze skin were displayed on his forearms where his shirt was pushed up.

So much of him was the same, and yet so much had changed.

Scars nicked his lips and nose. The shirt he wore was missing buttons, threadbare holes on either elbow. Desmond cleared his throat and Kamari realized she had been staring.

"You have a lot of questions," he said, "and I promise, Kamari, I will tell you everything." He squeezed her hand. "I'm just so relieved you're here."

Her fingers warmed from his touch. "I thought you were dead, Desmond. For weeks I thought I'd never see you again."

The ship jolted to the left, sending her sliding across her seat. Desmond moved across to the bench and pulled her close to his side. "I *was* dead."

"What do you mean?" She kept her eyes forward, focusing on the wooden planks that lined the walls. The small porthole that for a moment had let in such abrasive light blotted out, leaving the small cabin murky and dark.

A deep sigh rumbled in his chest. "The voices in my head have been with me since I was a child, only growing louder and louder each year I aged. I never listened to them before, always pushed them away. But recently, they have been telling me things." She moved out of his grip enough to look up at him.

"What kind of things?"

"Things about Ravki. About water and *astra*. They told me the only way to keep you safe was to leave, to find this place and I know I shouldn't have gone without you Kamari. I know that now, but I thought I was doing the right thing."

There it was. What she'd feared and dreaded.

He left you.

She snapped her gaze to him and hoped he could feel the fire burning through her eyes. Through her heart. "Why didn't you just tell me?"

Desmond shook his head. "I thought I was protecting you. Saving you from whatever was pulling me under."

"And that was your first mistake, Desmond." She crossed her arms, narrowed her gaze. "Assuming that if you were being dragged down, I wouldn't want to be dragged down with you."

"Kamari." Her name was broken on his lips.

"What happened when you left?"

Desmond cleared his throat, she could feel his eyes on her as she studied the wall across from them, tried to make out the blurry shapes through the porthole window.

"I didn't make it far, the voices stopped outside the Citadel. I didn't have a clear path. I got hung up just outside the Outpost, thought for certain I'd meet the end, and that's when they saved me."

"They?"

Desmond's hand moved over her spine, wrapping her closer into him and her breath hitched. "The rebels."

Kamari sat straight looking at him again. "The rebels found you and saved you?"

He nodded, his eyes snagging on her mouth. "It's complicated."

"It seems we have time." She waved around the mostly empty cabin.

His lips quirked up. "I missed you so much."

"Desmond, tell me why the rebels saved you. How they found you."

He rested his head against the wall and closed his eyes. "The voices in my head were never just in my head, Kamari." He kept his eyes closed, like he didn't want to see her face as he spoke. Like he was afraid of how she'd react.

Did she not prove her boundless affection before? Did she not sit with him night after night when he couldn't sleep? "These"— he opened his eyes and ran his finger over the unusual markings on his forearms—"are not just birthmarks. They're symbols, linking me to my people. My *actual* people, not those in Vargah that claim I'm one of them."

"I don't understand."

"Ravkians, Kamari. These runes link me to my ancestors from Ravki. It was their voices I heard. It was *them* who told me of the *astra*. Of Ravki. Of the lies that have plagued Vargah. They've been waiting for years and years for someone to finally *listen*." When she said nothing, defeat slumped his shoulders. "I still sound mad."

"I'm just overwhelmed." She looked around the small cabin. To the porthole filled with darkness. "It's all so much." He pinched his eyes shut again and he looked so broken, so lost, that she couldn't help but slide toward him and wrap her hand around his. His breath hitched, and she knew he felt it too. That lightning connection that had always been instant between them. He took it a step further and wrapped his arms around her again and her body relaxed against his. "And so it's true? *Astra* grows in Ravki?"

"When the rebels found me, nursed me back to health, they told me the truth. That a long time ago, Vargah harvested *astra* and have been growing it under the city. They keep reservoirs of water they siphon directly from the mountains, only refilling them on Naming Day, giving the illusion that the goddess has blessed them. It keeps the people loyal. Hardworking. Scared."

With each word his voice grew more and grew dark, more hoarse. More hateful. "They use Celestria as a weapon. A threat to keep people in line, when really, they have more than enough *astra* to keep the kingdom cool and powered year round. Have more than enough water for anyone to ever go thirsty."

His arms tightened around her as her mind raced through all the new information.

The rebels.

Astra.

Water.

A lump grew in her throat.

Celestria.

"I would have followed you, Desmond," she said, her voice rasping and tired. "I would have followed you anywhere."

He kissed the top of her head. "That's what I feared, my love. I knew you'd insist on coming with me and I couldn't take that risk. I didn't know what was happening inside my head." He cast his eyes away. "Didn't know what I was capable of."

The ship rocked again, a slapping sound hitting either side. "You would never hurt me, Desmond."

He shook his head. "I tried to get to you as soon as I could. Tried to have them bring you to me."

"The women who tried to kidnap me?" she asked. He nodded, his hand finding hers. "Why didn't you come for me yourself?"

"I wasn't well for a long time." He turned to her, tucking his thumb under her chin. "From the moment I left the Citadel, all of my thoughts have been only of you. How to get you out. How to save you from them." He swiped a tear from her face, then kissed the wet stains on her cheeks. "Whatever they put you through, I promise I'll make sure the punishment is fit."

Silence stretched between them, other than the odd, foreign noises of the ship as it sailed and so much of Kamari was relieved to be in his arms. And another part of her hated that he didn't trust her enough to tell her of the voices. Tell her that he was leaving.

"Aesira found it, you know."

"Hm?"

"Ravki, from your journals." She peeled herself away so she could see him. "The place of your ancestors."

"That isn't possible."

"Well she did. She wrote to me." She dug into her dress pocket and pulled out the crumpled paper, her heart stinging when she caught sight of Aesira's penmanship.

Desmond scanned the paper, his brows furrowing deeper and deeper until he sighed and his face smoothed. "This isn't Ravki." He handed her the letter. "What she found is likely the encampment Ravki used during the Great War over the Whispering Mountains. It's been abandoned for decades." The ship skidded to a stop and shouting above the deck trickled down the cracks of where they were hidden. "We'll talk about this more later. We're here."

Desmond pulled Kamari to her feet, running his fingers through her hair, touching lightly along the redness of her neck where the rope had bitten her skin. "I owe you so much." Before she could say anything, he was pulling them up a small, wooden ladder. Her legs were weak from days being cramped in the bottom of the ship but with Desmond's help, she made it to the top.

She shielded her eyes from the sun, salt and open air rushed her as she stepped onto the deck.

"Come," Desmond said, guiding her to the ship's edge.

A gasp tore up her throat, her eyes stinging from the light of the sun, the unfamiliar rush of cold wind and what she saw over the edge—

She'd expected to see a dock atop sand, like those in Vargah or Novaria but instead, the ship sat in an unending pool of water. She clutched Desmond's arm, her mouth dropped open.

"It's an ocean," Desmond said. "Water as far as the eye can see."

Tears pricked Kamari's eyes and she spun every which way, looking for land. Looking for sand. For any sign of the desolate world, the only one she'd ever known. Her throat was dry, closing in on her, leaving room for only one broken word to slip through her lips. "How?"

Desmond wrapped his arms around her as they watched the blue water of the ocean move with the breeze and overhead the roar of ancient beasts—*dragons*—not one but many, as they swooped and dotted out the brightness of the sun. "I told you there are secrets Kamari, some buried so deep even the gods can't find them. This is only one of them."

He tilted her chin and kissed her lightly on the forehead. Her body, her mind, all weightless and free of thought. She could not comprehend what she was seeing. Could not fathom how one moment she was set to die in the sand and in another, she was here, surrounded by the most precious resource her kingdom had ever known with her husband she thought to be dead.

In the distance she could hear faint whispering, like voices caught on the wind, and through it all only two words rose to the surface.

Rebel King.

"This way." Desmond led her by the hand to the end of the ship, where a smaller boat sat in the water with several people seemingly waiting for them inside. They glanced at each other, the whispering louder than before.

Rebel King.

Desmond squeezed her hand, pulling her attention. "Let me show you the real Ravki."

Acknowledgements

Here we are, my dearest readers, at the end of another book. Creating the world in City of Lost Kings has been such a dream. Hands down, my favorite book to write yet. It was a story that sat in the back of my head for almost a year before I began writing. It first came to me when I was still drafting Through a Somber Sky and I knew I had to put it on hold until the Enchantress Awakens series was complete.

When Through a Somber Sky released, I didn't write a word for months and at one point began to worry I'd never write again. Enchantress Awakens was such a close project to me that I feared I'd poured everything I had into it, leaving no room for anything else.

But Stone, Aesira, and Kamari were always there, waiting for their turn. So, I decided to trust myself, and one day began to listen to them. Began to write again. After that initial break through, the words came fast and easily. The vision was clear. Their motivations, flaws, joys; all of it.

I hold so much love for them and this world. Even the monsters I hold close to my heart.

This story pushed me in so many ways; creatively and as a writer. It's a story of hope and love and loss and defiance and sisterhood. It is the story that most reflects who I am as a writer and that is both exhilarating and terrifying and I can't wait for you to see what comes next for our crew.

I owe my thanks to so many people for helping make this book a reality:

To my husband for standing by me, always rooting for me.

To my family, for being my number one fans.

To my editor, Sara, for helping make this story the best it could be.

To my alpha and beta readers; Sarah, Cassandra, Krystal, Michelle, and Brit. Thank you endlessly for reading my early drafts and keeping me afloat with your enthusiasm about this story and these characters! You've championed them from the first, messy pages to now and I'm so thankful to each of you.

To you, the reader, for picking up this daring little book and giving it a chance.

OTHER BOOKS BY

KRISTEN R. MOORE:

Through the Wicked Wood
As the Moon Falls
Through a Somber Sky

About the author:

Kristen is a part time author in the PNW. She lives with her husband, son, and three fur babies. When she isn't writing or reading, she's hiking the woods, enjoying the river, finding new trails with her little one, and almost always drinking a coffee. Films, books, and music play a huge role in her writing, as well as nature and mythology.